BULLETPROOF
BARISTA

BULLETPROOF BARISTA

CLEO COYLE

BERKLEY PRIME CRIME
New York

BERKLEY PRIME CRIME
Published by Berkley
An imprint of Penguin Random House LLC
penguinrandomhouse.com

Copyright © 2023 by Alice Alfonsi and Marc Cerasini

Library of Congress Cataloging-in-Publication Data

Names: Coyle, Cleo, author.
Title: Bulletproof barista / Cleo Coyle.
Description: New York: Berkley Prime Crime, [2023] | Series: A coffeehouse
mystery; 20
Identifiers: LCCN 2023022560 (print) | LCCN 2023022561 (ebook) |
ISBN 9780593197592 (hardcover) | ISBN 9780593197608 (ebook)
Subjects: LCSH: Cosi, Clare (Fictitious character)—Fiction. |
Women detectives—Fiction. | Murder—Investigation—Fiction. |
Coffeehouses—Fiction. | LCGFT: Detective and mystery fiction. | Novels.
Classification: LCC PS3603.O94 B85 2023 (print) |
LCC PS3603.O94 (ebook) | DDC 813/.6—dc23/eng/20230526
LC record available at https://lccn.loc.gov/2023022560
LC ebook record available at https://lccn.loc.gov/2023022561

Printed in the United States of America
1st Printing

Book design by Kristin del Rosario

To every comedian who'd kill to make us laugh.

AUTHOR'S NOTE

Bulletproof Barista is the twentieth entry in our Coffeehouse Mysteries, simultaneously marking our twentieth anniversary celebration of the series itself. As our longtime readers know, our caffeinated stories are often inspired by events that happen in and around our New York City home. This time our creative inspiration didn't come from a sudden eureka moment but over years of working in the volatile profession of making art in a city that often doubles for an elaborate movie set.

In our own Queens neighborhood, location shoots have become so common that we hardly blink when signs are posted announcing production work—no parking because trucks and trailers, cameras and equipment will soon be appearing.

So it is that *The Amazing Spider-Man* lives in a modest home not far from us. Just up the street (in *Changing Lanes*) Samuel L. Jackson was reunited with his wife and kids in front of our favorite Peruvian-style chicken joint. Film crews have transformed a vacant storefront around the corner into an outdoor café, shot footage for an action thriller at our subway stop, and given Jennifer Lopez a *Second Act* in our local Irish pub. All of which helped inspire the question of what would happen if Clare Cosi welcomed a film crew into her Coffeehouse world.

Our second inspiration for this story is our shared admiration for comedians. Great comedians are great artists. They're brave and irreverent. They are wry observers, social commentators, and ego checkers—today's version of a court jester. And like the court jesters of old, they're needed more than ever to keep all the kings of our world (as well as ourselves) in perspective.

Though we are always inspired by the many gifted comedians we admire, this is a work of fiction, and any resemblance to actual persons, living or dead, is purely coincidental.

For this story's coffee inspiration, we happily acknowledge Dave Asprey, the American entrepreneur and author who invented bulletproof coffee. For more information on Mr. Asprey's recipes, books, and coffee, visit his website at bulletproof.com.

As for other aspects of the story, though we've researched processes and procedures for accuracy, we also plead the author's defense that in the service of fiction, rules occasionally get bent.

A showbiz shout-out goes to our publisher and everyone whose hard work transformed our manuscript into this beautiful publication. We're especially grateful to our excellent editor, Tracy Bernstein, who helped strengthen our story and keep us on track.

Applause once again goes out to our brilliant cover artist Cathy Gendron for creating another gorgeous Coffeehouse Mystery cover (her twentieth, too)!

To John Talbot, our literary agent, we continue to treasure your steadfast support and consummate professionalism. May our longstanding friendship continue for another twenty years.

Finally, we extend our gratitude to those we could not mention by name, including friends, family, and so many of you who read our books and send us notes via email, our website's message board, and social media. Your encouragement has lifted our spirits countless times over these past two decades, and for that we cannot thank you enough.

Whether you are new to our world or a devoted reader, we invite you to join our Coffeehouse community at coffeehousemystery.com where you will find bonus recipes, our latest book news, and a link to keep in touch by signing up for our newsletter. May you eat, drink, and read with joy!

—Alice Alfonsi and Marc Cerasini
aka Cleo Coyle, New York City

Show business is an industry that runs on egos
—and coffee.

—Jerry Sullivan, *I'm Still Standing*

BULLETPROOF BARISTA

Prologue

⨀⨀⨀⨀⨀⨀⨀⨀⨀⨀⨀⨀⨀⨀⨀⨀⨀⨀⨀⨀⨀

Evil is not something superhuman, it's something less than human.

—AGATHA CHRISTIE, *THE PALE HORSE*

Queens, New York
Three Weeks Ago

One screw loosened. Then two. Then three . . .

The Player suppressed a laugh at the simile—

Like a screw loose in the head. Ha ha!

Once the screws were wobbly and the trap was set, the Player climbed down from the soundstage cage. In the shadows, the Player waited as the room came alive, an ironic thought, given this setup for death.

In came the troupe with the grips and the gaffer, the costumes, worn denims, tattoos, and T-shirts. The star was here, too: Mr. Jerry Sullivan himself.

Soon the real show would begin.

Below those loosened lights, a dozen hearts were still beating. Any minute now, one could be stopped. This gamble tried the nerves, but it was also a thrill. With quickened breaths, the Player watched for the right moment.

On a stage like this, grips placed the camera where the director directed. And the framework of lights, suspended from the ceiling, let the cinematographer sculpt every shot.

A *bounce board* threw more light on the subject.

A *flag* here or there diffused the glare.

The trap the Player set was a form of art, too. The tiny explosive was ready. And now—

BAM!

The squib went off, and the bank of lights fell with a shattering crash. Beneath it: a smashed body, broken bones, and the seeping of blood.

"It's Norman!" Jerry Sullivan shouted. "Noman's under there!"

Screams ripped the air. Such shock! Such horror!

What a good joke. The Player silently snickered. *The comedian finally gets a real punch line.*

As the crew rushed forward, the Player sank back. A flood of relief kept the giddiness at bay. In an artificial room, control was easy. A location shoot would be harder to manage. (The real world always was.)

Not to worry, the Player decided. The solution was simple, like the one used on set, when black boards were brought in to block excessive glare.

No light would be shed on these "accidental" acts. If anyone suspected, they'd be in danger, too.

One

If it wasn't for the coffee, I'd have no identifiable personality whatsoever.

—DAVID LETTERMAN

Greenwich Village, New York
Present Day

AFTER I tied and retied my ponytail, slipped into a fresh Village Blend apron and straightened it, I wondered if I might look more "managerial" without it, so I took it off. That's when I noticed the Appalachian Trail of wrinkles on my thin cotton sweater and put the apron back on.

Esther Best watched this anxious process with a critical eye. As I slicked back my ponytail (yet again), my most outspoken barista finally spoke.

"I hope you're finished fussing, Ms. Boss. It's distressing to see a manic Clare Cosi." With a twist of her zaftig hips, Esther punctuated her statement by sliding a wrought iron chair into place.

"But I'm not manic," I protested as I reapplied lip gloss while checking my reflection in the espresso tamper's chrome.

"Okay, I'll be blunt. You're acting bat guano crazy! You're behaving like a refugee from a 1950s sock hop who's about to meet Elvis."

"I'm about to meet Jerry Sullivan, Esther. Jerry *is* my Elvis. And he'll be right here, in our coffeehouse, any minute!"

"Oh, come on. It's not like he's a superstar recording artist or something. He's just a comedian."

"Jerry Sullivan is not *just* a comedian. When I was growing up, he . . . well, let's just say he means a lot to me . . ."

Secretly, I feared I'd be tongue-tied the moment I met him, but I hoped that someday I could tell the man how much his comedy meant to a girl brought up in a struggling corner of Western Pennsylvania. Despite the dreariness of mill town life, my mother's desertion of me and my father, and eating my feelings through a chunky monkey childhood, Jerry made me laugh, no matter how low or unattractive I felt. His humor reassured me that I wasn't crazy simply because I thought the whole world was.

"Look at her!" Esther threw up her arms. "Ms. Boss is actually gushing."

"Maybe I am. But in my view, Jerry Sullivan deserves a little gushing—and fussing. And, by the way, if you're so blasé about his visit, why did you and Nancy come in *two hours* early?"

Tucker Burton, my trusted assistant manager by day and off-off-Broadway's favorite thespian by night, leaned his lanky form against the coffee bar, flipped back his floppy brown mop, and drawled—

"You tell 'em, Clare. Show business runs on fandom like yours."

"And mine!" Nancy Kelly, our youngest (and most enthusiastic) barista, shook her wheat-colored braids. "I mean, okay, I don't know much about Jerry Sullivan's history, but I *do* know he's the star of *Only Murders in Gotham* and he's coming to *our* coffeehouse!"

And why not? I thought. Our century-old shop was a singular destination with its restored plank floors, cozy fireplaces, and romantic wall of French doors. But the Village Blend's atmosphere was only part of its charm. Our coffeehouse served some of the finest sourced beans in the world *and* boasted a colorful history with roots that ran directly through the bohemian life of Greenwich Village.

For decades, aspiring actors, writers, musicians, and artists had sipped espressos at our marble-topped tables and crashed in our upstairs lounge when they couldn't make it home (or pay the rent). We had so many framed sketches, paintings, and napkin doodles from patrons who'd made it big that I'd become a curator as well as a master roaster, rotating the displays on our walls like the director of a pop art gallery.

On the other hand, as New Yorkers themselves could tell you, movie shoots were commonplace all over our five boroughs: from Times Square to Wall Street; the Brooklyn Bridge to Highbridge; a stoop in Woodside, Queens, to the steps of the Metropolitan Museum. It seemed inevitable that our Village Blend would one day become a shooting location. And I had to admit, the timing was fortuitous.

The rise of remote work had emptied many of the offices around us, and foot traffic was down. I knew that being featured on Jerry Sullivan's show would not only reraise our local profile, but would also make us a national, even international, fan-tourist destination.

"I cannot *wait* to meet him!" Nancy cried (interrupting my wishful retail thinking).

Esther rolled her Goth-lined eyes. "Forgive the exuberance of my star-struck roommate over a single streaming season of whodunit dramedy. Nancy is thrilled when that awful mime on Christopher Street pays us a visit."

"She has every reason to be thrilled," asserted Dante Silva, my *artista* barista. Born and raised in a little New England town, Dante was a fine arts painter who continually found outlets for his talent, including designing the mélange of tattoos on his arms, which he folded now in mild annoyance. "You might be blasé about meeting celebrities, Esther, but I'm excited, too. I've been a Jerry Sullivan fan since I saw *Chucklehead* in the fifth grade. My friends and I went to our quad cinema three times in one week just so we could see the movie again."

Esther smirked. "Not much to do in Rhode Island, eh? Well, now we know why the Michelangelo of Latte Art came in early."

"Just like you, Esther," Dante countered.

"It was Nancy's idea. I only came because I didn't want her riding the subway alone—"

"Um. We *walked*," Nancy said.

"Enough!" Tucker clapped his hands for silence. "Wanting to meet a celeb is perfectly understandable. And by the way, Dante, on that list of Jerry Sullivan movies, don't forget *Fatherhood* and *Daddy Plans a Wedding*. Even the sequel, *Daddy Plans Another Wedding*, has its moments."

Esther raised an eyebrow. "I'm surprised at you, Mr. Off-Off Broadway. I thought you were a nonconforming bohemian thespian, but it sounds to me like you're a fan of Jerry Sullivan, too."

"Of course," Tuck replied with a finger snap. "He has impeccable comic timing. And you know I've done more than cabarets and experimental theater. I've scored series television and soap roles for years. Heck, I've even done reality TV and game shows."

"Oh, now I get it!" Esther stabbed the air with an accusing finger. "You're excited because *Only Murders in Gotham* gives speaking roles to real New Yorkers, and you're angling for a part."

Tuck stood tall. "An actor is always looking for a new challenge—and it never hurts to be cast in a hit show."

"Which he will be," I informed them all with a mama bear–proud grin.

"What? Really?!" Nancy clapped her hands. "Tucker, you didn't say a word! How did it happen?"

"Our bighearted boss sang my praises to the location scout and casting director. I sent over my demo reel and landed a speaking role—a *very* small one."

"Who cares how small it is!" Dante slapped him on the back. "You'll be in a hit streaming show, filmed at the Village Blend. That's fantastic!"

"Well, I'm less than impressed," Esther replied with a huff.

Nancy rolled her eyes. "That's because you never watched *Only Murders in Gotham*. And you should. It's so much fun! The show starts with a murder, but the story has lots of twists and turns that keep you guessing the whole time—and you never know which cast member is going to drop dead next."

"Yeah." Dante nodded. "And they shoot everything at real New York locations. The entire first season was filmed in and around the Dakota building on 72nd Street. It was cool to see the John Lennon tribute mural I painted. You can spot it in the background of the outdoor scenes. Last week the construction crew finished their restoration and tore down the temporary plywood walls. But thanks to *Only Murders in Gotham*, my mural will live forever in the digital realm."

"I binge-watched the first season," Nancy confessed, "but I couldn't figure out who the killer was. And I *totally* love Kylee Ferris in the show."

Esther turned to her roommate. "You're two for two, Nancy. An old comedian and a bubbleheaded teenage pop star."

"Kylee Ferris is *not* a teenager. Not anymore. She's the same age as me."

"Chronologically or emotionally?" Esther huffed.

Tuck shook a finger in Esther's face. "Now I'm surprised at you."

"Why is that?"

"You're a slam poet, aren't you? You should appreciate good wordsmithery. And the writing on Jerry's show is tight and clever. With all the daydreams his character experiences, the audience is always on the edge of their seats, trying to guess what's real and what's not—"

"Exactly!" Nancy clapped her hands. "You just *have* to keep watching and waiting for the giveaway, that moment when you realize it's all in Jerry's head. Or not."

"The first season's climax in Central Park's Strawberry Fields was inspired," Tucker said. "Jerry's ad-libs are great, too."

"So entertaining," I agreed. "And did you notice? Jerry *cowrote* every episode. He really is a genius. I even remember Jerry from before he made any movies. When he was on *The Coffey Break*—"

Nancy blinked. "He did a show about coffee?"

"Coffey with a *y*," I explained. "*The Coffey Break* was a sketch comedy hour hosted by an older comedian named Dan Coffey. Jerry Sullivan was the costar."

Esther shook her head. "Nope. Never heard of him."

"I've seen some sketches on YouTube," Tucker said. "That slapstick thing they called *Lean on Louey* was sidesplitting: Three Stooges with a *Godfather* twist."

"I thought the TV detective spoof *Just One More Thing* was funny, too," I said. "Especially if you ever watched *Columbo*."

"The only thing I didn't love were those sketches with the smarmy *How's This for a Deal?* character." Tucker mock shuddered. "They were just creepy."

"Well, it all sounds funny to me," Nancy said. "Why haven't I ever heard about this show?"

"It aired many years ago," I told her. "Before Jerry became a stand-up sensation, and before all the movies. There weren't many episodes, either. The show was canceled in the middle of the first season. One week it was on, and the next week gone. Low ratings, I guess."

"Well, Mr. Sullivan has a hit now," Nancy proclaimed. "And he's going to film an episode right here in our—OMIGOSH, LOOK, EVERYONE! HERE HE COMES!"

With all speed, Nancy straightened her blue Village Blend apron and swept back her braids. Dante joined her on the lookout at our line of French doors, where together they scanned the side street.

"Where is he? I don't see him!"

"There! That big limo." Nancy pointed. "That's got to be him."

It was too late to fuss any further with my apron and hair. All I could do now was dab on fresh lip gloss and approach our front door.

"Which limo?" Dante asked.

"I'm pretty sure Nancy meant the one that just rolled *completely past* our shop," Esther cracked.

Nancy's shoulders sagged. "Esther's right. Maybe we closed the coffeehouse for nothing and Jerry isn't coming after all."

Just then, a blazing red e-bike braked in the bicycle lane outside our Hudson Street entrance. The rider, tall and trim in denims and a black leather jacket, had his face shielded by a scarlet helmet with a tinted visor. As I watched, he rolled his ride onto the sidewalk. When the man pulled off his helmet, I immediately recognized the strong jaw, piercing gray eyes, wry grin, and signature silver hair of my idol.

Jolted, I had to bite my cheek to keep from screaming like some sock hop fan meeting Elvis. (Okay, so Esther was right.)

My heart began pounding and my mouth suddenly went dry as Jerry Sullivan placed his helmet under his arm and approached our front door. For a moment, I completely froze. It was Tucker, veteran of stage and small screen, who pulled us together with the clap of his hands—

"Showtime, folks!"

Two

⟨decorative divider⟩

"SHOULD we act nonchalant?" Dante whispered.

Swallowing my nerves, I said, "Just be yourselves," hoping to take my own advice as I unlocked the front door.

With my staff flanking me, I greeted Jerry Sullivan as he walked in. I was glad my voice didn't quaver when I calmly said—

"Welcome to the Village Blend, Mr. Sullivan. I'm Clare Cosi."

Extending my hand in greeting, I was equally happy to see it wasn't shaking like a leaf in a nor'easter.

Jerry beamed, flashing that same crooked smile featured on the famous poster for *Chucklehead*. His gray eyes were bright with warmth as they gazed into mine, and my breath caught when he gripped my hand.

I couldn't help it.

On the screen, Jerry Sullivan displayed undeniable charisma. In the flesh, his presence was almost overwhelming. The man radiated dynamic energy. I could *feel* it. And though he was two decades my senior, I found him magnetically attractive. Old Hollywood had two words for what I was experiencing: *Star Quality.*

"How's this for a deal?" Jerry said—and my smile widened at the reference to that old sketch. "You can call me Jerry if I can call you Clare. Is it a deal, Clare?"

"Deal, Jerry."

Relieved I'd managed to greet this comedy icon without making a fangirl fool of myself, I moved to introduce my baristas—and backed into a wrought iron chair. Legs tangled, I landed on my posterior with a horrified "Whoof!" followed by my reflexive "Son of a bunny!" Both of which were drowned out by the earsplitting clang of the metal chair hitting the floor.

A pair of arms quickly reached down to untangle me from the chair. I was sure my face was cherry red when I realized it was Jerry himself who was helping me to my feet.

"I'm okay, I'm okay."

Though he tried to put on a concerned face, Jerry couldn't stop himself from laughing. "That was some pratfall, Clare. You may be a natural comedian. Would you consider repeating that stunt for my show? It's a great opportunity. You'll be getting laughs from Seattle to Singapore."

"I'll stick with roasting coffee, if you don't mind. It's the business I know." Rubbing my rump, I felt the heat on my cheeks (the ones on my face) and declared—

"Wow, that was embarrassing."

"And with that, my dear Clare, you just summed up what life is like in *my* business."

The comedian's gaze swept past me and my baristas, to scan the Village Blend's interior. His smile deepened, though his sharp gaze seemed to cloud a little with sadness or maybe regret? I couldn't tell which.

"This place looks shinier than I remember. But it hasn't changed." Then that wry grin returned. "It's kind of like visiting your old elementary school. Everything's the same, yet different somehow . . . smaller."

"Then you've been here before?"

Jerry nodded as he continued to look around. "Many years ago . . ."

I was surprised by that. *Really* surprised.

In our shop's vast array of Village Blend memorabilia, I'd seen nothing from Jerry, no photos, artifacts, or props. And we had so many! Carol Burnett had gifted us an autographed *Playbill* from *Once Upon a Mattress*; Joan Rivers had left a feathered boa; Richard Pryor, a cigar and fedora; Steve Allen, a pitch pipe; Dom DeLuise, a signed rubber chicken. Even Lenny Bruce had autographed a witty (albeit slightly obscene) napkin doodle.

I was such a Jerry Sullivan fan that I would have remembered a used Kleenex if he'd left one. But there was nothing in our collection. Nada. Zip. So, naturally I was curious about any history he had with our shop.

I was about to ask for more details when my question was cut off by a loud thump. Another red e-bike had hopped the curb. The driver—barely in control—struck our wall. Helmet askew, the man tumbled off the seat, and the bike crashed to the sidewalk.

"Yow! I better see if that guy needs help." Dante bolted through the door.

"Oh, he'll be okay," Jerry called. Then he faced me. "That's my new out-of-diapers assistant the production company foisted upon me. Three weeks ago, Norman, my brilliant, eagle-eyed assistant from our show's first season, was badly injured in a soundstage accident, and Drew was pro-moted to his position by the production office. Ah, nepotism. Holly-wood's favorite flavor." Lowering his voice, he added, "Drew Merriweather is cute as a baby owl, but a tad slow on the uptake. You've been warned."

While Dante righted the bike, the breathless young man who'd crashed it burst through the door.

"Sorry, Jerry, I—"

"Should learn to keep up!" Jerry interrupted. "Show business waits for no assistant, Mr. Merriweather."

Behind his oversized horn-rimmed glasses, the young man's green eyes flashed in his peach-skinned face, but he immediately swallowed his irritation.

"So, this is your staff," Jerry said, facing my baristas. I was about to introduce them when Jerry approached Esther.

"*This* young woman needs no introduction," he said. "Last month, I watched Ms. Best perform at the Metro Slam Poetry Fest."

Esther blinked. "You did?"

"I was in the audience—incognito, of course—though I doubt anyone in that young crowd would have recognized an old fart like me. My niece performed, too, under her stage name, Golden Felicia."

Jerry took Esther's hand.

"The poor girl was shaky, though she did a competent job. But you, Ms. Best, were spectacular. You owned that audience."

For the first and probably the last time in her adult life, our resident urban poetess blushed.

I tried to introduce the rest of my staff, but Jerry was way ahead of me.

"I'm thrilled to meet you, Mr. Silva," he said as he shook Dante's hand and complimented his self-designed tattoos. "I loved the tribute mural you painted across the street from the Dakota."

"I appreciate it, Mr. Sullivan. It's gone now, but the mural will always be seen on your show."

"It's not *that* gone," Jerry replied. "I bought it from the construction company that hired you to paint it. Do you want it back?"

"Um, ah, I don't know," Dante stammered. "I'd have nowhere to put it."

"Well, it's in storage at Silvercup Studios in Queens if you ever want to show it."

Jerry moved from a speechless Dante to a grinning Tucker.

"Mr. Tucker Burton," Jerry said, clasping his hand. "I'm sorry I missed *Some Like It Tepid*, but I heard that cabaret show was a hit."

"A modest hit," Tucker replied.

"Hey, a modest hit is better than an undeniable flop. Take it from the guy who starred in *Daddy Plans Another Wedding*."

Though Nancy didn't have a résumé, Jerry made her feel like a star, too, telling her how her fresh face and cute braids would have put her in the running for Judy Garland's role in *The Wizard of Oz*.

"Or a Flying Monkey," Esther added, but not out loud. She mouthed the wisecrack to me, which told me how well Jerry was doing in winning over the staff. Esther's cynical mind hadn't lost its acidity, but she was impressed enough with our celebrity guest to apply a filter.

Meanwhile, Jerry joked good-naturedly with everyone, putting us all at ease. He also thanked Dante for rushing to assist his new assistant, though Jerry took a few more jabs at poor Mr. Merriweather's lack of motoring skills.

"Would you like a tour?" I asked. "Or would you and Mr. Merriweather prefer refreshments first? Coffee? An espresso?"

Jerry snorted. "Mr. Merriweather is barely out of the maternity ward and only drinks bottled water—or almond milk formula."

Drew Merriweather, still seated at the coffee bar, sighed and shook his head. I thought he was going to offer a comeback, but the assistant's phone rang—or rather, played the theme for *Only Murders in Gotham*—until Merriweather took the call.

"Hey!" Jerry cried, pointing to our chalkboard. "You have bullet-proof butter coffee on the menu."

"We added our version of the drink for the keto crowd, but lots of people are drinking it now. We use high-fat butter from grass-fed cows, of course, and cinnamon for flavor and satiety."

"I'm sold, Clare!"

"Do you have a coffee you prefer?"

"What would you recommend?"

"We have a lovely estate roast from Kenya. It was sourced by our shop's own coffee hunter, Matteo Allegro, and the beans make a rich and voluptuous bulletproof."

"Voluptuous!" He waggled his eyebrows. "Sounds kinky."

"Lush and well-rounded," I quickly clarified.

He laughed. "Sounds perfect."

A minute later, Jerry was moaning in ecstasy. "Oh, Clare, this is the best cup of coffee I've had in ages—"

"Jerry!" Drew Merriweather interrupted. "It's Tina Bird on the phone."

Jerry waved his assistant away. "Another production glitch? Chirp all about it with Tweety Bird, Drew, and tell me later. I'm too busy enjoying caffeinated bliss."

Giddy with pride, I asked, "Would you like another?"

"Listen!" Drew said. "Tina called to warn us that Lizzy Meeks got onto the set *again*—"

"What?" Jerry's face flashed with anger.

"That was forty minutes ago. Studio security tried to grab her, but Meeks got away."

"Is this production cursed? Or am I being sabotaged? Whatever it is, I can't take much more of it."

"It's a screwup, Jerry. That's all. But it gets worse. Lizzy Meeks used her phone to photograph the shooting schedule and the call sheets off the big board. That means she knows where you are right now, and she's probably on her way. You don't want her to ambush you like she did at the Met last week. It was a miracle no one took a picture—"

"No picture, no bad press," Jerry said.

"Yeah? Well Lizzy probably figured that out herself. This time she might bring friends with smartphones."

Jerry offered me a strained smile. "I guess we should go."

Merriweather snatched his helmet and hopped off the stool.

A minute later, I escorted Jerry and his assistant out. I was dying to ask why exactly he was desperate to avoid this Lizzy Meeks. Was she an overly aggressive journalist? A celebrity-obsessed podcaster? A rabid fan? A psycho stalker? Or maybe a jilted lover?

At the door, Jerry shook my hand again.

"I'm sorry to leave early. But I'm looking forward to seeing you tomorrow. We're only shooting the sidewalk scenes—along that great line of your shop's French doors—but maybe we can talk coffee between takes."

As the two boarded their e-bikes, I heard Drew Merriweather speak.

"Lizzy is acting deranged. You should get a restraining order against her."

Jerry snorted. "A restraining order against the president of my own fan club? How's that going to look? Talk about bad press!"

The bike lane on Hudson Street was crowded, but Jerry and Drew easily broke into the flow. As I watched my favorite celebrity disappear with the traffic, Tucker touched my shoulder.

"Clare, I can't believe you turned down a role in *Only Murders in Gotham*."

"Excuse me?"

"Jerry wanted you to repeat that hilarious pratfall on his *hit* show. He was serious. Why didn't you accept?"

I thought the answer was obvious, until I realized that Tucker was staring at me, not as my assistant manager, but with the incredulous expression of a working actor, one who'd never understand. With a shrug, I tried anyway—

"Let's just say I value my dignity more than stardom."

THREE

∽∽∽∽∽∽∽∽∽∽∽∽∽∽∽∽∽∽∽∽∽∽∽∽∽∽∽∽∽∽∽∽∽∽∽∽

AFTER Jerry said goodbye, we reopened the shop and went back to work, flying high with a sense of anticipation for the week ahead.

Over the next few hours, I pulled espressos and kept a wary eye on the female clientele, continually wondering if one of them was Jerry's fan club president, Lizzy Meeks. I wasn't sure what to look for, of course. Would Jerry's "world's biggest fan" be wearing a *Silly for Sullivan* pin from his concert tours? An *Only Murders in Gotham* T-shirt? Or maybe a screwdriver-in-the-head prop from Jerry's stand-up days?

I pondered the possibilities until the end of our abbreviated afternoon rush. That's when I took a break from espresso making to work the register.

My first customer, a thirtysomething woman in a pin-striped business suit and designer heels, didn't order coffee. Instead, she posed a question.

"I didn't expect to find your coffeehouse open," she began. "Has Jerry Sullivan been here today?"

"Oh, you must have seen our sign," I replied. "Filming doesn't start until tomorrow, but our Village Blend truck will be parked nearby to fulfill your coffee needs while the shop is closed."

"I don't care about that," she said briskly. "I have it on good authority that Jerry was here today."

Her urgent tone made me take a second look. Her sad, brown eyes met mine.

"My name is Lizzy Meeks," she said. "I'm president and CEO of the Jerry Sullivan Fan Club."

Her pale right hand reached across the counter while her left uneasily worried the strap of the Birkin bag slung over her scarecrow shoulder.

Despite the tension Lizzy Meeks radiated, I wondered why Jerry Sullivan was in such a rush to avoid her. Ms. Meeks didn't seem threatening in the least. When I shook her hand and introduced myself as "a big fan," she seemed almost relieved, like she'd found a kindred spirit.

"Are you a member?" Lizzy asked. "Because if you're a fan, you really should join."

She reached into that bag and handed me a slick brochure with catalog items listed inside—hats, pins, posters, calendars, coffee mugs, bumper stickers, comic props, hoodies, and more.

"That's the club's most recent collection of offerings. You can see on the back page that an annual membership is only twenty-five dollars, and you'll get a personally autographed picture of Jerry just for joining. Members also get special discounts on Jerry's merchandise. And you can bid on exclusive memorabilia, too."

As she spoke, I leafed through the pamphlet. Tucker appeared at my shoulder, and Lizzy didn't break stride as she passed him a brochure as well.

"A premium membership is only ten dollars more and you get free shipping on all orders. Premium members also get first dibs on Jerry's stand-up show when he returns to the Winner Hotel and Casino in Las Vegas."

Tuck scanned the catalog pages. "Do you sell *Only Murders in Gotham* T-shirts?"

Lizzy's expression froze. When she spoke again, her tone was far less enthusiastic. "That's not really Jerry's show. Kylee Ferris is the star."

"Kylee Ferris?" I said, surprised.

"Kylee's only a costar," Tuck countered. "She doesn't have top billing."

Lizzy grimaced. "No, she doesn't have top billing, but that washed-up teenage pop star gets *all* the press and media attention. Fawning features in *Variety*, *Rolling Stone*, and the *Hollywood Reporter*. Next month, she'll be on the cover of *Vogue*. She's raking in the dough on downloads of the theme song she wrote for the show, and a fashion line featuring ready-to-wear versions of her costumes is launching next month with her name on the label. Kylee is reaping tons of merch benefits from being cast in Jerry's show."

"Merch?" I repeated. "As in merchandise, right?"

"Yes, Ms. Cosi, merchandizing has become an important revenue stream for any celebrity. But Jerry has been shut out of that stream for *Only Murders in Gotham*. The production company signed those rights away to the streaming service. It controls everything."

"I didn't realize—"

"It's true!" Lizzy cried, her voice becoming tighter and more strident. "If you were a real fan, you'd understand this small-screen series baloney is a step *down* for Jerry. He should be making feature films or returning to Vegas where he's not playing second fiddle to a little diva whose music career nose-dived after high school graduation."

I shot a glance Tucker's way and could tell he was feeling as uncomfortable as I was. But there was no stopping Lizzy Meeks. She leaned close—

"Did you know that Kylee Ferris told an interviewer that she had to *Google* Jerry Sullivan when she was hired for the show because she had no idea who he was! Frankly, I don't believe her. And even if it were true, and she was that cinematically illiterate, why say so in an interview? To make Jerry look less important than her, that's why."

"Appalling," Tucker offered.

"I know! She's such a little brat—"

"But if that's all true," I cut in, "why would Jerry put up with it?"

"Even big stars like Jerry make bad decisions. I tried to tell him that there was something *very wrong* with this show. That he was being used to carry the water for a lesser talent." Lizzy smirked. "But Jerry can be so stubborn. If you knew him like I do, you'd see. I've tried to explain that fans want to see him in his own movie, not playing a second banana to a reheated teen idol. But Jerry—he just won't listen. I'm determined to convince him, though."

She paused, and her expression turned sly.

"So, will Jerry be here tomorrow? I know this coffeehouse is going to be closed all week, but is Jerry involved in the filming? Will he be shooting alone, or will Kylee be here, too?"

"I really don't know," I replied, giving Tuck a warning look.

"But surely you must have some idea!" she pressed.

"I'm afraid we don't," I asserted—though I did, of course.

Turkey Shoot Productions, the company that made *Only Murders in Gotham*, had the use of the Village Blend for the next seven days, and Tucker and I were fully aware of their shooting schedule.

Lizzy's professional expression twisted into a scowl. Narrowing her eyes, she clearly suspected I was lying to her, which I was. After all, it wasn't up to me to share production information!

"I understand what's going on here," she spat. "You're using Jerry, too, to push this stupid coffeehouse." She snatched the brochure from Tucker's hand. "It sickens me to see that you are exploiting Jerry Sullivan just like everyone else."

"That's a terrible accusation," I returned. "And if we're being blunt, it seems to me that *you* are also exploiting Jerry." I waved her fan club brochure. "The annual membership. All this stuff you're selling. How much of this 'important revenue stream' does Jerry really get?"

Lizzy's self-righteous fury melted for a moment into blank confusion.

"What I do, I do for Jerry!" she returned defensively.

Tuck arched an eyebrow. "Really?"

"Of course!" Clearly rattled, Lizzy backed into a waiting customer. "It's my destiny. I was put on this earth to help Jerry nurture his genius, not exploit him for my own selfish gain."

I was about to argue that point but didn't get the chance. The woman turned on her designer heels and bolted for the exit. At the door, she called over her shoulder.

"I'm right. You'll see! This show is cursed! Jerry needs to get out before his career is ruined. He doesn't want to believe it. But I'll prove it to him, and to you. Just wait!"

With that, Jerry Sullivan's number one fan vanished into the autumn dusk. Tucker and I exchanged bemused glances.

"What do you think of that, Tuck?"

"All I can say is . . . *Cock-a-doodle-doo.*"

"Excuse me?"

"I'll give you a hint. The Sixty-Third Academy Awards."

"Sorry, Tucker, I don't follow."

"That was the year Kathy Bates won the Oscar for playing Annie Wilkes, the psycho fan in *Misery.*"

"She crowed like a rooster?"

"You haven't seen *Misery*? Oh, Clare, you have to screen it. Then you'll understand."

I nodded politely, but I didn't have time to "screen" anything. Tomorrow morning, the Village Blend was destined to appear on its own Hollywood screen. And if I wanted my beloved coffeehouse to be ready for its close-up, I was in for a late night and little sleep.

Four

~~~~~~

By six AM, I was out of bed, showered, and dressed for the day. Like a child on Christmas morning, I flew down the back steps.

Peering through the spotless Village Blend windows, I saw the studio trucks were already parked on our block. Though the sun had barely risen on this cool autumn morning, the blue sky was clear, and the fall leaves around our shop were at their most colorful. Our spick-and-span coffeehouse was ready to shine like a star!

Though today's filming was an "exterior" scene, taking place on our side street sidewalk, our shop would be open to the cast and crew. Like a fangirl, I was hoping Jerry Sullivan would drop in to say hello.

For a few minutes, I watched members of the production staff unload spools of wire and cases of equipment, then I started my own work, humming happily as I turned up the pressure on the espresso machines. (They were never off entirely. We had two machines, and we shut them down in rotation—one every three days—to thoroughly clean them.)

Recalling Jerry's enjoyment of my bulletproof keto coffee, I fetched a tub of high-fat butter from our cold storage in the basement, moving it to our shop's undercounter fridge, along with quarts of cream and fresh milk, all of it purchased from a dairy farm in Pennsylvania's Amish country.

Tucker arrived to help me right the chairs. As we finished, roommates Nancy and Esther came in together. Nancy was as chipper as always, but Esther—never a morning person to begin with—looked tired.

"I couldn't sleep," she confessed. "I was so shocked by Jerry Sullivan's compliments that I decided to repeat the performance he saw at next week's New Voices of Brooklyn Poetry Slam, and I had to rehearse."

As my baristas donned their aprons, I asked Tucker to brew a pour-over pot of the beans I'd freshly roasted. Matt had sourced them on his last trip to Indonesia, and I was anxious for the staff to sample the coffee before I put it on our chalkboard.

While Tuck went to work, I climbed the spiral staircase to my small office, which was tucked away on our second-floor lounge, a casual space with a cozy fireplace, standing lamps, and eclectic mix of comfy furniture. Customers enjoyed relaxing on this floor, but we also used it for private parties and special events.

I wondered if *Only Murders in Gotham* fans would book the floor in the future—and that's when my mind returned to the unhinged president of Jerry's fan club.

As wrongheaded and disturbed as Lizzy Meeks seemed, she did ram home an important point. The Village Blend would likely benefit from exposure on Jerry's show, maybe the same way a little-known cupcake bakery became an international destination after being featured on *Sex and the City.*

Given what that could mean for our business, I felt a keen managerial need to see that Jerry's shoot went smoothly. Unfortunately, I felt an equally ugly premonition about Lizzy's warning. The woman was absolutely convinced that something was "very wrong" with the production of *Only Murders in Gotham.*

I wanted to dismiss it. Yet Jerry himself had expressed concerns. He'd even used the word *sabotage . . .*

Distracted by these worrisome thoughts, I absently opened my office door and—let out a piercing squeal!

I quickly slammed the door again.

"Clare! What's wrong?" Tuck called. Alarmed, he came running with Esther right behind him.

"There's a naked ex-husband in my office!"

Five

~~~
@@@@@@@@@@@@@@@@@@@@@@@@@@@@@@@@@@@@@@@@
~~~

Slowly, the office door opened again. To be honest, Matt wasn't completely naked. His muscular arms and chest were bare, and darkly tanned from his recent trek across the coffee-growing highlands of Tanzania. His beard had gone mountain-man wild, and his dark hair was flyaway, but he'd modestly covered his black bikini briefs with the invoice file from my office desk.

"What's the matter with you, Clare? Didn't you see that it was me?"

"I saw *plenty*."

As I averted my eyes, Esther snickered, and Tucker herded her away. When they hit the spiral staircase, I faced Matt again.

"I'm surprised to find you here."

"I've been in and out of airports for eighteen hours, with one delay after another. I only arrived at LaGuardia three hours ago and decided it was too much trouble to schlep all the way to Brooklyn, only to come back here a few hours later, so I crashed in your office."

"Why do you want to be here at all?"

"So I'd be around to see the movie people."

"Then you better get dressed, unless you're planning on appearing in a nude scene."

Matt flashed his toothy smile. "You know me, Clare. I'm always up for anything."

"Well, this is a G-rated show, so cover up, please!"

"Sure, but I need a shower first." He lifted one arm and sniffed. "I think I'm a little ripe. Can I use the bathroom upstairs? The Flatfoot isn't around, is he? The last time I surprised your NYPD Boy Scout up there he put me in cuffs."

"That was a long time ago—and a misunderstanding. But you're in luck. Java and Frothy are all alone in the apartment. And last I checked, cats don't carry badges or guns."

"Your fiancé is gone?"

"For a week. Mike went to Virginia to speak at a conference, and he extended his stay on some official police business. He's due back tomorrow. But *do* put on some clothes before you go up. I don't want your hairy chest and scruffy beard scaring my girls."

"Very funny."

"Was it really? *Funny,* I mean. I need to be funny this week."

"Why?"

"Because I don't want Jerry Sullivan to think I'm a caffeine-pushing dullard. You either. He's quick-witted, Matt, so sharpen up."

"For that I'll need some of that caffeine you push."

"That's something I can help you with. In fact, we're about to sample the outstanding Sumatra you scored. Join us downstairs when you've washed away your jet lag—and trimmed that beard."

"Have a heart, Clare, and bring a fresh cup up to me in the shower?"

"Sorry, I've seen enough half-naked ex-husband for one day."

"Oh, come on. Admit it. I gave you a thrill."

"What you gave me was close to a heart attack."

"See that? You admit it involved your *heart.* I knew you still had feelings for me."

We both laughed at that one, and I conceded his sense of humor was presentable, even if he wasn't.

"Come on, Clare, last chance. Are you *sure* you don't want a peek of me in the shower?"

Waving him away, I headed back downstairs. Before hitting the coffee bar, I glanced through the front windows to see if any of the film crew was heading our way for a morning brew—and stopped dead.

"What is *that*?!" I cried, pointing to a huge silver truck parked directly in front of our Hudson Street entrance. The vehicle was an obvious food truck, with its side service window open. I could plainly see an espresso machine inside.

"That's the craft services truck," Tucker replied.

"Craft services?"

"That's right. They're caterers hired by the producers to supply the meals and snacks to the cast and crew during filming."

"But not the *coffee*! I thought *we* were going to do that!"

"That's because you know Jerry's movies, but you don't know the movie *business*."

Six

꩜꩜꩜꩜꩜꩜꩜꩜꩜꩜꩜꩜꩜꩜꩜꩜꩜꩜꩜꩜꩜

I SHOOK my head at the humiliating news. "I cannot believe Turkey Shoot Productions hired someone else to make coffee while they're filming at a landmark coffeehouse."

"It's probably a union thing. Or the other thing."

"What other thing?"

"No matter where a production company shoots, they will make sure coffee is *always* available. You know the old adage, don't you?"

"What adage?"

"Hollywood runs on money and egos, but a movie shoot runs on caffeine."

Tucker's adage didn't help.

With one glimpse of that craft services espresso machine, my own pathetically small ego (along with my "get closer to Jerry" scheme) dropped through our restored plank floor and landed with a splat in my basement roasting room.

I had been fantasizing about plying Jerry Sullivan with our freshly roasted coffee and beautifully baked pastries, along with providing a sympathetic "personal barista's" ear while he filmed in and around our shop.

It was my (apparently delusional) way of fast-tracking some kind of rapport between us. And okay, given the ravings of Lizzy Meeks, I thought it was my best chance to find out whether the production was really under some kind of cloud or—as Jerry himself put it—being sabotaged.

It wasn't much of a plan, but it was all I had. And now even that pathetic strategy was ruined by a shiny silver food truck staffed by a slender, blond, black-aproned barista—

Hey. Wait a minute! I thought. *Why do black aprons seem so ominously familiar?* When I remembered, my situation went from hopeless to soul-destroying.

"Oh, no," Esther shrieked. "It's those lousy rats from Driftwood Coffee!"

Nancy blinked. "What are *they* doing here?"

"*They* have obviously been hired to supply craft services for Turkey Shoot Productions," Tucker replied.

"And now they're squatting right in front of *our* coffeehouse," Nancy said with a shake of her braids. "This is a big, smelly pile of rotten bananas!"

"I smell a pile of something, too," Tucker said, "and it ain't fruit."

Esther pinched her nose. "I think it's their coffee."

I couldn't have agreed more.

THE bitter relationship between the Village Blend and Driftwood Coffee had been building for years and lately had gotten worse.

Around a decade ago, Driftwood didn't enter the scene so much as burst upon it, with a lot of flash, a million-dollar public relations campaign, and a dashing spokesmodel CEO who paraded his good looks and second-tier coffee products on all the local news shows.

"Second-tier" (by the way) was not meant as a snarky insult, but a simple statement of fact. Because of their many stores, Driftwood bought their beans in bulk and roasted them in large, homogenous batches.

The Village Blend, on the other hand, prided itself on using Grade 1 beans—specialty shade-grown coffee sourced by Matt and his importing business from small farms and cooperatives around the globe. They were then roasted fresh in small, custom-designed batches by me, the shop's master roaster.

Driftwood's elaborate commercials *implied* they were in the business of serving high-end specialty coffee, but that was not the case. There simply weren't enough Grade 1 beans, or small-batch roasting models, to meet their corporate cups-per-hour profitability demands.

Degrading a superior product was the primary reason why the Village

Blend's octogenarian owner would never agree to franchising our business, no matter how many times she was approached or how big the offer.

The flamboyant, French-born Madame Dreyfus Allegro Dubois, or simply "Madame," as she came to be known over the many decades she ran this coffeehouse, also happened to be Matt's mother, and my former mother-in-law. I was wary when she insisted on turning over the running of the business to the two of us, but the woman had always been uncannily wise, and she'd been right about me and Matt, despite our divorce.

Though our marital union hadn't lasted, our business partnership was functioning beautifully, and the reason was simple. Matt and I were fully dedicated to seeing the Village Blend's legacy continue at the highest level. We also loved Madame and respected her advice, including her outspoken views on franchising—

"Matt's grandfather started this coffee business over a century ago," she often reminded us. "His late father and I poured blood, sweat, and plenty of tears into keeping it going as a vital part of this Village community. As long as I breathe air, I will never allow anyone to corrupt its excellent offerings or its good name."

That sentiment was all well and good, *in private*. But when the *New York Times* published a profile of Matt's mother and the Village Blend's history, things got hairy.

Madame's words about Driftwood's "Exchange Grade" coffee beans and their bulk roasting had the Driftwood CEO seeing red. Her remarks were innocently spoken, meant to explain why our coffee was continually voted the best in the city; why gourmet restaurants served our signature beans; and why she eschewed franchising, beyond our single second shop, currently managed by my daughter, in Washington, DC.

Driftwood didn't see it that way. After that public slight, they had an official hate on for us. If they did acknowledge the existence of the Village Blend, it was only to disparage us—or outright rip us off.

Whenever we came up with a new beverage idea, named a blend, or sourced a novel coffee, Driftwood would immediately imitate it, cheapen it, and then claim it as their own, all the while pretending we didn't exist.

When the foodie press wrote up Matt's meticulously sourced Ambrosia beans, for example, Driftwood released its new blend "Ambosia"— yes, leaving out the *r* along with the quality.

They criticized us for "overcharging" on Kona beans. Yet, as Matt countered in an interview, their KONA in big caps was followed in very small letters with the word *blend*—because it had very little actual Kona in it!

And the feud escalated.

Every December, we featured a different menu of holiday-inspired latte flavors that we famously called Fa-la-la-la-lattes. New York's food writers covered us with fun annual pieces, reporting on our offerings and lauding us for the wholesome ingredients we used. Social media always gave us a boost, resulting in lines around the block, local TV news coverage, and customers taking selfies.

One year, *New York* magazine photographed me and my staff, working at our coffee bar, declaring Clare Cosi "the Dominique Ansel of coffee" and our Fa-la-la-la-lattes "drinkable Cronuts."

After the fawning magazine piece appeared, Driftwood launched a splashy publicity campaign for their "Ho-ho-ho-lattes," completely missing the charm of alliteration, not to mention (as Esther pointed out) the Urban Dictionary definition of "Ho."

Driftwood not only copied our holiday menu, but they bastardized our drinks, using cheap corn syrups doctored with imitation flavorings instead of quality ingredients like the local honeys, artisanal chocolates, and pureed fruits, which went into our handmade syrups.

The latest hit in this ongoing rivalry was against our baristas.

In all the years Driftwood had been doing business in our region, they'd never once bothered to enter the Tri-State Latte Art competition. This year, however, they'd imported a ringer from Seattle in an attempt to snatch our Best in Show title. The man they entered was a West Coast champion for *another* coffee company. Suddenly, the man was hired by Driftwood, living in New York, and entering our local competitions. Suspicious, to say the least!

Thank goodness, our Dante—fine artist that he was—won anyway. Sadly, their ringer did manage to beat our Esther out of second place and a nice monetary prize.

Feelings were still raw over that one, and that bitterness was on full display in my coffeehouse right now.

Seven

〰〰〰〰〰〰〰〰〰〰〰〰〰〰〰〰〰〰〰

"THIS is sickening," Esther moaned. "Look at them swanning around in their Darth Vader black aprons, brewing espressos on *our* turf, and all the while they're laughing in our faces."

"I'd avoid using gang-sounding words like *turf*," Tuck advised. "This isn't *West Side Story*. We're not the Sharks, and they're not the Jets—or is it the other way around? Anyway, you don't want to get us into a *rumble*, do you? The hardened gangs we have today aren't exactly the quaint, Damon Runyon–esque kiddies of the celluloid kind, you know."

Esther didn't care, she just kept on ranting—

"What is that white stain on the front of those Darth aprons, anyway? It's located where their hearts would be if any of them actually *had* one."

Nancy squinted through the window. "It kind of looks like a map of their arteries, but you're right. I don't see anything that looks like a heart."

"It's a piece of driftwood," Tucker informed her flatly. "You know, like their name—"

Esther sniffed. "Well, I wish they'd *drift*."

"I have to admit the embossing is nice," Tucker said with a shrug.

"They even parked rudely," Nancy declared. "Their truck is blocking our sign."

"I'll bet those creeps would chain our door and set fire to the place if they thought they could get away with it," Esther added. "Look at that little blonde inside the truck. She keeps staring through our window and laughing. There, did you see? She did it again!"

Esther caught the eye of the blonde in question. My insidiously clever barista displayed a friendly smile and offered a wave. All the while Esther muttered under her breath.

"That's right, sweetie, I'm waving at you, but what I'd really like to do is drag you out of that truck by your nose ring."

The mood was getting ugly, and I knew things were bound to get uglier if I didn't put a stop to it. So, despite my own frustration with the situation, I felt I had to say something to smooth our troubled waters.

"Let's dial it back, okay? I know Driftwood is our competition, but we should be big about this. The production company hired them to provide craft services, so there's nothing we—"

Tuck cried out in horror. "Is that Driftwood barista tapping the fire hydrant for water? He is. He's tapping the *fire hydrant* for water!"

I watched as a young barista attached a standard garden hose to the hydrant's nozzle, then handed the other end to the blonde inside the truck. She signaled a moment later and the man opened the tap.

"Rank amateurs," Esther huffed. "Unfiltered city water will scale up their espresso machines faster than melted lard will clog a refrigerated drainpipe. If they're that sloppy, they might as well use coffee vending machines."

"Who might as well use coffee vending machines?" Matt asked, buttoning a blue linen shirt as he stepped off the staircase. His dark hair was still damp, but he'd slicked it neatly back, and he'd trimmed and tamed his beard—with a good bit of it lining my bathroom sink, no doubt. (Reminder to self, clean all evidence of ex-husband before fiancé gets back!)

"It's Driftwood Coffee," Tuck informed Matt. "One of their trucks is parked in front of the coffeehouse."

Matt scowled. "Why?"

"They're providing craft services for *Only Murders in Gotham*."

Matt took a breath and blew it out, then in a noble attempt to shrug it off, he spoke in a surprisingly reasonable tone.

"Look on the bright side. It's Saturday, so most of our regular customers won't even see that truck."

"That's right," I added. "Because our regulars will be getting coffee from our Village Blend truck when Dante opens in an hour."

"Maybe Driftwood's coffee truck will *catch fire* and we can replace it with ours," Esther said. "It's a tough town. I'll bet that can be arranged."

Matt shared a look with me, that *uh-oh* parental glance we often exchanged when raising our daughter, Joy.

"Let's put our anger aside, Esther," Matt counseled. "Sometimes you have to live and let live."

Thank goodness Matt's here, I thought. *He's another voice of calm and reason to back me up.*

"I'll talk to Jerry," I offered. "Ask for the Driftwood truck to be relocated somewhere else—"

"Yeah, like Poughkeepsie," Esther cracked.

"—after Jerry arrives at the shoot, I mean."

"Clare, it looks like Jerry is already on location—" Tucker held up his phone. "I can't believe what Driftwood Coffee just posted on Twitter!"

Tuck's screen displayed a photo of Jerry Sullivan sipping orange juice from a clear plastic cup bearing the Driftwood logo.

I peered out our front window, hoping to spot my silver-haired idol, but there was no sign. All I noticed was a burly man with a salt-and-pepper beard who *had* to be from the film crew. Who else would wear a yellow-and-purple LA Lakers jacket in the center of Knicks and Nets land?

As I watched, the bearded Lakers man shared a flirty grin with the barista who'd so gotten under Esther's skin. The young blond woman with the nose ring handed him a Driftwood takeout cup with the words FRED and DOUBLE ESPRESSO printed in big, bold marker. He winked and began to drink.

"I was wrong," Nancy said as she gazed at the screen. "You *can* read the Village Blend sign, except for a tiny part that's blocked by Jerry's Driftwood cup."

My ex-husband's face flushed, but instead of boiling over, Matt applied enough mental pressure to tamp down his anger. I continued to be impressed with his control, but I remained wary.

Matt may have matured into a worldly wise coffee importer, fluent in dozens of languages, but at heart he was still an extreme-sports adrenaline junkie. Sure, when it's your job to convince cherry farmers—from Guatemala to Rwanda—to trust you, patience and understanding become necessary virtues. But back here, in New York, Matt was no wet espresso puck. This city would grind you up and spit you out if you didn't stand up for yourself and your business.

My ex could be pushed only so far before he'd explode.

"Driftwood is trying to rattle our chain," Matt finally declared, clearly irritated. "But we can't let them get to us. This is the Village Blend's day to shine. We can't let Driftwood get us all hot and—"

"Look at that!" Nancy pointed. "They're putting up a Driftwood Coffee sign right in front of our door!"

Through the window I watched the burly man in the Lakers jacket step aside while two black aprons raised the Driftwood banner over the food cart's service window.

That did it.

"Why, those dirty sons of—" Matt's face went red, his hands clenched into fists, and his muscular body was about to charge when I grabbed his arm.

"Wait!"

"No way, Clare!" He was still moving toward the exit—and practically dragging me with him. "Do you see what they're—"

"Shut up, Matt. Will you please stop and look!"

"Look at what? I saw the sign."

"Not the sign!"

I pointed and my ex finally spotted what I did.

Double-Espresso Fred, the burly, bearded man in the LA Lakers jacket, was swaying on his feet. Fred's flirty grin for the Driftwood barista was gone, replaced by a look of dazed confusion.

The man retched, but nothing came up. Then his eyes glazed as the remainder of his Driftwood drink spilled on the sidewalk. Clutching his chest, the big man followed his paper cup to the pavement.

Eight

꩜꩜꩜꩜꩜꩜꩜꩜꩜꩜꩜꩜꩜꩜꩜꩜꩜꩜꩜꩜

Matt slipped my grip. This time I let him go.

"Tucker, call 911!" I shouted as I followed Matt through the door. "Tell them it's a medical emergency!"

The burly man was sprawled on his side, his bearded cheek flat against the cold concrete. His complexion had a bluish tint, and it didn't look like the man was breathing. The only sign of life was an occasional spasm that would rack his whole body.

Two Driftwood baristas—both shocked into paralysis—stood over the unconscious man. The blonde with the nose ring leaned out of the truck, gawking.

Matt pushed the black-aproned boys aside, knelt on the sidewalk, and gently turned the stricken man onto his back. While he checked the man's nose and mouth for obstructions, I faced the blonde in the truck.

"What happened?" I demanded.

"He fainted or something."

Matt began performing CPR, and I knew this was an "or something" situation, not a fainting spell.

I pointed to the takeout cups on the counter, all of them full and capped with plastic lids, crew names printed on the side.

"Were these drinks made using the first espressos out of that machine today?"

The girl just stared at me, her jaw slack.

I pointed to the man on the ground. "Did he drink one of the first pulls of the day?" I repeated loudly and slowly.

The blonde snapped out of her funk and nodded.

I turned to the crowd and spoke loudly. "If anyone grabbed an espresso drink from this truck, dump it right now. It could be tainted."

Two men in the crowd immediately dumped their cups—one of them did a nearly comedic spit-take first.

I knelt beside Matt.

"I don't think this is a heart attack, Clare," he said, still working the unconscious man. "There's no obstruction I can see, but he can't seem to breathe."

"He might be poisoned. If the cleaning fluid for the espresso machine wasn't flushed out properly, he could be having a reaction to peroxide or even sulfuric acid."

Matt nodded once and kept on working. Tuck appeared with a stack of folded towels, which he slipped under the victim's head. As my ex continued to apply CPR, the stricken man's chest began to rise and fall as oxygen finally filled his lungs. Otherwise, he remained unresponsive.

Someone who didn't get the memo stepped around us to take an espresso off the truck. I jumped to my feet and swatted his hand aside. With a single sweep of my arm, I spilled the rest of the cups into the street.

Beside me I heard Matt's grunt. "Come on, keep breathing."

No one around us crouched down to help, yet a wall of phone cameras was aimed in our direction. I did my best to ignore them.

A single siren was approaching fast, and I was thankful this was a quiet Saturday morning, and not a busier weekday.

The siren's scream intensified, then abruptly ended, and two paramedics pushed through the barricade of raised phones. As they jumped into action, Matt stepped back, his face flushed from his efforts.

The next few minutes went by in a blur. The medics stabilized the man, loaded him onto a gurney, and then into the ambulance. Several uniformed police appeared and shooed away the crowd with familiar yet eerily ominous words—

"Show's over, folks."

As the crowd broke up, I felt a little dazed, unsure what to do next.

Matt put a hand on my shoulder. "You okay?"

"Sure, *I'm* okay. I'm just worried about that poor man."

"Well, worrying never solved anything. Look, your staff is waiting for you." He pointed to the shop, where my baristas were standing together, their faces grim. "Didn't you promise them a Sumatra tasting?"

"I promised you, too," I said. "You saved that man's life, Matt, and you haven't even had your morning coffee."

"So let's remedy that," he said. "And get on with our day."

Nine

⊶⊷⊶⊷⊶⊷⊶⊷⊶⊷⊶⊷⊶⊷⊶⊷⊶⊷⊶⊷⊶⊷⊶⊷⊶⊷⊶⊷⊶

FIFTEEN minutes later, as we finished the tasting, the bell over our entrance rang. A member of the film crew stuck his head through the door and asked if the Village Blend was open for business. We'd already watched the Driftwood truck pack up and leave after the medical incident, but the film crew still lingered.

Matt and I exchanged surprised looks—and then I smiled.

"We'll be open in five minutes!"

Refreshed and invigorated by the superb beans Matt found among the smallholder farms on the largest of Indonesia's Sunda Islands, we all went to work. Nancy ran the register, Esther and I pulled espressos, and Matt doled out goodies from our bakery case. I never saw a group of people consume so many pastries, doughnuts, muffins, and cookies so quickly.

By noon, word came down from on high—the shoot was canceled for the day. Suddenly, the crew was breaking down the equipment and reloading it onto the trucks. By two PM, the film crew was gone, and the sidewalks flowed with normal foot traffic. In all that time I saw no sign of Jerry Sullivan, or Drew Merriweather, his assistant.

As my staff and I worked through the afternoon, we were oblivious to the fact that the footage of the medical emergency in front of our legendary coffeehouse had gone viral. Not until a pair of NYU students ordered takeout cappuccinos did we have a clue. Esther chatted them up as she prepared their drinks, and one of them surprised us with the viral video news.

Apparently, interest was amped up after New York One reported the incident occurred at the location shoot of *Only Murders in Gotham*.

There were quite a few phones out there, so a number of dramatic recordings hit the social media platforms. As soon as the students left the shop, Nancy, Tucker, and Esther dug out their phones and searched the net. Matt folded his arms and feigned disinterest.

Esther struck digital gold first. "Urban Gossip has a video, but no names. The title is 'Real Life Drama as Anonymous Citizen Gives Aid to Sick Man on Movie Set.'"

Tuck peeked over Esther's shoulder at the screen. "I must say, Matt, that your tan contrasts nicely with that powder blue shirt."

Matt shrugged off the compliment and groused about the headline.

"*Citizen*? How do they know that I'm actually a citizen? I could be a migrant or a tourist from Mesopotamia."

"If it's any consolation, they referred to you as a *Person* on WPIX News," Tuck offered. "And another local station has you on their Twitter feed."

"Okay, enough," Matt insisted.

"Any word on the man's condition?" I asked. "His name? What happened to him?"

Tuck sighed. "Nothing I can find. Only that the victim was rushed to a hospital."

"Look at this!" Nancy cried. "They're calling you both *Good Samaritans* on the Good News Network. That's so sweet."

We were staring at Nancy's phone screen with our backs to the door when the greeting bell rang.

"And look here," Nancy cried. "The first commenter on Reddit called you heroes!"

"What a joke," an angry but soft-spoken voice mocked.

I turned to find a beam of Golden State sunshine had entered our coffeehouse. On this cloudy Manhattan afternoon, the man literally radiated West Coast ambiance. His cascade of spun-gold hair gleamed brighter than his polished ivory teeth. Eyes as blue as a Pacific sky stared at us with open animosity.

I instantly recognized this Blond Adonis of Caffeine (in the opinion of the ladies on *The View*, not mine) as the CEO of Driftwood Coffee.

Cody "Drifter" Wood, former champion surfer and current coffee entrepreneur, was flanked by an entourage consisting of two young, equally blond and tanned toughs in hoodies and a young woman with tattoos on her neck and face.

Cody Wood's bluer-than-blue eyes didn't waver as he shook his head.

"Heroes?" he scoffed. "For smearing the good name of a superior coffee company? Dudes, the way I see it, you are slanderers!"

"Looks like there's going to be a rumble," Tuck quipped.

"Slander?" Matt shot back. "Now that's ironic coming from the guy who sat on the stage at the World Coffee Forum and talked about a certain coffee hunter who was really just a fading playboy. I believe you even suggested he should source Viagra instead of coffee cherries—"

Ouch, I thought. *That one was below the belt—in more ways than one!*

My ex bared his own white teeth. "Of course, you did it all without actually naming me, which would be actionable slander. But everyone in that audience knew to whom you were referring."

Cody ran fingers through his golden locks.

"Dude, not cool what you did out there on the sidewalk. Suggesting our coffee was to blame for that old fart keeling over—"

Matt silenced him with his hand.

"No, you're right," my ex said. "Putting aside that your machines might not be maintained to a high standard, I'd say that keeling over is a perfectly understandable reaction—"

"What do you mean, Allegro?"

"That anyone with good taste, or even taste buds, would naturally retch after swallowing that swill you call coffee—"

"Swill!" Blondie blinked. "Dude, you are so totally off base. Driftwood buys only *premium* beans—"

"Save it for your commercials. You buy Grade 3 beans in bulk. Then you roast them at a temperature rivaling the surface of the sun, giving you exactly two styles, too damn dark and burnt to hell, which you mask for your customers with copious amounts of steamed milk and flavored corn syrups."

Cody Wood shook a finger at Matt. "Now *that's* slander."

"No, that's where you and I differ," Matt said. "I state the *facts*, which contradict your misleading PR, so you *have* to call it slander."

Cody Wood's yellow mane shook like a shaggy sheepdog's as he turned to address his crew. "Are you getting this, Dallas? Pinot? Ventura?"

"Oh, yeah," one of the young men said with a smirk. Only then did I realize that all three members of his posse were recording the scene with their phones.

"Hey, Blondie, I'm getting it, too," Esther declared, waving her own phone.

"And me!" Nancy added.

"Me too," Tucker said. But as he fumbled to pull his phone from his pocket, he dropped it. "Dangit!"

Meanwhile, the bell over the door dinged as new customers entered. Nobody moved, or even looked in their direction. Instead, Cody faced Matt again, and puffed his machine-toned chest.

"At Driftwood, *we* employ the best roasters in the business. Not our bimbo ex-wife—"

"Okay, Beach Bum, now you crossed the line!"

Matt clenched his fists and stepped forward. I tried to stop him, but he slipped my grip. Golden Boy dropped into a martial arts crouch, and the posse backed away as Matt charged.

"Cease fire! Cease fire!" Jerry Sullivan shouted as he jumped between the two angry alphas. "Back to your corners, boys!"

Drew Merriweather was there, too, waving the blond hoodies back while his boss did all the yelling.

"There's been enough fighting in this coffeehouse. Take it from me, I know from experience, it never ends well—"

I blinked at Jerry's words. *What did he mean by that?* Before I could ask, he raised his voice another few decibels.

"Now listen up! Right this second, I want you *all* to put your phones away."

I nodded to my baristas, and they tucked their phones into their aprons.

It took a sharp second look from Jerry to get the Driftwood posse to comply, but they finally did.

When all was calm, Jerry approached me. "Clare, I came to tell you that our production will resume working tomorrow morning, six AM sharp, and we're going to need your full services."

"Excuse me?"

"I'm afraid it will be double duty for your baristas, Clare. I want them as extras while we're filming inside the coffeehouse, but I also want you and your staff to provide craft services temporarily for our crew—"

"What?!" the no longer soft-spoken Cody Wood bellowed.

Jerry faced Driftwood's CEO. "I just came from the hospital where the ambulance took Fred Denham, the member of my film crew who nearly died in front of your truck, but instead was saved by these two—" Jerry gestured in our direction. "The doctors told me that he nearly succumbed to what they believe was anaphylactic shock caused by a reaction to a toxic substance he'd consumed. And the only thing Fred consumed today was your espresso."

"But this bunch is to blame, Jerry. Someone from the Village Blend must have sabotaged us," Cody Wood ranted. "Tampered with our espressos, so they could make a big show in public with that viral video—"

"Ridiculous," Matt spat.

"That's the only answer. I'm telling you, Jerry, you can't fire us." Cody was pleading now. "Remember, we have a contract—"

"Which you violated when you poisoned my property master and armorer," Jerry replied. "Anyway, it's too late. Tina Bird and our legal counsel agree with me that Driftwood Coffee has become an insurance liability."

"I want a payout, then."

"No payout, Cody. Now you can go quietly, or Turkey Shoot Productions can issue a press release about why you were fired. What will it be?"

Cody Wood's expression was stony, though he clenched his fist when he stared at Matt.

"This isn't over," Cody muttered.

"Yes, it is," Jerry declared.

As we watched, Cody led his posse out the door. When they were gone, Jerry faced me again.

"I know it's asking a lot, but I need you, Clare. Frankly, I wanted you to have this job ever since I tasted your coffee. So, do we have a deal?"

A deal. The words of Jerry's old sketch came back to haunt me. This time there was no crooked grin. The funnyman's mouth was turned down, and his eyes were practically pleading.

I glanced at my staff. Matt was still distracted (and openly giddy) from watching Driftwood get fired, but my baristas' heads were all bobbing in excited nods.

"Yes, Jerry. You've got a deal," I said, and the silver screen smile was back as he shook my hand.

ten

❧❧❧❧❧❧❧❧❧❧❧❧❧❧❧❧❧❧

"I SURE could use another one of those Americanos, ma'am."

This marked the third visit to my coffee bar by the doe-eyed young woman in ragged denims and a faux-vintage bowling shirt. Attractive even without makeup, her laid-back Southern sweetness and melodious voice seemed out of place amid the tangled chaos of cables, lights, cameras, and equipment—never mind the shouts, the frenetic activity, and the bursts of profanity exploding from members of the crew.

It was seven AM, the second day of location shooting, and the Village Blend was now occupied territory—leased and managed by Turkey Shoot Productions for the week.

My "customer" with the slight Southern drawl had been carrying around a tattered and heavily annotated script since she'd arrived on set, so I figured her for an intern or some sort of assistant.

Coincidentally, Tuck had just passed me my own personal Americano before rushing to our basement for more milk.

"Here you go. Enjoy it," I said as I passed it on.

"Oh, I will! Your coffee is amazing! Much better than that craft services stuff, Ms.—" She squinted as she read my name tag. "Cosi. Why, what a cute name."

She introduced herself as "Kay."

"Well, Kay, we make our espresso drinks fresh—to order. We never serve stale coffee or leave drinks sitting on the counter. Our baristas are well trained, and we're vigilant about safety procedures, so you have nothing to worry about, okay?"

"That's good to know!" Kay nodded, looking relieved. "Thank you for the reassurance, Ms. Cosi. You don't mind if I rest my bones at this really nice coffee bar, do you? I want to avoid all the craziness."

"Please, make yourself comfortable, and feel free to call me Clare."

Tall and slender, she claimed a bar chair, crossed her long legs, placed her script on the counter, and tied her baby-fine strawberry blond hair into a ponytail.

"Say, Clare, is this real marble? It's such a lovely color."

"Yes, it's actual Italian marble and very old."

After finishing with her hair, she began leafing through the script. A few minutes later, she sighed and looked up.

"I'm so glad I stayed in the trailer yesterday." Kay shuddered. "I'm happy that Fred is going to be okay, but ever since my father passed on to his heavenly reward, I panic when I see someone get sick like that."

"It was pretty shocking."

Kay shook her head. "I haven't been on that many sets in my life, Ms. Cosi, but I hope they're not all this dangerous."

"Dangerous?"

"Well, maybe just accident prone." She leaned across the counter. "On the very first day of shooting this second season on a soundstage in Queens, Jerry's assistant broke his leg in two places. A bank of lights dropped on him from the ceiling. It happened right in the middle of the set."

"That's terrible. This wasn't Drew Merriweather, though?"

"No. His name was Norman. He was a guy Jerry had hired himself. A sweet fellow, too. He was with us through the whole first season."

"And Drew came along when?"

"Right after the accident. They replaced Jerry's guy with Drew, bumped him up from some gofer position in the back office."

"I'm sorry—*who* exactly hired Drew?"

She shrugged and shook her head. A moment later, a member of the production staff touched her arm and pointed to a guy standing in the center of a crowd of crew members.

"He needs you over there for a setup."

The "He" was the show's director, Sebastian Albee, a mochaccino drinker in his early thirties who (coincidentally enough, considering his preference for chocolate-flavored coffee) reminded me of Willy Wonka.

Maybe it was his Technicolor wardrobe: a purple runner's jacket over lime-green pajama-style pants and red high-top sneakers. Or maybe it was his thick, high crown of beige-ish hair that—combined with his rail-thin physique—gave him the appearance of a walking porcini mushroom. Either way, the guy's personality was intense. When he wasn't chewing on his thumb in a state of totally absorbed focus, he was speaking and gesticulating with great earnestness.

"I'm coming, Sebastian." Kay drained her cup and sighed. "Duty calls. But thanks again, Ms. Cosi—"

"Clare."

"Clare it is!"

Tucker reappeared with a gallon of milk in each hand, and I helped him reload the undercounter fridge.

"Guess who I caught trying to sneak in our back door?" he asked.

"I don't know. A member of the paparazzi?"

"Nope."

"The Driftwood legal team?

"Guess again."

"A Jerry Sullivan stalker?"

"Close enough. Here's a hint. *Cock-a-doodle-doo!*"

"Lizzy Meeks? What did she want?"

"She said she forgot her pass and didn't want to trouble anyone on the production crew."

"You didn't let her in, did you?"

"Don't worry. I remembered that unhinged conversation she had with us yesterday—and the fact that Jerry is trying to avoid her. So I told her she would have to go around to the trucks in front and get a new pass because it wasn't up to me to admit her."

"What happened next?"

"She objected and tried to get by me, but I blocked her, sort of edged her out the door, and locked it behind her."

I sighed with relief. "Good. I'm glad that's over."

"And I was glad to see that you were having a much more positive interaction."

"You mean with that Kay girl? Yes, she and I had a nice little talk. She's very sweet—"

"That Kay girl?" Tuck raised an eyebrow. "Is that what you said?"

"K-A-Y," I spelled. "It must be short for Katherine. Why are you giving me that weird look?"

I turned from Tucker to scan the room for the young woman. She was still talking to the porcini mushroom man, which I found curious, given the director's status here. Odder still, Willy Wonka didn't appear to be tossing off orders to her. Instead, he was concentrating with engrossed interest on every word Kay spoke.

"What do you think she does?" I asked Tuck. "Is she a script girl, an assistant? I don't think she's an intern. She looks too important for that."

"You're kidding, right?"

"What do you mean?"

"Well, first of all, you misspelled her name. It's not K-A-Y, it's simply the letter *K*, like on the cover of her first album."

"Album?"

"Yes, Clare. That's Kylee Ferris, this show's costar, arguably the *real* star if you want to go by the rantings of Lizzy Meeks—and a lot of the press and media coverage."

I was gobsmacked, especially given Lizzy's less-than-flattering description of Kylee as some kind of spoiled diva, which she clearly was not. Mostly, I was surprised at how different she looked and sounded from the character she played on-screen.

"In the show she's not a strawberry blonde. She has dark brown curly hair."

"It's a wig, Clare."

"I can see that now! She also talks with a Brooklyn accent."

"That's called acting."

"But I thought she was some kind of former teen pop star?"

"She was. And this is a smart move for her future. You know the old adage about acting and singing, don't you?"

"What adage?"

"You can turn a singer into an actor, but you can't train an actor to sing."

"I never heard that adage."

"Let me put it this way: Cher won an Oscar for her role in *Moonstruck*. Have you ever seen Clint Eastwood's musical numbers in *Paint Your Wagon*?"

"No, never."

"All I can say is, I'm glad Dirty Harry became a director."

"Speaking of directors, what do you think of Jerry's director?"

"You mean Mr. Sebastian Albee over there? He's one of the best young filmmakers in the industry. Two Emmy Awards already. Before that, he directed award-winning music videos. Prior to that, his animated shorts won prizes at prestigious festivals—"

A young man interrupted us and handed Tucker some papers.

"Those are your script pages," he said. "Jerry wanted me to apologize because you're getting them so late. Stuff is being rewritten constantly, and your scene was only finalized last night."

Tucker realized he was holding only three pages. "This is only one scene. Where's the rest of the script?"

"Oh, that's confidential. Performers get access to the shooting scripts on a need-to-know basis."

Tuck shrugged. "I assume I'm playing Leon the waiter?"

"Yes. Only you and Jerry are in this scene. Sebastian provided background notes in the margins to help you build your character."

The script boy left, and Tuck scanned the pages. Suddenly, he gasped.

"Juicy role?" I asked.

"So juicy I'm going to need a special costume prop," Tuck replied. "I'd better call Punch and have him bring over my magic box, pronto."

Punch was Tuck's special guy. He was also a brilliant cabaret performer and a local cult-celebrity in his own right who'd appeared in several of Tucker's off-off-Broadway productions.

Tuck speed-dialed his boyfriend. The conversation was short, and when it was over, Esther and Nancy approached him.

"I have a legal question, Mr. Showbiz," Esther began. "Can you tell me what this is exactly?" She displayed a double-sided sheet of paper covered with tiny type.

"*That*, my Goth princess, is a model release—"

"Why did I get one? I'm not a fashion model."

"You most certainly are not."

Esther's eyes narrowed. "What's that supposed to mean?"

Tuck dodged the second question by answering the first. "That *little* form gives the production *big* legal protection in using your likeness and voice. Bottom line, sweetie, you have to sign it before you can appear as an extra."

"Wait!" Nancy cried, waving her own paper. "If I sign this, I'm going to be on Jerry's show?"

Tuck shrugged again. "Apparently. Matt just signed his, and so did Dante. I presume they will appear on camera, too, probably as extras."

Nancy burst into song as she danced a jig. "I'm going to be on Jerry's show . . . Jerry's show . . . Jerry's show . . ."

Esther rolled her eyes, but I was happy for Nancy. In fact, I was happy for all of my staff and Matt, too—even though I felt like I wasn't invited to the party.

I suspected I'd been excluded because I declined to fall on my rump for a worldwide audience. Maybe Jerry assumed I had no interest in being an extra in any capacity. Or maybe he was peeved that I didn't jump at the chance to be on his show, and he was holding a grudge. I hated to think it was the latter, but I didn't regret my decision.

After all, I was no actor. The spotlight was unforgiving. And if I died tomorrow, I would rather be remembered for serving up "Dominique Ansel" lattes than Lucy Ricardo pratfalls.

Eleven

A SHORT time later, Sebastian Albee was praising my assistant manager.

"You nailed it, Tucker," the director said. "Three walk-throughs and you hit your marks every time. Now let's see if Jerry is up to your high standards."

So many crew members were clustered around a trench-coated Jerry Sullivan that he had to raise a hand above a sea of heads to get Sebastian's attention.

"We're still waiting for the assistant property master," he called. "Along with my fedora."

"I have your hat, Mr. Sullivan," a member of the costume crew called from outside the circle.

Sebastian cursed. "Where the deuce is Hutch? We're burning daylight."

Tina Bird jumped in. "I'm on it."

When it came to "Tweety," as Jerry had dubbed her, size didn't matter. More petite than even me, she wore her yellow hair in a pixie cut and an *Only Murders in Gotham* T-shirt with the words *Production Manager* emblazoned in large letters across her back.

Incessantly on the move, from the trucks outside to the set inside, Tweety did indeed remind me of a little bird, flitting back and forth. But she was no lightweight. And the crew knew it. Whenever Ms. Bird came around, everyone became more businesslike, more organized, and a whole lot quieter.

I also noticed after Tina consumed her no-nonsense triple espresso, the crew's continuous coffee breaks ended, and the final setups began in earnest.

Esther joined me behind the counter, where we were out of everyone's way but could still see all the action.

"I heard Punch was here," Esther said softly.

"Tuck let him in through the back-alley door since he didn't have a pass," I whispered.

"Oh, that's why I found the back door wide open."

"What do you mean *wide open*?"

Esther shrugged. "When I found it that way, I shut it again."

"Did you notice anyone in the alley before you shut the door? Or near the back pantry who shouldn't be?"

"Like who?"

"Like a slender brunette in designer heels and business attire."

"Um, no. I mean no one like that was near the pantry, and I didn't bother looking in the alley. I just shut the door and locked it. Why did Punch have to sneak onto the set, anyway?"

"He brought Tuck's 'magic box'—that's what he calls it. It's really just a Pullman suitcase full of makeup, prosthetics, and costume props."

Esther made a face. "That's odd. Tucker is all made up now, and he doesn't look any different."

I agreed.

When Punch had first arrived, the pair retreated to our basement roasting room. (The actual stars had their own dressing rooms in trailers outside.) In the meantime, I couldn't help wondering what Tuck and Punch were doing downstairs, and how they planned to transform Tucker into "Leon"—maybe a fake mustache and slicked-back hair? Perhaps a scar on his cheek?

But as Esther said, when Tuck returned, he didn't look any different, though he *did* adopt a surly attitude suitable for a haughty waiter.

Sebastian Albee was pleased. Before Jerry even came to the set, he had Tuck snarl into the camera, laugh dementedly, and look bemused—reaction shots, the director said, to be edited in later.

Then, about an hour ago, Jerry Sullivan arrived, and Sebastian began to set up an elaborate scene. Two cameras would be used, since Jerry and Tucker would be standing on opposite ends of the room. Tuck wouldn't let me see his script, so I had no idea what was about to happen.

After the makeup people finished fussing with Jerry and Tucker, the costume crew fitted Jerry with a fedora comically large enough to rival a sombrero. Then everyone stepped off camera. But there was still no sign of the property master.

"Are we ever going to do this?" Jerry asked.

Suddenly, a young Black man with dyed red Rasta locks burst through the coffeehouse door.

"I'm here, I'm here!" he cried. Hutch Saunders clutched an aluminum case with both hands. "Sorry it took so long. The case wasn't locked up like it should have been. I found it dumped in one of the equipment trucks!"

Hutch brushed his red locks aside and set the metal case on a table. When he opened the Pandora's box, I saw a very big handgun nestled in molded Styrofoam.

"Look what Clint Eastwood sent over," Jerry cracked. "I guess he wanted to 'make our day.'"

The crew laughed, but not Tweety Bird.

"Are you sure that gun is big enough, Sebastian?" she asked (sarcastically).

The director shrugged. "Jerry's script called for a quote, unquote, 'comically large gun.'"

Esther leaned close to me. "That gun is way more scary than it is funny."

A second later, the production manager echoed her concern. "That certainly looks like a real gun."

Hutch grinned. "That's because it *is* a real gun."

Tweety frowned. "Are you sure that thing is safe? Fred Denham is still in the hospital. I still say we should have waited for him to be discharged or hired a replacement armorer."

"Relax," Hutch said. "I helped Fred pack the blank and load this gun yesterday morning before he got sick. It's just a little gunpowder and a cotton ball, that's all. There'll be a big flash and a little noise—so little you may need a Foley guy to dub in a gunshot in postproduction."

Tweety looked doubtful.

"Scout's honor," Hutch said. "Fred and I were *real* careful."

Sebastian Albee clapped once. "Okay, then. Everyone take your places, and let's try to get this on the first take."

The director positioned four extras at tables near Tucker and briefed them on their actions. As he did, Esther leaned close again.

"Am I seeing things or are two of those extras *Driftwood baristas* from yesterday?"

"They must have signed releases before their company was fired. I guess the director thinks they have the right look for this particular shot."

"Shot is right," Esther groused. "I wish someone would shoot them."

"I'm going to assume you mean with a camera, which is about to take place," I warned. "So zip it before they kick us off the set."

I was relieved to see Esther follow my advice, and together we watched the director add two more extras to his shot—Matt and Nancy—whom he positioned at a table right behind Jerry.

Matt looked totally calm, cool, and collected (of course), but Nancy could barely contain her excitement. She gave us a little wave, and we waved back.

Finally, Sebastian Albee addressed Tucker.

"This is a going to be one of Jerry's fantasy scenes. Jerry came to this coffeehouse to talk to Leon. Leon, meanwhile, is deliberately ignoring Jerry. Jerry gets so infuriated he pulls that ridiculous gun out of his trench coat and that's when he shoots you."

Tuck nodded. "Got it."

"As you know, we're not using explosive squibs or blood bags," the director continued. "This is not supposed to be realistic. We're going for a 1940s movie vibe. No blood, not even a bullet hole. And I want you to really ham it up, Tucker. Give us a little Jimmy Cagney mixed with Paul Muni in *Scarface*."

"How about this?"

Tucker proceeded to clutch his chest, stagger, reach out one arm as if pleading with heaven—with a tortured expression to go with it. After a few long beats, Tucker slowly sank to the floor.

"Almost perfect," Sebastian said. "But I want you to stretch it out a little longer. This is comedy. Don't be afraid to look stupid."

"Let's do it," Tuck replied.

Camera operators stepped behind both cameras, and the sound guy donned earphones. Someone threw a switch, and the center of my coffeehouse was bathed in light.

Hutch struggled to slip the weapon into Jerry's trench coat. The handgun's barrel was so long that the material barely covered it.

"Don't worry about recoil, Mr. Sullivan," Hutch said. "Fred and I went light on the gunpowder."

With that, the assistant property master stepped off camera.

Now two actors and six extras became the center of the universe.

"Quiet on the set!"

Esther poked me with her elbow, and we shared excited looks.

"Rolling, one!" called the first camera operator.

"Rolling, two," said the other.

A man stepped into the shot holding a clapper board with a digital clock ticking away in big red numbers.

"Scene eleven, take one, mark!"

I literally jumped when he slapped the boards together.

Sebastian waited a beat and whispered, "Action."

As the shot began, Jerry's gaze was focused on the floor, his face hidden by the oversized fedora. Slowly, he raised his head until he was staring at Leon (played by Tucker) across the half-empty room.

"Hey, Leon," Jerry called. "Since you won't serve me, I'm going to serve you—"

Jerry whipped out the oversized handgun, aimed, and pulled the trigger.

In the confined space of the coffeehouse, the explosion was literally deafening—so loud the sound man ripped the earphones from his head.

As the echo faded, everyone remained frozen in place.

Jerry had displayed a look of instant shock when the gun jerked in his hand, but poor Tucker had no time to register any emotion. There was no hammy performance, either. Instead, my assistant manager was *blasted backward*, crashing into a table before falling to the floor.

The sight was sickening, and I knew at once it wasn't make-believe.

I saw the ragged hole in Tuck's apron, right over his heart, and I felt as though my own heart stopped beating.

I wasn't the only one paralyzed. Everyone on set stared with gaping mouths, trying to process the shock of what they'd just witnessed.

As a puff of gray smoke rose from the wound and Tucker lay still as death, it was Esther who broke the spell. No longer willing to be "quiet on the set," our urban poet let out an outraged scream.

Shaken out of his shock, Jerry Sullivan released the gun. It clattered to the floor. Behind him, Matt and Nancy jumped to their feet, and others moved toward Tucker's side. But it was Esther who got to him first. She dropped to her knees and cradled his head.

"Tucker! Wake up! Please, wake up!"

Through runny black eyeliner, Esther's cries melted into frightened sobs. But her expression of shocked grief turned to startled relief when Tucker suddenly gave a loud moan.

Matt, Nancy, and I reached Tuck as he rasped—

"I think I hit my head."

In a failed attempt to sit up, Tuck tumbled onto his side. I heard a click as the spent bullet fell from his ravaged apron to the hardwood floor.

"How . . . How is this possible?" Esther asked.

Matt picked up the bullet and immediately dropped it again. "Ouch, that's hot!"

Nancy stared at the object on the floor. "Is that what blanks are supposed to do?"

"That's not a blank," Matt said, exchanging a look with me. "That's a real bullet. So what the hell was it doing in Jerry's gun?"

An ominous silence followed. Then Tucker sat up, with Esther's help. He rubbed the back of his head and the hole in his apron at the same time.

"I think I cracked a rib . . ." Tucker tore away the tattered apron and opened his ruined shirt, revealing the "magic box costume prop" that had saved his life.

Beneath his clothes, my brilliant barista was wearing a dark gray bulletproof vest.

TWELVE

ESTHER gently applied an ice pack to the lump on Tucker's head. He winced at the touch.

"How are you doing?" Tina Bird asked.

"I'm a little dizzy," Tuck replied. "And my ribs hurt."

"We're going to get you to a doctor soon," she promised.

"A good doctor in a *private* clinic," Jerry added, exchanging a meaningful look with Tweety. "Someone who will be discreet."

Meanwhile, Sebastian examined the ragged tear in the bulletproof vest. "Why were you wearing this?" he asked.

Tucker frowned. "Three reasons. Jon-Erik Hexum, Brandon Lee, and Halyna Hutchins."

For a beat you could hear crickets—or you would have, if there had been any crickets inside our coffeehouse.

"Who are they?" Nancy whispered to me, Matt, and Esther.

As quiet as she tried to be, Tucker heard her.

"Three people who died from gun accidents on sets," Tuck said and moaned again.

"Tucker should be at a hospital right now," I insisted. "He needs a chest X-ray—"

"And that lump on his head should be checked, too," Matt added. "Tuck might have a concussion."

Jerry waved us back. "Easy, easy, Tuck will get all that care and more. My assistant is making the arrangements now. Tucker won't have to wait for hours in an ER, either. He'll be treated the moment he walks through the door."

Drew Merriweather pocketed his phone, pushed up his horn-rimmed glasses, and hopped off the coffee bar chair.

"It's all arranged, Jerry," he said. "They're ready to receive him, and we've got a luxury SUV outside to take Tucker uptown."

Jerry nodded. "I'm going with him."

"I hope it's a large vehicle," I said. "Because I'm going, too."

THE ride turned out to be roomy enough to accommodate Esther and Drew Meriweather as well. Matt and Nancy remained behind to look after the coffeehouse—and share shifts with Dante, who was currently serving our regular customers from the Village Blend coffee truck.

I wanted to have a talk with Jerry, but he rode beside the driver and spoke into his phone the whole trip.

The SUV rolled up Broadway, around Columbus Circle, and past Lincoln Center. We stopped on 68th Street, in front of a glass-and-steel office building. On the sidewalk, Jerry steered us away from the main entrance to a windowless, featureless steel door with a small brass plaque that read *Bedford-Barton Wellness*.

He pressed the bell, and we were admitted.

With a name like Bedford-Barton Wellness, I expected a health spa. What I found instead was a small, ultramodern, and very private medical facility with two doctors on duty, several nurses, technicians, diagnostic machines, and even rooms for extended stays.

A nurse sat Tucker in a wheelchair and whisked him off for an exam, including X-rays and a CAT scan. Jerry guided the rest of us to a small waiting room with modern furniture, a refreshment bar, and a flat-screen television streaming nature videos with calming ambient music.

When Jerry and Drew sat away from us and began speaking in hushed tones, Esther leaned close.

"What is this place?" she whispered.

"It's a concierge emergency room," I whispered back. "I read about these in the *Times* but never visited one."

"How expensive is it?"

"Upward of ten thou a year. And that's only for basic 24-7 access. Testing and treatment costs are extra."

Esther looked around the room and shuddered. "Sorry, but this place gives me the creeps."

"It's an ultraclean, state-of-the-art health care facility. How could it possibly give you the creeps?"

"It reminds me of the secret hospital in that classic horror film *Seconds*, where they turned a rich old man into Rock Hudson."

"Get a grip, Esther. This place isn't science fiction."

"Hey, when it comes to you and me—and anyone else in this town who *isn't* a one percenter—it might as well be."

With that, I couldn't argue. Everyone in New York knew emergency room walk-in visits were all-day, camp-out affairs.

"When my boyfriend needed stiches last month, it took so long to get Boris through the process, I had to bring his lunch and dinner to the waiting room. I was ready to buy a sleeping bag when they finally treated and discharged him."

"Well, I'm glad Jerry brought us here," I said, "because Tuck is being seen right away. I'm guessing he's using his personal membership account, which is nice of him."

"It's not that nice."

"What do you mean?"

"I mean, the guy's got to know that Tucker could sue the pants off him and the production company."

"He could," I said. "But he won't."

"What makes you so sure?"

"Tucker once told me about an actor friend who sued after an on-set injury. He was blacklisted ever after. In Tuck's view, the guy should have taken the standard insurance payout. Now he'll never work again. Tucker said he'd never launch a lawsuit that could kill his acting career. He loves it too much . . ."

After a few more minutes of waiting, Jerry left the room. Drew was alone now, and on the phone. Esther started texting Boris, and I checked for messages on my own phone.

Sensing someone's approach, I looked up and found myself gaping with complete surprise into the gently wrinkled face of my former mother-in-law and current employer, the legendary owner of the Village Blend herself, Madame Blanche Dreyfus Allegro Dubois.

"Oh, Clare," she said, "I came as soon as I heard the terrible news."

I was doubly surprised to see the woman because I didn't call her, and it wasn't like Matt to phone his mother over this kind of thing. (The Matteo Allegro I knew preferred to keep risks to himself and bad news in mothballs.)

In all honesty, I might have agreed to keep Matt's mother in the dark on this one. But that was hardly an option now. Facts were facts, truth was truth, and my beloved mentor was standing right in front of me expecting both.

Thirteen

~~~~~~

"I KNOW we must wait for the doctors to tell us how our Tucker is doing, but how are you faring, dear? You look a little shell-shocked."

Madame's arrival was so unexpected, it took me a moment to reply.

As I gathered my thoughts, I couldn't help admiring her elegant outfit. As stylish as ever, my octogenarian employer was swathed in cashmere today. Her car coat looked as soft and creamy as cappuccino foam, the perfect blank canvas for the vibrant colors of her silk scarf.

Forever the art school dropout, I immediately recognized the scarf's print as one of Georgia O'Keeffe's works. The deep purples in the modernist masterpiece brought out the stunning violet hue in Madame's eyes, one reason her intense gaze—framed by her sleek silver pageboy—had such a beguiling effect, especially on men.

Age was of no consequence when it came to Matt's mother. I'd seen young men stop and spin to hold doors for her; middle-aged men insist on buying her drinks at the bar; and older men court her like royalty.

Make no mistake, however. Beneath all that cashmere, a spine of steel had been forged over years of recoveries from pain and loss, beginning with the deaths of her mother and sister during their family's flight from Paris.

As Nazi tanks rolled in, young Blanche was whisked to a new country with a new language and no mother or sister to comfort or counsel her. After becoming a woman, she found true love, only to lose it too soon when Matt's father was killed. Then she struggled for years to keep the Village Blend afloat while she finished raising Matt.

That's one reason she kept her coffeehouse doors open for all those struggling artists, actors, musicians, and comics working the Village clubs and theaters. She knew what it was to feel alone in the world. To have a dream and lose it. To fight for your place and still be rejected. Then find the energy to begin again, after a long, hard day . . .

Looking concerned, Madame sat down beside me.

"Are you all right, Clare?"

"I'm a little shaken up, I guess."

She took my hand. "I'm glad I came, then."

"How did you even know to come here? Was it Matt? I thought by now you and your friend Babka were on your way to her house in East Hampton."

"Jerry phoned me about the accident as I was heading for the helipad. Babka's delaying the flight for me. She doesn't mind. I turned my driver around and here I am."

That's when I noticed Jerry hovering close by.

"I knew Blanche would want to know," he said.

The way he said "Blanche" intrigued me, as if they were old friends. But until this moment, I thought the pair had met only once—at a New York charity function where Jerry supposedly first proposed the idea of using the Village Blend as a location for his show's second season.

It was Esther who blurted out the question. "Hey, how long have you two known each other, anyway?"

Madame shared a mysterious glance with Jerry, who answered—

"For more years than you've been alive, Ms. Best."

Of course, I wondered why Madame had never mentioned knowing Jerry Sullivan from the old days. But this wasn't the time or place to grill her on her personal history. When a nurse appeared at the door and gestured to Jerry, I watched with hope, praying there was good news.

But there was no news. Instead, the pair disappeared around the corner.

"I'm sure Tucker will be fine," Madame said, as her violet gaze studied my worried frown. "Jerry tells me that firearm incidents are common and that even blanks can be dangerous—"

"This wasn't a blank," I quickly informed her. "Someone loaded a real bullet into that gun. Tucker would be dead now—and Jerry would be in police custody—if Tuck hadn't had the foresight to wear a bulletproof vest."

Madame expressed surprise, then frowned. "Are you certain it was a real bullet, Clare?"

"When your son picked it up off the floor, the bullet was still hot."

"Look who's back!" Esther cried.

Jerry returned with Tucker beside him.

Esther rushed to her friend and went in for a big hug. Tucker winced.

"Gently, Esther. Gently," he pleaded.

"You're okay?" she asked.

"He's aces," Jerry answered. "No concussion, and no broken ribs. He has a hell of a bruise though."

"They gave me a painkiller," Tuck added. "Which hasn't quite kicked in yet."

"Is Tucker being discharged?" I asked. "If he is, we should take him home right away."

"Let's hold off on that for a few minutes," Jerry said. "We need to talk about something first."

With a stony expression, he closed the waiting room door for privacy. Then he spoke.

"We can count our blessings that Tucker is okay. What happened at your coffeehouse today was a terrible accident—"

"That was no accident," I asserted. "Someone deliberately loaded that gun with a real bullet."

"You don't know that," Jerry countered. "All kinds of things could have happened. Hutch could have grabbed the wrong case. He told everyone he had to look for the gun. Maybe he found the wrong one."

"He should be questioned," I said. "Along with your production's armorer, Fred Denham."

"Fred is still in the hospital from that awful coffee poisoning yesterday. And Tina Bird will question him when he's well enough. In the meantime, she's questioning Hutch right now. She's the production manager. And she's responsible for getting to the bottom of this thing."

"You mistake my meaning. The police should be doing the questioning. NYPD detectives should be on this case—"

Jerry's face went pale. "I am begging you not to pursue that. Calling for that kind of investigation could end this season, and probably the show."

"But why?" Madame asked.

Jerry rubbed his cheeks with both hands. "For about a dozen reasons, Blanche. Calling in the law means delays, safety reviews, and tons of red tape, never mind what the police might find—which is probably nothing more than a stupid mistake. We can't let that happen, because the whole production will fall apart."

"How, exactly?" I asked.

Jerry began ticking off fingers. "Our director, Sebastian Albee, is eager to make a feature film after this gig. Sebastian is one of the reasons our first season was a smash hit. With a major delay, we could lose him."

He counted off another finger. "Kylee Ferris is blazing hot at the moment, thanks to being cast in the first season of my show, and she's been fielding offers like crazy. A delay could give her agent leverage in breaking her three-season contract."

He sighed as he went to a third finger.

"And then there's Billy Saddler—"

"Billy Saddler? Wow!" Tucker said, impressed. "He's had a great career, starting with those old network TV days on *New York Comedy Night*. Everyone loves Billy. What does he have to do with this?"

"Billy's been semiretired since he hosted the Oscars three years ago," Jerry said. "I did a lot of fast-talking and called in a favor to convince him to appear in our next four episodes. Billy is due on set next week, but if there is a delay, he's gone, too—back to his happy life in Barcelona where he and his young, pregnant wife run an art gallery."

Jerry took a breath. "And finally, there's the insurance."

Esther blinked. "Since when does State Farm tell Hollywood what to do?"

"Since forever," Jerry replied.

Tuck jumped in. "You can't make a television show or movie without insurance, Esther. All kinds of coverage, too. On the actors, the project, even against future lawsuits."

"Tucker is right," Jerry said. "And we've already had two *on-the-record* injuries filming the first four episodes. My original assistant is now at an upstate clinic learning to walk again. And as I mentioned, Fred

Denham is lying in a hospital bed at Mount Sinai. At this rate, we're due for three more incidents before the season wraps."

"That's absurd," Madame said. "You don't know that's going to happen."

"Neither does the insurance company, but that's how they are going to see it. Without insurance, this show becomes a write-off. Do you want to be responsible for that, Clare? Blanche? Anyone?"

I didn't know how to reply, and nobody else did, either. Fast-talking Jerry didn't give anyone a chance to, anyway.

"Do you really want to put those camera operators, sound and light technicians, grips, and production assistants out of work? Not to mention our postproduction people. And think about this. If there *is* an investigation, this show becomes a black mark on all of their résumés. Some of these people may never work again."

Jerry was quiet for a beat. When he spoke again, his tone was different, cajoling.

"How about we make a deal?"

Fourteen

~~~~~~

MAKE a deal.

That's what Jerry wanted to do, which seemed innocent enough. After all, dealmaking was the lifeblood of this town—anyone doing business (legit or otherwise) in the City That Never Sleeps could tell you that. Deals were proposed, accepted, and rejected every hour of every day.

Unfortunately, the first "deal" Jerry had offered me involved falling on my rump, so naturally, I was skeptical.

Esther was, too.

"What kind of deal?" she instantly asked.

"I fired the caterer yesterday," Jerry reminded us. "The Village Blend pinch-hit today, and everyone is happy about it—well, everyone but the Driftwood baristas we kept on hand as extras—"

He flashed a frozen grin.

None of us laughed.

"Okay, bad joke. Anyway, your coffee is outstanding, and your bakery goodies are delicious. Why don't you guys continue to provide our craft services? I'll have a contract drawn up right away. I'm sure you can find a vendor who can add premade sandwiches and wraps, some soups, and container salads to your menu. You've obviously got the coffee and espresso drinks covered and all the cold drinks in your customer fridge. It's great money. After we wrap at your shop, you can use your coffee truck to provide the refreshments for our other location shoots, and the Village Blend will be in the credits of every season two episode."

Jerry faced Madame. "It's the kind of international exposure your legacy coffeehouse deserves, Blanche." He paused before adding, "And you *know* I owe you."

Madame waved her hand. "We talked about that. You don't owe me anything."

"Yes, I do. You know I do. After all these years, this is my chance to make amends."

Tucker, Esther, and I shared curious glances at that admission. I was dying to pursue it, but Madame caught my eye and gave a little shake of her silver pageboy that clearly said—

Not now, Clare. Leave it alone.

While I bit my tongue, Jerry barreled on.

"And, Tucker—" He faced my wounded assistant manager. "I want you to take on a new role. It will be a better part, and you'll appear at least once in each of the next four episodes."

Tuck's jaw dropped. "Gulp," he quipped.

"And you, Esther. How would you like to do a slam poetry reading on our show? There's a scene in a bar coming up, and I think you're the perfect replacement for the torch singer. One script change is all it takes, so what will it be?"

"Gulp," Esther echoed.

"And you, Clare. You can appear in your Village Blend apron, without falling on your ass! I promise. We'll even shoot B-roll for intercuts of you making espresso and those famous lattes of yours. Do we have a deal?"

I realized I'd just witnessed Jerry "perform" two out of three of his old sketches from *The Coffey Break*. He'd bludgeoned us with guilt about the fate of his crew, mimicking the way his comic character used to bludgeon the poor guy in *Lean on Louey*.

Then he'd played the smarmy *How's This for a Deal* guy—to perfection, in my opinion, because it was clear he'd won over Madame, Tuck, and even the ever-skeptical Esther.

Now I was waiting for the *Columbo* joke, and Jerry didn't disappoint.

After everyone voted yes, except yours truly, who abstained, Jerry was obviously relieved.

"I promise you won't regret your decision," he said. "But before we say good night, *there's just one more thing—*"

Here it comes.

"Tina Bird is back at the Village Blend giving the same warning speech I gave you, and hopefully everyone will agree to remain mum. And that means you all, too. I'm not kidding. You can't mention what happened today. Not to a soul. Not your mother, your lover, your anybody."

Jerry pointed. "You have a boyfriend, right, Tuck?"

Tuck nodded.

"You can't tell him what really happened—"

"But Punch is going to see the bruise on my chest—"

"Tell him you fell down the steps, tell him you impaled yourself on an espresso machine. Make something up. You don't want to worry about him telling anyone else and risking a shutdown of the set—and your new part, do you?"

"Okay, I'll make something up. But I don't like it," Tuck replied.

"Same for you, Esther. Boyfriend, girlfriend, or spouse, you can't say a word."

"I don't like it, either, but I won't tell Boris."

"And Clare. Do you have a spouse?"

"Fiancé. He's a lieutenant in the New York Police Department."

"Oh, jeez." Jerry's eyes went wide. "You *really* can't tell him."

"Wait a minute," I said. "What about the police who are routinely assigned to New York location filming? Weren't there any cops on duty today?"

"Two uniformed police are assigned to us for crowd control on days when we shoot outside. But we weren't shooting outside today. During Tucker's scene, they were on the sidewalk. As far as they know, Tucker was a stuntman, and everything went as planned. So, there's no need to blow this up into something bigger than it is. Please, I'm begging you . . ."

I mulled over Jerry's offer, which I had not yet accepted.

This opportunity for the Village Blend was a rare one, I had to admit, but the *Lean on Louey* guilt trip that Jerry laid on us all was what ultimately persuaded me—along with Tucker's and Esther's pleading eyes. It was too much to bear. I told myself Tuck wasn't hurt, so no harm was done, but I still didn't feel good about this. It felt like a deal with . . . well, not a devil, more like a slippery Santa's elf.

In the end, for the sake of everyone else, I accepted—but with a caveat of my own.

"I'll go along with this charade, as long as you accept that I'll be doing my own investigating."

"Your own investigating?" Jerry blinked. "I don't understand."

"You don't have to. Just give me some latitude on the set, especially if people complain about my nosiness."

"Hold on." Jerry lifted his palms. "How is this 'nosiness' going to manifest itself exactly?"

"Some of it will be innocent questioning. And some observational."

"Sorry." Jerry still looked perplexed. "What is *observational* detecting?"

"Spying!" Madame clarified. "It's a marvelous idea. Clare has a genuine knack for amateur sleuthing."

"I thought she had a knack for roasting coffee and inventing lattes."

"That too," Madame replied. "But then you play piano and golf, don't you? You don't *just* make people laugh."

"I see your point. I just don't see sleuthing as a weekend hobby."

"Oh, pooh. Anyone who enjoys crosswords or putting together puzzles is playing a deduction game. Clare simply helps out friends and family when they find themselves in hot water. I've even assisted her when the game is afoot."

"The game is a what?"

"Why, Jerry, I'm surprised at you," Madame scolded. "Don't you know the famous saying from Sherlock Holmes?"

"Actually, Madame," Tucker interjected, "the original is from Shakespeare. *Henry IV, Part 1*, Northumberland says, 'Before the game is afoot, thou still let'st slip.'"

"Well, of course!" Madame said. "Holmes would have been well versed in Shakespeare."

Jerry held his head. "Forget the foot! The toes. And *this* heel. You folks don't need to get in the game. You don't need to do a thing—other than keep my production caffeinated. Like I said, I already asked Tina Bird to question the crew."

"But who will question Tina?" I calmly asked.

"What do you mean?"

"How can you be sure Tina Bird doesn't have a secret motive for sabotaging this set—or you personally?"

"Secret motive?" Jerry threw up his hands. "Clare, where are you getting this crazy conspiracy theory stuff?"

"From you."

"Me!"

"On the day we met, you used the word *sabotage*."

"As hyperbole! I also used the word *cursed*. But I'm not superstitious. Or paranoid. I'm a comedian." He blinked. "On the other hand, most comedians are superstitious and paranoid. Could be the drugs."

We all stared at him.

"People, I'm joking!"

"Be as witty as you like," I said. "We can always use a laugh. But I'm sure your assistant Norman isn't laughing. I heard about what happened to him a few weeks ago on a soundstage—"

"The studio investigated that. Burn marks indicated that a power surge brought down those lights. We moved to another soundstage, and everything went smoothly after that—"

"Smoothly!" I cried. "Take another look at Tucker. Consider where you'd be if he hadn't had the foresight to make himself bulletproof."

Jerry sighed. "What happened to Tucker was awful. *Unacceptable.* And I assure you nothing like that will happen again. I'm hiring more security guards for our set. *And* I'm writing real guns out of every episode for the rest of the season. We don't need guns on the set anymore—or an armorer, which means Fred Denham will simply return to his primary job as property master . . . when he's out of the hospital from that coffee poisoning, anyway."

"What about my fantasy death scene?" Tucker asked, clearly disappointed.

"Oh, you'll get to play it, don't worry."

"But you said no guns."

"No real guns. It's a fantasy sequence. And a comedy. We'll use a squirt gun or maybe a paintball gun. Don't worry. I promise it will *kill*!" Everyone gasped, and Jerry cringed. "Oh, whoops. My bad on the comedy slang. It will be *hilarious*, a real crowd-pleaser, guaranteed."

He faced me. "So you see, Clare, there's no reason to be paranoid. I'm sure nobody is out to intentionally sabotage our set. It's just showbiz snafus. Careless crew members and foul-ups. It's as common as caffeine on a movie set."

I took a breath. "Okay, Jerry, let's say you're right. Then you have nothing to worry about when it comes to me poking around, because I have no agenda. I have nothing at stake here except watching out for the health and safety of my baristas and your production crew for the length of your shoot—excuse the pun."

Jerry folded his arms.

"Look," I pressed, "all I want is the truth—to get to the bottom of what exactly happened today. And why. That's my only concern. Give me some leeway to question your people, and I'll agree with your decision not to officially notify the police."

He rubbed his face again, nodding under his hands.

"Fine, Clare. You've got yourself a deal."

Fifteen

WHEN we left the exclusive wellness facility, Jerry insisted on taking Tucker home in the luxury rent-a-car. And since Esther wouldn't leave her fellow barista's side, she joined them.

I wanted to get back to the shop, as soon as possible, and I expected Madame to be rushing to the helipad, where her old friend was waiting. But instead she insisted on giving me a ride downtown.

Climbing into her limo, I suspected that she wanted to talk privately, and I was right. No sooner had we settled into the plush back seat than Madame turned to face me.

"Clare, tell me straight—" Her gloved fingers gripped my arm, and I held my breath, ready for a bombshell. "Are you comfortable with managing the craft services contract that Jerry is offering us?"

"Oh, is that all?" I sat back. "The Village Blend has been catering private parties and community events for years. I've got a great list of vendors I can tap for the extra fare, and our baker will be thrilled to double our orders."

"Then we're set?"

"Piece of cake—and really tasty cake, too. So there's no need to worry."

"Excellent, my dear, I knew I could count on you. Feel free to use my connections. I've got lots of friends in this town, as you know, and they'll be happy to help. And, *please*, if you find you need anything, anything at all, be sure to let me know."

"I'll let *your son* know. Matt promised to be on hand and helpful during the location shooting process. I just hope he's okay with the extended craft services contract. It will be a nice boost to our quarterly bottom line, but if he's serious about helping out, it will ground him for the duration."

"I'm sure Matt will do the right thing. Finances aside, I do hope this experience is a positive one for you both."

"*And* the legacy of our coffeehouse," I added.

"That too. You can't buy exposure like this—" Madame paused and locked eyes with me. "As long as it's *positive* exposure."

My spine went stiff at that. "You're referring to what happened with Driftwood Coffee on the set yesterday, aren't you?"

She nodded. "Everyone's talking about it—and not just in the coffee trade."

"I know. Those mobile phone videos went viral, and it seems the whole world covered it."

"From coast to coast," Madame said pointedly. "And Driftwood's business is sure to suffer. Not that it doesn't deserve to. But, given everything that's happening . . ."

As her voice trailed off, she gazed out the car window, and I knew where her thoughts were going. Adding things up myself, I took a stab at a theory.

"Given what happened to Tucker, I'm sure you're wondering—as I now am—whether that coffee poisoning yesterday was really an accident."

"Go on," Madame prompted.

"Fred Denham is the show's armorer, which means he's the very man in charge of keeping all the firearms safe. Yesterday, he collapsed after drinking tainted coffee. As a result, he wasn't on the set today when Jerry shot Tucker with a bullet that shouldn't have been in one of Fred's guns."

"It could simply be an awful coincidence," Madame argued. "And perhaps the production should have waited for Mr. Denham's return before forging ahead without him."

"Perhaps," I conceded. "Maybe it was just bad judgment, a coincidence that feels like a conspiracy. I just hope we're all making the right decision not to involve the police."

"You heard Jerry. No police," Madame insisted. "And you know how

Matt feels about law enforcement. My son's not a fan of officials with badges and guns in *any* country."

"You don't have to remind me," I said. "I realize he's had plenty of disillusioning experiences—"

"Including being shaken down for bribes," Madame interjected. "And—

"Being falsely arrested," I finished for her. "Once by my own fiancé."

"Well, that one was forgivable, considering the circumstances. We won't hold that against your gallant Lieutenant Quinn," Madame said with a wink.

"You and I won't. But, believe me, Matt will—for the rest of his natural life."

"No matter," Madame said, waving it off. "Just be sure to keep your eyes open. Jerry has agreed to let you do some digging. But by all means, stay safe. And, Clare . . . do what you feel you must, no matter what we promised Jerry." She paused a moment and regarded me. "Come to think of it, your promise wasn't exactly the same as ours, was it? You promised you wouldn't *officially* notify the police. You promised nothing about talking to them *unofficially*."

"You noticed that, did you?"

She nodded with approval. "Smart girl. Always keep your options open. And I trust your judgment. If you believe *unofficial* police advice and support is needed, well . . . a little pillow talk will solve that, won't it?"

Madame's tone was suggestive, and I squirmed in my seat.

"I'm too old to blush," I told her.

"No, you're not. You're doing it right now." She gave me a little smile. "But you know how I feel. Your blue knight is worth blushing over." Her violet eyes danced. "He's quite a hunk of man, I must admit."

"Okay, that's enough. And since you've broached the subject of personal relationships, I'm going to go there."

"Go where?"

"Before today, I thought you barely knew Jerry Sullivan. Clearly, that's not the case. You two have a history."

"Of sorts."

"So what did he mean by that comment he made to you?"

Madame arched a silver eyebrow. "What comment would that be, dear? He made quite a few."

"When he offered us the craft services contract, he looked directly at you and said: 'It's the kind of international exposure your legacy coffee-house deserves . . . and *you know I owe you*.'"

"Yes, he did say that, didn't he?"

"Well, what did he mean that he *owed* you? And that he wanted to make amends? Amends for what?"

She waved a gloved hand. "Oh, that's just the new Jerry trying to make up for the old Jerry."

"The old Jerry? How old? Are we talking about those *really* early Greenwich Village stand-up years? Did you know him as far back as that?"

"I did. He was a bit of a cad when he was young. He made some terrible missteps. And a number of enemies."

"Were you one?"

"Oh, no. Never! I was only ever a fan of Jerry's. He was so talented. Anyone could see it. But talent alone won't save you in show business—or any business, come to think of it—and that's a hard lesson for some young people to learn. Anyway, Jerry learned it. And he's not young anymore. He's worked hard, paid his dues, made a great success of himself, and matured quite a bit along the way."

"Well, if you were such a fan, and he was a Village Blend regular, then why isn't there any evidence of him in the shop's memorabilia?"

"I did have some Jerry memorabilia from those days and some from Dan Coffey—"

"Dan Coffey! Jerry's old comedy team partner?"

"That's right. I even had some props from their old TV show."

"*The Coffey Break*! I remember that show. It was great! But I never saw any memorabilia in our storage. Where is it?"

"I disposed of it. All of it."

"Really?" I was so shocked that I couldn't speak for a moment. "Why would you do that? Did something terrible happen?"

Madame looked away. "It's ancient history, Clare. Suffice it to say, Jerry and Dan broke up. Dan never came back to the coffeehouse, and I lost touch with Jerry when he left for the West Coast. I thought he was gone for good and I'd never see him again—until we reconnected at that charity event. He's been quite gracious since then."

I wanted to grill Madame with more questions, but she was anxious to get back to the helipad.

"Babka's a good friend, and she was kind to hold the private helicopter for me. But her patience is limited."

And so, apparently, was Madame's—at least when it came to discussing her past dealings with Jerry Sullivan.

Sixteen

~~~~~~

WHEN Madame's driver dropped me off on Hudson, the studio trucks and dressing room trailers were still lining the block. I didn't see any production people around, though I noticed a young security guard in a gray uniform slowly pacing the sidewalk.

Using my key, I entered our closed shop. Inside, cameras and lights were still set up, but the place was empty.

Matt heard the bell ding over the door and emerged from the pantry with one of our Coffee Cake Streusel Muffins in hand.

My mouth watered at the sight. I hadn't eaten for hours, and that tender, buttery cake, layered with cinnamon streusel and topped with a sweet kiss of vanilla glaze, was enough to make a girl swoon.

Matt's bearded face took a bite, and his full mouth garbled a greeting.

"Glad you're back," he said. "Esther called and told us Tuck is okay and going home. I sent Nancy home after that."

"Are there any muffins left?"

"Sorry, last one."

"Figures. It's been that kind of day." I shrugged off my jacket. "So, have you been bribed to keep quiet like everyone else around here?"

"I was warned to keep quiet, just like everyone else who signed those consent forms. Ms. Bird reminded us all about a little nondisclosure clause on that form that could lead to big lawsuits if one were to violate it. So mum's the world, unless you want to spend ten years in civil court."

He checked his phone. "I've got to go, Clare. I have a date."

"But we need to talk—"

"It can wait."

"No, it can't."

"Sure it can—" Matt stuffed the rest of that delectable little cake into his mouth, wiped streusel crumbs from his beard, and grabbed his jacket. That's when I grabbed his arm and dragged it back to the coffee bar. (Matt wisely followed his arm.)

"Sit down and listen. We've got some planning to do . . ."

Taking the bar chair next to him, I gave Matt the lowdown on Jerry's offer of a craft services contract, which included the Village Blend being listed in every episode's credits.

"Good job, Clare. You talked him into it?"

"The other way around. Jerry himself made the offer as an incentive to keep us all quiet about the set shooting. Apparently, it's also some kind of grand gesture to help 'make amends' to your mother."

"Make amends? To *my* mother?" Matt blinked. "For what?"

"I don't know. Something happened between them years ago, something Jerry obviously regrets. Do you have a clue what it could be?"

"No idea. Mother never spoke to me about Jerry Sullivan. Not in her entire life—well, until recently when this set-jetting opportunity came our way."

"Set-jetting? Don't you mean JET-setting?"

"I do not." Matt's fingers tapped across his phone screen. "SET-jetting is what fans do when they travel to different locations used in their favorite films and TV shows. See . . ." He showed me a browser search with all kinds of *set-jetting* results, and asked—

"Remember when Nancy took that trip to Forks, Washington?"

"Oh, right. Her big *Twilight* movie locations tour. I doubt we'll be anywhere near that big."

"Hey, every little bit of notoriety helps."

"Not in Driftwood's case, as your mother already pointed out."

"We're *nothing* like Driftwood," Matt spat. "We don't tap hydrants with garden hoses for our water, and we don't poison our customers with cleaning fluid. You should be proud, Clare. You've trained our baristas to the highest standards."

"I am proud—of all of us, including what you do to fill our roaster downstairs with the best cherries in the business. And Jerry's offer is too good an opportunity to pass up, but we can't afford to let anything go wrong with this job or we might suffer the same fate as Driftwood."

We both fell silent at that ugly prospect.

I leaned closer. "Matt, Jerry denies that his set is being sabotaged, and maybe it's not. But if we're going to be part of this production for the duration, we have to take every precaution, which means I'll need all the *trusted* help I can get."

My ex took a breath and nodded. "All right. I'll cancel my flights and reschedule any sourcing trips."

"Thank you! That's just what I was hoping you'd say."

"Hey, you know me. When you need me, I'm there for you."

"A positive development in your character," I couldn't help pointing out. "You have to admit, you weren't always—you know—*there* for me, which wasn't so easy with a little girl at home, missing her daddy."

"Let's not get into ancient history. The little girl turned out fine, *better* than fine, and is running her own shop in DC. Meanwhile, you and I have plenty to focus on in the here and now."

"You're right," I said. "Let's start with getting our catering equipment out of storage at your Brooklyn warehouse. Can you move it here by morning?"

"Sure. I'll have my warehouse guys help. But what's your plan for expanding our menu in less than twenty-four hours? Film crews can't live on espressos and pastries alone—although they are darn good espressos and pastries." He brushed the last of the cinnamon streusel crumbs from his shirt.

"I'm calling my catering vendors as soon as we're done talking," I said. "The only issue will be the short notice—"

DING!

"That's probably my date texting me." Matt checked his phone and frowned. "Nope, the alert wasn't for me."

DING! DING!

"It's my phone." I pulled it out to find messages piling up.

"What is it?" Matt asked.

"Your mother."

"She's texting you?"

"No. Her friends are. Wow! She's faster on the draw than either of us . . ."

"What are you talking about?"

I pointed to the phone screen. "Dennis Murphy is offering us his famous Grandma's pizzas *at cost*. And Babka is ready to supply—"

"Let me guess, babkas."

"Not just any babkas, Matt, the best in the city, and her most popular new flavors—Nutella Chocolate, Bourbon Praline, and Maple Cinnamon—plus a variety of sandwiches, wraps, salads, and soups from her restaurant, also at cost!"

"I'm impressed. But then, Mother always did have a golden tongue."

"More like a golden ticket."

"Ticket?"

"To the Willy Wonka factory. These great deals are contingent upon a public 'thank you' of their businesses in Jerry's episode credits."

"I think that can be arranged," Matt said.

"You do?"

"Sure, we'll pass the savings on to the production company, and if that's not enough to convince Jerry, my mother will *gently* remind him that he's trying to 'make amends.' Isn't that what you said?"

"She'll guilt-trip him?"

"Of course. Hey, the guy may have made millions with a bit about making deals, but my mother has actually made them for decades—and in the biggest city of hustlers in the world."

"You're right," I said with the unabashed pride of a loyal protégé. "No one puts Madame in the corner."

Matt pulled out his own phone, and together we split the return calls, finalizing deliveries for the next week, at least.

DING!

"What now?" Matt asked. "A deal for doughnuts?"

"Close," I said.

Reading the screen, I couldn't stop my thrilled little smile.

"Whoa," Matt said. "What's *that* smile for?"

Before I could block him, he grabbed my phone and read:

Hey, sweetheart, I'm parked out front.
Got something hot in there for me?

With a scowl, Matt handed back my mobile. "It's the Flatfoot."

"Will you ever stop calling him that?"

"What do you think?"

"I think Mike Quinn hasn't been a cliché flat-footed uniformed beat cop in decades. As a decorated detective lieutenant with the NYPD, he wears plain clothes, *and* he has nice big feet with high arches."

"If you're going to start gushing about the man's feet, I'm out of here."

"Your date is waiting, isn't she?"

"She'd better be," Matt warned, slipping on his jacket. "If she isn't, you owe me."

"What are you talking about? If she isn't there, all you have to do is swipe right on a new one."

"Very funny."

"Funny but accurate."

"I'll see you in the morning!"

"Bright and early, Romeo. And don't forget that catering equipment or I'm sending you back to Verona!"

"And don't *you* forget, Clare. Mum's the word to your big-footed boyfriend or Jerry will be sending us to civil court."

Seventeen

Sнов⊥ꙅ after my ex-husband walked out, Mike Quinn walked in—and the irony of *that* choreography was not lost on me.

Neither was the rare appearance of Mike's big grin.

I was used to the man's big feet, since they were attached to the big guy—well over six feet of him, a skyscraper compared to my puny five-two. The big grin, however, was a rarity, primarily because of the stresses, frustrations, and (at times) heartbreaking nature of his job.

Mike had been conditioned, as most cops were, to keep emotions in check and personal opinions under house arrest. It took time and patience to draw him out and get him to trust that I wasn't going to turn into his ex-wife, a young woman who'd become disillusioned with her "hero" cop, the one she fell for and quickly wed after he'd saved her from a creepy and dangerous stalker.

The fact is, I had little in common with Leila Quinn. For one thing, I wasn't a gorgeous model, brought up in wealth and luxury. Leila's sense of entitlement was so ingrained that she saw nothing wrong with being outspokenly "uncomfortable" with the "seedier" side of life, which was (frankly) the reality for most of us attempting to survive the perils of this planet (as Esther bluntly pointed out in that posh, members-only emergency room).

True, I prided myself on providing the highest quality coffee to my customers, many of whom were quite wealthy themselves. But the struggling coffee belt farmers we supported through Matt's global sourcing work decidedly were not, and neither were the hardworking baristas on my staff.

I had more in common with the "common" end of that spectrum, given I was a working-class kid from Western Pennsylvania who'd grown up helping my grandmother run our family's little Italian grocery.

I never knew what "class" we were. I was simply happy to help my *nonna* bake bread and biscotti in the early morning hours, and in the afternoon, after school, make Italian sandwiches and stovetop espressos for her customers, who included not only mothers and grandmothers, but also local mill and factory workers—a tough crowd that routinely filed in and out of the curtained back room, where my pop ran a small-time bookie operation for dubious associates (but let's not go there).

The point is, I was no cream puff glamour girl. Like many of the artists and writers who came to Greenwich Village before me, my roots were sturdy, planted deep in the rough realities of this world. And as Mike came to know me, he realized that I didn't need to live in Sanitized Land like his ex-wife. I *wanted* to hear about his daily grind, the good, the bad, the so-called seedy, and distressingly ugly stuff, too.

And, unlike Leila, I was proud of my fiancé, because Mike had dedicated his life to doing what he'd always felt a calling to do, even back in those early years when he was a New York firefighter, which was simply to save lives.

These days he did it by leading a specialized team of detectives nicknamed the OD Squad. Their citywide efforts, investigating criminality behind drug overdoses, were highly regarded, not only in the department, but also among addiction and recovery professionals in our state and local agencies.

Their work even earned the admiration of the US Justice Department, whose brass tapped Quinn for a stint in Washington, DC. But he wasn't happy there, and he returned to his hometown to resume heading his old team—which made me happy since I wanted to continue leading mine.

Now, as I watched his long legs make easy strides across my shop's polished plank floor, I couldn't help but smile. The sight of him coming toward me felt blissfully comfortable, like drinking a warm mug of mocha. I'd missed his broad shoulders, which nicely filled out his blue suit.

Jet-setting Matt, the adrenaline junkie, judged Mike Quinn (as his ex-wife had) to be a "square-jawed bore." And most people who saw Quinn on the street would likely think the same. But I knew what he carried beneath that staid business attire.

Strapped to his clean white dress shirt, a leather shoulder holster held a service weapon, which I felt against my ribs whenever he hugged me close. It was a physical reminder of the substantial responsibility of his work, and the weight of his worries.

Maybe if Quinn were the kind of cop who didn't care, his typically serious demeanor would be lighter. But he did care. About the cases and the losses. About the pain of the city and all of the people who lived in it—and I considered it my personal mission, almost from the moment we met, to help lighten that load or at least lift his mood, whether through a hot cup of coffee, a silly joke, or a warm hug.

Tonight, however, something had done that job for me—

"What's the reason for the big grin?" I asked.

"Seeing you again isn't enough of a reason?"

"No. But I'll take it."

Mike pointed to the lights and production equipment. "I see the film people arrived. Are they still around?"

"No. They all left for the day."

"And the shop's closed? I saw the sign."

"That's right. No customers. No staff. No film people. We're all alone."

"Good," Mike said.

The kiss came next, soft and warm, and then the rapturous hug.

As his strong arms pulled me against him, I curled my own around his neck. Then it was me who deepened the kiss. After my long and trying day, all I wanted to do was pull Mike's stalwart strength inside me.

I could tell he was surprised by my aggressiveness, but also pleased. A low moan escaped his throat, and I knew he was feeling the same delicious, almost painful need to get closer.

When we finally broke contact, we were breathing hard, eyes glazed, both a little light-headed from the heated connection.

"Do you want to go upstairs?" he whispered in my ear.

"Absolutely."

I didn't think it was possible, but the man's grin grew even bigger.

Eighteen

~~~~~~

I LOCKED the shop's front door, and we hurriedly climbed the back service staircase, up three flights to my duplex apartment.

Typically, Mike would start a fire in the cozy front parlor, and I would pour us some wine to help us unwind. But after a week apart, our need for each other burned so hot that we had no patience for preliminaries.

I locked the apartment door and barely turned around before Mike was there, pulling us back together.

It was a sweet reunion—and a relief to me.

The two of us had struggled through some rough patches recently, including a dry spell that made me wonder if we'd ever find our passion again. I even considered calling off our upcoming spring wedding.

But we managed to find our way back to each other and rediscover how good things could be between us. This romantic reunion was a beautiful example. Lack of passion wasn't a problem tonight.

Our clothes came off and we came together on the parlor's area rug, right in front of the cold fireplace. It was a chilly fall evening, but neither of us felt cold. We laughed about it as I pushed Mike's sandy brown bangs off his damp forehead.

"What got into you?" I asked.

"I told you," he said. "I missed you."

I stared deep into his arctic blue eyes. "You can't hide things from me anymore. What aren't you telling me?"

"Okay, Inspector, you got me. I saw you from the car, through the windows of your shop. You were sitting next to Allegro, your heads together, a little too close . . . I didn't like it."

"*That's* what this is about? You were jealous? After all this time and all we've been through, you honestly felt threatened?"

"Possessive is what I felt. I trust you, but not your ex."

"So the big grin was about you being happy to see Matt take a hike?"

"I'm always happy to see Allegro take a hike. But the grin was for you, Clare. Totally and completely."

"Well, whatever it was that sparked this fire, I'm not going to argue with the euphoric result."

"Me either."

I took a breath. "So? What do you want to do now?"

"Now?" he said in a playful tone. "Read my lips . . ."

Then he pulled my mouth back onto his.

I hadn't eaten. I had work to do. But I wasn't about to stop Mike's desire for an encore. It was like the glorious early days of our relationship, when we were still discovering each other, and I reveled in the thrill of it.

Twenty minutes later, my empty stomach started to rumble in protest.

"You need to eat," Mike said, curling a lock of my chestnut hair around an ear.

"I guess so."

"That wasn't a question, Cosi. I can hear how hungry you are."

"Honestly, Detective," I teased, "when I saw you walk through my front door, I was only hungry for you. But now—*yeah*, I could eat! Should I make a quick Skillet Lasagna? It's one of your favorites."

"No way. A little birdie told me you had a hard day. So I'm taking my honey out. Let's freshen up and get dressed."

A SHORT time later, I set the store alarm and relocked the coffeehouse, while Mike walked around the corner to grab his SUV.

The cool night air was refreshing, and I was glad to be going out. It felt freeing.

With our shop closed all day, our sidewalk in front was deserted. Not even that young security guard was around, not that I could see, anyway. Then, as I turned to follow my fiancé, I noticed someone exiting one of the darkened trailers half a block away. I didn't think that anyone from the production company was still on-site, so I called out.

"Hey, what are you doing?"

I couldn't tell if the person was a man or woman. They wore baggy clothes, a padded jacket, and a baseball cap under a dark hoodie. Whoever it was didn't turn around when I called. Instead, they instantly ducked between two trailers.

I stepped into the street to catch sight of them, but the person managed to slip away before I got a second look.

I did finally spot that security guard. He was leaning against a rent-a-cop car, flirting with a pair of giggling young women who were asking what movie was being filmed and what stars were in it.

"Excuse me," I said sharply as I walked up to the guard. "I just saw someone leave that trailer!"

Alarmed by my tone, the two young women fled the scene. The guard, now suitably irritated, challenged me.

"Who are you?"

"I run this production's craft services—and that coffeehouse—and I didn't think anyone from the shoot was still on-site."

"Well, if you know the production people, then who did you see?"

"I couldn't tell."

He scratched his head. "There are a couple of people in the costume trailer." He pointed to a mobile home at the end of the block. Its lights were still blazing.

Hands on hips, I stood my ground. "We should check things out anyway. Come on . . ."

The guard followed me to the darkened trailer. The door was closed but unlocked. He stuck his head inside, then closed the door. This time, he made sure it was locked.

"Nothing has been disturbed. It was probably one of the wardrobe people delivering a costume."

"Why weren't you watching the trailers?"

"I have been. And I will be all night."

"Alone? Just you?"

The guard folded his arms. "I have a partner," he answered tightly. "We spell each other. Right now, he's on break."

"Well, Jerry Sullivan promised he would hire more security for this set."

"He did. We have two more guys scheduled to start tomorrow. That's all I know."

I shook my head. Sure, Jerry was doubling the security—which sounded impressive—but it still only amounted to four guards. Would it be enough of a deterrent to a saboteur? And what about tonight?

Just then, Mike pulled up in his SUV and popped the passenger side door.

"Anything wrong?" he asked.

I frowned, not sure how to answer. The guard looked at me expectantly, but there was nothing more to say.

"Clare?" Mike called.

"It's okay. I'm coming."

I climbed into the passenger seat, slammed the door, and Mike gave me a look.

"Why were you talking to that security guard? And why do you look so upset? Is something wrong?"

"Let's just say, I have no *proof* that there is."

Mike frowned. "What kind of answer is that?"

"The only one I can give you at the moment."

"What's that supposed to mean?"

"It means what it means!"

"Why are you being so defensive? And evasive?"

"You know what, Mike? Right now, what I am is hungry. And so are you. Do you really want a fit of *hanger* to ruin our night?"

"No. I don't. And you're right." He squeezed my hand. "Let's get some dinner."

Nineteen

╔══╗

"THIS was a good idea," Mike said between bites of juicy burger and sips of creamy, cold vanilla shake.

We were both so hungry that I suggested we skip the formal dining scene and drive straight to Madison Square Park, where restauranteur Danny Meyer had erected a Shake Shack kiosk, his tribute to the great American roadside burger stand.

Around our little outdoor table for two, the fall night air felt crisp and clear, and I was glad to inhale the freshness of this restored city park, a six-acre oasis of green grass, colorful flower beds, wooden benches, and stately trees, surrounded by the stunning grandeur of New York's vertical forest.

Sitting across from the man I loved, beneath the strings of glowing fairy lights felt enchanting, almost romantic. With the skyscraper windows twinkling above us like stars, I could tell Mike thought so, too, even with me rudely stuffing my face in front of him.

"Night air is always so much nicer than day air," he said. "Ever wonder why?"

"I don't know," I said, cramming more hot, crispy fries into my mouth. "It's darker?"

Mike laughed. "Very scientific, Cosi. Actually, I think it has to do with solar radiation being gone and less likely to cause pollutants to be dispersed."

"Very romantic, Quinn."

"Stick with me, sweetheart. I'll sweep you off your metatarsals."

"It's okay, Detective. I think we proved it tonight: you don't need words to do that."

He returned my smile, but it was a tight one this time, and an odd expression of concern clouded his gaze. "So . . . are you feeling better now? I mean, I know you were feeling good about our little reunion—"

"I loved our little reunion."

"But then . . . what happened after, with the security guard. What was all that about? Did it have something to do with your so-called hard day?"

"Who said I had a hard day?"

"Don't you remember? Before we left, I mentioned a little birdie told me."

"I thought you were kidding."

"No. Read it for yourself."

He pulled out his phone and showed me a text message from (of all people) Madame!

Take care of our Clare. Treat her to a nice dinner.
She's been missing you. And she's had a very hard day.

I stared at the screen in disbelief.

Madame knew very well Jerry had warned me *not to tell* my fiancé about our bulletproof barista. Her own son's last words to me, before going off on his swipe-to-meet date, amounted to a warning to *keep my mouth shut.*

Yet here she was, prodding Mike into questioning me. Did she really want me to spill the beans? I had to conclude she did, given our limo discussion about . . .

"Pillow talk," I mumbled.

"What's that?"

"Madame is trying to get me to open up to you about some problems we had with the location shooting today." (I nearly choked on a fry at my own choice of words.)

"Okay," Mike said. "So why don't you open up?"

"It's complicated."

"It's not. I'm here. And I'm listening."

"I know you are, but . . . Look, it's like this. If you're listening as my fiancé, the man I love, that's fine. But if you're listening as a member of the NYPD, I can't say a word."

Mike leaned forward. "What happened today, Cosi? Something illegal?"

"Right now, I don't know what it is. I'm looking into it."

"All right. But . . ."

"But what?"

He held up his phone again. "Your own mentor didn't send this text lightly. Seems to me she thinks you should talk, and I should be in the loop—*unofficially*, if that makes you feel any better."

I sat back, trying to decide what to do. Absently, I sucked on my straw so long that my chocolate milkshake froze my head.

"Son of a bunny!"

"Brain freeze?"

I nodded.

"Eat some hot fries."

"I finished mine!"

"Here—" Mike slid over his paper tray, and I stuffed the last few of his fries into my mouth. I must have had chipmunk cheeks because he was clearly suppressing a laugh.

"Tell you what," he said. "While you're waiting for your brain to unfreeze on deciding what to disclose to me, why don't I give you something to consider. It's police business, so I shouldn't be sharing it. Not officially. But I'm going to trust you . . ."

"Trust me?" I garbled, then chewed and swallowed. "Trust me with what?"

"Information. Let's call it *background*. I'm going to share it with you confidentially, as a warning about the kind of people you could be dealing with in this show business crowd."

Twenty

〜〜〜〜〜〜〜〜〜〜〜〜〜〜〜〜〜〜〜〜〜〜

SWALLOWING the last of Mike's fries, I learned forward.

"Go on," I said. "I'm listening."

"Two months ago, I told you about a corpse dumped at a sheet metal factory in Hunts Point. Surveillance cameras revealed that the body was rolled out of a rental van."

"I remember. But I don't remember you mentioning anything else."

"The thirty-three-year-old man turned out to be a writer and actor with a list of credits in film and television, and we traced the van to a movie being shot on location in the Bronx. We questioned the production manager, who claimed the vehicle had been stolen. Since the victim had no direct connection to the movie shoot, that part of the investigation stalled."

"Was the man murdered?"

"He died of a drug overdose, but our toxicologist was unfamiliar with the substance that killed him. Two weeks later, a young actress was left unconscious at Beth Israel's ER. She survived, and the toxicologist determined that she was a victim of the same substance."

"Then you had a lead?"

"She refused to cooperate. Said it would ruin her acting career if she named names. But she did give us something. She said the people she partied with called the drug Funtenol."

"Fentanyl?"

"No. *Funtenol* is not fentanyl—and has zero fentanyl in it. It's simply a new designer drug. It's not as deadly as its namesake, but it's dangerous enough. Two more fatal overdoses were traced to this poison—a production assistant who consumed it at a party, and a set decorator who worked at the soundstages of a Queens film and television production facility.

"In each case, no one in the entertainment community cooperated with the police to help us track down the distributors of this garbage. Despite three deaths and a near-fatal overdose in this city, no one would talk, fearing their careers would be ruined."

Mike paused. "While I was at the conference in Virginia, I reached out to my counterparts in other areas of the country that see a lot of film production work, including Los Angeles, *obviously*, and also San Francisco, Atlanta, Pittsburgh, and a few other cities. I briefed them on what to look for and forwarded the toxicology reports. None of them caught this trend, but they're looking now. It will take time, but they're going to review OD deaths over the past six months and look for the pattern we're seeing."

I shivered, suddenly cold. I did have a light jacket on, but Mike noticed and draped his trench coat over my shoulders. I couldn't tell him it wasn't the temperature but the similarity to Jerry's pressure to *stay quiet* about the problems on our set that caused my reaction.

No, I hadn't seen any drug use, but the "code of silence" thing was unnerving and a reminder of why Tucker would never come clean about today's accident—the fear of being blacklisted.

"Let's head back to your place," Mike said, concern in his gaze. "Maybe in front of a nice, warm fire, with a glass of wine, your brain will unfreeze enough to tell me about your day."

Before I could answer, Mike's phone vibrated.

He checked the ID and held it up for me to see. "I'm sorry, Clare, but I should answer this."

"Of course," I said and leaned closer to listen in.

On the line was Sergeant Emmanuel "Manny" Franco, a young man who was not only a trusted member of Mike Quinn's squad, but a romantic interest of my daughter, Joy—a fact that proved to be the opposite of joy for her father.

But she was a grown woman now, and Matt had no say in our headstrong daughter's choice of whom she loved.

I myself had no problem with Franco. He'd proved himself to be the best boyfriend material Joy had ever known. And he always came through for Mike—and me. (I'd counted on him, more times than I could count.)

"What's up, Franco?"

"We have a hot tip, Lieutenant. You wanted to be notified."

Quinn's face hardened. "Another body?"

"No. This time it's good news. The opportunity we've been waiting for. An anonymous tipster divulged the location of a private party at a rooftop restaurant with a mother lode of Funtenol on the menu."

"When and where?"

"Right here in Manhattan. Right now."

"Is it confirmed?"

"Yeah, Sanchez infiltrated the party and validated the tip. He says there's enough up there for a distribution charge. He has photos, and we have a warrant."

"Who do we have on duty?"

"Sanchez is still undercover at the scene. DeMarco is with me in the car, along with two uniforms I pulled from the precinct. We're five minutes from the location. Since you're back from Virginia, we could sure use a guiding light—"

"Where am I going?"

"The Industrial Hotel on 38th Street. South of Bryant Park, between Fifth and Sixth."

I touched Quinn's arm. "I know the place!"

He didn't react to me. Instead, he told Franco—

"Got it. On my way."

He turned to me. "I'm sorry, sweetheart. But it looks like I'll have to put you in a cab."

"Oh, no, you don't. I'm coming with you."

"That's not a good idea."

Ignoring him, I jumped to my feet, handed him back his coat, and quickly cleared our table, shoving everything into the Shake Shack paper sack before tossing it, like a Brooklyn Nets center, straight into a nearby garbage can.

"Nice shot," Quinn said, rising. "But you're still not coming."

"You want to waste time arguing?"

I grabbed his arm and pulled him toward the SUV.

"Listen to me, Mike. I *know* the place. And I know I can help. Let's go!"

Twenty-one

~~~~~~

THE lieutenant knew I meant business.

He didn't want to waste time debating or leave me alone in a city park at night. So, with a resigned exhale, Quinn unlocked the SUV.

We slammed our doors and clicked on our seat belts, then he threw the motor into gear, hit the police lights, and raced up Madison Avenue.

"Can you get Franco back on the line?" I asked.

Quinn didn't hesitate. He hit speed dial and then the speaker. "Franco, Clare is with me. She has something to say."

By now, the sergeant knew me well. "Hi, Coffee Lady," his deep voice rumbled. "What have you got?"

"Listen, Franco. I know a spot where we can hook up without attracting attention. There's a loading dock in back of the hotel. You get there through an L-shaped alley off West 38th Street. There's a tall security gate blocking it."

"Got it. Thanks for the heads-up. Meet you there!"

Quinn snorted as he ended the call. "You're full of surprises, Cosi."

"I told you I could help."

"And you knew about this alley *how?*"

"The rooftop restaurant you're going to, Metropolis, serves Village Blend coffee. They get our freshly roasted beans delivered every two weeks. I've made the drop-off myself, more than once."

"Okay, but I know you. Coming along with me is more than a thrill ride."

As Quinn hung a sharp left to cross town, I squirmed in my seat. He wasn't wrong about my motive—

"I want to see for myself, okay?"

"See what?"

"If what you shared on background is true—that people in the film community are partying with this new drug—I want a front row seat for what you're dealing with, including what this drug looks like and its effects. For the sake of my coffeehouse and its staff . . ."

"All right, Cosi, but favors go both ways. I'm going to want some answers on what you're trying to hide from me."

"Okay, okay," I said, and meant it. After all this, Mike deserved some trust on my part. "I'll come clean later—"

Time was up anyway. We were already rolling past the Industrial Hotel's brightly lit glass-and-steel entranceway. Like many structures in New York, the place was a repurposed factory. In this case, one that sat at the heart of the old Garment District.

Last century, this fifteen-story building housed dingy dressmaking sweatshops. Today, with its chic rooftop bar and restaurant, neo-industrial décor, and proximity to Times Square and the Theater District, the Industrial was one of the hottest watering holes in Midtown.

As Quinn pulled up to the alley I'd described, we knew Franco and his team must have arrived ahead of us, because the security gate was wide open.

Quinn steered us into the narrow passageway between two tall buildings. After a sharp left turn, we arrived at an open space. Franco's unmarked police car was parked beside the yellow-painted pavement lines that designated the area for loading dock work.

Surrounded by towering concrete walls, the place felt unpleasantly claustrophobic. Sergeant Franco and the other officers appeared in the headlight glare. Though the autumn chill was mild tonight, inside this artificial canyon it was cold enough to see the officers' steaming breath.

There were no friendly greetings. The three men and one woman had quietly donned tactical gear and were checking their service weapons. Quinn retrieved his own vest from the back seat and checked the automatic in his shoulder holster.

When he exited the vehicle, I followed.

Manny Franco, his shaved head reflecting the dim light, gave Quinn an update.

"The loading dock doors are secured by a padlocked gate, so nobody is getting in or out through there. The only other place of entry is a sliding door—"

I spoke up. "That's not a door. It's a service elevator."

Franco frowned as he took a closer look. "This would be a nice way to get to the roof in a hurry, but the call button is locked."

Disappointed, Quinn rubbed the back of his neck.

"Okay, no back door," he began after a pause. "So let's do it like this—Franco and DeMarco will stay here in case someone uses the elevator. The rest of us will go in through the lobby and find out what we're dealing with. I don't have to tell you all to keep your ears to the radio."

I was hoping to be ignored, but Quinn glanced my way next.

"Clare, I want you to get back inside the SUV and stay there."

"But—"

"Consider it an order."

"Fine."

As if that weren't enough, Quinn gave Franco additional instructions.

"Make sure Clare stays inside that vehicle, even if you have to cuff her to the steering wheel."

"Will do," the grinning sergeant replied.

Twenty-two

FRUSTRATED, I climbed back into the SUV and slammed the door. I waited until Quinn was out of sight before I cracked the window. I wanted to listen to the action, but all I heard were gripes from Franco and De-Marco about some undeserving cop at another precinct who won the state lottery, and how unjust the whole world suddenly seemed.

Lucky for me, their commiseration was soon interrupted by a call from the boss.

"I talked to the night manager, who assured me the service elevator is closed for the night," Quinn said. "He also reports there are upward of fifty guests on the roof."

"Not good odds, Lieutenant," DeMarco cracked.

"Doesn't matter. We're not arresting the attendees. We're looking for the perp or perps distributing or selling the drug. If they don't give themselves up, and no one points them out, we'll do a systematic bag search. And I need you both for crowd control."

"On our way, Lieutenant," Franco replied with a grin. Detective De-Marco slapped Franco's back, delighted to get back into the game as well. DeMarco moved at once, while Franco paused at the SUV's open window.

"Keep your head down and stay out of trouble, Coffee Lady."

Then the pair disappeared around the L-shaped corner.

I sat on my hands and did nothing in that miserable pit for what felt like an eternity—though my phone clocked it at a mere five minutes. I was eaten up by curiosity and peeved that I might be missing something. I was very tempted to get out of the vehicle, go around the corner, and peek into the hotel lobby to see if anything was happening.

I resisted the urge and was glad I did when, minutes later, headlights stabbed through the darkness as another vehicle entered the alley. Though it was still around the corner and out of sight, I could hear the engine as it approached.

Unsure what to do, I ducked.

White light scoured my vehicle's interior as the newcomer pulled up beside the loading dock. I held my breath and waited for the doors to open and someone to get out. But the car just sat there, its engine idling.

Then I heard another sound. I recognized it as the cumbersome rumble of the service elevator doors opening—the very elevator the night manager assured Quinn was "closed for the night."

I dared a peek.

Bright light spilled from the elevator's interior as two figures emerged.

I caught my breath when I recognized both—

Director Sebastian Albee and former pop star Kylee Ferris hurried across the yellow pavement and into the waiting sedan.

Though my glimpse was brief, Albee's signature mushroom cap hair on his beanpole body was easy to spot, and Kylee's pretty face and strawberry blond hair were brightly illuminated by the interior light when the car door was opened.

I tried to get a peek at the driver, too, but the visor was down, blocking his or her face.

I ducked again as the car slowly turned around inside the narrow confines of the alley. I raised my head in time to see red taillights vanishing around the corner, but too late to catch the license number.

Alone once more, I took stock of what I'd just witnessed.

Of course I was shocked to see that two invaluable members of Jerry's show had apparently just fled a drug raid. Whatever problems beset Jerry's production, I didn't consider drugs one of them. Could I have been wrong?

The other surprise was seeing the director and Kylee together. Did they meet up at the party, or did they come as a couple? And if it was the latter, what did that mean? Anything at all?

After a few moments, I realized that all that pondering nearly cost me an opportunity. The elevator doors were still wide open and ready for another passenger.

I was next in line.

Twenty-Three

~~~~~~~~~~~~~~~~~~~~~~~~~~~~~~~~~~~~~

As soon as my half boots touched the yellow-painted pavement, the elevator doors began to close.

"No, no, no!"

I barely managed to slip through the narrowing crack before the doors closed completely, and I banged my left elbow in the process. Gritting my teeth to keep from crying out, I leaned against the scratched and dented wall of the gray steel box as I massaged my throbbing arm.

There were only two unlocked buttons on the control panel—one marked *Ground*, the other *Roof*.

I didn't need to press either one. A few seconds after the doors closed, the ancient car shuddered and began its creaky ascent. The elevator—likely installed when this building was built—rose as slowly as you'd expect a centenarian to move, so the journey to the rooftop restaurant took a full minute. That was just long enough for me to wonder what I was getting into. Not that I regretted my rash decision—what good would that do now?—but I did worry that I might end up in the middle of a riot.

That seemed to be the case when the elevator jerked to a halt.

As soon as the doors rumbled open, I was bowled over by a rushing tide of white-jacketed sous-chefs, line cooks, dishwashers, and a black-clad waiter or two. Panicked, they were seeking escape from arrest. I fought my way through the mob and stumbled into the vast fluorescent whiteness of the kitchen as the elevator doors closed behind me.

The path to the cooking stations was littered with debris—marijuana, pipes, tiny vials of white powder, pills, even a magic mushroom or two—all of it the personal stash of the kitchen crew, discarded in their headlong flight from the police.

The late chef and global food critic Anthony Bourdain wrote candidly about the rampant drug use in many big-city restaurants, and here was the proof of what I already knew. Despite the evidence, these hardworking employees had nothing to fear from Quinn and his team. The OD Squad wasn't looking to arrest common users. They were after much bigger fish.

I followed the illicit trail past the refrigerators, prep tables, grills, and ovens. When I reached the serving window, I spied the swinging door that led to the dining room.

Oddly, I heard no sound—no party chatter, no music, just dead silence. There was no window on the door, so I opened it a crack and peeked through.

The rooftop restaurant continued the hotel's retro-modern theme, with naked brick walls, a green stone floor, and steel support beams holding up a glass roof. At least thirty people were standing around under the night sky, but the scene was anything but celebratory. The crowd was a mix of young and old, all well-dressed, and all seemingly transfixed—watching something I could not yet see.

A grunt cut the silence. Then I heard Franco. "How long since the last dose?"

"Two minutes, twenty seconds," Quinn replied.

"His breathing is still shallow. DeMarco, another Narcan—"

Narcan. I knew that name. Almost everyone did. Administered as a nasal spray, it was the most effective treatment for an opioid overdose, its very existence a sad statement about our times.

Every public school in New York City now had a supply on hand. Quite a few bars and restaurants kept the drug in their first aid kits. At the Village Blend we stored two bottles behind the coffee bar. And right now, someone in this restaurant was being treated with it to counteract a possibly lethal overdose.

I slipped through the door. No one noticed. They continued to stare at the man on the ground. Franco was kneeling beside him, and DeMarco handed him a new dose of the drug.

Quinn stood a few feet away, with his back to me. He was timing the dose with his watch. Two other officers, a young man and woman, stood on the opposite side of the restaurant, blocking the exit.

I scanned the faces in the crowd, looking for any other members of Jerry's cast and crew, but there were none—none that I recognized, anyway, since there were crew members with whom I'd never interacted. *And,* I had to acknowledge that with Sebastian Albee and Kylee Ferris rushing down the service elevator and out the back door, there may have been more cast members who'd left by the lobby, before the police arrived.

Franco finished administering the second Narcan dose. He checked the man's pulse and his breathing.

"I don't know if he's going to make it—"

Someone in the crowd cried out. A woman sobbed once.

"The paramedics are in the elevator now," DeMarco told him.

Franco removed the nasal sprayer to begin CPR, and the man's face was finally revealed. Despite the waxy complexion and the open, unseeing eyes, I recognized the victim immediately.

It was Jerry Sullivan's old friend, the comedian he'd hired as a guest star, funnyman Billy Saddler, late of stage, screen, and network television—and now, unless the paramedics could save him, quite possibly just late.

Twenty-Four

"Here you go . . ."

I handed Mike a glass of ruby red port and collapsed next to him on the sofa with mine. He'd started a fire, and we sat in complete, exhausted silence for a full minute, doing nothing but sipping those sweet Dionysian spirits and warming up.

For the last few hours, after Billy Saddler was rushed to the hospital, Quinn and his team had taken names and questioned the guests at the rooftop party. I lurked and listened until finally, he gave me a ride home.

"Okay," he prodded. "Now it's your turn."

"My turn?"

"A favor for a favor. Remember? I brought you to the party, *literally*. Now what have you got for me?"

"I feel like a police informant."

"And so you are."

Despite the crackling flames in the fireplace, Mike Quinn's arctic blue gaze gave me a slight chill, until one corner of his mouth twitched up.

"Come on, Cosi, don't make me use cuffs."

The teasing look he was now giving me sparked a different kind of heat—one with a magnetic pull.

I shifted uncomfortably on the cushions. With the adrenaline still flowing from the police raid, my head felt light. Resisting the wretched need in my core to make love to the man, I took a fortifying hit of the fortified wine.

"Don't kid around," I said, voice suddenly hoarse. "This is hard enough."

"Hey, it's just me. You still love me, don't you?"

"With all my heart."

"And you trust me?"

"I do."

"Then tell me what you're holding back . . ."

Clearing my throat, I finally gave in to Madame's idea of "pillow talk," even though we weren't in bed—*yet*. (The sofa pillows would have to do.)

I started with the so-called accident I was told had occurred on a soundstage set three weeks before in Queens, where a bank of lights fell on Jerry Sullivan's old assistant.

"Apparently, this guy Norman was injured pretty badly and is recovering at a clinic," I explained. "Jerry claimed the accident was investigated by the studio and the cause was chalked up to an electrical surge. Now he has a new assistant named Drew Merriweather, and I overheard Jerry complaining to him about other things going wrong, saying it felt like the production was under a curse—or being sabotaged."

Quinn nodded. "You were *told* about this soundstage accident, which makes it hearsay. Was there anything you actually *witnessed*?"

"Yes. Two incidents. Yesterday, on the first day of the location shoot here at the Village Blend, a man named Fred Denham, the set's property master and armorer, collapsed after drinking a double espresso from Driftwood's coffee truck—"

"Wait. Why was Driftwood serving coffee in front of your shop?"

"They were already under contract to provide craft services for the production company."

"I see. So what exactly happened to Denham?"

"The espresso he drank was tainted . . ." I explained the particulars and how he was taken away by an ambulance. "He's still in the hospital," I said.

"And was the set shut down?"

"For one day. Jerry fired Driftwood and asked the Village Blend to step in temporarily and provide refreshments for his crew, which we did, beginning today when Jerry resumed production with a scene that involved him firing a gun—"

"Wait. Without the armorer present?"

I held up my hand. "I know it's a violation, but Hutch, Fred Denham's assistant, claimed Fred had prepared the weapon himself and he'd watched him do it. He insisted there was no reason not to trust the safety of the weapon, except it turned out there was. The gun was loaded with a real bullet that could have killed Tucker, if he hadn't worn a bulletproof vest under his clothes."

"Oh, for the love of—" Quinn's poker face finally broke. "I can't believe what I'm hearing."

"I pushed for a police investigation," I said quickly, "but Jerry begged me not to make any calls. He said what happened was a freak accident, and in return for Tucker's troubles, he offered him a bigger part in the show and the Village Blend a craft services contract for the rest of their New York location filming with a credit on every episode of this season's production."

Quinn put down his port and sat up straight. "Do you realize what you're telling me, Clare? You and your staff are no longer witnesses. By agreeing to keep your mouths shut—and for a bribe, no less—you've all become accessories after the fact."

I put my own glass down. "Accessories to *what* exactly? The reality is, Tucker would never press charges. He wouldn't risk being blacklisted by other productions. If you or any of your fellow officers pushed him, then he'd claim the whole thing was a planned stunt and that's why he wore the vest."

Quinn rubbed his forehead in frustration. And I knew why—

If Tucker refused to provide supporting testimony, then there was no crime, or at least no real case for charges and prosecution.

"What about *future* gun safety?" Quinn challenged. "What's being done?"

"Jerry is banning all firearms from the set. The show is a murder mystery with comedic, over-the-top fantasy sequences, so he's going to replace real guns with squirt or paintball guns."

Quinn calmed down after that, pausing a moment to add things up. Finally, he said—

"So that's why you confronted that security guard tonight? You think someone is intentionally trying to sabotage the production."

"Let's just say *that's* what I'm trying to figure out. Jerry says, when it comes to any production, there are always accidents and screwups. But

I'm more than a little skeptical—and that's making me paranoid. When I noticed a shadowy figure hurrying out of a darkened trailer, one that I thought should have been locked, I made the guard check inside. But everything looked fine. He locked the trailer in front of me before I left with you."

"So *none* of this was about drugs on the set?"

"Drugs? No!"

"You didn't see *anyone* on this Jerry Sullivan production using or distributing Funtenol?"

"Is that what you thought I was trying to hide from you?"

"Since it's my squad's primary concern at the moment, yes. I told you the show business and film production communities are the primary users. They're partying with it—and the overdose cases are mounting. You saw the dangers with your own eyes. Billy Saddler nearly died tonight. I've got a detective at the hospital, waiting for a chance to talk to him. He hasn't come around yet, and he still may not recover."

"It's tragic, I know. But . . . you don't actually know that he collapsed because of the drug. What happened could have been from natural causes. A stroke or heart attack."

"We'll have to wait for the medical report, but the witnesses confirmed that he was using before he collapsed."

I sat back, took a breath. "About that party . . . I have something else to tell you. I know you and your team took statements from everyone in the restaurant. But you didn't talk to *everyone* who was there."

Intrigued, Quinn leaned forward.

"Go on," he said. "I'm listening . . ."

Twenty-Five

≈≈≈≈≈≈≈≈≈≈≈≈≈≈≈≈≈≈≈≈≈≈≈≈

As Mike Quinn leaned forward, I leaned back.

My body's reaction came a beat before I understood the reason for it. And that reason hit me with a knife-sharp strike, cutting through the fog of the port and the cloud of my affection for the blue-eyed hunk of a man sitting next to me—

What I was about to reveal could have ugly ramifications for Jerry's show, which is why I paused to reconsider my decision to disclose it.

I mean, did my Mike really need to know this?

The internal struggle must have been apparent on my face, because Mike immediately backed off, which shouldn't have surprised me. After years honing his skills in police interview rooms, he'd learned that establishing trust and employing rational arguments yielded far more answers than head-on force. He'd told me as much (more than once), which is why I knew his calm, quiet reaction to my reticence was more than organic. It was ingrained.

"Whoever you saw," he said with the persuasive purr of a seasoned detective, "you don't want them to end up like Billy Saddler, do you?"

"No, of course not."

"So what could it hurt to tell me what you know? Who did you see, Clare? It wasn't your ex-husband, was it? The former drug addict?"

"Oh, please. Matt was nowhere near that party. He went on a swipe-to-meet date hours before—and he's been clean for years."

"Okay, so it wasn't Allegro. Then I guess you'll just have to decide whether you want to trust me again . . ."

I took a long hit of the sweet-tart port and considered my options.

Mike went quiet as I thought things through. He didn't push. He simply waited.

Finally, after I weighed his unsettling warning about Billy Saddler against the dangerous consequences that could result from my not telling him, I spilled . . . (the truth, not my drink).

"All right, Mike, here it is. When I was waiting in that alley, I saw two members of Jerry Sullivan's production come down in the service elevator. They must have been fleeing the rooftop party, slipping out the back of the restaurant when they saw you and your team coming in."

Very slowly this time (so as not to spook me), Mike leaned closer and softly asked, "Who were they?"

"The director of the show, Sebastian Albee. And Jerry's costar, Kylee Ferris."

"Did they appear to be under the influence?"

"I don't think so," I said before something else occurred to me. "Could one of them have been your anonymous tipster? Maybe that's why they left so fast—because one or both of them knew a raid was coming."

"Could be, or . . ." Mike picked up his glass again. Sipping and thinking, he sat back in silence.

"Or what?" I prompted.

"Or Jerry's director and costar could have left the back way because they wanted to smuggle out a substantial amount of the drug with them."

"What makes you think that?"

"Billy Saddler was the one who brought the Funtenol. That's what the witnesses claimed. They said he was passing it out like Willy Wonka tossing chocolate bars."

Quinn's comparison wasn't random. Back at the hotel, I had asked to see what the drug looked like, and Franco showed me a handful of chocolate squares embossed with the word *Fun*. Though the drug itself was a white powder, looking much like cocaine, he told me that—unlike cocaine, which was typically snorted or injected—Funtenol was consumed orally.

The new drug was a stimulant, giving an "up" feeling, which is why partiers used it, and why people who worked long hours (like production crews on film sets) took it. And because it was orally consumable,

Funtenol could be dissolved into liquids or baked into brownies. Tonight, Billy brought it as a Willy Wonka edible.

Considering the drug was a stimulant, I had asked Franco why they'd used Narcan on Billy. "I thought Narcan only worked to reverse overdoses from opioids."

"When we can't be sure what the victim took, we always try Narcan," he'd told me. "It can't hurt them, and it's always worth a try to save a life . . ."

Now I closed my eyes and lamented what I knew. "Mike, please tell me this won't be in the papers."

"The statements were taken in confidence. No one's talking to the press. But Saddler being rushed to the hospital, that's going to be news."

"As an overdose?"

"The most anyone can factually report is that he collapsed at a party. Anything else would be speculation."

"That's not very reassuring since speculation is reported all the time. So now what? I mean, now that you know Jerry's director and costar were almost certainly at that party, what's the next step?"

"I have an idea about that . . ."

Mike's blue gaze became intense again. I shifted uncomfortably, but not because of a magnetic pull.

Now that he brought up my ex-husband—and current business partner—it occurred to me how Matt would react if he knew what I was doing. After his dire warning to keep my mouth shut, I truly couldn't have opened it any wider.

I faced down the detective. "You are not going to raid my coffeehouse set, are you?"

"No, of course not."

"Then what are you going to do?"

"I'd like to put Sergeant Franco undercover with you."

"Emmanuel Franco? Undercover in my coffeehouse?"

"He did it once before, as you recall. You trained him, didn't you?"

"To bus tables! I don't let new baristas pull a single espresso shot for a customer until they've spent three months training."

"So he can bus tables again—and help with other things. Put an apron on him and have him do whatever you let rookies do."

"It's not going to work, Mike. Every member of my staff who has a pass for the production set downstairs has gone through vetting. They've signed consent forms with nondisclosure agreements, which I am violating right now, by the way—"

"NDAs don't apply to illegal activity—"

"What illegal activity? We already established there isn't any. At least, none that any prosecutor could actually make stick. And with everything that's happened on Jerry's set, do you imagine he's going to let me suddenly bring in a muscle-bound barista who looks like a gangbanger?"

"Take it easy, Clare."

"You're also forgetting that my ex-husband can't stand Emmanuel Franco, despite the fact—scratch that—because of the fact that he's dating our daughter. Matt would never allow it!"

"Okay, okay. I hear you. Calm down . . ."

Mike rose and retrieved the bottle of port. He refilled my glass. I didn't object to the refill, but I was skeptical as to why—

"You think getting me soused will get me to agree with you?"

Mike arched an eyebrow. "If only it were that easy . . ."

I smiled at that. And so did he.

"Look, I'm not the enemy. I'm not trying to get you drunk for nefarious reasons. Or pressure you into a situation that you think is unworkable or ill-advised. I just don't want us to fight."

"Neither do I."

"So here's what we're going to do," he said as he refilled his own glass. "We're going to take our drinks upstairs to the bedroom—and stop talking for a while. Okay?"

Ever the persuasive detective, Mike finally got the answer he was hoping for.

Twenty-six

∽∽∽∽∽∽∽∽∽∽∽∽∽∽∽∽∽∽∽∽∽∽∽∽∽∽∽

Morning came too soon.

I woke to find Mike already up and gone for the day, but he'd left a sweet note on his pillow—

Need a date for dinner? Call me.

I smiled, considering he could have texted me the message. But he wanted me to have the note, something to hold, to touch—like his touch last night. Remembering, I closed my eyes and smiled wider.

Filled with renewed confidence, I kicked off the covers.

In almost no time, I showered and dressed. Then I floated down the service stairs. Okay, not literally, but that's how it felt.

I'd slept in, so I expected the shop to be filled with film production activity by now. Strangely, it wasn't.

"Hello!"

Calling out, I moved from the back pantry into the service area behind the coffee bar. The morning sun was shining through our French doors, drenching my coffeehouse with a gorgeous golden light. It was perfect for filming, and the camera equipment from Jerry's show was all set up, but strangely, the place was devoid of life.

Where was everyone? Had something happened? Something bad?

Suddenly filled with dread, my mind placed me back on the street last night. Once again, I saw the darkened trailer and that shadowy figure hurrying out and slipping away, like a slinky serpent . . .

This morning, the trailers were still parked outside. But I didn't see that security guard. I didn't see any security. Not even uniformed police for crowd control. No cast or production crew. No Matt or Tucker. No Esther, Nancy, or Dante.

Could they be upstairs, on the second-floor lounge?

That's it, I thought. They must be having some kind of staff meeting.

I hurried across the shop to the spiral stairs. My feet clanged on the wrought iron steps, but as I crested the top, I heard nothing. No voices, no moving of furniture. Entering our lounge floor, I saw no signs of life there, either.

Perplexed, I began to cross the deserted space, dodging café tables, standing lamps, and comfy chairs, when I noticed my office door ajar and the soft glow of artificial light shining inside. Alarmed, I called out—

"Who's there? Who's in my office?"

"It's me, Clare."

"Jerry?"

I pushed open the door to find Jerry Sullivan himself sitting in my creaky wooden desk chair, his sneakered feet on my desk, his long, jeans-clad legs crossed. The sleeves of his V-neck sweater were pushed up to his elbows, and his hands held a document.

As I entered the office, he lowered the paper, and his sharp gray gaze, beneath his signature silver hair, fixed me with an unnerving stare.

"I've been waiting for you."

"Why? And why are you here in my office? Where is everyone?"

"They're gone, Clare. I sent them away. They're not coming back."

"Why not?"

"Because of you. You and your big mouth."

"Wh-what are you talking about?" I stammered.

"Don't even try that lie with me. I know you talked to your cop boyfriend . . ."

Oh, no! No, no, no . . .

A horrible shock of betrayal went through me as I realized what must have happened. While I was sleeping, Mike must have acted on the information I gave him about Sebastian and Kylee being at that party. He must have sent detectives in to raid the production trailers, looking for that terrible new drug. He must have questioned Sebastian and Kylee and cornered Jerry about that accidental shooting on set!

I felt sick to my stomach as Jerry rose from my chair.

"You ruined everything!" he cried, his fury mounting. "You blabbed to a cop. You violated your NDA. We're going to sue you personally for everything you've got. And as far as your precious Village Blend is concerned, we are done filming here. We're pulling up stakes. Your shop is off the show, and so is your staff, including Tucker. He's cut from the cast as of today."

"No, Jerry. Wait!" I cried as he moved to leave. "Listen to me. It's not Tucker's fault. It's no one's fault but mine!"

"That's right. And you're going to stop talking right now because I'm going to make sure of it."

With uncanny speed, Jerry moved in close.

"What are you doing?"

Arms outstretched, he reached for me. I tried to dodge what was coming, but he moved too fast, backing me against the wall.

Face red with rage, he looked almost inhuman. His eyes went wide, practically popping in his head, as his hands gripped my throat and began to squeeze. I tried to kick, to punch, to peel his fingers away, but my efforts were feeble, useless!

Desperate to cry out, I couldn't. My voice was cut off. I couldn't scream or shout or make a sound. He was choking the life out of me!

With my eyes, I tried to plead with him to stop, to understand—

I didn't mean any harm in telling Mike! I wanted the opposite! I was trying to protect my staff and the production's cast and crew. I was trying to help!

It didn't matter.

Jerry didn't care.

His fingers felt like ten boa constrictors, tightening and tightening until I could no longer breathe or put up a fight.

With my air cut off, my mind shut down. Like the end of a scene on the silver screen, my eyes stopped seeing, and the room slowly, inevitably, faded to black.

"CLARE, wake up! Wake up!"

I opened my eyes. The horrible red rage of Jerry's furious face was replaced with the calming blue of Mike's concerned gaze. I glanced around and realized I was in my own bedroom, under the covers with my fiancé next to me.

"You were moaning and crying out in your sleep," he said. "You were having a nightmare."

I touched my throat. The dream was so real, I wasn't sure if I could speak—

"Jerry . . ." I croaked. "Jerry Sullivan was choking me."

"What? Why?"

I told him. I told Mike the whole fantastic dream, including the cutting feeling of betrayal when I thought he'd called in the OD Squad cavalry to raid Jerry's trailers and my coffeehouse.

When I was finished, he put his arm around me. "Come on, lie back . . ."

I did, but I was still a bundle of anxieties as I rested my head against him.

"Listen to me," he began, his deep voice creating a gentle rumble in his chest. "I am not going to betray your confidence. Or raid your coffeehouse. Or Jerry Sullivan's trailers. I am not going to question anyone you may or may not have seen exiting that party. And I am not putting any of my detectives undercover in your shop. Do you know why?"

"Why?"

"Because I don't have to. You're already there."

"Me?"

"As you well know, law enforcement relies on information—like that tip my squad received about the rooftop party where Billy Saddler collapsed. Sure, much of the info that we act on is gathered through our own efforts. But a good deal of it is provided by informants and concerned citizens—you being a textbook definition of the latter. Well, almost . . ."

"Almost?"

"As a rule, I don't sleep with my informants."

"Let's hope not."

"Listen, Clare, I know how concerned you are about the safety of your staff as well as Jerry's people. That's why you grilled that security guard in the street, isn't it?"

"Of course."

"You're also the best snoop I know."

"Thank you."

"So, as of this moment, I am unofficially deputizing you as an adjunct member of my squad."

"Good grief," I muttered. "Madame's pillow talk has gone to a whole new level."

"What's that?"

"Nothing. And I can't argue with your logic. In fact, I already warned Jerry I would be investigating whether someone was intentionally sabotaging his set. I'm just not sure where to start."

"You start with the obvious. Who brought the gun to the set?"

"The assistant property master, a young guy named Hutch Saunders."

"Start there. Ask some simple questions. Watch how he responds. Is he evasive, hostile? Try to determine if his answers check out, whether he's lying about anything."

"Okay," I said. "I'm also going to talk to those two I saw fleeing that rooftop party—Kylee Ferris and Sebastian Albee."

"They may be guilty of absolutely nothing related to your set sabotage, but if you can get them talking, they might give you a lead on who to question next."

"Go on," I said. "What other advice do you have?"

"Just a few reminders. Things you already know about how we operate. Questioning a pair of suspects should be done separately. That way you can compare their stories. If they differ—"

"One of them is lying."

"If you know the true story, then that will confirm it. And you were an eyewitness, in the back alley behind the hotel. You saw Sebastian and Kylee leave together. See if they come clean about that. You'll also want to keep an eye out for drug use or distribution—you don't want another Billy Saddler–type OD in the middle of your coffeehouse."

"No, but I can't be everywhere at once, Mike."

"Of course not. But you can use your people."

"My people," I echoed, realizing Mike was right—and not just about the drug thing. With Driftwood coffee baristas on our set, and all that anger over our winning their craft services business, I couldn't rule out competitive sabotage to our own food and beverage service.

"Keep in touch," Mike said softly, "and I'll do whatever I can to keep you and your people safe without jeopardizing your coffeehouse or the success of Jerry's production. Okay?"

"Okay."

"Now get some sleep."

With that, I didn't argue.

Yawning, I relaxed into the warmth of Mike's big body, feeling a little better about the week ahead. Deep sleep came quickly, which was a mercy, because in just a few hours, a very long day was about to start.

Twenty-seven

Not far away, in a New York hospital, a text message was typed and sent. It consisted of four simple words—

We need to talk.

The Player, busy at another location, heard the mobile alert and glanced at the screen. This wasn't good, the Player thought. Things weren't going as planned. But then when did things ever go as planned?

You better answer me.
Or I'm going to talk.

"What to say? What to say?" the Player muttered. *No. What to do? What to do?* the Player thought.
Finally, the Player typed—

Sit tight. We'll work this out.
Can't talk now. Will be in touch.

Mind over matter, the Player decided.
When you matter, no one minds.
Well, now is the time to matter.
And act. To cover your tracks.

Twenty-Eight

~~~~~~

"Keep your mitts off that muffin!"

At Esther's barked command, the Driftwood blonde with the nose ring literally jumped backward.

Esther offered her a sunny smile.

"Use tongs," she suggested, gently setting a blueberry muffin on the young woman's plate.

Breakfast was on at the Village Blend, and I was relieved to see that Esther was doing exactly what I asked: keeping a sharp eye on the extras from Driftwood Coffee. Nancy promised to do the same. Like a bloodhound with braids, my youngest staff member was downstairs, following the other Driftwood extra everywhere he went.

With my baristas on food and beverage security duty, I was confident that no one would be poisoned—not by the Driftwood people, anyway. In fact, things were humming along quite smoothly on our first day of craft services. We'd set up shop on the second floor, which provided more than enough room for Jerry's people to eat, drink, and merrily lounge.

I didn't know how Matt's dinner date went (I didn't pry), but my ex had pulled up to our coffeehouse at six thirty AM with a van full of catering supplies and equipment. In record time, Dante and Matt had unloaded the van and set everything up.

Word that Dennis Murphy's famous Grandma's pizza was on the lunch menu spread like wildfire through the ranks, and crew members were already looking forward to it. In the meantime, Jerry's people downed plenty of Village Blend coffee and feasted on our breakfast pastries, including our fresh-baked Strawberry Shortcake Muffins, Irish Oatmeal Cookie Muffins, Cherry Streusel Pastry Cake, and the unique babkas sent over by Madame's good friend, along with lunch items like wraps and salads.

As our first official craft services breakfast drew to a close, Jerry Sullivan called everyone together for an announcement—and I could tell by the somber expression on his face what was coming.

"This news hasn't hit the press yet, so keep it quiet as long as you can. Billy Saddler had a health episode last evening, probably pushing too hard after a long flight. Exhaustion and dehydration, you know? Anyway, he's in the hospital—"

The word *hospital* caused an uneasy murmur through the room.

"Hey, don't worry! It's all good. He'll be well taken care of while he recovers and gets the rest he needs. In a few days, he's going to be back to his zany old self, and we'll be having a grand time with Billy right here on this set!" Jerry clapped his hands. "So let's have a freakin' fantabulous day today! Okay, everyone?"

"Okay!" crew members returned.

"Yeah!"

"All right!"

Everyone appeared pumped up by Jerry's speech, which I knew was a complete fabrication. Even if Billy Saddler was in recovery, his collapse had less to do with jet lag than a new designer drug.

For a minute, I wondered if Jerry himself knew the truth or was simply spinning a fiction he hoped would become fact. Then I saw the tell—

The comedian's frozen smile remained in place only long enough for the production people to break up and head downstairs. As his expression collapsed, he exchanged an anxious look with Tina Bird, who gave him a hapless-looking shrug in return. That's precisely when he realized this moment of truth was being witnessed—by me.

"Hey, Clare—"

"Jerry!"

With his comedic mask back in place, Jerry slowly approached. His gray eyes were sharp, conveying no warmth, and I couldn't help flashing on that nightmarish image of his enraged face as he tried to choke me to death.

"Just wanted to say, outstanding job on the breakfast! Those Irish Oatmeal Cookie Muffins are ingenious and yummy. You've given me a *new* favorite way to get fiber in my diet. And that Sumatra is the best I've ever tasted—"

As he reached out to pat me on the shoulder, I reared back. I couldn't stop my automatic reaction, and Jerry immediately apologized.

"Sorry, sorry! Didn't mean to invade your space."

"No! It's okay. I just—"

"No need to explain, Clare. Plenty of people don't like to be touched. Believe me, I understand. Keep your hands to yourself, Jerry—" His frozen smile suddenly melted into a genuine one, and his gaze warmed. "I've just been around a long time, and old habits are hard to break. Forgive me?"

"Nothing to forgive. I'm just a little tense this morning."

"Sure, you've got a lot to manage. So I'll let you get to it . . ."

As Jerry strode away, I let out a relieved breath. Feeling my heart pound, I couldn't ignore the irony. A few days ago, it was pounding with excited anticipation. I couldn't wait to meet Jerry Sullivan in the flesh. Now my own central nervous system was prodding me to keep my distance from the star.

While I didn't for a moment believe Jerry would physically harm me, I did feel the ugly pressure to keep my mouth shut—about Billy Saddler and anything else that didn't fit the fabricated public image of everything being fantabulous on Jerry Sullivan's show.

Of course, I hadn't forgotten my pillow talk discussion with Mike, or Jerry's own agreement to let me investigate Tucker's shooting. Nothing had changed on that front, and I wasn't going to simply let it go.

First on my list to question was Hutch Saunders, the young guy with the fiery-red Rasta locks.

As assistant property master, Hutch was the one who'd handed Jerry the loaded gun, and I wanted to hear how he'd explain his mistake, whether he would be evasive or cooperative—and whether he himself had some secret suspicions that he was willing to confide.

Unfortunately for me, when I tried to find him, I learned he was gone from the set.

Apparently, Jerry had been unhappy with the selection of squirt guns Hutch had rounded up. For today's scene, he picked out a neon green

Super Soaker, but for future filming, he sent the rest back and told Hutch to go shopping for "funnier guns."

With that opportunity delayed, I moved on to my goal of questioning Sebastian Albee and Kylee Ferris about attending (and secretly fleeing) Billy Saddler's drug-fueled bash.

Since director Albee and I would be working together tomorrow, I knew I could quiz him then.

In the meantime, I devised a strategy for approaching Kylee at lunchtime. For that I would need my youngest barista, Nancy—

And a couple of mouthwatering slices of Grandma's pizza.

Twenty-nine

꩜꩜꩜꩜꩜꩜꩜꩜꩜꩜꩜꩜꩜꩜꩜꩜꩜꩜꩜

THE rest of the morning, everyone was focused on refilming Jerry's coffeehouse shooting scene—this time, as promised, with a gun that wouldn't require a bulletproof vest.

Tucker gave a wonderfully comedic performance as the victim. As soon as the water cannon hit from Jerry's neon green Super Soaker, Tuck went into over-the-top melodrama mode, and his "death throes" lasted for almost a minute. When Sebastian Albee yelled, "Cut!" the entire crew burst out in laughter and applause.

They filmed the scene four more times, blow-drying poor Tucker off between each take, until finally, the director called for a one-hour lunch break.

At that point, the stampede was on, and I feared our wrought iron spiral staircase wouldn't bear the number of people clanging up to our second floor for pizza. Slices were doled out and the cold drinks and iced lattes flowed. Everyone seemed happy, though a number of crew members outspokenly longed for beer to go with their pizza. (I would have found a way to serve it, but Tina Bird had banned the consumption of alcohol on the set.)

Jerry skipped lunch altogether and retired to his trailer with Tweety in tow, and I suspected they wanted enough privacy to check up on what was happening with Billy Saddler.

In the meantime, I was told that tomorrow Sebastian Albee wanted to oversee some filming of yours truly whipping up espressos and lattes to be edited into scenes where needed. Since that would take our first-floor beverage service offline for craft services, I asked Matt to set up two Rocket portable espresso makers on the second floor.

As for Kylee, she was scheduled to shoot her scenes this afternoon and had remained in her trailer all morning, which meant it was time to implement my scheme.

"Nancy, I'm betting you'd love a posed picture with Kylee Ferris, right?"

Her face brightened. "Sure would!"

"Let's take some pizza to her trailer, and I'll ask Kylee to pose with you."

"Would you, really?"

"Of course, come on . . ."

I placed two piping hot squares on a plate and covered them with foil. Nancy grabbed a cherry soda from the portable refrigerator—

"I saw Kylee drinking a cherry soda in an old interview on YouTube. I'm betting it's still her fave."

Plate and cold bottle in hand, Nancy and I ventured outside.

The trailers didn't have names on the doors, only numbers. Tucker informed me that only trailers used on studio lots had names identifying them. On location shoots, for security purposes, names were never affixed to trailers.

I had to ask a crew member to point out Kylee's trailer, and I immediately realized it was the very one that mysterious figure had entered last night.

We knocked and Kylee opened the door. Her fine, strawberry blond hair was coiled tightly in back of her head (likely readied for her curly brunette wig). The style would have been unflattering on many women, but it simply made Kylee's high cheekbones and large amber eyes look all the more striking. Dressed casually in worn jeans and a simple baby blue sweater, she smiled when she recognized me, greeting me with her laid-back Southern drawl.

"Hey, Clare, what have you got there?"

"Your lunch. Dennis Murphy's famous Grandma's pizza."

"You're welcome to come in. Jerry mentioned you might be stopping by to discuss some things with me . . ."

She stepped aside, and Nancy and I entered.

The trailer was comfortably furnished. A vanity with a lighted makeup mirror sat near the back. A set of clothes on a hanger, wrapped in plastic like dry cleaning, dangled from a wall hook, and I assumed that was her costume for today.

Mounted on another wall was a flat-screen TV. Playing now was one of Kylee's scenes from the first season of *Only Murders in Gotham*. Today's script pages lay scattered across a sofa, all covered with handwritten notes.

"Wow, you can stream in here," Nancy marveled.

I introduced my barista and handed over the pizza and cherry soda. Kylee set the pizza aside. But she immediately twisted off the soda bottle cap and took a satisfying drink.

"Oh, that's good. My favorite."

"Nancy knew it," I said. "She may be your biggest fan. She's also too intimidated to ask, but I think she'd love to get a picture of you two together."

"Why, sure!"

Kylee rose, put her arm around Nancy's shoulder, and smiled while I snapped a few quick pictures with Nancy's phone.

"That's very nice of you," I said. "Now we should let you eat!"

"I'm so nervous I don't know if I can eat," she confessed.

"Nervous?" I prodded.

"I can sing my heart out, but this acting thing . . ." Kylee shook her head.

"I think you're marvelous," Nancy gushed. "At singing and acting."

"You two are so, so sweet!" She took another happy swig of soda. "It's nice to have people to 'girl talk' with, you know? I don't have any friends or family here in New York."

"Well, feel free to 'girl talk' with us!" Nancy said.

"That's right," I seconded. "We'll be feeding and caffeinating you for the rest of your location work, so if you have any special food or beverage requests, just let me or Nancy know, okay?"

"I'm easy. And I'm glad you two will be around. You know, last year my agent convinced me to take this part, but I nearly quit on the first day."

"Why?" Nancy and I asked together.

"Lots of reasons. Let's just say, some people weren't as nice to me as you two."

"What people?" I asked. "Are they still here?"

Kylee tensed up at that question, and I knew I'd made a mistake. I pushed too hard, too fast. It was a blunder Mike Quinn never would have made.

Was it too late? I wondered. Did I botch my Cosi version of a police interview? Or was there still a way to fix this?

Thirty

∂⌒∂⌒∂⌒∂⌒∂⌒∂⌒∂⌒∂⌒∂⌒∂⌒∂⌒∂⌒∂⌒∂⌒∂⌒∂⌒∂

"I'M sorry for prying," I quickly told Kylee. "As a manager, especially of young women, I'd want to know if anyone on the set is inclined to engage in harassment."

Kylee shook her head. "It was nothing like that. It was just a difficult time for me. I wasn't very confident."

"But you didn't quit," I said, hoping to regain her trust. "And I heard Tucker mention there are rumors that you're going to win an Emmy."

Kylee frowned. "If I do, it's really Sebastian's Emmy."

"Sebastian Albee, the director?" Nancy asked. "Why would you say that?"

"Because it's true." Kylee rolled her pretty eyes. "I was such an amateur last season. It's embarrassing now."

"I don't believe it," I said.

"Me either," said Nancy.

Kylee laughed. "Believe it! I spoke my lines like a zombie and actually looked right into the camera like a doofus. I dropped in and out of character, and the Brooklyn accent was a real challenge. Before the show began, I studied with a voice coach and did the accent perfectly at the table read, but on the set, in front of the camera and lights . . ." She shook her head. "I was freezing up."

"What did you do?" Nancy asked.

"After that first awful day on the set, Sebastian came to my trailer with a Blu-ray of a movie called *Moonstruck*. Have you ever seen it?"

Nancy and I both nodded.

"We watched the movie together, and when it was over Sebastian explained that Cher—do you know her? She was a big pop star once."

"Uh, yeah," I said. "I think I've heard of her."

"Well, Cher wasn't a professionally trained actress, either. She was a singer first, but director Norman Jewison made her work hard to hone her skills, until Cher could hold her own beside amazingly talented actors like Nicolas Cage—"

"And Cher won an Oscar for Best Actress," I said.

"Exactly!" Kylee beamed. "Sebastian promised to give me the same help. He began to work with me that very night. After every day of work that first season, Sebastian would coach me in private on how I should approach the next day's shoot. It was Sebastian who gave me the confidence to step into the role and he showed me how to make it my own."

"You think highly of him, then?"

"Oh, I do. Any praise I get, any awards I win, it's all because of Sebastian. I'm still not sure I can act without him directing me."

"Do you two still work together after hours?" I asked.

Kylee nodded.

"I'm asking, because a friend told me you were at a party last night with Sebastian. Is that right?"

"Sebastian wanted to introduce me to Billy Saddler—it was his party."

"So I've heard."

"Tina Bird was there, too," Kylee said. "And so was Drew Merriweather, Jerry's assistant. I was surprised to see Drew at that party without Jerry. I don't know why that happened. I guess Jerry couldn't make it."

"That's odd, considering his speech this morning."

"Hey, I would have skipped it, too, if I could have."

"Why didn't you?"

Kylee shrugged. "Sebastian said I had a lot of scenes with Mr. Saddler coming up, and he wanted to introduce me, sort of break the ice."

"And did you?"

"Barely." Kylee shook her head. "Sebastian and I ended up taking the back elevator out of there. We got out fast."

"Why?"

She lowered her voice. "There were drugs at the party. A lot of them. And I knew I had to get Sebastian out. After all he's done for me, I couldn't let him risk his career by giving in to temptation."

"Temptation?" I pressed. "Is there a problem I should know about? Maybe I can help."

Kylee leaned close and spoke in a low whisper. "Sebastian has—I should say had—an addiction problem. He's clean now, but because of his reputation he almost didn't get the job on *Only Murders in Gotham*. The insurance company balked; the backers were dubious, so he almost lost the gig."

"But he did get the job in the end."

"It was only after Jerry threatened to quit the project that the money people agreed to green-light Sebastian, but on the condition that he stay away from drugs. And he has, he really has."

"But you were afraid for him last night?"

Kylee nodded. "Sebastian is a genius, Clare. But he's also a tortured man. His last project before *Murders* fell through; the one before that was a surreal comedy that broke his heart. The film was a critical success. That's why Jerry hired him. He called it an inventive masterpiece; the studio called it a financial disaster. Now poor Sebastian's nearly broke and stuck in a totally loveless marriage—"

Nancy and I exchanged looks. It was clear to us both that Kylee had strong feelings for Sebastian. Whether it went beyond friendship or some innocent crush, who knew. But the passion she had for him was impossible to miss.

"It's also been a tough second season," Kylee went on. "Did you know the cowriter on our show was fired?"

"I didn't know," I said.

"It was Jerry's doing. He insisted that the scripts Tate Cabot wrote were flat and unfunny. But Sebastian claims Jerry was jealous because Cabot was giving all the best lines to me."

"Well, it was a good thing you and Sebastian left the party," I said. "I heard the police arrived and ended the fun."

"I know." Kylee actually shivered. "If Sebastian was caught up in that, he would be out of a job today."

"Well, he wasn't, thanks to you," Nancy declared.

"You're a sweet thing for saying so," Kylee replied. "But it was Tina who warned us."

"Tina?" I blinked. "Tina Bird warned you about the police coming?"

"Yeah, that's right."

I couldn't believe what I was hearing. If Tina Bird knew the police were coming, then she must have been the OD Squad's anonymous tipster. But why would Tina have tipped off the police? Why would she want to jeopardize the reputation of Jerry's big guest star?

"I don't know how she knew, but Tina did us a real favor," Kylee said. "Hey, you know what? The aroma from that pizza is driving me crazy. I think I will have a slice."

"Great!" I said. "But I don't see any table."

"It's right here. This fold-up table thing is so clever. It even has a cubby shelf behind it for condiments and stuff—" Kylee pointed to a panel on the trailer's wall. "I just have to lower it."

She unfastened the latch and the table dropped down along with a hissing, spitting *live snake!*

Kylee wheeled backward in horror and screamed.

When Nancy saw the writhing reptilian coils on the tabletop, she made it a duet.

Thirty-one

〰〰〰〰〰〰〰〰〰〰〰〰〰〰〰〰〰

"THIS sick stunt has Lizzy Meeks written all over it," Jerry Sullivan raged. "I will not have my cast terrorized by that unbalanced woman!"

Cast and crew were present for this hastily called meeting on the main floor of the Village Blend—all except Matt, Nancy, and the Driftwood extras, who had been sent upstairs for a "break."

Tina Bird sat at the coffee bar, a scowl on her face, arms folded across her chest. Jerry's personal assistant Drew Merriweather stood behind his boss.

"Rest assured, I've fired the losers who were supposed to be providing security," Jerry continued. "I've brought in another company. Their security staff will be here before we close down for the day."

I was the reason for that particular change.

After Kylee discovered the snake, I reported what I'd seen the night before. Jerry wasn't happy to hear that some stranger may have entered Kylee's trailer, or how lax the security guards behaved. His response was immediate. And I was glad new guards would soon be on duty.

"What about this Meeks woman?" Sebastian Albee demanded. "Will you have her arrested?"

Jerry threw up his arms. "Without solid evidence I can't."

"She terrorized our star and disrupted the shooting schedule," Sebastian argued.

And it was obvious that Kylee Ferris had been terrorized. She sat at one of our tables, still in tears, while Sebastian tried unsuccessfully to console her.

Even after New York City's Department of Health and Mental Hygiene came to collect the slithering serpent—pronouncing it "large but harmless"—Kylee refused to return to her trailer.

"Who knows what other thing could be crawling around in there?" she cried. "That horrid woman must be stopped."

Meanwhile, Drew Merriweather, wearing a smug *I told you so* expression, faced his boss—

"Kylee's got a point, Jerry. Something has to be done about Lizzy Meeks."

"Yeah," Jerry replied, hands on hips. "And you're going to do it."

"What?" Drew's smug expression collapsed.

"You have Lizzy's phone number and address. Find her. Talk to her. Figure out what we can do to make peace. She's still steamed about my break from the Vegas show. Fine. Find out how to appease her: an autograph session on the merch she handles, a fan club tickets-only party with a reading from my book, *I'm Still Standing.* Something!"

"But I hardly know the woman—"

"Listen, Drew," Jerry growled. "Before you came along, Norman took care of things when Lizzy got out of hand. You took over Norman's job, right?"

"Right."

"Then do it."

Drew Merriweather slunk away.

"Now let's all get back to work," Jerry continued, his tone more subdued. "Our director says, given this interruption, he'd like to rearrange the schedule and do some reaction shots next. As we all know, Sebastian likes to be hands-on, even for B-rolls." He turned to Kylee. "Are you up for a few reaction shots?"

She shook her head. "Sorry, Jerry—and Sebastian. I want to go back to my hotel and pull myself together. If you have an exterminator check my trailer, I promise I'll be here in the morning, ready to work."

"Do you want me to go with you?" Sebastian quietly asked.

Kylee shook her head. "No, please. I don't want to hang you up, too. Stay here and work with the other actors. I'll have the driver take me back to the hotel."

The director frowned but nodded. "Okay, let's do this. After I get the reaction shots, I'll work with Clare on the B-roll coffee footage today instead of tomorrow. That way we won't lose any time on the schedule."

"Right!" Jerry said, clapping his hands. "Kylee's leaving, but the rest of us can make some progress. Everyone, take a ten-minute break. Then be back here ready to work!"

As the meeting broke up, I noticed Jerry putting his head together for a quiet discussion with Tina, after which Tina hurried out of the coffeehouse.

Curious about that (and wanting to speak with Jerry about a host of other things), I lured him to the coffee bar by offering him a freshly made bulletproof special.

He laughed at the irony of the drink, but he took a seat.

Nancy and Esther came downstairs to make drinks for the rest of the crew, and I moved around the coffee bar to deliver Jerry's butter coffee personally—

"Jerry, I'd like to talk to you about Lizzy Meeks."

He clutched at his hair. "I'm getting a migraine."

"You are not, and you need to hear me out."

With a resigned sigh, he took his coffee from me and proclaimed—

"Speak on, Macduff."

Thirty-two

∽∽∽∽∽∽∽∽∽∽∽∽∽∽∽∽∽∽∽∽∽∽∽∽∽∽∽∽∽∽

As Jerry sipped my bulletproof special, I took the seat next to him and confided—

"I actually met Lizzy Meeks. She stopped by the Village Blend after you visited us that first day—"

"And your conclusion?" he asked. "Mmm . . . superb coffee, by the way."

"Thanks. And my conclusion is that Lizzy thinks the world of you—"

Jerry cut me off with a fluttering-lipped Bronx cheer. "And what about the snake, Clare? Do you have a grand conclusion about that?"

"I admit, Lizzy doesn't have much love for Kylee, okay? I'll give you that. But it makes no sense to me that she would ever try to hurt you."

"So?"

I lowered my voice. "So putting aside the question of the snake, I don't believe Lizzy was the one who put a live bullet in that gun. If Tucker had died or been seriously injured by a gunshot wound that you inflicted—intentionally or not—you would be facing some serious charges right now. How would that help Lizzy? She's no fan of this production or Kylee's, but she's the president of your fan club and makes money from it. What would it profit her to put you in prison for manslaughter?"

"Who said she would? Not me!" Jerry sharply returned and then quickly lowered his own voice. "I never said Lizzy or anyone else put a live bullet in that gun. Not on purpose. It was obviously a freak accident."

Jerry took a long gulp of his bulletproof special and sighed. "Tweety Bird turned out to be right. We should have waited for Fred to get out of the hospital. Or hired another armorer for the set. Hutch Saunders is too young and inexperienced. He wasn't up to the job."

"Since you brought him up, did Tina Bird grill Hutch yet? Did he explain what happened? Or have any suspicions on who put the bullet in the gun?"

"I don't know. You can ask Tina herself when she gets back. She's dealing with some issues at . . . the production office in Queens."

The way he hesitated made me think she was doing something else entirely. Like maybe checking up on Billy Saddler at the hospital?

That whole Billy Saddler thing was turning into a mystery, as well.

According to Kylee, Tina was not only at the party last night, but also the one who warned her and Sebastian to leave the party by the back elevator, just before the police arrived.

It sure sounded as if Tina was the person who anonymously tipped off the police about the drugs. The coincidence of the "Bird" lady being a stool pigeon was not lost on me.

What I didn't know was why.

Nothing added up. And since I had no actual proof of Tweety singing to the cops, I didn't mention it to Jerry.

"You know what, Clare?" Jerry declared after my long silence. "Don't worry about what Hutch may or may not have said to Tina. You talk to Hutch yourself. He should be back on set this afternoon. And with that red rooster comb on his head, he's easy to spot even in a crowded room."

Jerry downed his drink. "Excellent, as usual. Now I better go and whip this scurvy bunch of buccaneers into ship shape."

Stepping into the middle of the room, he put two fingers in his mouth and gave an earsplitting whistle. Then he clapped his hands, and everyone jumped into action.

Thirty-three

〰〰〰〰〰〰〰〰〰〰〰〰〰〰〰〰〰〰〰〰〰

"Let's do the reaction shots first," Sebastian said. "Then we'll get to Clare behind the coffee bar . . ."

As anxious as I was to speak with Hutch Saunders and Tina Bird, I knew neither was on the set at the moment, so I'd have to bide my time. But, thanks to Sebastian Albee's announced shooting schedule, I knew that time wouldn't be a total loss.

If Sebastian was going to work with me this afternoon, then I would have the man's undivided attention. He couldn't walk away, and I could get some questioning in.

While I waited for my chance, I did some observational work—what Mike Quinn would probably label background.

From what I could see, Sebastian was not only an intense director, he was also a meticulous one. I remembered Jerry's exact words—

"As we all know, Sebastian likes to be hands-on, even for B-rolls."

I wasn't entirely sure what a B-roll was, but I assumed (from Jerry's statement) it was something Sebastian didn't have to film himself, something he could delegate to an underling. But he didn't. Which meant control was important to him.

That assumption proved itself true as I watched him work.

Sebastian oversaw everything. He supervised, chewing on his thumb, while hair and makeup did some touch-ups on the extras. And he broke in often with advice to the cinematographer as the lighting was adjusted.

When everything was set up precisely as he wanted, Sebastian turned his attention to the extras.

"Once I get each of you set up, I want you to stay put. Don't move off your marks. Got it?"

Everyone nodded.

Nancy was the only one who didn't. She looked nervous, and I suspected she was still a bit shaky from the snake incident. Maybe that's why Sebastian decided to work with her first.

"Nancy, I don't want you to worry about sound," he said. "We're not using microphones, just this single camera . . ."

The cameraman winked at Nancy, and she returned the gesture with a pained smile.

"Stay in character," Sebastian cautioned.

"Character?"

"Look . . ." Sebastian's voice became softer yet more animated. "You just saw a barista shot and killed. He died in front of you, and the guy who shot him is standing five feet away." Sebastian leaned so close that Nancy backed away. "If you don't think someone getting shot is frightening enough, then think about that scare you experienced in Kylee's trailer. Imagine that horrible, hissing snake is right in front of you . . ."

Beside me, Tucker whispered, "Did you ever think you'd see Nancy Method acting? Next thing you know she'll be talking like Marlon Brando."

Esther suppressed a giggle.

The clapboard clacked. The director softly spoke, "Action."

And Nancy froze.

"Keep shooting," Sebastian whispered to the cameraman as he studied her performance on a small screen monitor.

Nancy resembled a statue of a shell-shocked Heidi for a moment—and suddenly we all heard the sound of a hissing, clicking, and riled-up rattlesnake!

Nancy paled, her expression horrified, her jaw slack, eyes wide with terror. And through it all she bravely remained rooted in place as instructed.

"Cut!"

Sebastian grinned and held up his phone screen. He'd used his browser to call up a YouTube video of a hissing rattlesnake.

The director stepped around the camera and hugged Nancy. Her performance—more accurately her reaction—was so on the mark she was finished after the first take.

Impressed, I now had a clue how Sebastian had patiently worked with Kylee to get the performance he needed out of her.

Matt was next, and his reaction shot was completely convincing, without any audio prompts. Again, the director got what he wanted in a single take. Sebastian sent Matt to the sidelines, and my ex joined us at the coffee bar.

"That was a first-rate performance, Mr. Boss," Esther gushed. "Where did you dig up that look of sheer, abject horror?"

"Truthfully? I imagined the taste of a Driftwood espresso."

Thirty-Four

~~~~~~

"Okay. That's it for today's extras," Sebastian announced when all the reaction shots were finally finished. "Now it's Clare's turn. Let's get the lighting set up . . ."

"Break a leg," Matt told me as hair and makeup swooped in on me.

"And don't fall on your rump," Tucker added with a wink.

Everyone had to vacate the coffee bar while lights and a reflector were brought in. When that was finished, Sebastian agreed with his cinematographer on a handheld camera.

"It's too tight to use a camera dolly," he said.

After that, Sebastian chewed on his thumb as he studied the composition of the picture on his monitor.

"Okay, Clare, we're not using microphones. We'll dub the sound of the machines later. Mostly we'll be shooting your hands, so you can hum a song or talk if that helps allay any nervousness."

While the camera was readied, I took the director's advice and talked—

"I heard you and Kylee were at a party together last night."

Sebastian winced, then buried his surprise.

"We were at the same party, but not together," he said, his gaze never wavering from the monitor.

"Kylee really admires you. She told me so. She believes you're the reason for her success."

"The director's job is to get the best performance out of everyone," Sebastian replied. "Kylee's a natural. She just needed to regain some confidence in herself after . . ."

Sebastian's voice trailed off. Then he cursed.

"There's still too much glare off the espresso machines. Clare's hands look like skeletons. Let's get some negative fill."

As the gaffer went to work, Sebastian ordered me to remain in place while he continued to stare at the video screen.

"After what?" I asked.

"Excuse me?"

"You mentioned that Kylee needed to regain her confidence after something. After what?"

"I guess I meant after her musical career stalled," the director replied before moving to speak to the camera operator.

For the next hour, I pulled espressos, steamed milk, whipped up lattes, and used a French press. Sebastian would mutter a few instructions now and then, looking for interesting angles, but he remained seated, eyes on the monitor.

"Okay, that's a wrap," he said finally. "Good job, Clare."

As the camera operator backed off, Sebastian rose and stretched.

"Do you miss Los Angeles?" I asked.

"I live in Santa Barbara," Sebastian replied. "But I admit it doesn't feel like it. I've been working in New York City and living out of a hotel for months."

"You must miss your wife, your family?"

"I don't have children."

"Well, that is a long time to be separated from you wife—"

Suddenly irritated, Sebastian became surly.

"Is this an interview?" he asked. "Because if that's what you want, you'll have to go through my agent."

"Sorry, I didn't mean to pry—"

"People judge you," he told me, his gaze unnervingly penetrating.

"What?"

"That's why I don't share details about my personal life."

I quickly tried to reestablish trust, as I had with Kylee, but Sebastian Albee brushed me off. Tossing back his crown of porcini mushroom hair, he announced to the crew—

"I'm taking ten. Feel free to do the same . . ."

As I watched his rail-thin body stride away, I remembered Mike

Quinn's advice about interviewing Sebastian and Kylee. He told me to do it separately, which I had.

He also said if someone lied, they likely had something to hide.

Kylee Ferris gave me open, honest answers.

Sebastian Albee, for whatever his reasons, did not.

Thirty-Five

The ten-minute break called by the director stretched into twenty, and Tucker and I pulled twice that many espresso shots. One crew member grabbed two cups at a time.

"These people sure do love their caffeine," I whispered to Tucker.

"Remember what I told you? Movie shoots run on it, honey!"

As Tucker and I continued to distribute our legal stimulant, I couldn't help recalling the talk I had with Sergeant Franco about the stimulating effects of the illegal drug Funtenol. (The irony didn't escape me.)

Finally, twenty minutes stretched into almost thirty. By two PM, Sebastian Albee—who had disappeared into his trailer for the entire break—was calling everyone back to the set.

This time Jerry was the star, and Tuck and I watched him work.

For this sequence, he had a series of comedic monologues, staged as one-sided phone conversations, and they were fascinating to watch. Like a chameleon, Jerry transitioned with ease through a range of emotional expressions—anger, surprise, puzzlement, satisfaction.

"Sullivan really is amazing," Tucker whispered. "His performance is like a body language line-o-rama."

"Good job, Jerry. No, great job!" Sebastian Albee was beaming. His mood, ever since he'd returned from his afternoon break, was noticeably changed.

While he was working with me, the director had been surly and looked exhausted. After the break, he was so "up," I considered the reason why.

In the morning, I'd served Sebastian espressos. But this afternoon, I hadn't seen him take any coffee. So I couldn't help wondering whether he'd consumed something else in his trailer.

Kylee had confided that Sebastian had struggled to overcome a drug addiction. Had that Billy Saddler party set him off again? And had Mike Quinn been right when he threw out the possibility that Kylee and Sebastian had left by the back elevator to secretly smuggle out some of the party's drugs?

Whatever the truth, my silent speculations were interrupted by the director announcing the day's shoot was over.

"We'll pick up with Kylee's scenes in the morning," Sebastian said.

As the crew began to secure their equipment, I noticed a red cockscomb bobbing past our front window. A moment later, Hutch Saunders and his fiery Rasta locks came bounding through the door.

In his arms, he held a plastic milk crate full of the "funnier guns" Jerry had asked him to round up. He dropped the crate of paintball sprayers and water cannons beside the sound equipment, then he climbed the stairs to our lounge.

Finally, I thought. This was the perfect opportunity to grill the very person who'd put a real bullet into Jerry's hands.

I left Tuck in charge of the coffee bar while I took the back stairs to the second floor. With the crew hard at work downstairs, our second-floor catering area was mostly deserted.

Esther and Nancy were already cleaning up when Hutch arrived. He grabbed a cold bottle of soda from our fridge and two slices of pizza from under the warming lights. Then he settled into one of our lounge's comfy armchairs.

I was glad to see that a few more slices of Grandma's pizza were still up for grabs. I put a slice on a plate for myself, figuring if we were both eating the pizza, I'd have a good start to the conversation—food talk.

Hutch chose a seat that faced the fireplace. I took the nearest chair, which was more or less back-to-back with his. I began to eat and was about to turn around and strike up a conversation when Hutch's phone buzzed.

With a frustrated sigh, I sat back and listened while he answered with his phone speaker on.

"Hey, Fred," he garbled, his mouth half-full. "How's the hospital food?"

I leaned closer when I realized the "Fred" that Hutch was speaking with was Fred Denham, the armorer who'd been poisoned on the very first day of shooting.

"The gruel here is so bad, I want out," Fred replied.

"That's a real shame. Too bad I'm eating a slice of Grandma's pizza. Dennis Murphy's gourmet stuff."

"Don't torment me, Hutch."

"Hey, you have a Central Park view, don't you? And you have your meals brought to you in bed. People pay big money for that."

"I'm in the hospital, Hutch. That costs big money, too."

"So, you'll be back on set in a day or two?"

"I'm not coming back," Fred replied after a cough. "I need a vacation. I called because I want you to lock up my kit—"

"Done, my man. Your stuff is back at the studio behind lock and key. But why aren't you coming back?"

"Tina Bird told me about that barista who caught a bullet in the chest. I don't want to answer a lot of ugly questions."

"Nobody's blaming you and nobody's asking questions," Hutch insisted. "At least, nobody asked me much. Just Tina. Anyway, the guy wore a protective vest. No harm done. Jerry took him to a private clinic and hushed the whole thing up to avoid insurance hassles."

"That really worked, huh?" Fred sounded skeptical.

"It worked because Tina swore everyone to secrecy. If anyone blabs to the press, Tina will make darn sure they'll never work again."

"All the more reason I want out of this production. You can do my job. You're welcome to it. I'm leaving town as soon as possible."

"Where are you going?" Hutch pressed. "When will you get back?"

"Can't talk now," Fred replied. "The nurse is coming with some forms I have to sign to get out of this place."

The call ended. Hutch sat back and munched on his pizza. And I jumped out of my chair, my decision instantly made.

I could talk to Hutch another time, but this was clearly my one and only chance to talk to Fred Denham, the armorer responsible for providing and prepping that gun.

"Esther, do you know where Matt is?"

"He went to help Dante in our coffee truck—"

I started for the stairs when Esther stopped me. "But he's not there!"

"Then where is he?"

"Mr. Boss said our truck was running low on cups, so he took the van to Brooklyn for a supply run."

"How long ago did he leave?"

"About fifteen minutes."

"Darn it." While I wanted to bring Matt along for backup, I knew I couldn't risk the wait—and a trip to Brooklyn and back would take more than an hour.

"What is it?" Esther asked. "What's wrong?"

"Could you keep an eye on things here? I have to go out for a while."

"Sure, but where are you going?"

"I need to speak with someone before he skips town."

Thirty-Six

~~~~~~

I tore off my apron, grabbed my jacket and handbag, and slipped out the back door. I ran past the dumpsters, and out to the street, where I hailed a cab.

Thanks to Manhattan's afternoon traffic, simply crossing the island from the west side to the east took a maddening thirty minutes—maddening because I knew those "forms" Fred Denham was ready to sign involved his discharge.

If the show's armorer left the hospital and then skipped town, I would lose my only opportunity to ask him some "ugly questions" about my barista catching a bullet in the chest.

At least I'd overheard Hutch Saunders mentioning Central Park during his conversation with his boss. That little clue was a big help since there were a few Mount Sinai hospitals on the island of Manhattan but only one in close proximity to the park.

When the cab finally turned onto Madison Avenue and headed north, we started to make progress, but it still took more than twenty minutes to make it all the way uptown. Then, a block from the hospital's main entrance, I spied a burly figure on the sidewalk. I recognized the heavyset build, the salt-and-pepper beard, and the yellow-and-purple LA Lakers jacket, the very one Fred Denham had worn on the morning he'd been poisoned.

Cut loose from the doctors, Denham clearly had somewhere important to go. The property master was moving at a fast pace—in the opposite direction, unfortunately.

"Stop the cab! Stop!" I cried from the back seat.

Two things happened next.

The traffic light in front of us turned green, and an ambulance with flashing red lights pulled up to the taxi's rear bumper. The ambulance driver blasted his siren, but there was nowhere for the cabbie to pull over. My driver hit the gas and raced uptown for an entire block, letting the ambulance make its turn and pull into the loading zone in front of the hospital emergency room.

I threw too much money at the cabbie, bailed out, and hit the sidewalk running. Thanks to my weekly swimming routine at the Y, I had the stamina to do it, if not the footwear. My half boots clicked and clacked like tap shoes on the concrete, garnering stares from people I passed.

By now, daylight was gone. With the cloud cover above, night had settled faster than usual over the city, but at least Denham's loud Lakers jacket was easy to spot. I kept my eyes firmly fixed on the purple-and-yellow figure as he passed under one glowing streetlight after the other.

Suddenly, I lost sight of him. I soon realized he'd turned right on a narrow residential street I didn't even know existed.

Gustave L. Levy Place was a tree-lined lane with one-way traffic spilling off Fifth Avenue. As a delivery truck moved up the block, I caught sight of Fred Denham, illuminated by the truck's headlights.

It seemed to me that he was walking faster now. There was no way Denham could know I was following, so he wasn't trying to get away. He simply walked with determination, like he had an appointment to keep.

I jogged by beautiful apartment buildings with doormen, a charming fruit stand, and the entrance to an exclusive private school. I was less than half a block away from Fifth Avenue when I saw Denham run across the street against the light, then hang a left.

I noticed something else. Denham was talking on his mobile phone. Even from a distance I could see the illuminated screen, though I couldn't read it.

Fred was now heading south, walking parallel to Central Park, with me less than half a block behind him. We were on Museum Mile, a stretch of Fifth Avenue boasting six major museums, the grandest being the Guggenheim and the Metropolitan Museum of Art.

Our coffee truck had served attendees of the annual Museum Mile

Festival for the past three years, and I knew unless Denham hopped over the low stone wall and chanced a twenty-foot drop, he could enter Central Park only on 97th Street. I was confident I would catch up to him by then.

Now I was within hailing distance. Huffing and puffing, my legs turning to jelly, I did just that.

"Mr. Denham! Mr. Fred Denham!" I called. "I'd like a word with—"

He glanced over his shoulder, spotted me, and took off running.

"Son of a bunny!"

I realized my mistake. Hutch had warned Fred about Tina's threat. Nobody was to breathe a word about the on-set shooting on pain of being blacklisted. Clearly, Fred mistook me for a nosy reporter!

Throwing my handbag over my shoulder, I started running again.

For a heavyset man just out of the hospital, Fred Denham moved surprisingly fast. As I feared, he bolted through the 97th Street entrance and into the maze of pathways and trees that marked this area of Central Park.

I was practically staggering when I crossed the threshold—only to face not one, not two, but three possible directions the property master could have bolted to escape me, including an off-path journey into the deep shadows of the East Meadow.

The entire area was dark and deserted. There was no sign of Denham in any direction, and no one to ask if they'd seen him. With a groan, I dropped onto an empty bench.

I was just about ready to give up all hope when two gunshots exploded in the night.

The shots came close together, the echo bouncing off the stone wall that bordered Fifth Avenue. The gunfire was so near I caught a glimpse of the flashing muzzle through the trees.

Overcome by a mixture of worry and curiosity, I launched myself off the bench and farther into the wooded park.

ThIRTY-SEVEN

꧁ ꧁

FINDING Fred Denham didn't take long. The man was flat on his back beneath a tree near the footpath. No one else was in sight.

I recognized Denham by his Lakers jacket. Except for fingerprints or "distinguishing marks," there was no other way to do it. Even dental records would have been a challenge since the property master's head had been blown into raw red chunks and scattered around the blood-soaked corpse.

I risked a closer look—too close. My foot brushed a piece of scalp and skull. Feeling sick, I whirled around and bent over, nearly revisiting my Grandma's pizza. Instead, I swallowed hard and fumbled with my handbag to pull out my phone.

"Don't do that," a shaky voice commanded.

"Hands up!" commanded another.

I turned to find two uniformed police officers facing me with weapons drawn.

"Don't shoot!" I cried, throwing up my hands. I waved the one holding my phone. "I was trying to call 911."

The cops were obviously rookies. A tall, blond one with a ruddy complexion seemed too young to have graduated high school, never mind the police academy. His partner, a small, compact brunette with *L. Wu* on her name tag, didn't seem much older.

"I heard shots, and I ran toward the flash," I explained.

Officer Wu eyed me skeptically. "You ran *toward* the shots?"

I had no shorthand to explain anything, and after a clumsy silence, the policewoman waved her question aside.

"Do I have your permission to search your purse?" Officer Wu asked.

I immediately handed it over, along with my phone. She rifled through my stuff, then passed the purse to Officer B. Dowell. Wu's partner accepted my personal property absentmindedly, while he reported the crime to dispatch.

"I'm going to pat you down," Officer Wu said. She followed through, though we both seemed pretty embarrassed about the whole thing.

"CSU is on the way," Officer Dowell announced. "And a pair of detectives are just up the street. They should be here any minute."

Officer Wu produced a roll of yellow police ribbon and cordoned off the area using trees for posts. Officer Dowell handed back my purse, pointed to a bench, and told me to sit and wait for the detectives.

Anything "interesting" in New York City will attract a crowd, and within minutes of the tape going up, curious citizens approached the murder scene. More than one of them had their phone cameras raised and ready.

"Back away," Officer Wu said. "This is a crime scene."

Some retreated, but others pushed aggressively forward, right up to the *Do Not Cross* barrier Wu had created.

"Please keep your distance," Officer Dowell requested, without much authority.

Nobody cared and nobody moved, not until the night was shattered by a woman's bellowed command—

"You heard the *Home Alone* kid! Back off or we'll put all of you in cuffs for hindering a police investigation!"

The crowd scattered to the four winds as Lori Soles and Sue Ellen Bass barreled forward from the opposite end of the footpath.

The Fish Squad had arrived.

The sight alone gave me great relief. I was well acquainted with Soles and Bass, and happy to (excuse the pun) hook up with them again. We'd worked together a few times, even found ourselves at odds once or twice, but I considered them allies in this particular situation.

Both were tall and dressed alike, though their temperaments were different. Lori Soles with her cherubic blond curls was the cooler head. Sue Ellen Bass, a straight-haired brunette, was more confrontational. But the two had been partnered for so long, they reminded me of a married couple, even reading each other's thoughts and finishing each other's sentences.

Because of their last names, the pair had been dubbed the Fish Squad by their peers. Mostly, they ignored the nickname, but if someone on or off the force used it with disrespect, it was Sue Ellen who'd deal with them. The more volatile of the two, she was more likely to send the culprit to the ER than HR.

They strode toward the crime scene in their black slacks and dark blazers, gold shields and service weapons clipped to their belts, in plain sight—"for intimidation purposes," Sue Ellen Bass once told me.

With Officer Wu beside me, I did not rise and greet them. Instead, I watched while Officer Dowell met the pair on the path. The three immediately huddled in quiet conversation.

When the huddle broke, Sue Ellen approached me.

"If it isn't Clare Cosi, present at another crime scene," the detective began. "What brings you all the way up here to this land of money and culture? A visit to the Guggenheim, perhaps?"

I pointed to the dead man. "He did," I said, and began to rise.

"Where are you going? Keep that posterior glued to that park bench until I say otherwise."

While Sue Ellen kept me occupied, Lori Soles donned gloves and fished though the dead man's pockets.

"I assume you know the victim." It was not a question.

"His name is Fred Denham. I helped save his life a few days ago, when he suffered a health emergency in front of my coffeehouse."

Sue Ellen frowned. "Well, you sure didn't do him much good tonight."

"I guess not."

"What kind of health emergency?"

"He was poisoned by tainted coffee. And before you ask, that coffee did *not* come from my Village Blend."

I explained what I knew about that. Then we both watched Lori pull a bloodstained paper of some kind out of the late man's Lakers jacket.

"So how exactly do you know Drop-Dead Fred, Cosi?" Sue Ellen pressed.

"Mr. Denham was the property master and armorer on a film crew that's shooting inside the Village Blend this week. We're providing craft services."

Sue Ellen glanced again at the corpse. "That jacket tells me he's from out of town."

"I assume so. But I can't confirm that."

"You two decided to meet in Central Park why?"

"No, no," I replied. "Fred was just discharged from Mount Sinai. He was being treated for the poisoning I mentioned. I wanted to talk to him at his bedside, but he was already on the sidewalk when I arrived. I had to chase after him."

Lori joined her partner. She had several evidence bags clutched in her hand. She and Sue Ellen exchanged glances.

"From Mount Sinai to this location? You followed him for a long time," Lori noted.

"Let me guess," Detective Bass cracked. "He forgot to leave you his vegan menu."

"Mr. Denham had a head start. I only caught up with him on Fifth Avenue."

"And that's where you had your talk?" Sue Ellen assumed.

"No. We never talked. He ran away from me," I said. "He was in a big hurry to get somewhere. I think he was meeting someone in the park. He was definitely talking on the phone before I caught up with him. I could see the illuminated screen."

Again, the detectives exchanged glances.

"I found no phone on the victim," Lori Soles replied. "No wallet, either. Just a hotel key card and the printout of an e-ticket itinerary for a flight to Barbados leaving tomorrow morning." Lori paused. "It looks like your friend ran into a mugger."

"Makes perfect sense," Sue Ellen agreed. "Man in a loud and expensive sports team jacket that screams out-of-towner—"

"He flashes a very expensive phone in a shadowy part of the park," Lori added. "And suddenly an armed robber gets in his face. He resists—"

"And BAM!" Sue Ellen cried. "One less tourist in the city."

"I don't think that's what happened," I said. "Fred's death might have had something to do with the production itself."

"What production would that be exactly?" Lori asked.

"*Only Murders in Gotham*," I answered. "They have an office in Queens, or you can come to my coffeehouse tomorrow and talk to the people who worked with him."

"No need," Sue Ellen said, "except to find out the next of kin."

"The production manager should know," I said. "Her name is Tina Bird."

"We'll contact her, then," Lori replied.

"What are you going to tell her?"

"That her property master is the apparent victim of a mugging gone wrong."

"I don't think it's that simple," I said.

"Let's say you're right, Clare," Lori conceded. "Who do you think Fred was meeting?"

"I don't know who, and I don't know why," I confessed.

"I do," Sue Ellen declared. "Fred met the wrong mugger on the wrong night."

I wasn't ready to take more abuse, so Lori's next words came as a relief.

"I thank you for providing the man's name and occupation, Clare. Without a phone or ID, we would have spent hours trying to determine his identity."

"Maybe that's what his killer wanted . . ."

Sue Ellen shook her head. "The killer or killers got what they wanted— this man's phone and his wallet. If they were a little smarter about it, they might have gotten that nice Lakers jacket, too."

I wanted to persuade the detectives otherwise, but I had no evidence, no real hook—nothing beyond the suspicious incidents surrounding Jerry Sullivan's production—to convince the Fish Squad that I was right.

"Go home, Clare," Lori commanded. "We know where to find you. And thanks to you, we know where to find the victim's employer. We'll notify the production company. If we need more from you, we'll talk again."

And with that, the Fish Squad cut me loose and tossed me away.

Thirty-Eight

〜〜〜〜〜〜〜〜〜〜〜〜〜〜〜〜〜〜〜

FEELING a little dazed, I followed the footpath back to the 97th Street entrance and left Central Park just as the Crime Scene Unit arrived. An EMS truck pulled up behind it, along with a parade of police cars.

The spectacle gathered a curious crowd, but it all looked surreal to me. I trudged past the circus and down Fifth Avenue feeling a strange disconnection from the traffic and the pedestrians, the city noise, and the bright streetlights. When an unnatural chill settled over me, I cursed.

Finding a bench, I sat down and took some deep, shaky breaths.

I'd been fine interacting with the police and detectives. But the adrenaline rush was fading, and a mild shock was setting in.

I tried calling Mike Quinn, hoping my fiancé was free to talk, though he was still on duty. That hope was dashed when my call went directly to voice mail.

Okay, Clare, pull yourself together . . .

With slow, deliberate steps, I continued walking downtown until I spotted a cab pulling to the curb in front of me with passengers getting out.

"Taxi!" I called, hurrying to slip inside the open door.

The warmth of the cab's back seat felt like a comforting blanket, and I shut the door with relief. The driver, a young guy with a thick, dark beard and yellow turban, was apologetic when he heard my destination.

"If you're going all the way downtown, ma'am, I should warn you, there was a multicar collision on the FDR, so it's out. And traffic isn't moving on the avenues, either. Broadway's the best bet, but it's going to be a long trip."

I didn't care how long the trip would take. I was grateful to be inside this cab.

"Thanks for the warning," I told the driver, "but I'm feeling too shaky to take the subway. The scenic route is fine with me."

As we pulled away from the curb, I tried to reach Mike again, and I failed again. I didn't want to ponder Fred Denham's puzzling murder alone. I needed to talk with someone about what happened, if only to help me sort things in my own mind, because I knew I wasn't thinking straight.

These unexplained events, piling one on top of the other, had convinced me this production was either being sabotaged or suffering a curse of stunning coincidences.

In desperation, I called my ex-husband.

"Hey, Clare. Where did you go?" Matt asked, sounding upset. "When I got back to the coffeehouse, Esther told me the shoot was over for the day and you'd gone off to some mysterious meeting. Are you okay?"

I told Matt everything that happened from the moment I left the Village Blend right up to Fred Denham's murder and its aftermath. I didn't hold back the graphic details, either.

"The man's head was literally gone," I rasped, "along with his phone and wallet. If I hadn't been there to identify him, Detectives Soles and Bass still wouldn't know who Denham was."

After a moment of stunned silence, Matt found his tongue.

"Clare, you *do* realize that if things had gone differently, I could be identifying *your* corpse?"

"Don't be dramatic. It's over now, and—"

"And *nothing*! Really, what were you thinking? Wait. You *weren't*. At least admit that. I can't believe you ran *toward* the gunshots. You are acting—" What followed was a string of curses in three different languages that ended with the word "—crazy."

"Will you calm down? Despite the Fish Squad's hasty conclusion, I don't believe Denham was killed by a random mugger. I think someone set him up and lured him to his death. I *saw* him talking on his phone the whole way there."

"So what? I walk and talk on my phone all the time—as do millions of people. It doesn't prove a thing. And it doesn't excuse or even explain your loco decision. You're the mother of my only daughter. How am I supposed to take care of Joy if you're not around?"

"Dial it down, will you? As far as our daughter, that boat sailed long ago, and *you* traded in your ticket for a series of . . . *whatever.* Joy's an adult now. She's been taking care of herself for years."

"But—"

"*Listen,* I want to talk about this murder, not our past."

"Fine," Matt said after an exasperated exhale. "Talk."

Thirty-nine

With Matt hanging on the line, I took a moment to breathe.

Gazing out the taxi's window, I realized the brightly lit skyscrapers and crowded sidewalks were barely crawling by. *This cabbie wasn't kidding*, I thought. With the FDR closed, Broadway really was a parking lot.

The meter continued to tick away, but I didn't care. I was safe and warm, and with Matt on the line, at least I could puzzle out a few theories . . .

"So here's what I'm thinking," I began. "A killer has to have a motive, right?"

"You mean like a mugger in a park? What could be the motive? I know! How about *robbery*? Wow. Case closed."

"Case closed if you're a detective who wants to get off the clock. But there's more here, and you know it."

"I *don't* know it," Matt returned. "If Fred Denham wasn't killed for his phone and his wallet, then who would gain by the murder of the property master? Answer—*nobody*."

"I'm sure the killer is banking on that convenient conclusion. But I don't think it's that simple. Remember, Fred Denham wasn't just the production's property master. He was also the set's armorer, responsible for the safety of all the firearms used in the show. And the man was poisoned *right before* he was supposed to be supervising the safety of the very gun that shot Tucker."

"So what does that mean? The same person who poisoned him, shot him? That seems pretty far-fetched, Clare."

"As far-fetched as the man running out of the hospital and into

Central Park at night with an e-ticket itinerary for a morning flight to Barbados in his pocket? This whole thing doesn't add up to random."

"Maybe not to you. But to me and to your Fish Squad, it does."

"Just humor me, okay? I mean, I do admit the only person who appears to be a suspect is the assistant property master, Hutch Saunders, even though he didn't act like he was in a hurry to get uptown."

"What do you mean?"

"The only reason I knew Fred Denham was leaving the hospital tonight was because I eavesdropped on Hutch's phone conversation. When he ended the call with Fred, he didn't jump up from his seat. I was the one who did. I was worried about getting uptown in time to talk to Denham before he left, and—"

I paused.

"What?"

"Now that I think about the timeline, I'm considering the bigger picture."

"What do you mean?" Matt asked.

"The production shut down and the cast and crew were relieved around five o'clock. That means *anyone* from the production could have gone uptown to meet Denham in the park—"

"But how? With all the traffic?"

"Easy. Subway."

I reminded Matt that Fred Denham wasn't shot until around six thirty PM, so if the killer was traveling from our Village coffeehouse location, then they had plenty of time to take the subway uptown, call Denham, arrange a rendezvous, and wait in Central Park to ambush the man.

"That leaves you with one big problem," Matt said.

"Really? Only one?"

"Yes, Clare. And it's a big one. Whoever this killer is, they planned ahead and beat you to the murder scene. That makes them smarter than you."

I couldn't argue that. And I knew Matt wasn't trying to be a wiseass. Well, not completely. He was trying to *warn* me. And I didn't take that warning lightly.

Whoever killed Denham meant business.

"You know what?" Matt said. "I know I told you to keep your mouth shut about the set shooting. But in light of Denham's death, I think you should talk to . . ."

Matt's voice trailed off, and I almost laughed when I heard him groan. He just couldn't bring himself to say the words. So I did—

"You think I should talk to my fiancé about this, don't you?"

"I think the police are already involved. And, *if* Fred Denham wasn't killed by a mugger—and that's a big IF—then things are getting serious. So, *yeah*, talk to your favorite Flatfoot about all this, as long as you can keep him on a leash."

I would have argued with the insulting order, but I knew what Matt was trying to say, and then he said it anyway—

"Look, I'm sorry, but we don't need the NYPD raiding our coffee-house and dragging a comedy legend away in handcuffs."

"I think we can trust Mike not to do that," I said with absolute certainty. (Which was easy to do since I'd already blabbed to the man, and he'd already promised me as much.)

"So now what?" Matt asked.

"Now, we keep providing the best craft services we can. *And* we keep our eyes open. With Mike helping, we might be able to turn up something that lets us figure all this out."

"Hey, what about the unhinged woman Jerry said left a snake in Kylee Ferris's trailer? I heard some people talking about her on the set. What's her name again?"

"Lizzy Meeks. She's definitely on my radar after that snake prank. But she's also the president of Jerry's fan club. If Tucker hadn't worn that protective vest, the bullet in that gun could have left Jerry facing a manslaughter charge. Why would Lizzy want to set up her meal ticket for a prison sentence? Unless it was just some kind of revenge play. I mean, as you've pointed out, the snake thing does suggest that she may be unstable enough to do almost anything. And then there's Hutch . . ."

"The kid who brought the gun to the set?"

"Yes, it seems to me only Hutch knew his boss was skipping town. Even though he didn't jump up right away after the phone call, he *could* have left the coffeehouse after I did."

"Yeah, but what motive could this Hutch kid have for killing his boss? Did he covet the property master job that much?"

"It does come with a major screen credit," I noted. "And more money. But that can't be the motive. Before Fred Denham even left the hospital, he gave the position to Hutch. I heard him do it during the phone call."

"How is this for a motive, Clare? What if Hutch *did* put the real bullet in the chamber? And what if Denham found out?"

"*What if* is the easy part. But what would Hutch accomplish by it? What was his motive?"

"Money. Hutch could have been *paid* to do it."

"Now that you bring it up," I said, "Fred Denham could have been paid to do it. But why? Who would pay to have some random extra killed? Or set up Jerry for a criminal charge that would surely shut down the production? What would be the gain? And wouldn't the armorer or his assistant be at the top of the police suspect list? Maybe that's why Denham was heading to Barbados."

"Maybe," Matt said. "Or maybe Driftwood was actually negligent and failed to properly clean their machines, which led to Fred Denham being poisoned and landing in the hospital, which led to the screwup on set because an inexperienced assistant brought the wrong gun—one with a bullet in it. Maybe Denham didn't want to face the music of the accidental shooting, so he was trying to skip town. And while he was leaving the hospital, a nosy reporter ran after him for a comment, so he ran into the park to lose her and got himself killed by a mugger."

"You're sending us in circles, Matt."

"Fine. Then after you talk to the Flatfoot, maybe you should grill Tweety Bird. I believe she's still *pecking* around for clues."

"If your jokes are going to be that lame, I'm hanging up now."

"Okay. Seriously. What are you going to do next?"

"I'm going to speak with Mike Quinn. Then I'll try again to talk to Hutch."

"And after you talk to Hutch?"

"I'll let you know."

When I ended the call, I realized my cab was passing through the heart of Times Square. The taxi stopped at a red light in front of ABC's Times Square Studios, home of *ABC World News Tonight* and *Good Morning America*.

I noticed the two news tickers that ran across the curved, ultramodern façade. They both displayed the same tragic headlines:

**. . . BELOVED COMEDIAN BILLY SADDLER
DEAD AT 59 . . . FATAL OVERDOSE KILLS
COMEDY LEGEND . . . WATCH NYPD
CONFERENCE LIVE . . .**

Between the twin scrolls, a television screen two stories tall and half a city block wide displayed the somber press conference.

The police commissioner was speaking at the podium. To her left, the chief of detectives and a deputy mayor looked grimly on. And standing alone at the commissioner's right was my fiancé—

Detective Lieutenant Michael Ryan Francis Quinn.

Forty

~~~~~~

When I finally exited the cab at the Village Blend, the time was almost eight o'clock. All the production trailers were dark, and I was in a hurry to get inside.

While fishing for my keys at the coffeehouse door, I was startled when a giant hunk of muscle in a gray security uniform emerged from the shadows. Unsmiling, he showed me a big, shiny badge.

"This is a secure area. What are you doing here?"

"I live here. I manage this coffeehouse and my apartment is upstairs."

He raised his phone and rattled off the names on his screen.

"I've got Matteo Allegro, Esther Best, Tucker Burton, Clare Cosi, Nancy—"

"I'm Clare Cosi."

He frowned. "I'll need to see a photo ID."

For the second time that evening, I handed over my New York State driver's license to a person in authority. And this time I didn't mind one bit. I was overjoyed that Jerry Sullivan had come through on his promise of more and better security.

While the guard checked my driver's license, I scanned the area and spotted three more guards lurking among the trucks and trailers.

"Sorry to inconvenience you, Ms. Cosi," the man said at last. He handed over my license along with a printed card.

"If you have any trouble, call that number on the card. We're right here, and we will respond immediately. No waiting for 911 to get their act together."

He touched the brim of his hat. "You have a good night."

I probably would. Nothing like a circle of armed guards watching your back to induce a sound, restful sleep!

I longed to fall into bed right now, but I was tense and upset; I needed a warm, relaxing shower first. And even before I could enjoy such a desperately needed indulgence, I had something to do.

With our cup supply running low, I would have to move up our standing order, and the vendor's info was in my office. I also wanted to sit down with my phone and get that security company's number on my speed-dial list.

My feet ached as I climbed the spiral stairs to the shop's darkened lounge. My office door was closed but unlocked. Mind on other matters, I absently opened it—and promptly jumped out of my skin!

"What are you doing here!" I shouted.

Someone was hiding in my office. Just like my nightmare—only it wasn't Jerry Sullivan sitting at my desk. It was his *cock-a-doodle-doo* fan!

The scarecrow-thin figure of Lizzy Meeks rose to her feet.

"Calm down," she said quickly. "I just want to talk."

"Stay back!" I warned, though I was the one backing away.

At my command, Lizzy froze in place and displayed empty hands.

"Stay where you are. I'm calling the guards outside!" I cried, but as I fumbled for my phone, the card with the security team's number fluttered into the shadows. *Great!*

Now I had two choices. I could run out the door and scream for a guard or I could call 911—which would let me keep an eye on Lizzy and (if need be) physically prevent her from escaping.

"Please, Ms. Cosi, I just want to talk," Lizzy said in a calm voice.

"We have nothing to talk about," I said, thumb poised over the emergency speed dial.

"But we do!" Lizzy insisted, her wide eyes pleading. "I know you want to help Jerry. I want to help Jerry, too. But we can't do it alone. We need to work together—"

Cock-a-doodle-doo! I thought. "How did you get in here?!"

"Please. Just hear me out. If you still want to have me arrested when we're through, I'll surrender willingly."

Lizzy finally stopped talking—which helped dissipate some of my shock and fear. She remained standing behind my desk, her pale hands wringing the strap of her Birkin bag. Wearing a dark sweater and form-fitting slacks, she seemed smaller, and I saw her lip tremble while she waited for my answer.

I realized at that moment I was the one feeling "cock-a-doodle-doo." Lizzy seemed calm, almost rational—except for one small detail.

"You *know* you're trespassing, right?" I said.

She nodded. "I was desperate, Ms. Cosi. I couldn't get near you because of studio security. This was the only way. There are things I know that you don't. Things you *need* to hear."

She admitted she's trespassing, I told myself, which meant Lizzy Meeks knew right from wrong—which was as good a definition of sanity as any other. And it was hard to resist the giant carrot she was dangling.

Did she really have information that would help me finally make sense of the twisted things happening on the set of this production?

Or maybe I was *cock-a-doodle-doo* for accepting Lizzy's insight at face value—never mind her help. Willing to test the waters, I began with a simple question, but one I was dying to know—

"How the heck did you get past Jerry's new security?"

"Well," she began, "I've been watching this place for a few days. I noticed the set closing down early, except for the wardrobe truck, which was still open, and the costume crew was working after hours. Meanwhile, a bunch of new guards were replacing the old ones. Everyone seemed distracted, and I saw my chance. I grabbed some costumes off the rack, held them in front of my face, and walked right through the front door. I looked like I belonged, so no one gave me a second glance."

"You've been hiding in my office for almost three hours?"

She nodded. "I heard one of your baristas telling someone on the phone that you ran out but would be back soon. I'm sorry. The door was unlocked. I didn't break in, I swear!"

This time I believed her. I *had* left the door unlocked after I grabbed my handbag in my rush to see Fred Denham. But could she be lying about the timeline? Though I didn't have a clue how else she might have gotten into my coffeehouse, Lizzy *could* have been the one who shot and killed Fred Denham in the park—and if she'd taken the subway downtown, she could have beaten me here, too.

"If you want me to believe you, then do what I say," I ordered. "Empty your handbag of everything, right now, on my desk."

"Why?"

"You could be hiding a weapon. Are you?"

"No! Of course not. Here, look yourself—" She held the bag out for me.

"Empty it. Or I'm calling the guards."

"Fine, I'll do it."

She poured the bag out, and there was no gun, no weapon, just the sorts of things you'd find in a handbag—a brush, makeup, pack of tissues, breath mints, a small notebook, a mobile phone.

Her clothes were tight fitting, and it was obvious she wasn't hiding a gun on her person.

"Unlock your phone for me," I demanded.

"Why?"

"You want me to trust you?"

"Okay, okay . . ." She unlocked the phone and handed it to me. "There's not much battery life left. I was watching videos to pass the time waiting for you."

I quickly checked her recent messages and phone activity.

There was no communication between her and Fred Denham that I could see. I saw plenty of messages left for Jerry (none returned). Calls to Grubhub, other people named Meeks (which I assumed were family members), calls to and from Norman (Jerry's old assistant), though nothing from Drew Merriweather, which puzzled me, given that Jerry directly ordered Drew to contact Lizzy.

I also saw calls to and from someone named Windham (which rang a faint bell, but I couldn't quite place it).

As the craft services manager, I'd already reviewed a roll call of cast and crew member names for menu requests (dietary restrictions and the like), and I didn't recognize anyone else from the production.

I took a breath and considered the evidence . . .

Lizzy *could* have erased any trace of her contact with Fred, just as she could have disposed of the gun before she'd come downtown.

Maybe I was *cock-a-doodle-doo* for not calling the guards, but Lizzy appeared frail physically—and emotionally. If she was willing to risk arrest to speak privately with me, I decided it was worth giving her the benefit of the doubt to hear what she had to say.

"If you've been hiding all this time, waiting for me, I'm guessing you haven't eaten lately, have you?"

She blinked, surprised at the question. "To be honest, I didn't have lunch, and I was hiding through the dinner hour, so . . . no."

"Then follow me. Let's see what's in the shop's pantry."

Forty-one

❧❧❧❧❧❧❧❧❧❧❧❧❧❧❧❧❧❧❧❧❧❧❧❧

Lizzy and I sat alone in the empty coffeehouse at the only occupied table in a shadowy sea of café tables.

Sebastian Albee would have loved lighting this, I thought.

The place was still and quiet—almost too quiet, save the muffled noises of passing cars on Hudson and the sound of my uninvited guest hungrily gobbling her dinner.

As I quietly sipped a fresh cup of my Fireside blend, I watched Lizzy polish off one of Babka's gourmet wraps—a lovely combo of fresh baby greens, creamy Jarlsberg cheese, and succulent slices of Babka's Roasted Chicken with Sweet Garlic and Citrus. I snagged Lizzy a snack bag of Terra chips and a cream soda, too.

When she finally dabbed her lips with a napkin, I poured her a hot cup of Fireside from my French press, slid over a plate of our Village Blend Chocolate Chip Cookies (with notes of caramel and sea salt), and leaned across the table's marble top.

Now that her supper is over, it's time Lizzy sings for it . . .

"Could you answer a simple question for me, Ms. Meeks?"

Lizzy shrugged as she reached for a cookie. "Okay."

"You claimed you were in my office for the past three hours this evening. Where were you *last* evening?"

"Last evening?" she mumbled between nibbling bites.

"Yes, specifically between seven and eight o'clock."

She sat back. "You'll think I'm crazy."

"Try me."

"Turner Classic Movies ran *The Road to Ballyhoo* last night. Do you remember it? Jerry actually *married* his costar, Brenda Tanner. For the first time ever, Brenda introduced the film herself for TCM, and I didn't want to miss that. I *had* to see what she'd say about working with Jerry." Lizzy shook her head. "I could immediately see why the marriage didn't last. She wasn't the right fit for his comic genius. Not at all—"

"Back up, please, Ms. Meeks, and forget the postmortem on Jerry's failed marriage. I don't care about the man's love life. I want to know where *you* were between seven and eight o'clock. You're saying you were *home*, watching *television*—"

"Not in my home. I didn't say I was home. I live in Las Vegas. I was in the apartment that I've been subletting in Chelsea. But, yes, I was alone, watching television at seven, waiting for my dinner to be delivered and the eight o'clock movie to start. Why do you want to know?"

"Because someone pulled an ugly prank on Kylee around that time last night."

"Really?" Lizzy's eyebrows rose. "What was the prank?"

"You don't know?"

"I have no idea, Ms. Cosi. Like I told you upstairs, I couldn't get near the set all day, and Jerry won't return my calls."

I told Lizzy about the snake in Kylee's trailer. "She was frightened so badly that she couldn't pull herself together. They had to postpone her scenes and revise the shooting schedule to make up for lost time."

"And I take it from your cross-examination that you think I pulled this prank?"

"Are you saying you didn't?"

She laughed. "I wouldn't waste my time. Not when *The Road to Ballyhoo* is on with Brenda Tanner providing commentary. Do you know there's not even a DVD or Blu-ray release of that movie? It's criminal. Jerry's fans have been demanding it for years."

This conversation was getting me nowhere, so I switched subjects.

"You told me you had information. Something you thought I should know. So what is it? What do you want to tell me?"

"I heard about yesterday's incident," Lizzy confessed. "I know a real bullet was fired instead of a blank, and the extra's life was only saved because he wore a bulletproof vest."

"Wait a second. Are you telling me you had no idea that a snake was left in Kylee's trailer, yet you knew about the bullet? How did you find out?"

"Someone who witnessed the whole thing told me about it. This person also said that Jerry told everyone that *you* were investigating the incident, which is why I came to you."

"You seem to know a lot."

Lizzy sniffed. "I used to know it *all*—when Norman was my window into Jerry Sullivan's life."

"Norman? You mean Jerry's original assistant?"

"Jerry's *friend*," Lizzy replied. "Norman worked with Jerry for nine years. And over those years, Norman became my friend, too. When my relationship with Jerry became . . . *complicated* . . . Norman would smooth things over. He helped me keep the fan club business on track, too, during those times when Jerry became temperamental or difficult."

"I heard what happened to Norman—"

"Did you?" Lizzy snapped. "Did you really? Or did Jerry tell you it was a terrible accident? A freak electrical surge?"

"You're saying it wasn't."

"It was not an accident—"

"You know this how?"

"While filming the first season, Norman formed a friendship with someone on the production. This person stuck by Norman after his injuries, and when they discovered the truth, they thought Norman should know what *really* happened, how it wasn't an accident at all."

Lizzy finished her coffee, and I poured her a refill.

"Do you know what a squib is, Ms. Cosi?"

I shook my head.

"It's a tiny explosive used to simulate all sorts of things on a movie set. They call things like squibs 'practical effects' because they're done right in front of the camera, not added later by a computer. Filmmakers will use squibs and a bag of artificial blood, for example, to make gunshot wounds appear real. Squibs can break bottles and windows, put holes in walls, even knock down furniture on cue. Some squibs are triggered through wiring. Others are wireless. They can be detonated remotely with a simple smartphone."

Lizzy paused and leaned toward me. "After Norman was injured, burn marks from a squib were found on the bank of lights that fell—"

"So, you're saying that those lights were dropped on purpose? By someone using a squib?"

"The so-called accident was certainly premeditated," Lizzy said. "The bolts holding the lights in place had been loosened, but the squib brought the whole thing down. Jerry learned the truth hours after it happened, but he managed to hush it up. Others know, too, but they're not talking, either."

Lizzy's eyes met mine. "Jerry did it again, right? After the incident with the live bullet, he covered it up, didn't he?"

That was precisely what Jerry did. But Lizzy knew the answer before she asked the question, so I asked my own question.

"You say Norman's *friend* still works on the set and is passing information to you?"

"Not to me directly. This person tells Norman. And Norman tells me."

"And not Jerry?"

"I told you; Jerry isn't interested in the truth. He wants bad things buried and the show to go on. Norman and I are on the same page. We want to protect Jerry. And you obviously do, too. That's why I came to you. I don't know how much longer Norman's informant is going to *keep* informing him. Since you're asking questions, trying to get to the bottom of things, we should work *together*. We could accomplish so much—"

"Whoa. Let's not hop the rails yet."

Lizzy frowned.

"Look, I'd like to trust you," I said. "Will you tell me the name of your source on the set?"

"No, I'm sorry. I can't tell a soul. I'd be risking their job. If Jerry found out, he'd be furious. He *might* forgive this person. Or he might fire them. Probably the latter."

"Okay, fine. Then at least tell me this. Is your informant *reliable*?"

Lizzy shrugged. "So far."

"Then Jerry is digging a pretty deep hole for himself. If this stuff he buried comes to light and a crime is involved, Jerry could look like an accessory after the fact. And there might be lawsuits, fraud charges . . ."

"It could ruin him, I know." Lizzy shook her head. "Jerry should never have broken his contract with the Winner Hotel and Casino. He claims he likes things uncomplicated, and he once told me that two shows a day, five days a week, didn't seem like work at all. Plus, he was a star in Las Vegas. That's why I don't understand . . ."

As her voice trailed off, she shook her head.

"Understand *what*?" I pressed.

"Isn't it obvious? What I don't understand is why Jerry gave up twenty million dollars a year to take on this stupid series. All the show has done is raise the profile of everyone around him."

Twenty million dollars a year *was* an incredible payday to give up. But Jerry must have had his reasons. And I couldn't help wondering (once again) what percentage of that bounty Lizzy was raking in with ticket sale commissions through her fan club.

I didn't ask that question directly because I was pretty sure Lizzy would go all *cock-a-doodle-doo* on me, just like the last time I broached the subject. Fortunately, I had a work-around.

"How did you become the head of Jerry's fan club?"

"Pity. That's how. After all that happened between us, Jerry felt sorry for me. He wanted to make it right, so he tossed me the fan club job. It was all he had left to give."

"I don't understand. What exactly happened between you and Jerry?"

Lizzy Meeks gazed at the empty plate in front of her for a long moment. When she raised her eyes, I was shocked to see the gleam of tears.

"Don't you see? Do I have to say it? Jerry and I . . ."

"What?" I pressed. "What about Jerry and you?"

"We were lovers."

Forty-two

∿∿∿∿∿∿∿∿∿∿∿∿∿∿∿∿∿∿∿∿∿∿∿

I REMEMBERED when I first heard the name Lizzy Meeks, just a few days ago. I wondered if she was a rabid fan, a psycho stalker, or even a jilted lover. If she was telling me the truth about her past with Jerry Sullivan, then Lizzy was all three.

Still, I had my doubts.

Was the "lovers" part real? I wondered. Or was it some kind of fantasy affair that was all in her head? Cautiously skeptical, I asked—

"How did you first meet Jerry?"

"Ten years ago, right after I earned my graduate degree, I moved to Los Angeles. I dreamed of becoming a screenwriter. I even shopped around a few scripts, but none of them were bought. So I supported myself with freelance writing. I wrote for advertising and production companies. I doctored scripts, wrote for entertainment websites, and published a few celebrity bio books. Everyone was happy with my work, and one job led to another and another, mostly through recommendations.

"One day I got a call to come for an interview for a ghostwriting job."

Lizzy's expression softened at the memory, and a decade of nervous tension seemed to melt away.

"You can't believe how thrilled I was when a secretary ushered me into Jerry Sullivan's office. I made a fool of myself, I was gushing so much. But Jerry didn't mind. He seemed to enjoy the adulation.

"He explained that he was looking for a ghostwriter to help him shape his memoirs, and a colleague suggested me. By this time, I had ghostwritten a memoir for a retired Oscar-winning actress, and I'd helped a young comedian streamline a bloated manuscript into a bestselling book, so I had the experience Jerry was looking for. He liked the ideas I threw at him that day, and he hired me on the spot."

Lizzy sat back and closed her eyes.

"The next four months were heavenly, the happiest time of my life. I worked with Jerry every day, talking with him, taking notes. At night I wrote. As we worked together, we fell in love—or maybe only I fell in love. But it didn't matter. Jerry was everything I wanted.

"Some of my friends thought he was too old, but I didn't care that I was half his age. To me, Jerry was timeless. So when he asked me, I dropped my own career ambitions and moved in with him."

She frowned. "That first year turned difficult. *Daddy Plans Another Wedding* was a terrible flop. The critics were cruel, and when Jerry's memoir *I'm Still Standing* was published a few months later, it was lost in an ocean of bad publicity, fallout from that dreadful movie.

"Overnight, producers stopped sending Jerry their hottest scripts, and no one in the movie business would hire him. Jerry got a few offers for television roles, but he hated the idea of doing TV again. Jerry wouldn't even let me write about his early television years in his memoirs. For some reason he was bitter about that part of his life."

"Is that why he went back to stand-up comedy?"

Lizzy nodded. "I was the one who pushed the hardest for that, and after his Hollywood dry spell went on for nearly two years, he finally listened. Jerry began writing new routines, primarily out of ideas we'd put into *I'm Still Standing*. I helped him refine those, too, and I went on the road with him when he tested his new act at dozens of little comedy clubs. He did that for nearly a year, until Morris Windham, the entertainment director of the Winner Hotel and Casino, saw him—"

"Wait!" The name *Windham* finally connected. "Isn't Morris Windham the *owner* of that hotel and casino?

"Yes, but his *son* works as the entertainment director. It was Morris Windham, Jr., who signed Jerry for six months, playing nightly in their largest theater. Jerry was a smash hit from day one, their biggest moneymaker in a decade, according to Mr. Windham. Six months turned into two years of sold-out seats—and millions of dollars. The hotel and casino saw a huge spike in its business, too."

"Sounds like a happy ending," I said.

"Until Jerry ended it! The Windham family signed him for *three years*. But Jerry found a legal loophole in the contract that allowed him to leave the Windham family with an empty theater, just so he could do this stupid streaming show."

"Is that why Jerry is on bad terms with you? Because you want him to go back to the Vegas show he left?"

"It's more than that. I'm an ugly reminder of his Hollywood low point—the movie flop, his failed memoir, that long dry spell when no one would cast him, even the yearlong struggle to prove himself as a headlining stand-up comedian again."

She laughed, but the edge was bitter. "You should know Jerry by now, Ms. Cosi. He likes to bury the ugly stuff. Sweep it under a rug. Forget it ever happened, and convince everyone else to forget, too. So you see? Just like that, I was also forgotten."

"But he gave you a job. And he hasn't fired you."

"Like I told you, it was a pity play. The fan club was in trouble, but I turned it around and made it pay. Under my direction, that club has become a major revenue stream. I know he does appreciate that. And believe it or not, that's enough for me."

Lizzy stared at me across the table.

"Listen, I know Jerry and I will never have the same relationship that we once shared. But can't you see how a woman could work with an ex-lover who she still cares deeply about, out of mutual respect and a common goal?"

In her infinite wisdom—or abject insanity—Lizzy had come to the one person who could understand her, because if she was *cock-a-doodle-doo*, for working with (and still caring about) her ex, then so was I.

Despite my failed marriage with Matt, and all the hurt and anxiety he caused me over the years, we still had a strong bond of respect and affection.

"Okay, Ms. Meeks. You've been forthcoming, and I appreciate it. Now what do you want from me?"

"I want you to be my eyes and ears, the way *Norman* was. Someone is wrecking Jerry's production. Right now, you are in the best position to stop it."

"How?"

"You have to watch people, discover their true motives. There are people around Jerry who have been acting strangely."

"People? What people?"

"Tina Bird, the production manager, for one." Lizzy locked eyes with me. "She's not to be trusted."

"I planned on talking to Tina. What do you want me to ask her?"

"Don't ask her, Ms. Cosi. *Watch* her."

"Watch her? Why exactly? Why don't you trust Tina?"

"She's been lying to Jerry. My source says she *tells* people on the set that she's going to the office in Queens, but she goes to the back door of a Broadway theater instead. She's up to something. I know it's true because I followed her—"

"You followed her?" I shifted uncomfortably. This conversation was starting to feel unhinged.

"Last week she went there twice." Lizzy held up two fingers and nodded conspiratorially. "She goes to the stage door and knocks to get in. There is no title on the marquee, and it looks like the venue is between shows, so I don't know what's going on."

"I see," I said carefully (so as not to set her off). "Who else do you think I should watch?"

"Fred Denham. You should talk to him when he's released from the hospital. He's the go-to guy on using squibs, and he loaded that gun—"

"There's no talking with Fred Denham," I interrupted, watching her closely. "He was murdered in Central Park this evening. The police believe he was the victim of an armed robbery."

Lizzy wasn't as surprised as I thought she'd be—or *should* be.

"That was no random robbery," she whispered while slowly shaking her head. "*Someone* wanted him dead. This whole thing has become a lot more dangerous for Jerry." Lizzy's eyes met mine. "And maybe for *you*, too. Be careful, Ms. Cosi, *you* could be next."

I wanted to trust Lizzy. But those words ("you could be next") sounded less like a warning than a threat. And my patience with her had worn out.

I rose. "It's getting late, and I've got work to do."

"All right, okay . . ." With obvious reluctance, Lizzy stood and shouldered her handbag.

With brisk steps, I walked her to the back door.

"Thank you for dinner, Ms. Cosi," Lizzy said as she handed me her business card. "And please keep in touch. I have eyes and ears on the set, but I don't know how long they'll last . . ."

"I'll consider it, Ms. Meeks. I can't promise anything."

"Suit yourself," she replied shortly, feeling my chill. "Just watch your back. And don't trust anyone."

Relieved to see her go, I shut and firmly locked the back door. With everything I'd been through, I wasn't sure what to make of Lizzy's bizarre visit. But her last piece of advice I would take—

I wasn't going to trust her, either.

FORTY-THREE

∿∿∿∿∿∿∿∿∿∿∿∿∿∿∿∿∿∿∿∿∿∿∿∿

AFTER the stressful events of the last twelve hours, I took solace in the quiet climb up the back stairs to my duplex apartment.

The silence didn't last.

The sound of my key in the door set off the outraged demands of two hungry felines . . .

MRRROW! MRRROW! MRRROW!

"Take it easy, girls! Your grub-bub's here. Follow me . . ."

As low as I felt, given poor Fred Denham's horrible fate and sad Lizzy's troublesome statements, I couldn't help but feel my spirits lift, just a little, at the sight of two flagpole-straight tails following me, one behind the other, like two ducklings paddling to keep up with their mommy.

When we reached the kitchen, my furry girls arched their backs and rubbed against my pant legs, leaving evidence of their names behind. Java marked me with her espresso brown coat, and Frothy left fluff as white as milk foam. (Together, it seemed to me, they made a perfect cat cappuccino.)

I opened their favorite Fancy Feast flavors. As they smacked their kitty lips, I realized that I myself hadn't consumed much of anything all day, beyond a few bites of that Grandma's pizza slice—and after finding Fred Denham in that awful state, I'd almost lost it. But seeing Lizzy enjoy her Babka wrap brought my appetite back.

I checked the time, wondering when Mike would show for dinner. I was about to call him when I saw his text—

Tied up here.

Will drop by late to . . .

Love you.

The suggestive note lifted my low spirits another notch, though I was disappointed that we wouldn't be sharing an evening meal. I wanted to speak with him about everything that had happened today, including and especially Fred's murder, but it would have to wait.

"Well, girls, it looks like you two are my dinner date."

Java and Frothy lifted their heads at the sound of my voice—and went directly back to eating.

Good idea.

With the speed of a hungry mouse hunter, I pawed through my fridge for a leftover love connection. *This will do nicely,* I decided, grabbing the foil-wrapped package. *With thanks to my pride named Joy . . .*

My daughter and I had shared a quick FaceTime call earlier in the day, and I was looking forward to a longer catch-up session soon. These days she was as busy as I was, but she was happy in her work managing our DC coffeehouse and its upstairs jazz supper club, and I wasn't surprised. All her life, my daughter had found joy in the kitchen.

When she'd been accepted to a prestigious culinary school here in New York, we were both ecstatic. Unfortunately, the school administration kicked her out for reasons that had nothing to do with the culinary arts—unless you counted the murdered chef she was accused of killing. (But that was an entirely different story.)

Anyway, thanks to her grandmother's connections in Paris, our girl landed a job on the kitchen staff of a charming bistro in Montmartre. Joy worked her fanny off there, learned plenty, and contributed some wonderful fusion ideas of her own. It was an experience she said she'd never forget. And I was the continued beneficiary of her tasty recipes—like the one I was pulling out of the fridge tonight for my improvised dinner.

After unwrapping the leftover roast beef, I cut thin slices and warmed them in a skillet with a generous pour of au jus. I split a crusty roll; slapped the warm, moistened beef on the soft, pillowy-white insides; and transferred the remaining au jus into a small bowl.

Joy's version of a French dip was one of Mike's favorites, and mine, too. The rump roast was a no-fuss deal, and the au jus was a snap to make on the stovetop.

The first night we had it, I made Joy's "Cold Oil" *Pommes Frites* as a side, but I was too impatient to make those homemade fries tonight and immediately started dipping and eating my sandwich while still standing at the counter.

After a few sloppy, satisfying bites, I poured a glass of Shiraz and sat down at the table to inhale the rest of my mouthwatering meal.

When my mobile phone vibrated, I was a little annoyed at being interrupted, but after checking the caller ID, I answered immediately.

"Madame?"

"Hello, dear."

"Is everything all right?"

"I was about to ask you the same question."

"Oh," I said. "Well, the answer to that is relative . . . and disturbingly complicated."

Forty-four

~~~~~~

Between bites of the French dip (with apologies for chewing as I talked), I recounted for Madame the incidents associated with Jerry's production, including (so far)—

One terrible accident (Norman).

One bulletproof barista (Tucker).

One snake-scare (Kylee).

One poisoning and gunshot victim (Fred Denham, DOA).

And an OD'd guest star (RIP, Billy Saddler).

"When you put it all together, that's quite a list, Clare!"

"I know. And Jerry has 'reasonable' explanations for most of them."

"But you don't believe that."

"At this point, I don't know what to believe."

"Well, the reason I'm calling is because of the last man on your list. That famous comic actor—"

"Billy Saddler?"

"Yes, dear. I saw the police commissioner's press conference this evening, and given what was announced to the public, I'm quite concerned."

"Oh, I see . . ." I took a breath in preparation for a somber discussion. "I'm so sorry for your loss, Madame. Were you very close friends with Mr. Saddler?"

"Me? Heavens no!"

"Wait. What?"

"I don't know Billy Saddler. I never met him."

"Then . . . *what* exactly is upsetting you?"

"I told you. The press conference. And, by the way, I thought your blue knight looked quite handsome, standing there next to the commissioner, so tall and broad shouldered in his crisp navy suit."

"Thank you, I noticed Mike, too. But the truth is, I didn't view the press conference. I mean, I *saw* it—on a digital billboard while I was passing through Times Square in a taxi. But I didn't *hear* it. So what exactly happened?"

"The commissioner explained that before Mr. Saddler collapsed and was rushed to the hospital, witnesses confirmed that he had consumed quite a bit of a new drug called . . . oh, dear, now what was it called, it began with an F—"

"Funtenol," I said.

"Fentanyl?" Madame replied.

"No. There is no fentanyl in Funtenol. Fentanyl is a downer, an opioid. Funtenol is an upper, a stimulant, like cocaine."

"Oh, dear. That is exactly what I'm afraid of."

"What? I don't understand. I'm sorry, Madame, I'm trying to follow you, but I can't see what you're getting at."

"My *son*, Clare. I'm concerned for Matt."

"Why?"

"The commissioner used the press conference to warn the public about this new drug. She said your fiancé and his OD Squad are tracking its usage, which is limited at present, but they're trying to prevent its dissemination to the general public. Well, I can add two and two! The reason Billy Saddler was here in New York was to work with Jerry Sullivan on his show—a show for which you and Matt and our Village Blend are providing craft services. If Mr. Saddler attended a party where this drug was free-flowing, I can't help but think—"

"Okay, okay," I said, "I see where you're going. You're afraid Matt will be exposed to this new drug and fall off the wagon, right?"

"Precisely. His cocaine addiction nearly killed him."

"I know. But that was a long time ago. He's been clean for *many* years, and I don't think you should worry."

"Well, I think I should. And I think you should, too, Clare. If there are too many drugs flowing around Jerry's production, and the right pretty girl happens to offer my Matteo some of that poison during a weak moment, well—"

"You want me to keep an eye on him?"

"Yes."

"Then I will. I promise. I'll watch Matt for any sign of drug use—other than caffeine."

"Thank you, dear. I don't fault Matt's addiction to doppio espresso shots, only to dope."

By the time Matt's mother and I finished our conversation, I had polished off my French dip and a second glass of wine.

I had room for dessert and (while stifling a monumental yawn) considered one of the six Chocolate Espresso Cupcakes I'd set aside from our bakery delivery for my fiancé. But mostly what I wanted was a shower—and Mike's arms around me.

Since he wasn't here, a hot shower would have to do. So I skipped the cupcake and (with my cat cappuccino in tow) headed for the bath.

FORTY-FIVE

꩜꩜꩜꩜꩜꩜꩜꩜꩜꩜꩜꩜꩜꩜꩜꩜꩜꩜꩜꩜

"I'M sorry, sweetheart, I didn't mean to wake you."

"Didn't you?" I said, rubbing the sleep from my eyes. "Well, *that's* a disappointment . . ."

Mike Quinn returned my smile. Then the blue-eyed, blue-suited police lieutenant sat down on the edge of my bed. Shadows shrouded the room, but his stubbled jaw and loving gaze were nicely lit by the glow of the still-crackling fireplace.

"I tried to wait up for you," I said. "We need to talk, but—" My voice cut out as a yawn overtook me.

"It's almost one in the morning," Mike said, loosening his tie with one hand. "I didn't expect you to wait up. Hey, do you want some?"

"Want some what?" Pushing myself up to a sitting position, I saw Mike's other hand was holding out a napkin with a Chocolate Espresso Cupcake nestled inside. Obviously, he'd found the bakery box on my counter and eaten at least one of the half-dozen cupcakes. My first clue? The smudge of buttercream frosting at the edge of his mouth.

"You have it," I said. "I'll get crumbs in the bed."

"Suit yourself," he said with a shrug and then slowly—*painfully* slowly—lifted the cupcake to his mouth.

"Wait!" I said. "Who cares about crumbs! Let's share . . ."

"I knew I'd get you." With an amused smile, he broke the cupcake in half.

Finally, I had my dessert. And after we consumed that piece of edible joy, something even sweeter followed. First our lips came together and then we did. His cheeks were rough from the beard stubble, but I didn't mind. He tasted of chocolate, espresso frosting, and a bit of whiskey, which he likely poured downstairs to unwind. Well, *this* was a way to unwind, too. For him, and for me.

After all the hellish shocks of the day, the feel of Mike's strong hands and tender mouth was a heavenly gateway to forgetting, for a little while anyway . . .

Very early the next morning, I slipped out of bed as quietly as I could, letting Mike linger in dreamland.

When we finally drifted off in the wee hours, he'd looked happy but exhausted, and I knew he needed the rest. As for me, I hated leaving the big, soft bed and his big, warm body, but duty called.

After feeding my early-rising felines, I took a quick shower and pulled on jeans, a sweater, and my comfortably low ankle boots. With Mike still in a deep sleep, I wrote a quick note and left it on my pillow . . .

CALL ME. WE NEED TO TALK.
I'LL BRING BREAKFAST!

Downstairs, I accepted the bakery delivery. Then Dante and Matt arrived and got to work opening the coffee truck for our regular customers. I didn't expect to hear from Mike for a few hours, but he buzzed my phone before seven—just as Esther, Nancy, and Tucker arrived.

"I'm in your kitchen, making coffee," he said through a yawn. "We can talk anytime."

No time like the present, I decided.

Forty-six

⊙⊙⊙⊙⊙⊙⊙⊙⊙⊙⊙⊙⊙⊙⊙⊙⊙⊙⊙⊙⊙⊙⊙⊙⊙

Leaving Tucker in charge, I piled a selection of pastries into a basket and headed up the back stairs.

I found my fiancé at the kitchen counter wearing his NYPD sweatpants and a Police Athletic League T-shirt. His short sandy hair was sleep tousled. His jaw was dark from unshaved stubble. And he was in the middle of a huge, awkward yawn. I thought he was the most attractive man I'd ever seen.

As I walked in, he was pouring a fresh cup of my Breakfast blend. When he saw me, he pulled over a second mug and filled it.

We kissed good morning—long and sweet. It was hard to break away, but the minutes were ticking by, and I had work to do.

"I don't have much time," I said, setting the basket of croissants and muffins on the table. "But I have *a lot* to tell you. And ask you . . ."

As we ate our breakfast, I brought Mike up to speed on all the crazy happenings of the day before, including and *especially* the murder of Fred Denham in Central Park. I told him how Soles and Bass caught the case—and that both detectives believed Denham's death was the tragic result of a random mugging.

"But you don't."

"I believe it may be connected to the sabotage going on around the *Only Murders in Gotham* production."

"Well . . ." Mike paused to sip his coffee. "You'll need to prove that."

"I know, and that's where I need your help. Can you talk to the Fish Squad and let me know how the case progresses? What they turn up? I mean, why did Denham head into the park right after he left the hospital? It seemed to me he was hurrying to meet someone. Is that who he was talking with on the phone? Can the detectives get a warrant for his phone data in the cloud?"

"Good questions. And I'll ask them on *my* behalf, given Billy Saddler's death—and his connection to the production. Anything else?"

"One more thing. I think you were right."

"About what?"

"The party where Billy Saddler overdosed. I told you about Sebastian Albee and Kylee Ferris leaving the hotel restaurant by the service elevator, and you thought they might have done it to smuggle some of the party's drugs out with them."

"I remember."

"Well, Kylee Ferris was honest with me about how she left the party. Sebastian Albee was not. And I have to admit, he's acting like he's using again."

"What do you mean *again*?"

"Kylee confided that he's an ex-addict. He almost didn't get the job directing the show's first season because of it. Jerry vouched for him, and Sebastian could be in real trouble if anyone finds out."

"Tell me more . . ."

I gave Mike the lowdown on Sebastian's mood swing while he was directing me. How he'd been surly and irritable, looking exhausted—then took an overlong break and came back from his trailer up-up-up.

"How up?" Mike asked. "Like he'd taken a stimulant drug?"

I nodded. "Funtenol is a stimulant, isn't it?"

"It is . . ." Mike said and drew a long breath. "Clare . . . you don't re-ally want me to crack this open, do you?"

"No! The only reason I'm telling you about Sebastian is to get your advice. I don't want the set to be shut down *or* the Village Blend to be implicated in a future overdose death. You see where I'm going?"

Mike nodded again, and I confided—

"Matt's mother called me last evening. She saw your press conference, and now she's worried about her son's exposure to this new drug. Given Matt's past cocaine use, she figured this Funtenol stuff is right up his old addiction alley. I doubt very much he'd start using again, but to set her mind at ease, I promised I'd keep an eye on him. And, of course, I *didn't* tell her a thing about the show's director or the possibility that the drugs from Billy Saddler's party are floating around our Village Blend set. I didn't want her to worry."

"She's right to worry," Mike said. "And so are you."

"You're not exactly setting my mind at ease here."

"It's one or the other, Clare. I do have an alternative. I can assign Sergeant Franco to undercover duty as a member of your staff—"

"No. It won't work. I already told you all the reasons why—"

"Then here's my advice to you. Keep an eye on your ex-husband. But you'd better watch Sebastian Albee, too. What you saw with his behavior could have been an aberration. Or he could be at risk of overdosing, just like . . ."

Mike's voice trailed into a sigh, and I finished the sentence for him.

"Just like Billy Saddler."

Forty-seven

As I came down the steps to the Village Blend, I carried the weight of my talk with Mike. Walking into the shop, I found the mood had descended here, as well.

My baristas were diligently fulfilling orders, but the quiet murmurs from the crew were a stark change from the shouted commands and noisy laughter that usually started each day of shooting. The line at the coffee bar was almost solemn with mumbled drink requests replacing the fun banter Nancy and Esther had experienced on other mornings of the shoot.

Billy Saddler's death was pressing heavily on everyone. Listening to their conversations, I could tell they hadn't heard about Fred Denham yet, but the news would likely hit them just as hard when they finally did.

In the meantime, Billy's tragic passing was the top news story of the day. The network morning shows and cable news were airing video montages of his zany comedy routines, along with short clips of last evening's NYPD press briefing.

Copies of newspapers, with Billy's death in the headlines, lay scattered across our café tables and chairs. Someone at the soundboard was playing a local talk radio station's discussion about Saddler's demise in particular, and the history of celebrity drug-related deaths in general.

That radio was abruptly cut off when Tina Bird arrived.

Stone-faced, she skipped the coffee bar to huddle with Drew Merriweather at a corner table.

Moments later, through the French doors, I saw Sebastian Albee.

The director had his arm around a visibly upset Kylee Ferris, whose features were hidden by a headscarf and sunglasses. The pair rounded the corner to our front door, entered the coffeehouse together, and joined Tina and Drew at their table.

When Jerry Sullivan arrived, minutes later, all conversation ceased, and all eyes turned to the star. It was obvious this was the moment every member of the cast and crew had been waiting for.

After a deep breath, Jerry began his speech.

"You all heard the terrible news, so I'm not going to repeat it." He shook his head. "I'm truly sorry this happened. Billy was my friend, and I know a lot of you were looking forward to working with him. We all knew Billy the funnyman actor, but only some of us knew he was a brilliant writer, a comedic virtuoso, and one crazy son of a Sasquatch, too."

A few tension-relieving chuckles cut through the gloom.

"Billy Saddler was going to repeat his 'crotchety old man' routine for our show, a gag he was rightly famous for. For years, he had to put makeup and prosthetics on to look convincing for the old shtick. But the crotchety part?" Jerry smiled. "Well, that came naturally. So did Billy's razor-sharp wit and perfect comic timing. I want to tell you a story I never told anyone. About how me, Marty Long, and Billy Saddler almost drowned in the Colorado River—and even then Billy Saddler couldn't help but be funny . . ."

As Jerry spoke, the crew—most of them smiling by now—leaned forward in their seats.

"Billy was filming *Two Busted Bronco Brothers* with Marty Long, who played the other brother. They had this rafting scene coming up. So Billy invites Marty and me on a little rafting expedition. He's going to teach Marty how to white-water raft, right?

"So we get in this rubber boat and float down the river and the water is getting rougher and rougher, and we're getting thrown back and forth like Ping-Pong balls. Suddenly, we see some scary rocks ahead.

"Poor Marty's getting nervous, so he asks Billy how we should negotiate the rocks in the white water. And Billy says, 'Damn if I know, Marty. I figured you and me could learn together!'"

The crew burst out laughing, and Jerry started laughing, too, even as he continued the story.

"So naturally we crash and end up in the drink, and the three of us are all swept downstream for what feels like a mile before we finally manage to scramble ashore.

"Marty Long tells Billy that he saw his whole life flash before his eyes. Then I say to Billy that I could be dead now and in heaven for all I know.

"Billy looks at me real serious and says, 'That's impossible, Jerry. Didn't you read the reviews of your last movie? You're already in hell, dummy.'"

The crew roared, and Jerry joined them.

When the room quieted, Jerry launched into another story about the night Billy Saddler fell through a trapdoor in the middle of a sketch on live TV.

". . . So while the shocked cast members gather around the open trapdoor, Billy yells up to them, 'Hey! If you want to drop me from the show, just tell me! You don't have to *drop me* from the show!'"

The on-screen accident was famous, but Jerry's crew loved hearing him retell it, and they laughed and laughed, as if they'd never heard it before.

When the laughter finally faded, Jerry spoke again, only this time he was serious.

"It feels like that now," he said. "For me—and the whole world. Billy was here. With all of us. And now he's gone. He's left the stage. But let's not allow that to be the end. Let's make sure the laughter doesn't die with Billy." Jerry bowed his head a moment, then lifted it high. "I'm going to dedicate this second season of *Only Murders in Gotham* to the memory of Billy Saddler. Now let's make our work worthy of one of the greatest comedians who ever lived!"

The coffeehouse exploded in cheers and applause.

Esther, Nancy, Tucker, and I joined in the clapping. As the applause continued, Sebastian, Kylie, and Tina Bird all embraced a tearful Jerry in a four-way hug. Some crew members slapped Jerry on the back. Others wiped away their own tears.

Inspired by Jerry's impassioned speech, everyone went to work.

But as they took their places, I saw Tina Bird call Hutch Saunders over to the corner table. Jerry joined, and I closely watched the intense conversation that followed.

From Hutch's reaction, I was sure Tina had just told him about Fred Denham's murder. He swiped his scarlet locks aside and buried his face in his shaky hands. Both Tina and Jerry hugged the distraught young man, then Jerry gently patted him on the back.

When Hutch was dismissed, he bypassed the coffee bar and headed upstairs to the catering area.

With all speed, I went up the back stairs, determined not to let anything distract me from finally talking to Hutch Saunders.

While I felt terrible about the loss of his friend, I needed answers— and I wasn't backing down until I got them.

Forty-eight

⦵⦵⦵⦵⦵⦵⦵⦵⦵⦵⦵⦵⦵⦵⦵⦵⦵⦵⦵⦵⦵⦵⦵⦵

I FOUND Hutch Saunders on the lounge floor, facing the naked brick wall and the cold fireplace—the same seat he'd chosen yesterday, when he enjoyed a pizza lunch and took that final call from his late boss.

Today, Hutch seemed to have lost his appetite. He clutched a forgotten bottle of orange juice and stared at nothing. His stubbly cheeks accentuated the grim worry lines on his face.

Without hesitation, I stepped up to him.

"Mr. Saunders, I heard what happened to Fred Denham," I began. "I'm sorry for your loss. My name is Clare Cosi. I'm the manager here."

As we shook hands, his frown was replaced by an expression of bafflement. "I'm surprised you knew Fred."

"I didn't know him, exactly. My business partner, Matt Allegro, performed CPR on Mr. Denham when he collapsed outside, in front of the Driftwood truck."

"That's right. Now I remember. You were in the video," Hutch said with a nod. "When I saw Fred go down, I froze. I didn't think he was going to pull through, but he did with your help. Now he's gone anyway. I guess when your number's up, it's up."

"What did Tina and Jerry tell you about Fred's death?"

"Just what the detectives told them. That Fred was mugged, right after he left the hospital, and he was shot to death."

"Do you think the police are right?"

Hutch shrugged. "Sure. Why not? This is a nasty town—and Fred didn't have an enemy in the world. Even his bookie loved him—"

"His bookie?"

"Fred did a lot of sports betting. He's a lousy gambler but he always pays up."

"Was Fred doing any betting locally?"

"Nah, his regular guy is in Los Angeles, and that's only a phone call away." Hutch gave a sad smile. "At least Fred had a winning streak before he died. I mean, he must have. He bought a top-of-the-line phone and a new Lakers' jacket a couple of weeks ago."

"What else did Tina and Jerry tell you?"

"Only that I have Fred's job now." Hutch drained half his bottle of juice. "Miserable way to get a promotion," he muttered.

I knew I had to frame the next question delicately, and without sounding accusatory.

"Tina and Jerry promoted you, so they obviously don't hold you responsible for the shooting incident."

Hutch winced. "They should. I was worried about Fred and wasn't thinking straight. I went with him to the hospital."

I moved a chair closer and sat down.

"Could you tell me what you meant when you said, 'They should'? How is anything your fault?"

Hutch pointed into space. "You know that big white trailer at the end of the line? That's Truck One. It has a safe inside. All firearms, explosives, and squibs are to be locked up inside that safe at the end of the day. And Truck One doesn't stick around. It goes back to the studio in Queens every night."

"That's not what happened this time?"

"Truck One went back to the studio, but the gun wasn't in it. I should have stuck around and locked the gun box up. Instead, I went off with Fred in the ambulance, and someone else loaded that box into the prop truck."

"Then you believe the gun was tampered with?"

"Anyone could have gotten to it. Fred kept live ammo and blanks in the same case, so it was easy to replace the blank with a live round."

"But why would anyone do it?"

"Some wiseass finds a gun and starts playing with it, that's my bet. The prop truck is full of lots of cool junk. People screw around in there all the time, even people who shouldn't be there at all.

"The way I see it, the nice shiny gun box attracted the attention of one of our so-called security people, or it could have been a grip. Easy access, too. That box wasn't even locked when I found it."

Hutch frowned. "Anyway, nobody got hurt. And now the guns and squibs are going to stay locked up. Since Jerry wants toy guns instead of real ones and he won't wear a squib, no matter what, we probably won't have reason to unlock it again—*unless* he changes his mind, which he's been known to do."

At the mention of squibs, I remembered Lizzy, and how she insisted it was a squib that brought the lights down on Norman.

"So you *did* have squibs on the set, then?"

"Sure."

"And now they're locked up—"

Hutch was in the middle of a nod when Tina Bird interrupted us. With a scowl on her face and her hands on her hips, she glared at me first, then turned to Hutch.

"Jerry has been calling you for the last ten minutes. This is a hell of a way to start your first day as property master."

Hutch jumped to his feet. "Jeez, sorry, Tweety—I mean Tina. Er . . . I'll get right on it, Ms. Bird."

Hutch hurried downstairs. Tina lingered, looming over me. When everyone was out of earshot, she spoke.

"I need to talk to you, Ms. Cosi. And you'd better listen."

Her tone was surprisingly hostile, but I kept my cool. More curious than defensive, I leaned back in my chair and assured her—

"You have my complete attention."

Forty-nine

〰〰〰〰〰〰〰〰〰〰〰〰〰〰〰〰〰〰〰〰

I INVITED Tina to take a seat, but she curtly shook her head and wasted no time with pleasantries.

"Why are you harassing our crew?" she demanded.

I was taken aback by the accusation. "I'm *harassing* no one—"

"Sebastian Albee tells a different tale."

"Oh, please. Making conversation is not harassment. And Jerry knows full well what I'm doing, not to mention why I'm doing it."

"Well, I don't like what you're doing," Tina returned. "Just now, you kept Hutch Saunders from his job. We don't need more delays on this set. Or disruptions."

"Disruptions?"

"You seem to be around whenever there's trouble. The live round, Kylee's snake, and . . . everything else."

"Everything else? What is that supposed to mean?"

"Part of my job is protecting my cast and crew," Tina went on, ignoring my question. "That includes their privacy, and that's why I'm telling you to *back off.*"

I rose and stood toe-to-toe with the woman.

"Look, a valued friend and one of my employees almost died on this set. Just like you, my job is to make sure my employees are not in danger. That's why I'm looking for answers, and I'm not about to stop."

Tina folded her arms so tightly that she looked like she was wearing a straitjacket. The impatient tapping of her foot told me she wasn't listening to a word I said, only waiting for me to finish.

I tried again to establish trust—

"Why don't you and I work together," I said and immediately realized that I had made the same pitch to Tina that Lizzy Meeks had made to me!

It went over just about as well, too.

Tina scowled at the very idea of "working together," and her next question made me realize that she viewed me with the same level of mistrust that I viewed Lizzy Meeks.

"Ms. Cosi, when Detective Soles called me about Fred Denham's death, I was surprised to hear *your* name come up. Do you have an explanation?"

"There was nothing sinister in what I did. I simply wanted to speak with Mr. Denham before he left the hospital, but he'd already been released. So I tried to catch up to him on the street—"

"Sounds like you were *stalking* him. And *that* sounds a lot like harassment—"

"Excuse me, but—"

"No buts!" Tweety chirped. "From now on, please restrict yourself to craft services management duties only. If I find you bothering Sebastian Albee or Hutch Saunders or anyone else on our set again, I will have you forcibly removed."

"You can't do that."

Tina snorted. "Just watch me."

With that, she strode away, looking more like a cocky rooster than an angry Bird.

"Wow, what went on there, Ms. Boss?" Esther cracked when I joined her and Tucker in clearing the remains of breakfast. "You two looked so cute and tiny and cuddly as you squared off. Like a pair of attack hamsters."

"I thought there was going to be a rumble, for sure," Tucker quipped.

"No big deal," I said, shrugging it off. "Just a slight disagreement about managerial responsibilities—and a few ruffled feathers."

Fifty

~~~~~~~~~~~~~~~~~~~~~~~~~~~~~~~~~~~~~~~

RUFFLED feathers is exactly what I found when I grabbed the laptop from my second-floor office and took a "cooling off" break in my apartment upstairs.

"Hello, girls!" I called, coming through the duplex's front door.

Tails twitching, eyes wide, Java and Frothy were perched on the ledge of the window that led to my fire escape, where I kept a bird feeder during cold-weather months.

I saw Mike had refilled the feeder before he left, and I suspected he *re-fed* my cats, too, because they barely glanced my way when I came through the door, preferring instead to focus on the frantic fluttering of feathers around the fire escape feeder.

From the satisfied smirks on their furry faces and disinterest in picketing me for snacks, I just knew they'd *meowed* a second breakfast out of my easily duped fiancé.

"You buffaloed Mike, didn't you?" I accused the pair.

Of course, in their little cat minds, a hunted snack wasn't out of the question. If given the chance, they would relish chomping the heads off those unsuspecting sparrows and pigeons outside.

I knew *exactly* how they felt!

Though I'd kept my cool downstairs in front of my staff, I was still so infuriated by Tina's threats that I couldn't stop myself from picturing her fluttering around my fire escape—and letting Java and Frothy out for lunch.

"What do you say, girls? Want to work up an appetite for Tweety Bird?"

Keep it down! they seemed to reply with their stares before turning back to the sparrow and pigeon show.

I almost laughed. Before I climbed north to my apartment, I'd heard a crew person on the main floor make a similar demand—

"QUIET ON THE SET!"

The softer voice of Sebastian had followed, coaxing his players into—

"Action."

The voice of Jerry Sullivan and his raucous comedian character had come next, followed by the wry counterpoint of Kylee Ferris, playing her policewoman's part with a perfectly executed Brooklyn accent.

Good for you, Kylee, I'd thought. *Stay focused!*

Now, upstairs at my kitchen table, it was time for me to focus on work. Opening my laptop, I began by updating schedules and supply orders.

Forty minutes later, I stood, stretched, and brewed a pour-over pot of Matt's Sumatra at which point my mobile phone rang.

"Mike?"

"Hey, sweetheart, I didn't get a chance to kiss you goodbye."

"Criminal," I said, taking a fresh, delicious sip from my cup. "But I thought you'd stick around a little longer."

"No. Duty called—but, if you need me, I'm just up the street, at the Sixth."

"Actually, I do need you."

"What's wrong?"

"Nothing. I mean . . . what I need from you is *information.*"

"What's going on?"

I updated Mike on Tina Bird's threats, which seemed way out of proportion, considering the situation. And, though I still didn't trust Lizzy Meeks, I couldn't get her warning about Tina out of my head.

"What warning?" Mike pressed.

"Lizzy thinks Tina Bird shouldn't be trusted. She says she's up to something behind Jerry's back."

"What exactly is she up to?"

"Lizzy wasn't sure. She followed her to the stage door of a dark Broadway theater, but that's all she knows."

"That doesn't seem suspicious," Mike said. "Ms. Bird could be interviewing new actors for Jerry Sullivan's show, right?"

"No. That's not her job. And even if it was, then why keep it from Jerry? Why lie about where she's going?"

"Sounds like there's more than a few secrets being hidden on that set."

"And maybe one more."

"What do you mean?"

"Something I forgot to mention," I said. "When I questioned Kylee Ferris about Billy Saddler's party, she mentioned Tina Bird. I didn't think much about it, but now, with Ms. Bird threatening me so emphatically about asking questions . . ."

"Go on," Mike prompted, clearly intrigued. "What did Kylee say?"

"She said Tina Bird warned her that the police were coming to the party. Kylee said that's why she and Sebastian took the service elevator to the loading dock. Now, how would Tina know that you and your detectives were coming? Unless—"

"Unless Ms. Bird was the one who called us," Mike finished for me. "Or knew the person who did."

"Is that something you can help me with? Did your squad trace the call from this so-called anonymous tipster?"

"Of course we did. And it led to a burner phone, wiped of prints and left under a table at the hotel restaurant. A waiter said he saw the abandoned phone and put it in lost and found. And that's where we found it."

"That sounds oddly premeditated, doesn't it? Like a setup."

"Exactly like a setup," Mike said. "The question is why."

And to that, neither one of us had an answer.

Fifty-one

෧෨෧෧෧෨෧෨෧෧෧෧෧෧෧෨෧෨෧෧෧෧෧෧

The rest of the morning passed quickly, and noontime arrived with a tense crew of hungry mouths to feed.

Lunch was a variety of salads from Babka's, along with hot Chicken Marsala sandwiches on crusty Italian rolls and Three-Cheese Pizza Pinwheels, courtesy of Dennis Murphy, who, besides being a famous restauranteur, appeared to be a culinary psychic, sensing how tightly wound we all were and providing food accordingly.

The pinwheels and crusty Marsala sandwiches were both huge hits. Bellies full and palates satisfied, the cast and crew became boisterous again, back to their laughing, joking selves.

With lunch service done, we cleaned and reset the lounge. By the time the afternoon coffee break rolled around, I was happy to see trays of our lush, rich Chocolate Espresso Cupcakes and mouthwatering Caramel-Dipped Meltaways ready to go, but I noticed we were running low on my Kivu Lake Rwandan City Roast, our coffee of the day.

While Esther brewed the final batch, I headed downstairs to the roasting room. I was about to pull two ten-pound bags off the shelf when I heard footsteps on the basement steps above. Someone was coming to help me haul these heavy bags, I thought.

Then I spied high-top red sneakers and pajama-style pants on the steps. At the same moment I heard Sebastian Albee's voice.

"I'm glad you picked up," he said. "I was afraid I'd missed you."

I realized the director was on the phone, and he thought he was alone. I decided to keep him in the dark and slipped behind our big red Probat roaster before he had a chance to spot me.

"I'll take whatever you have," Sebastian said as he sat down near the bottom of the steps. "But it's got to be today. I can't wait. I'm under a tremendous amount of pressure and I feel like I'm going to crack. I really need this . . ."

Oh, God, I thought. *I was right. The director is hooked on drugs again, and he desperately needs a fix.*

"Are you sure no one will recognize me?" Sebastian continued. "This has to remain a secret. It could ruin my position on this project if word got out . . ."

A pause, then: "No, don't worry. No one can hear me. I'm calling from the basement of a coffeehouse."

There was a long pause while Sebastian simply listened. Finally, he let loose with a ragged sigh.

"Thank you for this. I really owe you," he rasped. "Three o'clock is fine. Text me that address and I'll be there . . . I can leave the set for a couple of hours before I have to start shooting the night scenes."

The director ended the call, but for a long moment the man didn't move. Neither did I. The roaster was cold, the ventilation system shut down. With only a soft murmur of voices wafting down from the coffeehouse, I scarcely breathed for fear he'd hear me.

Eventually, I heard a rocking movement. Then Sebastian Albee choked back a sob. Finally, he rose and slowly climbed the steps.

That poor man, I thought. *He sounds so stressed and desperate.*

Suddenly, I didn't care what Tina Bird thought or said. The director needed help. The man was crumbling under the strain, and the slave of some sort of addiction—most likely Funtenol.

Fortunately, I knew someone who could understand and empathize with Sebastian's misery, someone who'd been down the road of addiction and recovery and might be able to lend wisdom and support.

That person was Matt Allegro. The question was—

Would my ex-husband agree to join me in my mission?

I didn't know the answer, but the second I got out of this basement, I was determined to convince him.

Fifty-two

∽∾∽∾∽∾∽∾∽∾∽∾∽∾∽∾∽∾∽∾∽∾∽∾∽∾∽∾

WHEN the coast was finally clear, I hauled two bags of Rwandan up the basement steps and delivered them to Esther at the coffee bar.

"Have you seen Matt?"

"Mr. Boss grabbed a double espresso ten minutes ago. I think he went up to the lounge."

I checked my watch. It was almost two o'clock now. Depending on how far Sebastian had to travel to score his drugs, he might leave at any moment.

Matt needed to grab our van right now, so we'd be ready to follow the director's car.

But what if he walked? I suddenly wondered. Or took the subway? What if the director spotted our tail? After Tina's threats, it wouldn't be pretty.

So much could go wrong that I had half a mind to grab Sebastian and try to talk some sense into him before he even left the coffeehouse.

But if I did anything in front of the cast and crew, his secret would be out, and I would be responsible for the destruction of his career.

No, Matt and I would have to confront Sebastian Albee at the source, before he was about to purchase the drugs. Ideally, we could convince him not to buy the poison *and* finger a Funtenol pusher for Mike Quinn's OD Squad at the same time.

As I climbed the back stairs to the second-floor lounge, I shuddered at the thought of Funtenol being used inside my coffeehouse. I saw what happened to Billy Saddler, and witnessing another event like that was too disturbing to contemplate—which explained the stab of panic I felt a few moments later.

I found the lounge mostly empty. The lunch crowd had cleared off by now, except for a few stragglers. Nancy was in a flirty conversation with the gaffer, and my ex-husband sat at a table for two with none other than that blonde Driftwood barista (the one Esther had wanted to drag out of her truck by her nose ring).

I watched with shock and mortal terror as Nose Ring Girl offered Matt a chocolate square. When he reached for the poisoned sweet, I moved faster than I'd ever moved before.

"STOP!" I cried as I snatched the chocolate from Nose Ring Girl's hand.

Matt and the young woman gawked at me.

"And what is THIS?!" I demanded, holding the chocolate square above my head.

"It's Hershey's," the baffled girl replied. "Hershey's chocolate."

I looked at the chocolate square in my hand. The Hershey's logo was melting on my fingers.

"Oh. Sorry," I said, handing the crushed mess to Matt. "I . . . uh . . . I thought it had almonds . . . Matt is rather careless about his nut allergy, you see."

"Nut allergy?" Matt stared at me as if I'd gone over the edge.

"Forget about nut allergies, Matt. Something *terribly important* has come up and I need your help to deal with it."

Matt could tell by my tone that the situation was serious. He apologized to Nose Ring Girl and followed me down the back stairs.

"Clare, what in the world has gotten into you? Here I am trying to smooth things over with the Driftwood people—"

"So that's why you were sitting with Nose Ring Girl—"

"Stop calling her that! Her name is Serena. And what's with that nut allergy stunt? You know my only allergy is to *nutcases*, and you're acting like one!"

"Shut up and listen. Do you have the keys to the van?"

"Sure, but—"

"We may need it."

We reached the main floor of the coffeehouse—just in time to see Sebastian Albee walk out the front door and head up Hudson on foot.

"We're in luck," I said. "It looks like he's going to walk. And we're going to follow!"

"Why?"

"Because Sebastian Albee is in trouble. And we're going to help him."

Matt's expression was dubious. "Help him how?"

"By staging an intervention."

FIFTY-THREE

WITH a Village Blend take-out cup in hand, Sebastian Albee walked along Hudson Street at a brisk pace. Matt and I followed on foot, staying a cautious half block behind.

I noticed the director had done a quick change in his trailer, ditching his colorful Willy Wonka attire for scuffed running shoes, tight denims, and a gray hoodie that covered his mushroom top haircut. If I hadn't seen him leave our shop, I probably wouldn't have recognized him.

As we walked, I told Matt about the phone conversation I'd overheard between Sebastian and his drug dealer—and about the party I'd witnessed at the rooftop restaurant. I also confessed what Mike Quinn told me about the dangers of Funtenol.

"Now I understand why you snapped over a Hershey bar," Matt said. "But that doesn't excuse your behavior."

"I'm sorry I embarrassed you in front of . . . Serena."

"It's not that, Clare. I'm just disappointed. How could you think I'd start using again? You know I'm committed to dying clean—and at a *very old* age."

I was heartened to hear that, and my reply came naturally. "Message received. I'll stop worrying about you . . ."

I was not being truthful, of course. There are certain people in your life that you never stop worrying about. For me, Matt Allegro would forever be one of them.

We walked uptown on tree-lined Hudson Street for a short time, passing sights that gave the Village its charm: the Federal-style brick buildings, the boutique shops, the neighborhood pubs, the quaint eateries.

When Sebastian reached the next intersection, he turned right on Christopher Street and vanished.

"Hurry!" I said, knowing we could lose him completely if he ducked into a building or alleyway.

Matt was a few steps ahead of me. As he turned the corner, I rushed to catch up. But just as I rounded onto Christopher—

Whoa!

Matt's strong arm reached out and hauled me into a doorway. I was about to cry out when he put his hand over my mouth.

"Shhh!" he hissed in my ear. That's when I realized that Sebastian had stopped to check his phone screen—and I'd nearly collided with him!

We waited in the shadows of the doorway, just a few feet behind the man, until he finally took off again, this time incredibly quickly.

"Come on," Matt said, picking up his pace.

I had to race double time to keep up with my ex's long strides. Finally, the director walked by the façade of a large white-stone building with a steeple, one of the oldest churches in the neighborhood.

Between the church and the next building was a gated alleyway. The black iron gate was open, and Sebastian turned down the alley, vanishing from sight again.

We cautiously approached the mouth of the alley and looked down the narrow straight. A dozen or so men—young, middle-aged, and older—were lingering in the courtyard. All seemed tense, some smoking like chimneys. Sebastian Albee was among them, one hand shoved into the pocket of his hoodie, the other still clutching our Village Blend takeout cup.

"This is pretty brazen," I whispered. "They're just waiting around for the dealer to show up and start pushing poison—and this is happening right beside a church? It's appalling."

"I don't think that's what's happening," Matt murmured as we observed the group. "Let's step back."

We moved away from the alley's entrance, and Matt checked his watch.

"Let's wait here, Clare. It's a little after three o'clock now. Didn't you say that's when Albee was supposed to pick up his drugs?"

"That's right," I said with a nod. "But I didn't expect a crowd."

A minute later, we checked again. The men were gone!

"Where did they go?"

I didn't understand it. We'd been watching the sidewalk the whole time. No one came out of the alley. And no one new went in!

"Come on," Matt insisted. "Let's check it out."

We slowly walked down the narrow path between the buildings. Only scattered cigarette butts remained at the end of it. An unmarked basement door stood ajar. Matt pointed.

"Let's go inside."

"Do you think it's safe?"

"I'm pretty sure we're going to be okay."

Matt obviously knew something that I didn't, but before I could ask him what was up, he pushed through the unmarked door.

I had no choice but to follow.

On the other side, we found a shadowy hallway. That's when I caught a whiff of something unexpected—

"Coffee?"

"A Grade 4 or even 5 cup, likely brewed from beans that came out of a can," Matt replied. "There will be doughnuts, too."

A door opened across the hall and a smiling older woman approached us. "Are you here for the meeting?" she asked in a kind voice. "It's already started, but please go right in. It's through the second door on your right."

The woman pointed out the door, wished us a "blessed day," and went out the basement door that we came in.

"Okay, Matt. This obviously isn't the haunt of some sleezy drug dealer. So, what is it?"

My ex-husband led me down the hall. "This is a place I am quite familiar with—"

"You've been here?"

"Never here," Matt replied. "But I've been to dozens of places like it, in a dozen cities around the world."

We entered a tiny room adjacent to a larger space dominated by a circle of folding chairs. On a card table in this small room, an urn of fresh coffee had just finished brewing. There were doughnuts, too—still in their boxes, lids open—just as Matt predicted.

Matt sighed. "These places are all the same. The antsy chain-smokers outside, the cheap, plentiful coffee, the free snacks—"

"What is this place?" I demanded.

"It's a Narcotics Anonymous meeting."

Fifty-Four

⊚⌾⊚⌾⊚⌾⊚⌾⊚⌾⊚⌾⊚⌾⊚⌾⊚⌾⊚⌾⊚⌾⊚⌾⊚⌾⊚⌾⊚⌾⊚⌾⊚

OBVIOUSLY, I couldn't have been more wrong about Sebastian Albee and his intentions. Yet the snoop-dog in me wasn't willing to slink away.

"Let's go in," I whispered.

Matt caught my arm before I took two steps.

"That's an NA meeting, Clare, not a spectator sport. Everyone who's in there is in some degree of crisis. They're in that group to battle their personal demons and find comfort and support from fellow sufferers. You and I don't have the right to go in there."

Matt was correct, of course. But I reminded him that I was investigating two shootings—one of them fatal.

"I want to hear what Sebastian has to say," I quietly insisted. "What if his pain and suffering are all about the guilt he feels for shooting Fred Denham? Or what if he knows who did?"

Matt folded his muscular arms. "You really think that's likely?"

My ex and I went back and forth for a few minutes, but Matt's cooler head ultimately prevailed.

"Okay, I won't crash the meeting," I whispered. "But I'm going to hang around with the coffee and doughnuts and eavesdrop a little. It won't hurt anyone, and it might help me catch a killer. Since you don't want to invade anyone's privacy, what are you going to do?"

Matt shrugged. "I'll probably—"

I shushed him. "Wait! I think it's starting."

After a long prayer led by a man with a rich baritone voice, I heard the folding chairs buckle as the group sat down.

"Today we have a guest, someone from out of town," the deep voice continued. "I've spoken with his sponsor who tells me our brother is struggling with a number of issues we're all familiar with. Let's welcome Sebastian to our group."

While the men greeted the director, I whispered to Matt—

"Remind me. What does a sponsor do exactly? I remember you had one, but it's been so many years . . ."

"A sponsor is a member of the group who's been in recovery for a couple of years," Matt quietly replied. "Your sponsor is your confidant, someone who's been where you are and understands your situation."

Matt shook his head. "It's got to be tough on Albee. He's working nearly three thousand miles from his sponsor, at a time when that sponsor becomes the only person you can count on."

"I know you're speaking from experience."

"My sponsor saved my sanity more than once, Clare. We're—"

I shushed Matt again.

Inside the meeting room, Mr. Deep Voice spoke. "Let's let our guest introduce himself."

The chair creaked as Albee rose. "My name's Sebastian and I'm an addict. I say that every day because it took me a long time to admit the truth to myself. I've been clean for eighteen months and thirteen days, and I fight the addiction every day. I'm winning because generous, caring people like yourselves have shown me a new path to follow."

Sebastian paused. "I . . . I can't say it's been easy. I have a highly stressful job, and a lot of people look to me for support. My decisions affect all of their careers. They lean on me for strength—one young woman in particular—but I don't feel I have much strength left."

Sebastian Albee's voice became choked with emotion.

"During the past few days, the old craving came back. I beat the urge by having an assistant deliver a gallon of espressos to my trailer, where I meditated in private . . ."

I resisted the urge to smack myself in the forehead.

I'd wondered about Sebastian's mood shifts, from morning depressive to afternoon up-up-up. Now I understood why—and the explanation was perfectly innocent.

"Well, that's *one* mystery solved," I whispered to Matt.

In response to Sebastian's admission, some of the men spoke of their own weak moments and what brought them on. Finally, the group leader with the deep voice got Sebastian to talk about his current trigger.

"When I started on this journey, my sponsor warned me that some of my friends would no longer be my friends because I was living drug- and alcohol-free," Sebastian said. "I didn't believe him. That sounded crazy to me. Then it actually started happening. It was depressing to lose friends, but I've finally accepted it.

"And now . . . well, that same alienation has hit closer to home, and I'm not sure I can face it. My wife is an important woman. She's an executive at a major studio. She's hardheaded and pragmatic. Lately, she made it clear that she preferred the way I used to be. My wife just doesn't understand or relate to the path I've taken."

"Is there anything specific that you can pinpoint?" asked the group leader. "Anything you can work on as a couple?"

"I've been living away from my wife for months, working on a project here in the city. The separation is only making a bad situation worse, and I'm pretty sure she's going to ask for a divorce."

Surprised gasps and murmured sympathies followed Sebastian's heartfelt confession.

"I want to live the life I've chosen," Sebastian insisted. "It's the only way to fight my addiction. But I love my wife and I don't want my marriage to fall apart, either. I'm not sure what will happen. Or how I'll cope . . ."

The men commiserated with Sebastian, some offering advice, others their prayers and good wishes. Finally, the group leader's deep voice announced—

"I think Sebastian and all of us have forgotten our most basic tenet, so I shall remind us all—"

I could hear the men rising. I peeked into the room and saw the group gathering in a close circle, putting their arms around one another.

"Let us pray that we have the capacity to accept what we cannot change," he intoned, "and the courage to change what we can. We must live one day at a time. Use hardships as our pathway to wisdom. And whatever is in our futures, we pray for the strength within to face it . . ."

I pulled Matt's arm. "Okay, I've heard enough. Let's get out of here."

"Are you sure you don't want a doughnut first?"

"No thanks. I'm too stuffed from eating crow."

Fifty-Five

᷾᷾᷾᷾᷾᷾᷾᷾᷾᷾᷾᷾᷾᷾᷾᷾᷾᷾᷾᷾᷾᷾᷾᷾᷾᷾᷾᷾᷾᷾

Aғɪᴇʀ Matt and I returned from our "mission," I was glad to get back to work. There was plenty to do, because Jerry and his crew would be filming late into the night. And that meant we would be serving dinner as well as evening snacks.

As for Sebastian Albee, he returned from his Narcotics Anonymous meeting with renewed creative energy. He grabbed a triple espresso at the coffee bar and consulted at a table with members of his crew. Then he began lining up shots and wardrobe changes for the series of night scenes between Kylee and Jerry that would span several episodes.

Given what I'd learned, I felt a lot better, too.

It was a great relief to know that our director wasn't on drugs. Albee was the only individual I even suspected of narcotics abuse, and now that he'd been cleared, that was one worry I could put aside.

I knew Madame would also be relieved. She feared her son would be lured off the wagon. Now, at least, I could assure her of the resolve in Matt's voice this afternoon, when he spoke of staying clean for the rest of his life.

The dinner service prep went smoothly, and we had more than enough food to offer, including pans of meatless Baked Ziti from Dennis Murphy and sticky, succulent Garlic and Citrus Wings from Babka, a crowd-pleasing entrée that used the same excellent marinade as her restaurant's popular Whole Roasted Chicken. The crew had an extended three-hour break before their night shoot began, and they started chowing down immediately. Twenty minutes later, with the dinner rush calming, Dante texted me with a list of urgent needs for our coffee truck.

Happy to keep busy—and wanting to check our current inventory, anyway—I left Matt in charge of monitoring the lounge service and headed back down to our shop to load a standing dolly with supplies.

Tucker, who'd asked for the evening off, spotted me struggling and jumped in to help.

"Thank you," I said as he took control of the dolly. When we were through the front door and on the sidewalk, I noticed my assistant manager's change of wardrobe.

Tuck modeled his French blue suit, worn with an open-necked dress shirt and a colorful silk hanky in the lapel pocket. His shoes were blue high-top sneakers.

"You certainly look dapper tonight."

"I'm going to a dinner party with Punch and an important contact, but I'm way early, so why don't you let me help?"

With Tuck pushing the dolly, we covered the half block to the brightly lit coffee truck in minutes. Dante looked relieved to see us.

"We're down to our last dozen cups," he said.

"And our last few pastries," Nancy added.

"But you were stocked with enough treats to last all evening," I said, perplexed. "What happened?"

"A fire truck happened," Nancy said. "Those FDNY guys really know how to snack!"

"Yeah, they descended like a plague of locusts," Dante said with a snort. Then he noticed Tucker's attire. "Hey, look at you all gussied up in your fancy go-to-meetin' duds."

"Gussied up?" Tuck cried. "Go-to-meetin' duds? From whence did you steal those lines, varlet?"

"*The Beverly Hillbillies*," Dante replied. "It's freakishly popular lately, all kinds of memes and viral videos with dubbed dialogue. A friend asked me to design a Jethro Bodine tattoo, and I got hooked on those crazy old episodes."

Tuck nodded. "I've seen the Jethro T-shirts. With *Shucked* a hit on Broadway, I have to say I'm not surprised."

I folded the empty dolly and left it inside the truck. As Tucker and I walked back to the coffeehouse, he poked me and pointed—

"Looks like I'm not the only one who's *all gussied up* tonight."

Tina Bird was exiting the Village Blend. She'd shed her drab production manager's feathers for more gorgeous plumage—a silver pantsuit that shimmered in the streetlight's glow. Tweety seemed taller in high heels, too, and her slicked-back pixie cut and polished cosmetics looked as if they'd been done by the film's hair and makeup department.

She attempted to flag down a cab, which I found odd. Why not use the always-available studio car and driver sitting across the street? Could it be that Ms. Bird didn't want anyone at the studio to know where she was going on her three-hour dinner break?

Between Lizzy Meeks's accusations that Tina was "up to something" and that nasty pecking order fight I'd had with the Bird lady, I was curious about her destination—and why she was so "gussied up" for it.

Making a snap judgment, I faced Tucker. "How early are you for your dinner party?"

"About ninety minutes."

"How would you like to find out where Tweety is flying?"

A sly smile crossed Tuck's face. "If something's up, I want in on it. But we'd better move fast because she just caught a cab."

"We're in luck!" I cried. "There's another cab right behind hers."

Waving wildly, I flagged down the second taxi, and Tuck and I piled in.

"You've got to let me say it, Clare," Tuck pleaded. "It's a classic line. Let me deliver it once in my life."

"Be my guest."

With his game face on, he leaned toward the driver and pointed.

"Follow that cab!"

Fifty-six

∽∽∽∽∽∽∽∽∽∽∽∽∽∽∽∽∽∽∽∽∽∽∽∽∽∽

Ina Bird's destination turned out to be 44th Street between Eighth Avenue and Broadway, the heart of Manhattan's Theater District.

Tucker and I exited our cab just in time to see her walking through the double doors that fronted the smallest theater on the block.

"That's the Hayes Theater," Tucker said. "The most intimate venue on Broadway."

"What do you mean by intimate?"

"Less than six hundred seats."

Several larger theaters occupied both sides of 44th, and though curtain time was nearly an hour away for these big Broadway shows, ticket holders were already gathering on the sidewalks in front of the brightly lit façades.

Unlike the giant venues, the little three-story Hayes Theater, housed in a quaint colonial-style redbrick structure, had no title plastered across its darkened marquee. As we approached the entrance, we spied a stark black-and-white poster in its glass display window:

PROJECT NINE
EXCLUSIVE TEASER
SEVEN THIRTY PM
SERIOUS INVESTORS WELCOME

Uncertain what to do next, Tuck and I paused.

"I'd love to go in, but I'm sure Tina Bird would spot me in an instant. And it looks like this event might be by invitation only."

"It's not," Tuck said. "I've been to these things before—heck, I hosted a few myself. Somebody is trying to launch a new show. *Serious investors welcome* means you show your business card or who you're affiliated with. Believe me, if they're desperate to find funding, they'll take it anywhere they can get it."

"So, when they ask us, who are we supposed to be affiliated with?"

Tuck offered that sly smile again. "Don't worry about it, Clare. I have that covered."

I'd heard the same refrain from Matt more than once—and more than once things ended in disaster. So instead of barging in, I convinced Tucker to wait around while we counted heads.

"There are at least two hundred people in there now," Tuck said after fifteen minutes had passed. "I think we can lose ourselves in a crowd of that size. And if Tina spots me, so what? She knows I'm part of the New York theater scene. But you—" He looked me over and conceded. "Some sort of disguise might be in order."

"Okay, what do we do? Call Punch for the magic box?"

"No time. Give me a moment." He tapped his chin, considering my outfit. "Black cashmere sweater and black denims. Good enough for the role of 'my assistant,' but you're still going to need a little help to pull this off. Do you have lipstick?"

I fished through my bag and handed it over. Tuck told me to pucker up. Then he slathered on way more than I ever would.

"There," Tuck said with a satisfied nod. Next he yanked the long, colorful hanky from his lapel pocket and tied it stylishly around my neck.

"There's not much I can do with the hair—wait! I have it."

Tucker undid my ponytail, shook my hair out, and totally mussed it for a solid minute.

"What are you doing?"

"Look at your reflection in that window, and no thanks are necessary."

My hair was all over the place. Not sticking up so much as falling all over my face, like a scruffy St. Bernard.

"I look like I just crawled out of bed—after a nightmare."

"Precisely. It's Kurt Cobain hair with Billie Eilish flair."

"Who's he?"

"Never mind, sweetie. You look *somewhat* chic—and that's all anyone will see."

I arched an eyebrow. "Really?"

"Okay, okay. One more adjustment should help . . ."

He reached into his jacket and pulled out a pair of sunglasses in the same French blue as his suit and sneakers. He slipped the oversized specs onto my face.

"There!" He threw up his hands. "I don't even recognize you."

I swallowed hard and took Tucker's arm, hoping he was right. Because if Tweety Bird *did* recognize me, it would not be pretty.

"Okay, let's go," I said, forcing a confident stride.

Just inside the theater lobby, we were greeted by a tall young woman in a tiny red dress.

"Hello and welcome to Project Nine," she said brightly. "Who do you represent, please?"

Tucker handed her an impressive-looking embossed business card.

"Greg Armstrong," Tuck said. "Irregular Investments. And this is my personal assistant, Ernesta."

The woman slid Tucker's card into a folder and handed us each a program that resembled a *Playbill* but much thinner and printed in gray scale.

As we walked away, I leaned close to Tuck. "How do you know the real Greg Armstrong won't be here tonight?"

"Because I'm meeting him for dinner in an hour, about three blocks from here. He's interested in investing in my next cabaret show. Punch told him about the hilarious death scene with Jerry Sullivan in *Only Murders in Gotham*, and he can't wait to meet me. Strike while the iron is hot, you know? And, hey, if this show is any good, I'll tell him about it, too."

Relieved we'd actually gotten in, I glanced at the program.

"Project Nine?" I read. "Book by Laura Byron-Coffey. Ever heard of her? The name rings a faint bell."

Tucker shook his head. "There's a B-movie actress named Laura Byron. I wonder if it's the same woman?"

I read further.

"Music by Bennie Bennett? That name sounds familiar, too, but I can't quite place it."

Tucker opened the program, looking for bios of these two and finding none, only the names of tonight's performers and their backgrounds. There were a half dozen of them, and Tuck was familiar with a few.

"Hmm . . . okay," he said. "It says here the teaser will last approximately thirty minutes, and the title will be announced at the start of the show."

We were still standing in the theater lobby. Most of the people were clustering at the three auditorium doors, none of which were opened yet. My worries that Tina would spot me were quickly trumped by my desperate curiosity about this crowd, and I began to scan the faces.

To my shock, the first familiar face I saw belonged to Drew Merriweather. He'd exchanged his casual clothes for a sharp blue blazer and pressed khakis—and he was speaking quite familiarly with a well-dressed older man, a slick-looking character with a bronzed tan, perfectly coiffed salt-and-pepper hair, and leathery face. The man didn't strike me as a New Yorker. A tan like that was rare around the city, as was the silver-and-jade bolo tie.

I tugged Tucker's arm. "Who's that guy with Drew?"

He did a double take. "Oh, my, that's Morris Windham, Jr., entertainment director for the Winner Hotel and Casino in Vegas. I've never met him, but I've seen his photo in the trades plenty of times. Punch has a friend who plays Vegas clubs on a circuit, so he's especially tuned in to all the movers and shakers out there."

With that revelation, I insisted *we* move right now—much closer. With Tuck's help, we came within earshot just as the two men burst into peals of laughter.

"That's why you should listen to your uncle Morris," the older man said.

"You know I do, Unc," Drew replied, adjusting the horn-rimmed glasses on his baby face.

"And how's your mother? I haven't talked to Edith since the Fourth of July bash in Brentwood . . ."

As their talk became more personal, I guided Tuck away. The threat of discovery was too great. And I'd already learned everything I needed to know—that Drew Merriweather, Jerry's studio-assigned and not always trustworthy personal assistant, was actually the beloved nephew of a man who might be out for Jerry's blood over a broken casino contract.

Modern psychology would call what I experienced *cognitive dissonance*.

While the fan in me wanted nothing to be wrong with Jerry's production, the snoop in me was suddenly suspicious. I did a long, slow search of the lobby and was surprised (and actually relieved) to see that Lizzy Meeks wasn't present. She'd been pushing so hard for Jerry to return to Vegas that I thought she might have been part of this cadre.

Or maybe it wasn't a "cadre" at all. Perhaps Drew's family connections were what Jerry was referring to when he made that crack the first day I met him about nepotism being "Hollywood's favorite flavor."

Was Drew the informant who was *helping* Lizzy?

Now *that* made a kind of sense. Maybe that was why I didn't see Drew Merriweather's name on Lizzy's phone screen. No calls were necessary if Drew was communicating with Lizzy through their mutual friend Norman.

Or . . .

Maybe Drew never called Lizzy because he knew she wasn't the one who put the snake in Kylee's trailer. Maybe Drew knew that because he did it himself.

Lizzy made it very clear that the Winner Casino wanted their multimillion-dollar attraction back in their Vegas theater. Could Drew be working for his uncle? Secretly sabotaging the set and the show? That would be one surefire way to get Jerry back in Vegas. Or a flat-out revenge play, if they were bitter enough.

And if Drew was creating chaos at the behest of his uncle, did Lizzy know all along? Was her visit with me a way to deflect blame from herself and Drew, to keep her friends close and enemies closer—me being the latter since she knew I was trying to get to the bottom of all the sabotage on the set.

My head spun with speculations, but I had no time to take a breath because the surprises just kept on coming. In my zeal to steer Tucker and myself away from Drew Merriweather, I bumped smack into a jovial, heavyset man, who'd been addressing a small circle of attentive listeners.

"Excuse me, I—"

My mind instantly froze when I realized with whom I had just col-lided. I was suddenly standing face-to-face with the star of *The Coffey Break*, the prime-time network show that had launched Jerry Sullivan's career decades before.

I couldn't believe it! Gawking like an idiot, I stared in shocked silence at the legendary comedian himself, Jerry's old partner in the museum of television history, Dan Coffey.

Fifty-seven

⟡⟡⟡⟡⟡⟡⟡⟡⟡⟡⟡⟡⟡⟡⟡⟡⟡⟡⟡⟡⟡⟡⟡⟡⟡⟡⟡⟡⟡⟡⟡⟡⟡

Mʀ. Coffey was (of course!) a lot older now than in his early television days. His hair was mostly gray, but there was still plenty of it. And I immediately recognized his round, red face and ready laugh.

"Will you look at this?" Coffey cracked, pointing at me. "I've struck this poor woman into stone-cold silence. If only I had that power over my wife!"

As the crowd around the comedian broke up, Coffey craned his neck to scan the lobby.

"Where is Mrs. Byron-Coffey, anyway?"

He waved to a slender woman in a knee-length scarlet dress standing among another cluster of attendees. Realizing she'd been called out, Mrs. Byron-Coffey nodded her platinum blond head and offered her husband a crooked smile through red-lined and (definitely) Botoxed lips.

"There she is, folks," Coffey said. "You know I hardly recognize Laura these days. She's been locked up writing this play for so long I forgot I was married—which was very awkward when I brought that pair of coeds home from the sports bar on Saturday night."

More laughter, and a theatrical roll of the eyes from Mrs. Byron-Coffey.

"But she looks gorgeous tonight, am I right?" Coffey said with a wink. "Grace under pressure. That's why I love her."

The scarlet-draped woman on the other side of the lobby blew Coffey a kiss and everyone applauded.

"It *is* her," Tuck whispered.

"Who her?"

"Laura Byron-Coffey is Laura Byron, teenage star of the *Punkin' Head* horror franchise. Remember? Back in the 1980s—"

"*Punkin' Head?*"

"Yeah, an eternal demon with a pumpkin for a head kills teenagers every Halloween. Great campy horror. I think they made five of them!"

I waved the program. "Your scream queen is a playwright now."

Tucker sniffed. "We'll see."

"Oh, my God! That's who he is—"

"Who *who* is, Clare?"

"Bennie Bennett. The guy who wrote tonight's music was the bandleader on *The Coffey Break* all those years ago. He'd pop in and out of sketches— a real music personality, like Paul Shaffer on the David Letterman show."

Just then, ushers opened the doors, and everyone streamed inside.

The theater had two tiers, but only the bottom section was open. Two hundred or more people quickly found seats, most crowding near the stage. Tuck and I hung back a little, to better observe the crowd.

Almost immediately, the curtains parted and Tina Bird shocked the heck out of me by stepping up to the standing microphone. She introduced herself as the executive producer of Project Nine.

"Sounds like she's lining up her next job," I whispered.

Then Tina surprised me again when she acknowledged her "Uncle Dan and Aunt Laura," in the front row.

Dan Coffey and his wife stood and accepted applause.

"Holy cow," I whispered to Tuck. "Is everyone in show business related to everyone else?"

"Oh, honey." Tucker snorted. "Get used to it!"

Meanwhile, Tina continued with her list of thanks, including the theater, the performers, and everyone who decided to attend. She ended with a special shout-out to Tate Cabot "for his generous help in preparing the final draft of the book."

Tina gestured to a big blond man in the front row.

"That's Tate Cabot?" I whispered, shocked.

Cabot rose to his full six and a half feet, in cowboy boots. I'd noticed him in the lobby, wearing those boots and a Stetson hat, but I had no idea who he was.

The screenwriter now clutched his Stetson with both hands. He also sported distressed denims, a big silver belt buckle, and (like Drew's uncle

Morris) a bolo tie. Cabot humbly accepted the applause from the audience and quickly squeezed into his seat again.

"So *that's* the fired cowriter of *Only Murders in Gotham*?" I whispered to Tucker.

"That's him all right." Tuck read my mind. "I know, I know. As a cowriter on a Jerry Sullivan project, you'd expect less John Wayne and more Woody Allen, wouldn't you? On the other hand, Westerns are in again. And in that getup, Cabot should be a shoo-in for the head writer job on a *Gunsmoke* reboot."

"And now," Tina proclaimed. "I present Project Nine—"

Tina Bird moved stage left and took the mike with her. The curtain opened on a stark set—a couch and a chair on stage right, a kitchen table in a mock kitchen on the left.

"The setting is Arthur Avenue in the Bronx," Tina narrated. "The time is now. Our protagonists are Angela, Loretta, and Maria, three mature wives and mothers who face catastrophe when their husbands are sentenced to twenty-five years to life in a federal penitentiary.

"To feed their families—to simply survive—these remarkable women must take on their husbands' old jobs and become Mafia bosses themselves. And now . . . let's meet the women and hear the music of *Mob Wives: The Musical!*"

A burst of applause greeted the performers. Music played—a canned band but live singers.

The first number—"Fuhgeddaboudit!"—was sung by all three mob wives.

The overly made-up women lamented all they had to endure as "linguine-making baby machines" for their crime boss husbands—

"The late-night calls, the bloodstained clothes," they sang. "The mistresses, my friends deposed!"

The second song went to Angela, the stereotypical "fat Italian wife" who sang "I Drool for Gabagool," a sad tune about food addiction that ended with a lyric borrowed from *The Godfather*—

"Next time I'm gonna leave the gun *and* the cannoli. 'Cause I'm tryin' to lose a few pounds here!"

Loretta crooned about her family's secret shame in the desperate-to-be-poignant ballad "My Ma Was a Goomah."

When the young daughter of one of the mob wives falls for an up-and-coming soldier in a rival crime family, her mother, Maria, sings a heartfelt tune in full, operatic voice titled "Love Is Like Mozzarella"—

"Stretched thin but never breaks. So melty and chewy, it makes your heart ache."

When the curtain came down, I was (once again) speechless. And I wasn't the only one. Poor Tucker looked horrified. As sporadic and polite applause filled the auditorium, he leaned close and whispered—

"Clare, given your Italian-American heritage, let me just say, on behalf of every thespian in New York, I offer my sincerest apologies."

"It's okay, Tuck," I whispered back. "The *Godfather* movies were brilliant, and so was *The Sopranos*. Let's face it, Hollywood has made plenty of money on Italian stereotypes. Why not Broadway?"

"Are you kidding?" he hissed. "This *might* play as a campy cabaret spoof downtown, but not in a legit Broadway house. The critics would savage the fiasco. It would open and close in one week—or less."

"Hey, could that be what they're going for? A *Producers*-like scam? Nathan Lane and Matthew Broderick overselling the financial shares in an awful musical they expect to bomb so they can get rich off a bunch of saps?"

"If only!" Tucker waved his hand. "But look at them; they're completely deluded. They really think this will be a hit."

"Good grief, you're right," I said.

"I know I'm right. And given that lineup of tasteless lyrics, there's really only one song missing."

"What's that?"

"'Springtime for Hitler.'"

Fifty-eight

≈≈≈≈≈≈≈≈≈≈≈≈≈≈≈≈≈≈≈≈≈≈≈≈≈≈≈

"Let's get out of here," I whispered. "I've seen enough."

"Oh, sister, we both have!"

On the sidewalk out front, I returned Tucker's things.

"Would you like to join my dinner party?" he asked as he slipped his sunglasses back into his suit jacket and effortlessly arranged his pocket scarf.

"Thanks," I said, "but I better get back to the shop."

I turned to hail a cab and felt Tucker's hand drop on my shoulder.

"Clare, wait. I know you. And that look."

"What look?"

"An expression somewhere between perplexed and paranoid." He tossed his floppy mop in the direction of the theater we'd just left. "Are you going to tell Jerry about Tina's moonlighting?"

"Given the problems with the production, I think I must. Jerry should know what she's up to. Don't you agree?"

Tucker nodded. "Just be careful."

"What do you mean?"

"Clare, show business runs on two things—in addition to fandom and coffee." He flashed a smile.

"And those are?"

"Money and egos. Jerry Sullivan has plenty of money. That's not a sore point. But . . ." Tuck's smile disappeared. "The man clearly has a highly bruise-able ego."

"What makes you say that?"

"Do you remember that story he told about Billy Saddler and the rafting trip? I'm sure Jerry knew plenty of anecdotes involving Billy, but the one that stuck in his mind—to eulogize the man, no less—was the story where Billy took a cheap shot at Jerry over his failed movie."

"You don't think Jerry told it because he thought it was a good joke?"

"No. I think the reason that story among *all* the others stuck out in Jerry's mind was because it was a raw memory. And it was a raw memory because it was an attack on his ego."

Feeling a little lost, I shook my head. "What exactly are you trying to tell me?"

"That despite appearances, Jerry is not a rock. Like a lot of people in this business, he's really just a big egg with a thin shell. If you're going to tell Jerry Sullivan that he's been duped by an employee, he's not going to take it well. So be prepared. And since he won't appreciate an audience witnessing his embarrassment, be sure to tell him *in private*."

"I'll do my best."

Looking skeptical, Tucker pursed his lips. "Let me give you a Method acting prompt."

"A what?"

"When you talk to Jerry about all this, picture him as Humpty Dumpty sitting on a wall."

"Are you serious?"

"Dead serious."

"You're saying Jerry is a comedian that I *don't* want to crack up?"

"Listen, honey, a person can 'crack up' in more ways than one!"

"True," I said. "Then again, that's what I'm trying to prevent—for all of us."

"I know you are."

"You better get going, Tuck. Good luck with your investor, and I'll do my best to keep Humpty from going over the edge."

"That's my girl."

By the time I returned to the Village Blend, I was surprised to find a perimeter of police barricades set up for the night shoot, complete with a small army of security. Not only those muscle-bound members of Jerry's hired private security but also uniformed members of the NYPD.

I could see bright lights shining around our corner, but the production vehicles and barricades made it impossible to see much more. On top of that, a small but aggressive crowd had gathered in hopes of glimpsing celebrities, and I jostled my way through them.

"Excuse me!" I waved to a security guard. "I'm the craft services manager for this production. My name is Clare Cosi. Would you please let me pass?"

"Just a moment, ma'am." The guard texted a contact inside.

The reply came quickly.

"Sorry, Ms. Cosi, they're rolling. Nobody goes in after they start. And craft services is being managed by a guy named Matt."

"Fine," I told the guard, "but you can't ban me from the building completely. I live on the upper floors."

"If you do, then you know the production company legally leased this property, and I have to follow their instructions. I'd advise you to do the same and find something else to do for the next four hours or so. By then, they should be done filming for the night."

Stepping away from the crowd, I phoned Matt to let him know that I was locked out.

"Why are they filming now?" I demanded. "Sebastian gave everyone a three-hour break. I'm back with time to spare."

"Yes, but *Jerry* wanted to get started, so they shortened the break with no notice, and since you weren't back, I took over."

"I'm sorry, Matt."

"Where did you go so fast? I saw you and Tucker dive into that cab like you were a couple of Keystone Cops going after a bank robber."

"It's a long story—though we *were* in pursuit of a dubious individual."

"Well, tell me about it later. Tonight I'm in charge of the feeding trough as well as the caffeination. And these people drink so much coffee, I think they'd take it through IVs, if I had the equipment."

"I'm sorry I'm not there to help."

"Stop apologizing. I've got it covered. Compared to a day in the bush, this is a walk in the park. Dante volunteered to stay. He's having fun flirting with the girls on the crew and happy to make the overtime money. So take the night off, Clare. You earned it."

"Thanks. I owe you."

"That's right, you do," he teased. "And I'm going to *make sure* you pay me back."

There was glee in my ex-husband's voice, along with the typical Matt risqué insinuation—which reminded me that he was likely having just as much fun flirting with the women on the crew. But before I could manage a wiseass reply, he ended the call.

A night off, I thought to myself. It sounded almost surreal. After the intensity of the last few days, the very idea left me at a mental loose end. But not for long.

Texting Mike, I asked if my favorite NYPD lieutenant was free for dinner. (I wanted to see him, of course, but I was hoping for an update on the Soles and Bass investigation of Fred Denham's murder.)

The answer was a disappointed no. Mike wanted to get away, but he was tied up with a series of meetings at One Police Plaza and promised to check in later because (as he typed in all caps)—

WE NEED TO TALK.

I stared at those four words with apprehension. Mike Quinn would never send that message without a serious subject in mind.

I asked if he wanted to FaceTime now, but he begged off, texting that he had important info to share, and it was best to do it in person. Agreeing to meet later, he ended the chat.

That left me with one more throw of the dice.

"Hello, Madame?"

"Clare, my dear! What a pleasant surprise."

"Are you back from the Hamptons?"

"As of last evening. I'm so relieved to be back in the city. That ocean air is fresh but freezing at this time of year! I'm in my penthouse as we speak."

"What do you think of a girls' night out?"

"If you and I are *the girls*, I think it's a fabulous idea."

"Me too."

Madame paused. "You sound a little tense, Clare. Is there a purpose for our night out, other than camaraderie?"

"Now that you mention it, I'd like to know more about Jerry Sullivan. It's important, given what I'm discovering."

"You're curious about his early years, aren't you? The years he won't talk about—that terrible Dan Coffey incident."

"Incident? What incident? And why was it terrible?"

"I'll tell you about it, dear, but right now I'm famished. I'm perfectly willing to dish, but I need something on my plate first."

"That's the best idea I've heard all night."

Fifty-nine

~~~~~~

Two hours later, Madame, elegant as always in a vintage Dior sheath, was sipping an artisanal cocktail twenty-six floors above First Avenue.

"So, my dear, what is it you'd like to know? Now that we've cleaned our plates, I'm ready to dish . . ."

The plate cleaning, I had to admit, was pure pleasure.

I'd gulped down the bar's French onion sliders with roasted garlic mayo and a side of truffle fries while Madame had gone for the duck confit spring rolls, truffle mushroom ravioli, potato bites layered with crème fraîche, caviar, and chives, *and* the tiramisu for dessert. (She did say she was famished!)

We inhaled our dinner sitting side by side on a red banquette, overlooking the glittering grandeur of the city from atop the Beekman Tower, a landmark Art Deco building designed with Gothic attitude.

In my black sweater and slacks, I looked more like the help than a posh customer, but Madame had brought one of her chic hand-embroidered Kashmiri shawls and draped it around me with panache. (Problem solved.)

Ironically, the last time I was on this glass-enclosed Grand Terrace, I *was* the help. (The space was often rented for private parties, and the Village Blend had catered several.) Since then, the ownership had changed, and the terrace relaunched as a public cocktail lounge by the name of Ophelia.

The naming could have been ironic, given the original purpose of the hotel, which was to house sorority girls. Taking in the converted solarium's dazzling view of the city's East Side, I couldn't help reflecting on the Shakespearean reference to Hamlet's doomed girlfriend.

Having suffered the pain of the Danish prince's cruel indifference,

Ophelia would have likely jumped from this height rather than ended her life underwater. Then again, the bar's elaborate cocktails could have given the lovesick young woman the option to drown her sorrows, instead of herself.

That rather depressing thought brought me back to the deflating duplicitousness of Tina Bird—and the surprise of her relationship to "Uncle Dan" Coffey.

After bringing Madame up to speed with everything I'd witnessed this evening, including the lamentable lyrics of *Mob Wives: The Musical!*, I had to ask—

"What can you tell me about Jerry's past? I know decades ago he and Dan Coffey were a comedy team, and they worked together on Dan's old TV show—"

"*The Coffey Break*," Madame cut in with a pained look on her face. "Yes, I know all about it, I'm afraid."

"It's the '*I'm afraid*' part that bothers me," I said. "That's why I need you to dish. I understand Jerry refuses to talk about his early years, including *The Coffey Break*—why the show was canceled so abruptly and why he and Dan Coffey split as a comedy team. So what happened? And why won't anyone talk about it?"

"No one likes to recall bad memories, Clare, especially when they behaved badly. As for me, it was a heartbreaking moment in show business history, and it grieved me to have a front row seat for it. You see, the terrible split between the two happened on the very night their show was taken off the air forever. And it happened, I'm sorry to say, at our Village Blend."

"Really?" I was surprised to hear it, but I wanted to hear all of it. "How did Jerry and Dan get together in the first place?"

"From the beginning, then," Madame said, pausing to sip her drink. "I first met Jerry when he began doing stand-up comedy in the Village. I noticed him the very first day he came into the shop. He was such a handsome young man, yet his hair was prematurely silver. His look was quite striking, and his smile was—well, it was dazzling."

"It still is," I said.

Madame nodded. "Jerry worked hard on his act. He would perform at two or three comedy clubs a night and camp out at the Village Blend between sets." She smiled at the memory. "He'd often nap in one of our upstairs armchairs, and he'd ask me to wake him in time to make his next gig."

That struck me as odd. "Don't comedians usually hang out with other comedians between shows and sets?"

"Not Jerry. Though he was hardly a misanthrope, he didn't make friends easily. For someone who chose to be a performer, he was a very private individual. Eventually, over time, Jerry began treating me like his bartender. I got to know the young man very well. We became close friends."

Madame sighed. "I learned that Jerry wasn't good at being Jerry. He was only comfortable onstage—in character, as he put it. And he continually doubted his own abilities, though anyone could see that he was extremely talented."

"I don't doubt the talent part," I said, "but if he didn't interact much with other comedians, then how did he and Dan Coffey become a team?"

"Believe it or not, their collaboration began with an onstage fight at a comedy club."

"An actual fight, or an elaborate act?"

"It was no act," Madame asserted. "The act came later."

"What happened?"

"It was a Saturday night, and the club was packed. Both comedians were promised an eight-minute spot, but at the end of the night the master of ceremonies reneged, insisting there was only time for one comedian, and they had to work it out between them who would take the final time slot.

"Dan and Jerry *both* rushed the stage and fought for the microphone. Then they began trading insults. The audience thought it was an act, and because they got the best laughs of the entire night, the owner asked them to repeat it the next evening, and the night after that, and within a few weeks a comedy partnership was born."

Madame signaled for a fresh cocktail—and another rosé cider for me.

"After that, Jerry brought Dan with him to the Village Blend, but there was no more napping between sets. The pair became fast friends, cracking each other up. I brewed their coffee while they brewed up new routines, feeding off each other's imagination. And the coffeehouse was the perfect place for them, not just because of Dan's last name. Jerry confided that Dan Coffey was a reformed alcoholic, which is why he didn't like to hang out at the comedy club bars. Jerry didn't drink much, either. The two really were simpatico."

"How did they get a national TV show?"

"It happened fast. They'd been working together only a few months when a network executive caught their act—the head of prime-time programming, no less, a man named Fletcher Ulmer. He was looking to fill a summer spot on his network's schedule. He thought Dan and Jerry would work well, and cheaply, and that's how *The Coffey Break* was born."

"I saw the show when I was pretty young, and I assumed Dan Coffey was the star and Jerry Sullivan was his sidekick. But it sounds like they began as equal partners. I'm surprised Jerry allowed the show to be named after Dan."

"Jerry allowed a lot of things to happen that he didn't like or approve of—for a while, anyway."

"Such as?"

"Well, because Coffey was older and shrewder about the rewards of 'managing up,' he put in the time and effort to schmooze the network brass, and that's how he ended up with the titular role, even though Jerry did as much writing and performing as Dan."

"Is that why they fought? Over billing?"

"Oh, no." Madame shook her head. "Jerry didn't care about that. He only cared about making the audience laugh and whether the show was good enough. He agonized over it, and that's ultimately what led to the show's end—a bitter end to be sure."

"That sounds ominous. What happened exactly?"

"First you must remember that the show was broadcast live, with a few pretaped segments. It was a hit from the start. But *The Coffey Break* was also edgy. So edgy that one of the sponsors threatened to pull out. After the fifth episode, the network brass clamped down and insisted that all sketches be approved before they aired. Jerry told me that he hated watching his prime material being ground up into homogenized hamburger."

"What about Dan?"

Madame shrugged. "Dan didn't care about the oversight. He simply wanted to make the executives happy and have their show renewed for another thirteen episodes. But the tamer and less timely the sketches got, the less funny they were, and the ratings began to decline. Not by much, but enough so that Jerry became furious about the network censorship. Finally, on the night of their ninth show, he did something about it."

"Did Jerry and Dan air a sketch that wasn't approved?"

"That's what happened. But it was Jerry who did it. Dan didn't know a thing about it."

"How could that be?"

"As I said, the show was mostly live, but some segments were pretaped. Jerry's rejected sketch had been recorded on videotape, and he found a way to switch it with the approved one."

"What happened after that?"

Madame shook her head. "When Jerry's unapproved sketch aired, the fallout was devastating, for everyone."

"Go on. I want to hear every detail you can remember."

"All right, dear. Well, let's see . . . at the end of every broadcast, the cast and crew had a tradition of gathering at the Village Blend for a wrap party. Some of them brought their own flasks to sweeten the coffee, but I always turned a blind eye—just as I did on that hot night in August when they wrapped their final show—not that anyone knew it *was* their final show. Not at first . . ."

As she spoke, Madame stared into the distance, looking past the glittering skyscrapers toward the memories of her own past.

Sixty

The Village Blend
Many decades ago . . .

"BLANCHE, *ma belle amie!*"

A grinning Jerry Sullivan pushed through the coffeehouse door.

The slim woman with striking violet eyes stepped around the marble-topped coffee bar, returning his greeting with a smile.

"*Tu es en retard, mon amour,*" she said, retying her blueberry apron. "Your friends are already here."

"I know I'm late. Wardrobe change. Plus, those streets are pretty crowded for midnight. Don't people ever sleep?"

The newcomer, tall with an athletic build and silver-white hair, spread his arms wide to show off his untucked powder blue polo shirt.

Blanche Dreyfus Allegro folded her arms. "It appears you've joined the smart set."

Jerry waved away the compliment. "They wouldn't have me."

Blanche ran her fingers through her lush dark hair. Then she reached for an empty tray to clear a few tables. Jerry stopped her by taking her hand.

"You look absolutely delicious tonight, Blanche. Far too tasty to be a busboy."

Laughing, he took the slim, statuesque woman in his arms, spun her, and then caught Blanche in a clinch, until they were face-to-face.

"That's quite enough of that, Mr. Sullivan," Blanche said as she detached herself. "My, I've never seen you so exuberant. Did you imbibe on the cab ride down?"

"I'm high on life," Jerry cracked, adding a flutter-lipped Bronx cheer. "So give us a kiss, then!"

"I most certainly will not." Pushing her dark bangs away from her eyes, Blanche laughed through her mock outrage. "Why, I'm a respectable shop owner. And I'm old enough to be your—"

"Spectacularly attractive aunt who's not afraid to wear a miniskirt? Or perhaps my hot Parisian high school teacher, itching to show this innocent boy the ways of the red-light district?"

Blanche flattened her hand against his chest. "Or the way out the door if you're not careful."

Hiding a smile, she smoothed her short skirt and immediately changed the subject.

"The backstage crew and the performers are upstairs, and the band is over in the corner. But Dan's not here yet. Everyone's in very good spirits, I've noticed."

"They should be. Tonight's was the best show yet, and it went off without a hitch. And speaking of spirits, I'll need an Americano, *tout de suite, s'il vous plaît.* 'Cause it's been a long, exhausting day!"

Blanche snapped her fingers, and Nero, a burly barista who hailed from Sicily, went to work.

Jerry waved to someone climbing the spiral staircase, then accepted the coffee from the big man. He took a sip and grinned.

"I just spotted Andre from makeup. I'll bet he can Irish this up for me."

Blanche cocked her head.

"I'm sorry. I didn't quite catch that last part. And before you repeat yourself, please remember that the Village Blend does not have a license to serve liquor."

"I won't call the cops. I'm no rat." Jerry ran two fingers across his lips. "Not a peep, zipped forever."

Suddenly, a short, sallow man in a loud Hawaiian shirt slapped Jerry on the back.

"Hell of a show, Jerry. The guys, they all loved it."

"Thanks, Bennie. So, your bandmates are here?"

"Sure, Jerry. Every one of them."

"I hope to God they didn't bring their instruments—" Realizing the implied insult, he immediately switched tone. "I mean, you guys can't top tonight's performance. Your brass section's high notes gave me a nosebleed."

Bennie slapped Jerry again. "Always a barrel of laughs." The bandleader scanned the room. "Hey, where's Dan? He should have been here by now."

"As I was leaving the studio, Dan the man got summoned upstairs."

"To the executive suite? What for?"

"I imagine he's about to get a tongue-lashing from the Mrs. Grundy who runs Standards and Practices." Stifling a yawn, Jerry shrugged. "Listening to self-righteous blowhards is the price you pay for having your name on the masthead, I suppose."

Bennie's brow furrowed. "I'll bet it's over that corporate executive sketch. But you don't have to worry about S&P since the network approved the script, right?"

"Yeah, well . . . they sort of approved it," Jerry mumbled and looked away.

Bennie frowned. "What do you mean *sort of*?"

A young man descended the spiral staircase, only to stop halfway when he spied Jerry.

"Well, if it isn't F.U.!" The young man nearly doubled over with laughter. "How's it hanging, F.U.?" he bellowed in a voice loud enough to fill the coffeehouse.

The combination of those two innocent letters was toxic. At a table beside the French doors, a middle-aged woman and her companion looked up from their cappuccinos, clearly annoyed.

"Cool it, Gavin," Jerry hissed. "Not everybody's in on our joke."

Minutes later, Blanche was at the coffeehouse door bidding a regular good night when Dan Coffey appeared. Heavyset, with a round rubber face and thick, powerful arms, the television host looked more like a professional bouncer than a comedian. As he approached, he pushed through the nighttime crowd like a running back on the gridiron.

"Good evening, Dan," Blanche said, holding the door open.

There was no reply. Instead of his usual jovial greeting, Dan Coffey stared right through her. His ever-present Howdy Doody smile had been replaced by an angry grimace. His face was sweaty and flushed; even his bald patch, circled by a damp halo of hair, had gone red.

"Dan? Is something wrong?"

She touched his arm. He didn't pull away or brush her off. Dan Coffey was so fixated on finding one particular individual, he wasn't even aware he'd been touched.

In that perfectly ill-timed moment, Jerry rose from the band's table and crossed to the coffee bar for a caffeinated refill. Dan spied him and charted his target.

Jerry turned—soon enough to see the blow coming but without enough time to avoid it. Dan's meaty fist connected with Jerry's head in a resounding smack. Jerry slammed against the marble bar, his espresso cup shattering on the floor.

Suddenly, the coffeehouse was silent, the witnesses as stunned by the blow as Jerry.

Pushing away from the bar, Jerry whirled. "What the hell was that for?"

Instead of a reply, Dan roared as he body-slammed Jerry, pinning him against the edge of the bar. The air shot out of Jerry's lungs in a harsh rasp. Then Dan Coffey wrapped his big hands around Jerry's neck.

"Stop!" Blanche cried as she thrust herself between the tangling men. With a powerful shrug of his broad shoulders, Dan knocked Blanche to the floor.

The room exploded. With chairs overturning, Bennie and his bandmates jumped to their feet and literally pried Dan loose from the gasping Jerry. As soon as he caught his breath, an enraged Jerry launched himself at the already restrained Dan.

Jerry was quickly restrained in turn by Nero, the burly barista, who'd leaped over the bar and wrapped his thick arms around the comedian.

Jerry raged helplessly. "You son of a—"

"Funny man!" Dan spat. "Yes sir, F.U. Whatever you say, F.U. That is so F.U.!"

It took Blanche a moment to realize two things—first, that her nose was seeping blood. And second, that the furious star of *The Coffey Break* was quoting from tonight's show, specifically a sketch featuring Jerry, in which he played a network executive with the initials F.U. Pacing back and forth in his executive suite, F.U. pompously pontificated absolutely awful ideas for his network television shows while toadies responded as if they were hearing the most brilliant concepts ever uttered, all while sporadically shouting the executive's initials to great comic effect.

While Jerry's sketch was edgy, it was also hilarious, the kind of bawdy material teenagers and college students recited at parties and adults chuckled over around watercoolers the next day.

But Dan didn't care. He told Jerry he'd landed in scorching hot water because of it.

As Blanche tried to make sense of his fury—and stop her nosebleed with a stack of Village Blend napkins—Jerry shook off Nero's grip.

"Are you telling me you're this bent out of shape about another lecture from Standards and Practices? Just last week you said S and P stood for 'stupid and pointless.' Come on, Dan. If we listened to the suits, we'd be a laugh-free zone!"

Bennie's bandmates released Dan. He didn't lunge at Jerry again, though his nostrils flared like a maddened bull. Instead, Dan just glared at his partner.

"Do you really want to listen to the executive suite?" Jerry stroked his bruised and swelling cheek. "Those guys wouldn't know a joke if it bit them on the ass."

"S and P wasn't there, Jerry. When I got to my office, the head of network programming and two serious-looking lawyers were waiting for me—"

Surprised, Jerry managed a grunt.

"Yeah, you heard right. Fletcher Ulmer. F.U. himself. The president of prime-time programming. And guess what, Jerry? F as in Fletcher and U as in Ulmer *got* the joke. And old F.U. thinks *you* bit *him* on the ass."

Jerry's face fell even further. "You got reamed, then?"

"You could say that. I explained that you and Gavin made the tape, and I hadn't even screened it before it was aired—"

Jerry interrupted. "Of course you didn't screen it. You and Bennie were too focused on this week's *Lean on Louey* segment. That one-joke sketch got tired two shows ago. How many times are you going to pretend to beat on Bennie, huh—"

Dan talked over him.

"—Me, Ulmer, and the lawyers discovered something. The F.U. sketch was *rejected* by the network, but you switched the tapes anyway."

"The bit was funny! They were wrong!"

Blanche thought Dan was going to lunge again, but self-control prevailed.

"So," Jerry said. "What were the lawyers for? Is the FCC going to fine the network?"

Dan's gaze narrowed. "Those lawyers worked for the network, Jerry. They were there to dot all the i's and cross all the t's. That's *t* as in termination."

A collective gasp erupted from the musicians, cast members, and backstage crew surrounding them. Dan turned his back on Jerry and faced the crowd.

"That's right, gang. As of tonight, *The Coffey Break* is officially *canceled*. We've been yanked from the air. You, me, Bennie, and the band, the rest of the cast and crew, makeup, continuity, the director—you're all out of work—"

As Dan headed for the exit, he jerked his thumb in Jerry's direction.

"—and never forget you have that arrogant, scene-stealing *prima donna* to thank for it."

Sixty-one

࿅࿅࿅࿅࿅࿅࿅࿅࿅࿅࿅࿅࿅࿅࿅࿅࿅࿅

As my mentor concluded her story, I leaned back. She'd put me on the edge of our red banquette with her devastating tale of a shattered friendship.

"What happened after Dan left?"

Madame sighed. "Jerry tried to give a pep talk. He promised to save the show, that he would go to Fletcher Ulmer on bended knee and apologize. He said if that wasn't enough he'd take responsibility and fall on his own sword to save everyone's job.

"Of course, no one believed Jerry could change a thing, and they were correct. When Jerry went to the network offices, he was barred from entry. And though he begged for a meeting, Fletcher Ulmer refused to see him."

She paused to drain her drink. "It was too late to save the show anyway. The Hollywood press and New York papers were quick to publish news of *The Coffey Break*'s abrupt cancellation and why—the network's version, of course."

"And the network's version was . . . ?"

"They claimed the ratings were 'down' for the second week in a row, even though it amounted to something like half a point. *The Coffey Break* was replaced by reruns of a medical drama called *LA Metro General*."

"How did Jerry take it?"

"Hard, I'm sure. But I never found out. We'd been close before that horrible August night. After the show was canceled, and all hopes for a bright future *seemingly* lost, Jerry stopped coming to the Village Blend. He and Dan never even paid their wrap party tabs, which they'd run up with me for weeks. I got stuck with their IOUs. Later, I heard Jerry had moved to the West Coast."

Madame sadly shook her head. "He didn't even stop in to say goodbye."

I saw disappointment—or was it hurt?—in Madame's violet eyes. Yet strangely, I found myself rising to Jerry's defense.

"You know he must have been devastated," I said. "And humiliated. He was probably too ashamed to show his face again."

Madame nodded. "Since we reconnected, Jerry has said as much. And I do confess, after his feature film career took off, he sent me a very big check with a very big box of long-stemmed roses. But to be honest, I was hardly the only one to suffer from his rash decision. Everyone in the cast and crew lost their jobs, and many struggled for years. Dan Coffey never managed to resurrect his career to the same level, no matter how hard he tried."

"Did he try? I thought Coffey pulled the whole Greta Garbo 'I want to be alone' thing."

"Not true, Clare. Dan tried to make a comeback in television, but he was thwarted."

"How?"

"Fletcher Ulmer was a vindictive man and did everything he could to make sure Dan never worked at his network again."

"And Jerry?"

"He managed to escape Ulmer's wrath, perhaps because he immediately fled to the West Coast. Out of sight, out of mind, as they say.

"Dan Coffey continued to work the New York comedy circuit and managed to land some guest-starring roles in television shows—not on Ulmer's network. Jerry, on the other hand, stayed out of the limelight for several years. He carefully avoided TV appearances while he honed his skills in West Coast and Las Vegas clubs. Building on that success, Jerry made fresh Hollywood connections and launched his career as a writer and star of feature films."

"What happened to Fletcher Ulmer? Is he still around?"

"Ulmer retired," Madame said, unable to stop the little smile from gracing her face. "And, as Jerry likes to tell it, F.U. died of a stroke on a golf course when he heard Jerry's debut feature opened number one at the box office. The rest, of course, is entertainment history."

"Only to a point," I noted. "Clearly, this history isn't over. And from what I saw tonight, I'd say we're on a train ride to another collision between Jerry and Dan."

"If we are, then what do you propose we do about that?"

"I think I should speak to Jerry. Don't you? Tell him about Tina Bird and her relationship to Dan Coffey."

"Just be careful, Clare."

"That's what Tucker said. He wants me to think of Jerry as a big egg with a thin shell. Like Humpty Dumpty on a wall." I laughed at the "Method acting" prompt, but Madame looked as dead serious as my assistant manager.

"Tucker's a wise young man," she said. "Don't forget, I witnessed a man crack one night, all those years ago."

"You mean Dan Coffey?"

"That's right. It was Dan's name on the marquee, so to speak. Back then, he was the Humpty on the wall. And when *The Coffey Break* broke, the network sent Dan crashing to the ground. Now, all these years later, it's Jerry who's on the wall, high up and vulnerable."

"Okay, I hear you. I'll be careful."

"And so you should. The night Dan cracked, I ended up with a bloody nose. Thank goodness for the band and Nero, who kept the men apart. Otherwise, I think they might have killed each other."

Those last words gave me pause. "Do you think Dan still wants to kill Jerry? Could it be Dan causing these set accidents? Using his niece, Tina, to exact payback for all those years ago?"

"I honestly don't know. Dan certainly has a motive to hurt Jerry. Seeing him filming a hit streaming show back here in New York—and at the Village Blend, no less—well, it must be galling."

"Has Jerry said anything at all to you about what's happening now?"

"Nothing. We don't talk about the past, and he doesn't like to talk about his personal life. So there's not much to say, anymore. Just superficial pleasantries. Flirtations and small talk."

"How can we crack that wall, I wonder?"

"I did it once. As his barista. But I'm not Jerry's barista anymore." She gave me a wily smile. "*You* are."

"Me?"

"Of course." Madame leaned closer. "Jerry is still a very private man, but at some point everyone needs someone to talk to, so why not you?"

"But, given all your warnings—"

"Talk to the man, Clare. That was your plan, and it's a good one. The only way to help Jerry Sullivan is to talk to him and listen. Given what you've uncovered, and what you've pried out of me, you might be the only person who can do it."

Sixty-two

I EXITED Madame's car as close to the Village Blend as her driver could get me, which turned out to be two blocks away. She stifled a yawn before pecking my cheek and wishing me—

"Sweet dreams."

Recalling the nightmare of Jerry's hands around my throat, I didn't take that wish lightly. I also knew no dreams would be forthcoming for quite a while.

Though she'd invited me to spend the night at her penthouse, I was anxious to speak with Jerry about Tina Bird's extracurricular activities and expected to catch the comic star when his night shoot finally ended.

Hoping the production team would call it quits early (since they'd started sooner than expected), I flagged a security guard, a different one this time, but (alas) I received the same answer.

They were still rolling, and I was locked out.

With more time to kill, I texted Mike Quinn again. Those four words he'd sent came back to me: WE NEED TO TALK. He claimed he had some kind of information to share—and whatever it was, he wouldn't do it over the phone.

This time, luck was with me. He texted that he was right up the street, and I quickly headed up Hudson and hung a right on 10th.

THE brightly lit Sixth Precinct was busy tonight with cops and civilians filing in and out of the squat Bauhaus building's glass doors—a parade of drunk and disorderlies, domestic disputes, stolen car victims, and other typical activities of a Manhattan evening.

"Hey, Coffee Lady!"

The desk sergeant greeted me with a wave, and I returned it. Most of the Sixth's officers and detectives were regulars at the Village Blend, and I sometimes brought treats for them when I visited Mike.

Tonight, however, I was forced to come empty-handed, but they didn't hold it against me. As I crossed the lobby, uniformed officers called out greetings, and so did the plainclothes detectives that I passed going up the stairs.

Mike's OD Squad was headquartered here, in one section of the precinct's second floor, where his elite team of detectives shared desks around their lieutenant's corner office.

I waved to the two young detectives who were on duty tonight. Sergeant Franco was busy on the phone with paperwork in front of him, but he nodded in greeting, as did Detective DeMarco, who emphatically pointed me toward his commanding officer's lair.

I already knew the way, but the pointing told me that Mike was eager to talk. I found him busy on the phone, so I stood in the open doorway until he noticed me. When he waved me in, I closed the office door.

Mike looked tired. His suit jacket was off, but his leather shoulder holster remained strapped to his strong shoulders, leaving wrinkles in his white dress shirt. His tie was firmly knotted, but I suspected he was dying to loosen it and end his day.

Me? With one look at Mike's strong jaw, blue eyes, and powerful body, I was suddenly dying to end my own. I pictured my four-poster bed with him in it, close to me, under the covers. Too bad the blinds on his glass walls were open, which meant we had no privacy, so I kept my distance—even though I would have loved to cross the room, take his face in my hands, and gently brush my lips across his.

The look on my face must have given away the direction of my thoughts, because Mike—who was still on the phone—suddenly stopped talking.

When our gazes met, I slowly smiled.

"Uh, yeah. I'm here." Mike's deep voice had turned gravelly. "Sorry I was ah—*distracted* a moment . . ."

He returned my smile with a little one of his own and quickly finished his call.

"Hi, Clare," he said.

"Hi, Mike."

"You see those blinds on the window behind you?" he asked.

"Yeah."

"Do me a favor and close them."

Sixty-three

∿∿∿∿∿∿∿∿∿∿∿∿∿∿∿∿∿∿∿

AFTER a sweet private greeting, Mike broke contact between us with a tantalizing promise, against my lips, that he'd continue what he'd started—at a later hour and a more appropriate location.

He was right, of course, and I straightened my sweater, moved around his desk, and took a seat.

"Okay, Lieutenant," I said, doing my best to catch my breath and shake my head clear. "You wanted to talk?"

Mike nodded, leaning forward in his chair. "I have some information. It's not going to be made public, because we believe it involves a crime."

"Against whom?"

"Billy Saddler, the celebrity comedian who collapsed at that rooftop restaurant party. We initially believed Mr. Saddler overdosed on Funtenol."

"*Initially* believed. What do you mean? You don't believe that anymore?"

"Toxicology returned an unexpected result, strongly leading us in the direction of another theory."

"And what is that?"

"Mr. Saddler may have been the victim of a crime."

"What crime exactly?"

"Homicide."

The word left me speechless, but not for long.

First, I grilled Mike about those toxicology results, which (he explained) involved a fatal dose of *fentanyl*. Not the stimulant Funtenol, but the dangerous opioid that it was obviously named after. Fifty times more powerful than heroin, fentanyl was a drug that had killed countless thousands already. And now it had killed Billy Saddler.

I asked why Mike didn't believe Billy took the drug himself.

"Because we tested all the Funtenol that we confiscated at the party. Not a single piece was laced with fentanyl. We believe someone slipped the drug to Billy without his knowing. We can't prove it. Not yet, but that's what we suspect . . ."

Mike's questioning then turned to what I knew about Billy Saddler's involvement with the Jerry Sullivan show. And I shared all I knew, including possible motives for sabotage from a number of individuals.

Next, Mike opened a file with enlarged photos from Billy's party—photos that Detective Sanchez took undercover *before* the police arrived.

Using me as a witness, he asked me to identify anyone I was able to recognize. He took notes as I pointed out every player I knew—especially those who had a possible motive for sabotaging Jerry's show.

At the end of it, Mike once again proposed placing an undercover detective on my craft services team. This time I agreed. Given these dangerous new developments, I could no longer argue against it.

"Sergeant Franco?" I assumed.

Mike shook his head. "Franco might be recognized from the party. He went in as a cop. But Detective Sanchez never broke cover. He's a good man, Clare. You'll get along well with him."

We talked about the murder of Fred Denham, too, but it was clear that no viable leads had presented themselves in that investigation.

Since the dead man's wallet and phone remained missing, Soles and Bass agreed to seek a warrant to review any mobile data saved in the cloud. But while they waited for that data, they were *still* aggressively pursuing their Central Park mugging theory.

When our discussion was finally exhausted, I left the precinct without Mike. He had work to do with Sergeant Franco and Detective DeMarco, and I needed to get back to the Village Blend before Jerry left the set.

More than ever now, Jerry Sullivan and I needed to talk, and not just about Billy Saddler and Tina Bird.

In those photos from Billy Saddler's party, I pointed out people I'd expected to see—

Sebastian Albee

Kylee Ferris

Tweety Bird

Drew Merriweather

But there were three more attendees to that fatal bash who surprised me—

The first was Morris Windham, Jr., from the Winner Hotel and Casino. His family lost millions because of Jerry's decision to jump through a contractual loophole to star in his own streaming show.

The second person I was surprised to see was Lizzy Meeks. Like Sebastian, Kylee, Tweety, and Drew, Lizzy had left the party before the police arrived. But—

Since Lizzy had been banned from the *Only Murders in Gotham* set, I was shocked to see her at all. *Did she crash the party?* I wondered. *Or did someone bring her along as a guest?*

Another photo revealed a possible answer—

In a corner of the restaurant, Lizzy was having a cozy head-to-head discussion with a big blond man, the very same man I'd seen earlier this evening at that Broadway theater.

It was Tate Cabot, the cowboy-booted, Stetson hat–wearing Texas writer Jerry had fired off his hit show.

Sixty-Four

∽⃝∾⃝∽⃝∾⃝∽⃝∾⃝∽⃝∾⃝∽⃝∾⃝∽⃝∾⃝∽⃝∾⃝∽⃝∾⃝∽⃝∾⃝∽⃝∾⃝

After leaving Mike at the precinct, I returned to the coffeehouse to find the night shoot wrapped and the production crew gone. Only Jerry and Tina had remained for a private talk, but by the time I arrived it sounded more like World War Three.

"NO, TINA. ABSOLUTELY NOT!"

"Take it easy, Jerry. Will you LISTEN TO REASON!"

"Tina, you have no idea what you're saying. NO IDEA!"

Watching the pair fight, I felt as though I'd stepped back in time. Madame's description of how Jerry Sullivan and Dan Coffey nearly killed each other, in this very shop, seemed to be playing out anew. Only this time it was a much older Jerry and Dan's much younger niece.

"Just hear me out!" Tina begged. "Uncle Dan said you and he haven't talked in a long time. And this is the perfect solution for the show."

"Perfectly *insane*. There is no way. NO WAY!"

"Stop this!" Tina demanded. "You're being unreasonable!"

"NO WAY! NO HOW! NO WAY!"

Jerry was raging. His pale skin was flushed red; his eyes were practically popping out of his head. *Just like my nightmare*, I thought, and feared he was going to put his hands on Tina—who stupidly couldn't see him cracking and refused to back down.

I had to do something.

"HELLO, THERE!" I called. "Would anyone like a fresh, hot cup of coffee?"

The pair froze in place and blinked at me like a married couple embarrassed to be caught in an ugly public argument.

"You know what?" Jerry said, turning away from Tina. "I'd *love* one. Thank you, Clare."

As Jerry headed to the coffee bar, Tina, who was still wearing her silver pantsuit from the Broadway investor event, stood her ground and said—

"I don't want coffee. And I am not talking to *you* in front of *her*!"

"Too bad, Tweety," Jerry shot back, "because I love Clare's coffee, and I need a break. So if you want to keep chirping, do it somewhere else."

Clenching her small hands into fists, Tina glared at me, threw back her shoulders, and stormed out the door. I kept a wary eye on her yellow pixie head as it bobbed toward the wardrobe trailer and disappeared inside. Then I moved behind the counter and told Jerry—

"I'm flattered you like my coffee so much. One special bulletproof?"

"Not tonight," he said, settling in at the bar. "Give me an Americano."

"Sure, no problem . . ."

As I prepared Jerry's drink, and a double espresso for myself, I remembered Tucker's prompt and tried to picture my favorite comedian as a big egg, sitting on the edge, before I ever so carefully asked—

"Was that argument, by any chance, about Tina's moonlighting? Did she confess it to you? Or did someone else tell you?"

"Tell me what? I'm not following you."

I cleared my throat and bravely informed Jerry that I had followed Tina to the investors' preview in the Theater District.

Jerry waved his hand. "Oh, I knew about that."

"You did?"

"Sure. She cleared it with me, ages ago. That show's a real turkey, isn't it? Holy cow-patty, if there was ever a stink bomb ready to go off—"

"Wait. You knew about the show? But you *couldn't* have known Tina was Dan Coffey's niece?"

"Sure, I knew."

"You did?"

"You're surprised."

"Yes, very. Madame told me about the history between you and Dan. I thought you two never talked again."

"We never did. But what can I say? Tina was a fantastic production manager during our first season. That's why I didn't fire her after I found out about her relationship to Dan. She hired and trained a crack assistant, who helps out whenever she has to leave the set for her work on that theatrical catastrophe she's hoping to produce. Once it bombs, she'll be back, fully focused, for our third season. Of this, I have no doubt."

"You have a third season approved already?"

"Sure do. We're already casting for it."

"Then why were you two arguing?"

"With Billy gone, we're in dire need of a replacement guest star with a name, someone who can keep the publicity buzz going in the later episodes of the season. I wanted Marty Long, but he's tied up filming a feature. We can't wait six months. We needed somebody yesterday. And tonight Tina proposed a solution. She wants me to hire her uncle Dan."

"Dan Coffey? She wants you two to team up again?"

"That's right. She hit me in the face with it like a rubber chicken."

"You know we have one in our memorabilia. Signed by Dom DeLuise."

That cracked Jerry up—in a good way.

When he was done chuckling, I passed him his Americano. He sipped with happy relief, then slumped on the counter, resting his head on his arms.

"So good. Thanks, Clare."

"Savor the good, Jerry. Because I have some not-so-good news."

He let out a comic moan. "Have mercy, woman. I don't think I can take it."

"You'll have to, I'm afraid. For your own good. And the good of your production."

"All right. Hit me—just don't use Dom's rubber chicken."

Sixty-Five

After taking the seat at the bar next to him, I downed a fortifying dose of my freshly pulled double espresso and began breaking the bad news as gently as I could.

"I learned something unsettling tonight . . ."

Jerry buried his face in his arms. Then he flapped one hand for me to continue.

"The police believe Billy Saddler may have been murdered."

"Murdered?" Jerry sat up. "How?"

When I told him the details of the fentanyl poisoning, he shook his head. "You've got to be kidding me. Is *everyone* completely ignorant of comedy history?"

"Excuse me?"

"John Belushi, *Saturday Night Live* superstar, dead at the age of thirty-three from a *speedball*—a stimulant and opioid *intentionally* mixed together for a special kind of high."

"You think Billy took fentanyl intentionally? A drug that's fifty times more powerful than heroin?"

"Billy has struggled with drug addiction his whole life. I thought he'd kicked it, but clearly he landed in New York wanting to party like the old days, and he just couldn't handle it anymore. He fell off the wagon in a spectacularly stupid way. Or he got a bad piece of that other party drug, and he didn't know it was laced. Tragic, yes. Murder? No."

We're back to that, I thought in frustration. Jerry was trying to sweep the bad thing under the rug, cover it up and forget it, like everything else.

Nevertheless, for the next ten minutes, I told Jerry everything I knew about the trouble on his set, along with the motives for sabotaging it. He brushed everything off as "pranks" or "screwups."

"Jerry, I have to tell you something else you aren't going to like."

He grabbed his hair. "You're killing me, Clare."

"Jerry, believe me when I tell you, *that's* what I'm trying to prevent."

"Fine. I'm listening."

"I know Tina Bird was at Billy Saddler's party."

"Yeah? So were a lot of people."

"A lot of people aren't suddenly proposing that their uncle Dan take Billy's place in a hit streaming show."

"Wait a minute, wait a minute. You're saying—"

"Maybe Tina didn't mean to kill Billy, but she could have slipped him something that she thought would send him into the hospital for a while or get him in trouble with the law—enough fentanyl to take him out of the show."

"What you're telling me is outrageous!"

"What I'm telling you is Tina has a motive. She may have been the one to tip off the police, which tells me she didn't mean to kill Billy. She just wanted to get him into trouble."

Jerry shook his head. "You have quite the imagination."

"You obviously don't agree with my theory."

"That's just it. You have a theory—and no proof. The police don't, either, or I'd be talking to them."

"I'm sure the detectives on the case will want to talk with you—and the others who were at that party."

"That's fine. And I'll tell them what I'm telling you. Billy was a former drug addict who fell off the wagon and tragically died."

"So you don't suspect Tina?"

"No."

"What about Lizzy Meeks?"

"Lizzy? Why?"

"She was at the party, too."

"That's odd." He sat back. "She must have crashed it."

"Or come with someone else."

"Aaah!" Jerry jumped in his seat.

"What is it? What's wrong?"

He shuddered. "I thought I saw Lizzy's face peeking in your front window." He massaged his temples. "My nerves must be getting to me."

"I don't blame you. Lizzy nearly gave me a stroke by sneaking into my office upstairs. She doesn't appear all that stable."

"No. I don't think she is."

"I fed her some dinner, and she opened up to me about her past with you. She said you don't want to see her anymore because she reminds you of the bad times you went through."

"That's not why I don't want to see her! And it's not because she's frail or unstable. I'm not a bastard, Clare. I'm still working with her on the fan club stuff, and trying to remain a friend, but Lizzy . . ."

He shook his head sadly. "She wants something from me I can't give her."

"Which is?"

"Self-worth. And that's the problem with celebrity. We need our fans. But when fans need us too much, the relationship becomes toxic. And it's never about us, you know? It's always about them; the need they can't fulfill for themselves. I can give Lizzy a job. But I can't give her self-worth. She has to find that all by herself."

"Lizzy claims she has your best interests in mind. She still cares for you—"

"She latched onto me, and it turned sour, that's all. Maybe one day we can find some kind of equilibrium, but right now, I've got to keep my distance from her."

"I know she wants you to go back to Vegas. Lizzy feels she can't make money on this show, and her living depends on you returning to the theater at the Windham family's hotel and casino."

"Yes, I know. We've had that discussion. Many times."

"What about Drew Merriweather?"

"What about him?"

"Did you know Drew is a member of the Windham family?"

"Of course! I kid him about nepotism all the time."

"Hollywood's favorite flavor. I remember the joke."

He waved his hand. "Giving Drew a job on my production was a peace offering to the Windhams since they were so pissed about my leaving their show to do this one. Little Drew wants to be a big Hollywood producer someday, so I got him a job in our production office. With zero experience, he was a glorified gofer, and he hated it. So when Norman was hurt in that awful accident, Morris Windham *suggested* I promote Drew up the ladder. He's a powerful guy, so I did him the favor."

"And you trust Drew? You don't think he could be behind some of this sabotage, like the lights coming down on Norman, or Billy's death?"

"Hey, look, I'll be going back to Vegas—eventually. And when I do, after this hit show, Drew's family will be able to double the ticket prices. So what's to be pissed about?"

"Millions of dollars lost every year you do this show instead of theirs."

He waved his hand again. "Not convinced."

"What about Tate Cabot?"

"What about him?"

"He was at the party, too. And you fired him, didn't you?"

"That's a big leap."

"That's a motive. And what about Fred Denham's death?"

"Fred was always a little shady. Didn't Hutch tell you about his gambling habit? I'm sorry he was killed. That was awful. But the man went into Central Park after dark with an expensive phone and LA Lakers jacket."

"He had an e-ticket to Barbados in his pocket."

"Clare, you're reaching. These are all just theories. And what do you want me to do about it, anyway?"

"I'll tell you. I need clearance for a new member of my craft services team. He's going to start right away."

"Okay. I can help you with that. But what does that have to do with—"

"He's an undercover detective, Jerry. He's not looking to shut down this production, just keep it safe. If you agree to that, I'm sure the NYPD will appreciate it."

Jerry took a deep breath and drained his cup.

"Tell you what, Clare. You make me another Americano as good as this first one, and I'll agree to having a narc on the set."

"Thank you, Jerry," I said, moving to make him a fresh drink.

"Good grief, what next!" Jerry cried as he slumped back over the coffee bar.

Five minutes later, he found out.

Tina Bird was back.

Sixty-six

~~~
≈≈≈≈≈≈≈≈≈≈≈≈≈≈≈≈≈≈≈≈≈≈≈≈
~~~

Tweety Bird had changed her plumage, shedding her silver pantsuit for a pair of jeans, sneakers, and a hoodie.

"Jerry, I came to apologize," she began, voice now calm and respectful. "You've been very good to me, and I feel terrible about upsetting you."

"It's okay," Jerry said. "I *may* have overreacted."

"You have a right to be wary. I know the history between you and Uncle Dan was rocky. But he really does want to reconcile with you. He wants to make peace and try to be friends again."

"After all these years? Doesn't he still hold a grudge?"

"No. He has no anger toward you at this point. None at all."

"I don't believe it."

"It's true," Tina said. "I spoke to him on the phone just now, and he said he respects your feelings completely. He told me he looks back at those years and wishes he could have changed things. He says he took the top billing away from you. That you were the one who cared about the quality of the show—and that your success reflects exactly the high caliber of comedian you are. The biggest regret in his life was not listening to you. He says together you could have reached the stars. Stood up to the network. Or found another one that would have supported the vision you had for *The Coffey Break*. But with that punch in the nose that my uncle gave you, right here in this coffeehouse, he destroyed any chance for a future together, and that's what he still regrets."

I could see Tina's soliloquy genuinely moved Jerry.

"Well," he said, reluctantly. "I guess I *could* sleep on it."

"Sleep on this, Jerry. The publicity your reunion would generate could be enormous. Young people who watch *Only Murders in Gotham* will learn about *The Coffey Break* for the first time. They'll be searching the Internet for the old episodes. They'll put clips on social media, no doubt about it."

Jerry snorted. "Now that would be something: seeing the old sketches resurrected. Discovered and appreciated by a new generation."

"And your reunion alone will get us a higher rating on the later episodes of the season. It'll be like . . ." She snapped her fingers. "Dean Martin and Jerry Lewis reconciling after twenty years of not speaking."

"Yeah, they reconciled all right," Jerry said. "But they never *worked* together again, did they?"

"No, but think about this. Your reunion will take the focus of the critics off Kylee's performance and put it back on you. The show needs it, too, given the story line for the end of the season. Have you thought about that?"

A long, heavy pause came after those words: *the story line for the end of the season* . . .

"Yeah," Jerry finally said. "You are right about that. We do need something like this to balance out the second season's ending."

"So you'll think about it? Sleep on it, at least?"

Jerry nodded. "It's worth considering, I have to admit . . ."

Needless to say, this whole thing still sounded suspicious to me, especially in light of Billy Saddler's death.

"Well, I'm done in, ladies," Jerry suddenly announced, "and I have a lot to consider. So I'll bid you good night."

When Jerry went out the door, Tina faced me.

"I find it very curious, Ms. Cosi, that you're still here, making coffee, after everyone else is gone."

"It's my shop."

"You're still *snooping*, aren't you?"

"I'm still asking questions, if that's what you mean. And curious about all the so-called bad luck on this set."

"Just make sure *you* aren't involved with any future *mishaps.*"

"Is that a threat, Tina?"

"Of course not."

"Then why don't you sit down. I'll make you a drink, and we can talk."

Tina folded her arms. "Talk about what?"

"For one thing, about the identity of the person at Billy Saddler's party who tipped off the police and left a burner phone wiped of prints."

"I don't know what you're talking about."

"Then I'll tell you. Kylee Ferris was at that party. She said you warned her and Sebastian that the police were coming."

"Hey, listen. All I said to Kylee was that Sebastian shouldn't be there, given his drug addiction problems."

"Or . . . you wanted Kylee and Sebastian to go out the back way because they were valuable assets to this production. And, in your mind, Billy wasn't. With Billy arrested, you could propose your uncle Dan as a fast substitute."

"That's not what happened! If Kylee told you that crap about me knowing the police were coming, then she's got a faulty memory. Or she's lying."

"Or you are," I said. "Was the reward for helping your uncle Dan an executive producer position on his wife's theatrical project?"

"We're done here," Tina snapped.

"Why are we done? Don't you care about getting to the bottom of who's sabotaging this production?"

"That's not the issue," Tina spat, before turning from me and marching away.

"Then what is?" I called after her.

She paused at the door. "I don't trust you."

"Believe me," I muttered, watching her go. "The feeling is mutual."

Sixty-seven

TWO weeks later, Dan Coffey walked into our Village Blend, the very cof-feehouse where he punched Jerry in the nose and ended their friendship decades before. This time they came together in a very different way.

The cast, the crew, and the members of the press were all on pins and needles as the two men met for the first time since that terrible rift. Jerry and Dan seemed uncertain at first. But when they finally came face-to-face, and looked one another in the eye, their tension vanished.

Tears flowing, the two men embraced.

The entire cast and crew and all my baristas applauded and cheered while television cameras recorded the historic moment. Even Madame came to witness the reunion of Jerry Sullivan and Dan Coffey.

For more than an hour, Jerry and Dan answered questions from the media. Ten minutes into the press conference, they were already trading quips and tossing out jokes. As Tina Bird predicted—or *planned*—the articles and features that followed all made comparisons to the reunion between Dean Martin and Jerry Lewis after their twenty-year feud.

Ironically, a week after Dan joined the cast, Tina Bird said goodbye.

Tweety was flying to a new coop. An investor actually did come through for *Mob Wives: The Musical!* Their savior was Morris Windham, Jr., who was looking for a new act to fill Jerry's theater. The entertainment director immediately began peddling the show as "the campiest musical laugh-fest in Las Vegas history."

Meanwhile, Detective Sanchez had already joined our craft services team and fit right in. Raised above his family's neighborhood restaurant,

Sanchez had so much experience in food service that I forgot he was an undercover cop and treated him like any other member of my staff. He moved with us as we took our coffee truck and catering equipment to each new filming location.

Jerry and Dan worked together as if their rift had never happened. They laughed it up off camera, and their chemistry was clearly visible. The pair constantly came up with sidesplitting stuff that wasn't in the script and convinced Sebastian to film it.

A scene written with the Central Park Carousel in the background was transformed into a slapstick chase aboard the spinning merry-go-round involving Kylee, Jerry, Dan, and a pair of "bad guy" extras.

Tuck and I couldn't stop laughing at the *Breakfast at Tiffany's* spoof, which featured an Audrey Hepburn look-alike pepper spraying Jerry and Dan while they chowed down on Hotcakes Happy Meals in front of the famed jeweler.

Nancy was impressed by a scene shot in Bryant Park, where Kylee's character, Officer Polly Brightwell, restrained and handcuffed a suspect twice her size.

"I heard that Kylee spent time with a policewoman, learning the ropes," she marveled.

"Not to mention the *cuffs*," Tucker quipped.

While filming between the famous marble lions on the rainswept stairs of the Fifth Avenue library, Dan Coffey slipped and bounced down five steps on his rump. When he landed, Dan threw out his arms and cried, "Ta-da! Now *that's* what I call ad-libbing between the lions!"

"Comedy gold," Jerry declared.

"And one big pain in the tush," Dan deadpanned.

A FEW days later, Tucker and I were running our craft services truck in Washington Square Park and watching the comedians film a scene beside the fountain.

Esther and Nancy arrived early for their afternoon shift. As the pair sipped macchiatos, Nancy wondered if this season had a "happy ending."

"I'm wondering that, too," I said. "Do you know anything about this season's climax, Tuck?"

"I've heard whispers that it's going to be a bombshell. Why do you ask?"

"It's something Jerry said, back when Tina Bird was arguing with him about her uncle joining the show. Dan Coffey coming on board was supposed to 'balance out the second season's ending.' Now I'm wondering what needs to be balanced out. What could this season's ending be?"

"I don't know how the *first* season ended," Esther said. "In fact, I never even watched the show. What's the story about, anyway?"

"I'll tell you!" Nancy offered excitedly. "You see, Kylee plays this traffic cop from Brooklyn named Polly Brightwell. Her boring meter maid duties on the Upper West Side have her dreaming of becoming a superstar homicide detective. And some of those dreams are really elaborate and funny."

"I get it," Esther said. "Go on."

Nancy nodded. "One day, Jerry Sullivan, who plays a retired New York comedian, parks his car in front of a hydrant. He just wants to make a quick stop to pick up a slice at his favorite pizzeria. Kylee, playing meter maid Polly, is eating at the same pizza place. When she sees Jerry block the hydrant, she's outraged that a guy thinks he can endanger people with his arrogance, and she tickets him."

"Riveting," Esther cracked.

"Just *listen*," Nancy said. "While they're arguing, a body flies out a window and lands on the sidewalk! The overworked NYPD detectives who are assigned to the case rule the death a suicide. But Jerry knows the guy who went splat, and he doesn't believe he committed suicide. When he gets a letter from the dead guy, he's sure the man has been murdered."

"Okay, I'm hooked," Esther admitted. "Keep going."

"The detectives dismiss the letter, but Kylee buys Jerry's theory. She's desperate to prove herself to her superiors, so she works with Jerry, and together they solve the case!"

"Not bad." Esther sniffed. "I'd watch that. But it makes you wonder where the story can go from there."

"I know a little about this second season," Tuck said. "Jerry wants to leave retirement and try to make a comeback as an older Rodney Dangerfield–type comedian. He starts appearing at comedy clubs in the West Village, where Kylee, now a detective, is assigned to work—"

"Oh, *now* I get it!" Esther exclaimed. "That's why Sebastian had me do my slam poetry performance on a comedy club stage. Nine times in a row!"

"That's why," Tucker said. "And our Village Blend coffeehouse is where Jerry and Kylee meet and compare notes on another murder case. A fellow comedian of Jerry's dies onstage. Then he *really* dies because he's murdered."

"Did somebody mention murder?" Detective Sanchez asked. He had a big grin on his angular face.

"Hey, you're not working until later," I said. "What are you doing here?"

"I came to deliver the sad news."

"Sad?"

With a nod, he pulled me aside for a private talk.

Sixty-eight

෧෧෧෧෧෧෧෧෧෧෧෧෧෧෧෧෧෧෧෧

"These last couple of weeks have been fun for me, Ms. Cosi. You and your staff were great, and seeing all the filming was interesting. But this whole assignment has been a nothing burger." Sanchez gave a little shrug. "No drugs, no mischief, no crimes of any kind. Meanwhile, my squad is short-handed and needs help on other cases, so Lieutenant Quinn has agreed with me that my work is done here . . ."

Detective Sanchez's summation sounded like an echo of Detectives Soles and Bass. They had yet to recover or even been able to trace Fred Denham's expensive phone. And none of the dead man's credit cards had been used. Yet the Fish Squad still believed Fred was killed by a mugger.

In other words, the trail had gone cold.

Not even the cloud data provided a lead. They said none of the backup info on Fred's phone appeared threatening or out of the ordinary. Then again, on the day Fred was killed, no backup was made. Whoever took that phone made sure of it.

Soles and Bass did uncover one interesting twist, however.

It wasn't cleaning fluid in Driftwood's espresso machines that had sent Fred Denham to the ER that first day of our location shoot. The blood tests at the hospital revealed that Denham had been poisoned by *fentanyl*, the very same drug that had killed Billy Saddler—which convinced me, if not Soles and Bass, that Fred was not slain in a simple robbery but had been marked for murder before he'd ever set foot in Central Park.

As far as Detective Sanchez's departure, what could I say? He wasn't wrong. There'd been no sabotage, drug use, or accidents in the weeks since he'd joined us, and I told him that he'd be missed.

The detective's assessment did make me wonder if Tina Bird had been the saboteur all along. Ever since Tweety had flown west to produce that campy musical, Jerry's production had been free of drama—apart from the scripted kind.

Of course, I feared another explanation for all this calm.

It was possible that the saboteur was still among us.

When Sanchez first joined us undercover, Mike's squad had aggressively questioned everyone who'd attended Billy Saddler's party. At the same time, I had a sneaking suspicion that Jerry had let loose the rumor (whether intentionally or accidentally) that an undercover detective was working on my craft services staff. Why would he start such a rumor on purpose? It wasn't hard to guess since it wasn't in Jerry's best interest to have drug use or dealing exposed on his set. A warning in the form of a rumor would have served its purpose in cooling any bad behavior.

But with Sanchez departing, and the police seemingly satisfied with the answers they got, I feared trouble might begin again.

As that feeling of dread settled over me, I hoped I was wrong, and Sanchez was right.

Either way, I couldn't stop worrying. Or watching. Or wondering . . .

What would happen next?

TWO days after Detective Sanchez left us, I got my first clue.

We'd been filming in the park for almost a week, and the novelty had worn off. The last few days involved only Jerry and Dan, so Kylee's fans were no shows. Today the crowd was small, which was why one big, blond watcher stood out, despite his obvious efforts to be discreet.

Tate Cabot had left the Stetson at home, but his ruddy good looks were easy enough to spot as he furtively moved from one park tree to the next— and if I had any doubt about the man's identity, the cowboy boots were a dead giveaway.

Now why, I wondered, would Tate Cabot be lurking around the shoot of a show he was fired from? I had half a mind to walk up and straight-out ask him, but before I made a move, Tate made a phone call.

To my surprise, one member of our shoot—suddenly on his phone—broke from the rest and walked in the general direction of the fired screenwriter—

Baby-faced Drew Merriweather, wearing an open jacket over one of those Jethro Bodine T-shirts—the kind I'd seen young guys wearing around the Village—breezed right past our catering area. When the two men made eye contact, both pocketed their phones and headed down the same side path in the same direction, though not together.

"Hold down the foodie fort, Esther," I whispered. "I'll be right back."

I had to hustle down the path before I caught sight of them again. They were side by side now, in animated discussion, and a third person had joined them—

Lizzy Meeks!

This was starting to look unsettling, like a conspiracy. But what were they conspiring to do? Was Cabot eyeing revenge for being fired? Or was he trying to get back on the show?

And what about Drew? Was he the one feeding Lizzy news about the set? If so, was Drew doing it to help the production, or hurt it, so that Jerry would finally go back to being his family's comic cash cow at their casino in Vegas?

Either way, with Detective Sanchez gone, I planned to keep a close eye on Drew Merriweather.

Sixty-nine

꩜꩜꩜꩜꩜꩜꩜꩜꩜꩜꩜꩜꩜꩜꩜꩜꩜꩜꩜꩜꩜

For the final three weeks of filming, the shoot moved to an old factory near the East River in the borough of Queens.

The ten-story structure was being converted into luxury condominiums, and its primary advantage, aside from the low cost of leasing the industrial property, was the spectacular rooftop view of the Manhattan skyline across the water.

Sebastian Albee was thrilled to have that glittering skyline in his backgrounds, and the production crew was happy to be setting up three separate scene changes without a cumbersome shift of location.

A hand-to-hand fight would be filmed on the construction site around the building. A fake bar and restaurant would be built on a section of the roof. And an executive's corner office would be set up on the floor beneath—a floor destined for conversion into pricey penthouse apartments.

There were small inconveniences, of course.

Because of the construction, the building was currently off the grid—electricity, water, and power were disconnected. That meant gasoline-powered generators for power, and porta-potties for hygiene.

With the location's water coming from a tapped hydrant, I insisted we bring our own supply of distilled water for brewing. My decision turned out to be a smart one because our catering truck was assigned a spot—and a large tent—just outside the plywood fence surrounding the construction site. The spot was far from the water source (and fortunately, the porta-potties, too).

Sebastian felt the spectacular skyline views made all the challenges worthwhile. Even from street level, the towering skyscrapers across the river were impressive. I was here at the crack of dawn on that first day, and the sunup was breathtaking. I wasn't surprised to find out later that Sebastian and his cinematographer were on the roof, filming it.

After breakfast, Sebastian shot a fight scene in the middle of the expansive construction site. It was Kylee's big action turn, and the scene didn't involve Jerry. But he was here on location, holed up with Dan Coffey inside the fake corner office on the tenth floor, working on last-minute rewrites.

The morning was filled with shouts and grunts as the fight scenes were filmed. Each shot was set up by Sebastian and carefully choreographed by a stuntwoman. Professional stuntmen played Kylee's antagonists—

"Three highly inauthentic gang members," Esther Best quipped. "These guys dress like they shoplift at the Gap!"

At one point Kylee got very frustrated by a side kick she couldn't quite master. She ended up on the ground twice in a row.

"Sebastian, aren't you going to help me?" she demanded.

"Kylee, the drama here is physical," Sebastian patiently replied. "You need to listen to the stunt coordinator, all right? You can do this. Take a few deep breaths and try again."

Sebastian nodded to the stunt coordinator, who moved in to correct Kylee's stance and made her try the kick again.

All this production action was hidden from the public behind the site's tall plywood construction fence. But that didn't seem to matter to a certain segment of fandom.

By noon, word went viral that Kylee Ferris was filming here. A small crowd gathered—maybe thirty people, mostly young women. They were a peaceful lot and easily controlled by the two NYPD officers assigned to that duty.

Right before lunch service began, I checked out the crowd for myself and was surprised to see Lizzy Meeks among them. Wearing a bright red jacket and shouldering that same designer bag she'd clutched so anxiously the night I found her hiding in my office, she was apparently now doing her own reconnaissance. And she wasn't alone.

Drew Merriweather stood beside her, their heads together.

More than ever, I was convinced that Drew was feeding Lizzy information about the shoot, but now he was doing it *directly*, without Norman as a go-between. And once again, I wondered—

Was Drew trying to help this production? Or hurt it?

Aғᴛᴇʀ lunch break, a crew member showed up at the catering truck with pages for Tucker. I was recruited to be in the restaurant scenes as an extra, but I had no dialogue. Tucker did.

"Jerry has written some additional scenes for you," the young woman told him. "He's going to need you to join the cast tomorrow and the next day."

Tucker scanned the pages and grinned. "Three different setups, all with dialogue. I'm going to be a star."

"Who are you playing that you're in every restaurant scene?" I asked.

"Leon," Tucker replied. "The running gag for the dream sequences is that my character works at every eatery Jerry visits."

I called Matt and told him I'd need to pull someone from the coffeehouse for the next two days. After weeks of managing the Village Blend, Matt volunteered for the job.

"I need a change of scenery," he said. "But I can't show up at the crack of dawn. I have a very special date tonight."

"Of course you do. Just make sure you're on Vernon Boulevard by seven ᴀᴍ. It's going to be you, me, and Esther."

By late afternoon, the fights scenes were wrapped. The sun was setting in less than an hour, and the crew was losing the light, so they began to break down the equipment and move it into the trucks.

Jerry and Dan Coffey emerged from their fake office to hear Drew Merriweather announce that the carpenters had finished the rooftop bar.

"Anyone who wants a tour, follow me and Hutch to the elevator!"

Seventy

The elevator ride was a perfectly creepy affair. There was no car, just an open wooden platform inside a large steel cage. Only a small group of us was brave enough to join Drew and Hutch aboard the rickety contraption, including Sebastian, Jerry, Dan, Kylee, Tucker, and me.

Hutch threw a switch and the platform rumbled to life, creaking as it rose, herky-jerky on rusty rails. It was bizarre watching each floor go by—all of them with their interiors hollowed out and the walls stripped of plaster.

The outside of the brick-and-steel building was covered with thick construction mesh, so not much light penetrated the gloomy interior. The windows were glassless, and wind off the river whistled through the cavernous structure.

After a slow minute and a half, the platform jerked to a halt on the tenth floor.

"Over there, they built the fake office," Hutch said, pointing to a partitioned-off space on the opposite end of the vast empty floor.

Then Hutch and Drew led us to a steel staircase that reached up to the roof.

"Witness movie magic," Hutch declared.

He was not wrong. The flat tar paper had been transformed into what appeared to be a luxurious rooftop dining space. Tables and chairs had not yet been set up—too windy, Hutch said—but the tar had been paved over by a floor covering that mimicked multicolored stone. A fake barbecue pit was set up behind a fake oak bar, and he demonstrated that the pit smoked on cue—without fire or heat.

But again, the main attraction was an absolutely spectacular view of the Manhattan skyline.

"Look at that backdrop we've got," said Sebastian, nodding his approval. "It's perfect for the crucial scenes coming up."

"What's all that canvas for?" Dan Coffey asked, pointing to an eight-foot-tall fabric wall erected along one side of the roof.

"That's a windbreak," Hutch explained. "We may have to move it around depending on which direction the wind is blowing."

Sebastian was still admiring the view when his phone buzzed. I was close enough to hear him answer on speaker.

"Your wife is arriving from the airport, Mr. Albee. Our driver called to say he's just a few minutes away."

Sebastian glanced at Jerry, who'd overheard the call, as well.

"Take the elevator," he said. "Just make sure you send it back up when you get to the bottom."

"Will do," Sebastian replied.

As the director breezed past me, I saw tension on his face, and I remembered the anxieties he'd expressed at the Narcotics Anonymous meeting. He loved his wife, and was trying to work out their differences, but he feared she would ultimately want a divorce. Since then, I knew he'd jetted back and forth to California for short visits, but I'd never seen his wife visit the set before.

Concerned for him, and curious to get a look at his studio executive spouse, I circled the roof until I found a place where I could observe traffic down on Vernon Boulevard. With careful steps, I moved around the canvas windbreak, squeezing between the canvas and a two-foot brick wall that edged the building.

Without a safety rail, I felt a little nervous looking down, but I did anyway. I could see those fans gathered ten floors below. The group had grown in size since the last time I checked. The police had pushed them to the opposite side of the boulevard. Even from this height I could see Lizzy's distinctive red jacket among the crowd.

I saw the studio SUV approaching the building, presumably with Mrs. Albee inside. The gray-clad security men opened the gate, and the vehicle rolled into the construction site.

Holding my breath, I watched Sebastian cross the cracked pavement to meet his wife's car. The door opened and a lean, coltish woman with upswept raven hair stepped out of the SUV. From the anxieties Sebastian expressed, I expected her to greet him coldly. But she literally fell into her husband's arms.

They stood there, holding each other a long moment. Then they spoke a few minutes, and Sebastian, beaming with happiness, hugged his wife close. After a lingering kiss, he put her back in the SUV and climbed in beside her.

As they left the site, the fan mob craned their necks and raised their phone cameras, hoping to catch a glimpse or snap a photo of one celebrity or another.

As I turned to go, I was startled to see someone else on this side of the windbreak tarp. Kylee Ferris stood a good twenty feet away, so intent on watching the reunion of Sebastian and his wife that I quietly slipped away before she even noticed me.

Seventy-one

꩜꩜꩜꩜꩜꩜꩜꩜꩜꩜꩜꩜꩜꩜꩜꩜꩜꩜꩜꩜꩜꩜

At five o'clock the next morning, I thought I was the only person on the set besides the overnight security crew. I was about to test run the portable espresso machines when I heard a woman's voice—

"Sebastian! Over here."

The call came as a whispered hiss, but I recognized the voice as Kylee's. Alone inside the closed catering truck, I peeked through the tiny porthole in the back door to see what was going on.

Sebastian was walking away from the studio car that had dropped him off. It was a cold morning, and he wore an open anorak that flapped in the wind.

He was fast approaching my truck, and I stepped away from the porthole to give them privacy—and, okay, do a little curious eavesdropping.

"Over here," Kylee whispered again as the two of them slipped into the narrow space between my catering truck and the construction site's plywood fence.

I had cracked a high vent to let in the fresh morning air, which meant I could hear every word they said. Unfortunately, I was too short to peek through that vent without making a commotion, so I held my breath, stood very still, and listened.

I heard plenty.

"I'm glad you came early. I was worried *that woman* would hold you up, take you away from your work."

"That woman is my wife, Kylee. And Victoria understands the kind of schedule I keep. She has business of her own in the city—"

"Then you won't see her today?"

"Actually, I will. Victoria plans to drop by the set later."

"Well, when are you going to drop her?" Kylee asked with a shameless air of impatient contempt. "Or has she decided to serve *you* divorce papers?"

"We're not getting a divorce—"

"Don't say that."

"Kylee . . . don't."

"Oh, come on. You know you want me. Let's go to my trailer. Isn't it time you see what you're missing?"

"Don't do this, Kylee. I've told you. Many times. I'm a married man."

"But for how long? What do you think *she* was doing in LA while you were pulling your Mister Morality act with me?"

"Victoria isn't like that—"

"Of course she is. You've been apart for months. And a woman like your wife would be a magnet for male attention. So why not get even with her right now—"

"No. Kylee, please . . ."

"We can make her jealous, at least. All we have to do is show up somewhere together, holding hands. The press will do the rest—"

"That's not going to happen—"

"Why not? Come on, you're a free spirit. Let's do something really scandalous. Here, put your hands on me—" I heard Kylee take a few steps.

"Don't, Kylee! What are you—dammit, are you naked under that coat?"

"You want me to take charge? I learned plenty of moves from the stunt coordinator—" I heard a scuffle, and a body slammed against the side of the truck.

"Stop it. Put your coat back on—"

"Why? Don't you want me?"

"This isn't about *you*." Sebastian's patient voice was becoming surly. "Victoria and I are going to reconcile. She's transferring to a position here in New York so we can be close—"

"But what about *us*, Sebastian?"

"We're friends, that's all. Don't ruin it. Listen to me . . ." His tone softened again. "You're a fine actor. We can finish this season, and you can go make that movie you've been offered—"

"Only if *you* direct it. I *can't* act without *you*—"

"Of course you can—"

"I need you. I *want* you."

"We don't always get what we want. You have to grow up and face the fact that not everyone is going to fall in line with how you see things—"

"All I can see is what you're doing to me!"

"Stop it, Kylee. You're not a victim. You've had so many advantages and opportunities. Take it from an ex-addict: Don't feel sorry for yourself. Or give in to self-indulgent anger and resentment. They're the road to ruin. Focus on bigger things, new doors to open. Be brave. Be forgiving. Move forward. I know you can—"

"It's because of her, isn't it?" Kylee spat. "Because of Victoria—"

"My wife and I are reconciling, yes. But even if we weren't—"

"It's because of her. I know it."

Another bump against the wall—like a fist hitting it. Then I heard Kylee curse and footsteps on the cracked concrete.

I risked another peek through the porthole and saw Kylee running across the site toward her trailer as fast as she could manage on high-heeled pumps.

Sebastian's lean form walked away a moment later. Shaking his head vigorously with agitation, he disappeared into the privacy of his own trailer.

The scene was upsetting, and I had mixed feelings about having spied on the pair. I felt guilty for violating their privacy—even though I really had no choice, since I'd simply been doing my job inside the truck.

On the other hand, I couldn't help worrying about Kylee's state of mind. The way she threw herself at Sebastian, not seeing reality quite clearly, made me wonder—and worry—what she'd do next. And what she was capable of doing . . .

I had work to do, and I began to do it, though I felt a little dazed while I did. With thoughts racing, I tested the espresso machines and accepted our regular bakery delivery on automatic pilot. Then Esther arrived and helped me unload Babka's delivery van, but I hardly said two words to her. She didn't appear to mind since she wasn't exactly a morning person and hardly spoke herself.

While we ground fresh beans for our coffee urns and laid out the buffet table under the tent, my head continued to spin. I didn't know where to go with what I'd just overheard—or if I should go anywhere with it at all. I'd invaded Sebastian's privacy once already, and all it accomplished was disproving my misguided suspicions about him.

I'd nearly decided to keep my mouth shut about this morning's horrible scene when Matt arrived, right on time. Unfortunately, my ex-husband knew me too well, and after working under the tent for fifteen minutes, he pulled me aside.

"What's the matter with you, Clare? The crew is going to show up soon and you're walking around with your head in the clouds. Tell me what's going on."

I tried to brush it off, but Matt wouldn't take no for an answer.

With Esther inside the truck, waiting to pull espresso shots, I finally confided in Matt. After I recounted what I'd overheard this morning, I added one caveat—

"The only reason I told you about that *very* private exchange was because you already know enough about Sebastian's situation to advise me."

"Advise you about what exactly?"

"About what I should do next. Do I tell Jerry about Kylee's unrequited infatuation?"

"I don't see the point, Clare. What's going on between them sounds like the typical off-screen, on-set drama that's fodder for the gossip columns."

"But what if it's something more this time? What if Kylee's romantic delusion has something to do with the sabotage that's been going on since the shoot began?"

"Come on, that's pretty far-fetched. Tell me how Kylee's girlish crush gets Tucker shot? And I'd really love to hear you explain to Detectives Soles and Bass how Kylee's need for some kind of daddy figure connects with a robbery-slash-murder in Central Park."

Matt's words were a cold glass of reason dashed in my face.

"I sound crazy, right?"

"You said it, not me."

"Well, Matt, I think this whole shoot is driving me crazy."

Tucker arrived that moment, decked out in a waiter's uniform for his first scene. He filled his coffee cup with the freshly brewed Breakfast blend from our urn and joined us.

"Speaking of crazy, did you check the crowd across the street?" Tuck said.

"It's only seven thirty in the morning," I cried. "Fans are gathering already?"

Tuck nodded. "But I'm speaking of one fan in particular. Look across the street at the crowd. She's front and center."

I poked my head out of the tent. It didn't take me long to spot her.

"Lizzy Meeks again—"

"Again?" Tuck said, surprised.

"She was in the crowd yesterday, too. Wearing that same red jacket."

Tuck shook his head. "She really is *cock-a-doodle-doo*."

"Goodness knows why Lizzy is hanging around, or what she thinks she's doing."

Tuck raised an eyebrow. "Or what she's going to do . . ."

Seventy-two

At two o'clock on that bright, sunny, but windy and chilly afternoon, I was on the roof, shivering in a skimpy waitress miniskirt, black tights, and a flimsy blouse. Matt, who stood beside me, seemed no warmer in a chef's uniform, as he pretended to operate the barbecue grill that gave off smoke but no heat.

Tucker and the dozen extras sitting at tables were shivering, too. Though the set had outdoor heaters, they could only do so much.

Meanwhile, Hutch Saunders helped the grips move the windbreaking canvas wall for the second time that afternoon. This was done not to spare the cast from the cold blasts off the East River, but to keep the wind from blowing napkins off the table, rippling the tablecloths, or otherwise spoiling a shot.

"Sebastian picked a hell of a day to shoot a rooftop restaurant scene," Jerry complained. Under a blanket the comedian wore a white short-sleeved polo shirt. The extras were all dressed in casual attire, as well, because the scene was set in much balmier weather.

Apparently, the magic of filmmaking didn't extend to climate control.

Sebastian vanished the moment Hutch and the guys began moving the windbreak. He magically showed up twenty minutes later, at the precise moment they were finished.

His wife, Victoria, was with him, and I finally got a good look at Mrs. Sebastian Albee.

Tall and long limbed, she bordered on gawky. Though not traditionally beautiful, her striking, catlike eyes and full lips were nevertheless captivating. A formfitting business suit accentuated her trim figure, and stacked heels brought her up to the altitude of her creative genius husband.

Sebastian made a point of introducing us. Victoria Albee shook my hand and began to gush.

"Your espressos are incredible," she said. "And Esther, your barista, is charming."

It was the first time I'd heard *that* word used to describe Esther, but I was sure Mrs. Albee was sincere.

Her devotion to Sebastian was obvious, too. She touched him affectionately and often. And when they stopped to talk with Jerry, her long arm curled around Sebastian's waist as if she were afraid to let go.

During their conversation, my eyes drifted to Kylee. Wearing a strapless dress for the restaurant scene, she snuggled under a blanket like the rest of us. Kylee refused to even look at Sebastian's wife as he showed her around, and the director wisely spared both women an awkward introduction.

Like everyone else, Victoria Albee was smitten by the amazing view of the city and vowed to take pictures.

"The skyline is half-hidden now," Hutch told her. "We had to set up breaks because the wind coming off the water is a problem. But on the other side of that tarp, the view is awe-inspiring."

The cinematographer called out to Sebastian. Soon he and the director were deep in conversation over some problem. Sebastian called the other two camera operators over, and they all began to consult.

At that point, Jerry called for a break but asked that no one leave the roof. "Remember your places, everyone," he called. "And take thirty."

I'd planned for this contingency and immediately phoned Esther and told her to bring up the coffee cart. Even though reception was lousy to nonexistent, I managed to get through, but calls were only possible from the roof.

Minutes later, Esther arrived with the cart, and Tucker jumped in to help her set up. Immediately, the thirsty, cold extras surrounded our Village Blend pump thermoses for hits of hot, fresh caffeine.

With warm drinks in hand, they strolled around, took mobile phone photos of the skyline, or of themselves posing with Jerry and Dan Coffey, who both happily mingled with the extras.

Tucker was sipping hot coffee with Matt and me at the fake barbecue pit when suddenly a shrill scream cut through the murmur of the crowd.

"What was that?" I called.

"It came from over there," an extra replied, pointing.

What happened seemed clear. A section of the windbreak had been knocked over by a standing light that the wind had toppled. A large section of the canvas was now hanging over the edge of the building, threatening to fall to the ground at any moment.

We all heard another scream, then a woman's desperate cries for help.

An extra dared to peek around the leaning canvas. "Oh, God!" she cried. "Someone fell over the side!"

Suddenly, everyone seemed paralyzed—everyone except Matt. He immediately pushed through the throng while I followed in his wake. As the crew lifted the fallen light and dragged the windbreak back into place, Matt and I reached the edge of the roof and peered over the side.

Half a floor down, Victoria Albee was dangling from the construction mesh with one hand. She'd managed to catch the protective netting on her way down, but the fibers had dug into her fingers. Thin red rivulets threaded down her forearm. As I watched, one of her high heels dropped to the pavement ten stories below.

"Somebody get a rope!" Matt shouted.

Then, without hesitation and without a safety harness of his own, my danger-craving, rock-climbing ex-husband scrambled over the low wall and down the mesh as if it were a rope ladder.

In seconds, Matt was within reach of the terrified woman.

On the street below, the drama was clearly visible to the fans who gathered across Vernon Boulevard. Most were recording the action with their phones.

Up here, everyone was crowding the edge of the roof to watch as Matt seized Victoria's wrist just as she lost her grip. The extras gasped as the sudden jolt nearly yanked Matt from his precarious perch.

Though he could not move in any direction, my ex managed to hold the woman with one hand while he clung to the mesh with the other.

On the ground, the crowd pushed past the NYPD officers and bellied up to the plywood fence. I noticed Lizzy's red jacket was no longer among them, but I had no time to ponder that mystery.

Hutch Saunders and the stunt coordinator acted fast. Using secured ropes, they quickly moved down to parallel Matt and Victoria. Then all of them worked together to haul Sebastian's wife back onto the roof.

Sebastian rushed to his wife's side as Matt laid her limp form on a table someone had cleared. She was having trouble breathing—likely from shock and anxiety—and one of the extras, a nurse as it turned out, checked the cuts on Victoria's hand and wrist.

"She's going to need stitches," he announced.

Drew Merriweather phoned for an ambulance.

The crew and all of the extras were milling about—at least thirty people. I looked for Kylee among the throng, but she was out of sight.

Jerry, standing at the edge of the roof, turned to Hutch.

"Why in the hell wasn't that light secured?"

"It *was* secured," Hutch shot back. "Tight as a drum."

"Then why did it fall?"

"Think about it, boss," Hutch replied. "The wind is coming off the river, right? Only that light fell *toward* the river, which means it didn't blow down . . ."

Jerry frowned at Hutch's unspoken implication.

"Okay, Hutch," Jerry said after a long pause. "We can't sweep this one under the rug, so let's secure the set for the insurance people to conduct their investigation—"

Hutch scratched his head. "Secure the set how?"

"We're done for the day. Leave everything in place, but I want everyone in the cast and crew off the roof *now*."

Seventy-three

∽∾∽∾∽∾∽∾∽∾∽∾∽∾∽∾∽∾∽∾∽∾∽∾∽∾∽∾∽∾

FROM a hiding place, the Player watched Jerry search the roof.

So serious. So intense!

He checked the toppled light, the windbreak, and the spot where the woman went flailing over the side.

Ha ha! Bye-bye!

Well, almost.

The Player would have to try again. Something *new* next time. Something from the bag of tricks.

And the comedian just keeps looking. There's nothing to see! Stupid man. But if you come a little closer, you can go over the side, too . . .

That's when the Player saw. The comedian was not alone.

"Jerry! I need to speak with you . . ."

The woman was still here. The awful snooping woman. The coffee-pushing busybody who had the gall to bring a narc on the set.

Pushing *her* over the side would have been even more fun. But two people at the same time?

No. That won't work.

The insufferable comic and the nosy barista would have to be dealt with another way. The Player puzzled over this, but whatever was done had to be now. With everyone gone, no one would guess who ended their days.

The show would be over *for good*.

And the Player's desperate wish would finally come true . . .

Seventy-Four

"Jerry! I need to speak with you."

"What do you want, Clare?"

"We have to talk . . ."

When I first realized that Jerry was staying on the roof, I told Tucker to leave without me.

"Why?" Tuck demanded. "What are you going to do?"

"I have to speak with Jerry about what just happened. I think I know who was responsible."

"Oh, God." Tuck blanched. "Just remember, Clare, you're dealing with Humpty Dumpty."

"I don't care. Today someone was *pushed* off the wall, and I don't want to see it happen again . . ."

Despite my anxiety, I approached the lone figure on the roof. Jerry was busy intensely inspecting the area where the equipment fell. He still had a blanket draped over his shoulders, and now it blew in the wind like Batman's cape—or was he a caped villain? Would his reaction to my accusations make him want to strangle me the way he did in my nightmare?

When I approached him (cautiously) with my request to talk, I thought he was going to send me away, but then he nodded and said—

"Not here. It's too cold and I can't find any answers, anyway. Let's go to the office set."

Jerry led me down the stairs and past a rumbling generator powering the set above. In the far corner, three unused generators on wheels were lined up near a single door. Jerry squeezed between the equipment, pulled the door open, and ushered me inside. Though everyone was clearing out of the building but us, Jerry closed the door firmly behind him anyway "for privacy."

This old, stark factory storeroom had been transformed into a convincing corner office with bookshelves, framed prints, a faux oak desk (plywood covered with wallpaper), and a pair of real office chairs. A fresh paint smell lingered in the air. The quiet rumble of the generator outside was the only sound.

Afternoon sunlight streamed through the plate glass windows. Because those windows were on a different side of the building than the fake rooftop restaurant, we had a view of the glass-and-steel skyscrapers of Long Island City instead of the East River and Manhattan.

Jerry sat behind the desk, where he'd left today's script pages, covered with scribbled notes. I sat opposite him, in the other office chair.

"Okay," he said, "What's up, Clare?"

I told him about Kylee's inappropriate advances toward the director, and what I believed was the tragic result of her obsession—

"I believe Kylee tried to kill Sebastian's wife."

Jerry laughed.

"You don't believe me?"

"About Kylee's obsession with Sebastian Albee? Oh, yeah. About *that*, I believe you. In fact, I already knew about it. Sebastian confided in me. He needed advice, and we talked it all out."

"I need more," I said. "Given what happened between them this morning, I'd like to understand."

Jerry leaned across the desk. "Kylee was offered the lead in a feature film just before we began shooting this season. She really wants to accept the part, but she lacks confidence. Kylee has convinced herself that she can't act without Sebastian directing her. So she's been pressuring Sebastian to break his contract with me and direct her movie. But Sebastian doesn't want to do that. He says he owes me for backing him when nobody else would." Jerry paused. "The reasons for Sebastian's troubles are private. He had some issues. But it's not my place to—"

"Sebastian is a recovering drug addict," I said flatly. "And he's still struggling to stay clean."

"My, my, you *have* been a busybody."

"As I warned you I'd be. But what about Kylee?"

"She's become a real problem for Sebastian. He can't take the pressure she's putting on him. I went through this with Lizzy. That's what I told Sebastian. Kylee Ferris latched onto him the same way, and she won't let go. He's become an addiction as toxic as any drug. It's not about him, it's about her, and this show isn't good for her any longer. That's why Sebastian and I have written her out of it—"

"Wait. What?" I was genuinely shocked. "Did I hear you right? You're dumping Kylee from your hit show?"

"It was Sebastian's idea to kill her in the final episode. I've already signed Justin Trevor from that boy band, the Trevor Twins, to replace her in the third season. Trevor will play a young rookie cop assigned to solve the murder of Kylee's character. He ends up falling in love with a picture of Kylee, just like in that old movie *Laura*."

"Wait a minute. I thought Kylee had a three-season contract?"

"She does. Kylee will appear in the third season, in Justin's dream sequences. The best part is that we can film her stuff in a week. One week with a second unit director, and she's free. Free as a bird. Just like Tina, Kylee can fly off and do something for herself, make her big movie, whatever she wants to do—but *without* Sebastian, who wants to stick with me."

"Okay, what about the squib?" I asked.

"Squib?"

"You know what I'm talking about. I know you do. When you first started filming this season, it was a squib that brought down the lights on poor Norman."

"We talked about Norman's accident."

"It was no accident."

Jerry's eyes narrowed. "You're wrong—"

"No, Jerry. I believe Kylee tried to sabotage the show in the very first week of shooting. Lizzy tells me that Norman always watched your back."

Jerry nodded. "True."

"That's why Kylee got rid of him. She knew she couldn't get away with much with Norman's sharp eyes looking over everyone's shoulder."

"Don't be ridiculous. Okay, maybe the squib wasn't an accident. Maybe it was a sick prank. Like the snake in Kylee's trailer."

"I'm betting the snake was planted by Kylee herself. Think about it. She made certain I was there to see it."

"I don't understand. Why would she do that?"

"Because you told everyone that I would be asking questions about the bulletproof barista incident. She was guilty of putting that bullet in the gun, so she set up the snake, making herself look like a *victim* to deflect blame."

I paused as more connections occurred to me.

"I'll bet it was Fred Denham who found evidence of the squib after the accident, wasn't it?"

Jerry blinked.

"Wasn't it?"

"Yeah, it was Fred. But he said he didn't know how it got there or where it came from."

"I'm betting he *did*. Hutch Saunders, Fred's assistant, told me that Denham was a lousy gambler, yet he came into big money in the first couple weeks of shooting—enough to buy a fancy team jacket and an expensive phone. Hutch thought Fred was on a winning streak."

Jerry threw up his hands. "Maybe Fred was!"

"No, he wasn't. I believe Fred realized one of his squibs was missing. Either that or Kylee conned one out of him—maybe she lied about wanting it for a prank or a party. Either way, I'm guessing he figured out she was the one who set the trap that caught Norman, and Fred took a payoff to keep quiet about it."

"Come on, Clare—"

"Remember the day Fred Denham was shot? Kylee left the set early. She was so upset by the snake, she couldn't work. Or so she said—"

"The snake that *Lizzy* put in her trailer."

"I don't believe Lizzy had anything to do with it. Like I said, I think Kylee planted that snake. And not only to deflect blame away from herself. It would have given her a chance to act the part of the terrorized ingenue."

"Why? For what purpose?"

"So she could get out of filming that day and arrange a lethal meeting in Central Park with Fred—who was probably blackmailing her."

"This is crazy talk," Jerry said angrily. "Complete fiction. Like an episode of *Columbo*—"

"And speaking of *Columbo*, that's the *one thing* I can't figure out. The one flaw that botches up my whole theory."

"What flaw? That the whole thing is crackpot crazy?"

"No. It's about that real bullet that struck Tucker. Why would Kylee put it in the gun? What would it get her? Even if Tucker died, that wouldn't guarantee the show would end. Stuntmen are killed in film production accidents all the time, and the show goes on. It would make more sense to me if she'd set *you* up to take that bullet."

Jerry's jaw dropped. Then he went pale and sat back in his chair.

"What's the matter? You look like someone walked across your grave."

"I think you may be right, Clare. And if you are, then Kylee Ferris did try to put me in the grave."

"Finally?! What convinced you?"

"Kylee only saw Tate Cabot's version of the script—"

"What's the difference?"

"Tate's draft had the waiter, Tucker, shooting *me* in that scene. At the last minute—literally the night before—I rewrote the scene and switched roles so that I was the one shooting Tucker."

My breath caught.

"You were supposed to be killed with that bullet! Do you finally see, Jerry? Kylee tried and failed to kill you once. Get it through your head. You are not dealing with a *prankster* here. This is no screwup or accident. These are the actions of a cold-blooded *murderer.* The young woman is unhinged. She's cracking up. She wants what she wants like an unbalanced addict. She'll do anything to get it. And if Kylee gets another chance, and thinks she can get away with it, I believe she'll try to kill you again."

Suddenly, Jerry sat upright and sniffed the air.

"Clare, do you smell that?"

"What?"

"Smoke! I smell smoke!"

Seventy-Five

I SMELLED the smoke, too. An acrid, bitter stench like burning rubber.

"We better get out of here," I said, rising.

Jerry came around the desk and pushed on the door. It opened less than an inch before it seemed to hit a solid wall.

"The damn thing is blocked."

I joined Jerry and we both put our shoulders to the door, but it wouldn't budge.

Now we could see smoke through the window, curling in the wind like an ugly black smog.

"I can't get a signal," I said when I checked my phone.

"You can't. Not in here," Jerry said. "That's why I come here. For the privacy."

"Well, if we don't do something fast, we're going to die in privacy!"

Smoke was starting to fill the space. We'd be suffocating soon if we didn't burn to death first. I looked around for something heavy to break the window and decided one of the office chairs would have to do.

"Stand back," I cried. With all my might, I hurled the heavy chair against the windowpane. Apparently, all my might wasn't enough. The window cracked but didn't shatter, and the chair tumbled to the floor.

"Allow me," Jerry said, hurling the second chair. The window blasted outward with a satisfying crash and a shower of glass. As the chair dropped out of sight, we both rushed to the window, yelling our throats raw.

"Help! Help!"

"We're trapped! There's a fire!"

Unfortunately, the cast and crew, the food tent, and the fan crowd were on the other side of the building. All we faced was an expansive lot of overgrown weeds, and beyond that, a wall of tall skyscrapers. Not a pedestrian was in sight, let alone in earshot.

I hung out the window and tested the phone again. The bars barely budged. And I noticed the construction mesh that cocooned this building had been pulled aside to allow for the view from the faux office. But I could still reach that mesh, and I instantly decided we could use it like a ladder the way Matt did.

"Jerry! We can climb to the roof."

The comedian blinked like a deer in the headlights of an oncoming semi.

"I can't go out there," he said in an octave higher than the Vienna Boys Choir's.

"It's just one floor up. On the roof we can call the fire department. And we can reach the fire escape on the other side of the building."

Jerry stuck his head out the window, blinking against the smoke.

"Nope, no way. I can't do it. I can't!"

"Okay, Jerry. Calm down. It's okay. I'll climb up to the roof myself and come back down to free you. If my ex-husband can do it, so can I."

"What?!" he cried. "Are you and your ex part of a circus act? Tightrope walkers on the side, maybe?"

"No, Jerry. Just caffeinated overachievers."

With that, I shoved the phone inside my bra, kicked off my high heels, and stepped onto the ledge. I told myself not to look down, but of course I did look down—all ten stories down.

That's when the queasiness hit me.

With a shaky hand, I reached out and grasped the mesh. It was rough and hard, and I immediately wished I had gloves. But I tightened my grip until the mesh dug into my flesh. I stuck one stockinged foot into the mesh. Then, gripping the material like my life depended on it (which it did!), I pulled myself through the broken window.

Dangling ten stories in the air with no safety harness is a powerful incentive to move carefully and quickly. Using the Method acting prompt of a desperate monkey being chased by a fire-breathing dragon, I scrambled up to the roof in less than a minute.

Panting and shaky, I pulled the phone from my bra.

It had a signal!

I immediately called 911.

My waitress skirt was hiked up around my waist. I pulled it down as I stumbled into the middle of the empty restaurant set.

Smoke was rising all around me, but oddly there was still no fire. I ripped a tablecloth free and wrapped it around my face to filter the toxic fumes. I grabbed another for Jerry. My nose and mouth were protected, but my eyes were burning and there was nothing I could do about that.

I ran down the stairs, and that's when I found the fire. The generator that had been humming was burning now. Flames rose from its innards, and the rubber wheels had melted. The wooden floor around the device was just beginning to blaze, and the ceiling was smoldering.

I circled the fire and reached the fake office. Someone had wheeled all three unused generators in front of the door, one after the other.

Coughing, I pushed hard to budge the first one and move it out of the way. The second one was easier, but I was coughing up a storm by the time I moved the third.

"Jerry!" I called, pounding on the door.

He pushed it open. Jerry was coughing, too, and tears streamed down his face. I wrapped the second tablecloth around his nose and mouth, then grabbed his arm. My eyes were watering so badly now it felt like I was walking under ten feet of murky water. I managed to steer us past the flames and up to the roof.

We tossed aside the tablecloths and took deep breaths of cool, semi-fresh air.

I heard sirens.

"Come on," I cried, tugging a gasping Jerry to his feet. "The fire escape is over there. Let's get out of here."

JERRY and I were taking hits of pure oxygen from a tank in the back of an FDNY ambulance when the fire chief approached us.

"The fire is out, and it looks like arson, just like you said."

"How was it done?"

"Well, ma'am, it appears someone emptied a gasoline can on the generator. It caught fire, but since there wasn't much to burn, the fire spread slowly."

The firefighter looked up at the smoke still rising from the top of the building.

"You were in more danger of suffocating than burning to death. But you were both brave and resourceful, and you got out."

Jerry pointed at me as he took another hit of oxygen. "She was the brave one! I was a blubbering idiot."

"The fire marshal and an arson investigator are on the way," the firefighter said. "They're going to want some answers."

"And they'll get them," Jerry assured him.

"But we have to do something first," I said.

"What do you mean?" Jerry looked at me, puzzled. "We know who tried to kill us. Don't we?"

"Yes. But we have to prove it."

Jerry blinked his red and puffy eyes. "How are we going to do that?"

"I have a plan to expose our killer, but we're going to need help, and lots of it."

"Whatever you say, Clare. I'm in."

"I hope you are, Jerry, because now it's your turn to be brave."

Seventy-six

⚜⚜⚜⚜⚜⚜⚜⚜⚜⚜⚜⚜⚜⚜⚜⚜⚜⚜⚜

JERRY and I sat at a table inside the darkened Village Blend. It was well after closing time. The espresso machines were quiet, and the brick hearth was cold. Outside, the studio trailers and trucks were long gone. It was so late that traffic along Hudson was light and pedestrians rare.

To prepare for this showdown, Jerry had traded his smoky clothes for a white dress shirt and navy sports jacket. I'd replaced my waitress uniform with a sweater and denims.

Jerry poured more coffee from the French press while we waited in the shadows for Kylee Ferris to arrive. We knew she was coming because my call to her, thirty minutes ago, had awakened her from a sound sleep. That's when I'd delivered the dialogue Jerry and I had scripted together . . .

"I'M sorry I woke you, Kylee," I recited into my phone, "but this is important. We believe Lizzy Meeks tried to murder Sebastian Albee's wife earlier today. Then Lizzy set fire to the building and almost killed Jerry and me—"

"Oh, my!"

"Don't worry, Kylee. It's over now and we're both safe. But we want to stay that way and keep *you* safe, too."

"What do I do?" Kylee asked.

"Jerry and I both think Lizzy will come after you next. It's one AM now. Do you think you can get to the Village Blend in an hour?"

"Yes, I can."

"That's great. Lizzy has spies and we don't know who to trust, so Jerry and I will be alone. Together, the three of us will figure out how we can have Lizzy locked up before she kills every one of us."

Then I ended the call, and our wait began.

"What time is it now?" Jerry asked.

I checked my phone. "One fifty-six. Kylee should be here any—"

I stopped talking and we both watched a cab roll to the curb outside. Kylee climbed out. As I expected, she traveled incognito, in worn denims and a hoodie pulled over her head. A large leather handbag hung from her shoulder.

Jerry remained seated while I unlocked the door and admitted her. Kylee rushed to the table and put her arms around Jerry's shoulder.

"I can't believe what Clare told me! Are you both okay?"

"Sit down," Jerry said. "We need to talk."

Kylee unzipped her hoodie, hung her bag over the back of the chair, and sat down. I took the chair beside hers.

"What's the matter, Jerry?" Kylee asked. "You seem strange."

"You think I'm strange? Try this."

The gun appeared in Jerry's hand so quickly I didn't see where it came from. Kylee's mouth opened in stunned surprise when he leveled it at her heart.

"I know why you're really here, Kylee," Jerry said. "You came to kill us. Only I'm going to kill you first!"

"Jerry, what are you doing?" I cried, jumping to my feet. "This isn't what we planned. You'll be tried for cold-blooded murder!"

"I don't care," Jerry replied. "After all she's done, it will be worth it!"

"No!" Kylee cried. "You've got it all wrong, Jerry. I didn't do anything. It's your crazy fan club president, Lizzy Meeks, who's guilty."

Jerry snorted. "Lizzy was nowhere near the set when those lights fell on Norman. And Lizzy didn't shoot Fred Denham, either—"

"You're wrong," Kylee insisted, her pretty eyes pleading. "Whatever you think you know, Lizzy must have set me up to look like I'm guilty!"

"It's true, Jerry," I argued. "Kylee isn't guilty. I believe her. You should, too. You know Lizzy. She's crazy—"

"Get that handbag of hers and toss it over there," Jerry said, pointing to the far corner. "Kylee's got a gun in there, I'm sure of it."

Kylee shifted in her seat. Jerry jabbed the gun at her.

"Don't move," he warned. Then to me he said, "Throw the handbag, Clare, or I'll shoot her now."

"Fine." I tossed the heavy handbag away.

"Are you happy, Jerry? Kylee's got no weapon, if she ever had one. Now just put down your gun and we can work this out. Give Kylee a chance. Let her prove she's innocent."

Kylee nodded, tears slipping down her cheeks. Jerry sighed, shook his head, and reluctantly set the gun on the table.

"There. Now we can all calm down and talk like rational—"

Kylee snatched up the gun and waved it at Jerry, then at me.

A cruel, crooked grin replaced her crocodile tears.

"Sit down," she barked. "In that chair next to Jerry."

I did as she demanded. Now she had us both covered.

Kylee shook her head. "You are so stupid." Then she laughed.

Angry now, Jerry attempted to rise.

Kylee shot him.

Blood exploded from the horrific wound in his chest. Jerry fell back in his chair, then slid to the floor. A river of blood flowed across the restored plank floor.

"What have you done!" I screamed. "Kylee, why? Why did you do it?"

"To shut him up. Just like I'm going to shut you up."

Seventy-seven

〰〰〰〰〰〰〰〰〰〰〰〰〰〰〰〰〰〰〰〰〰〰〰

"Wait, wait," I cried, waving my arms in front of me. "Just tell me why!"

"Why? Because I've been trying to kill Jerry since the beginning of the season. Well, not really. I thought I could sabotage the show enough to kill it without killing Jerry, but that didn't work."

"Then you planted the squib?"

"Of course I did! I learned how they worked last season. And Fred Denham was hard up for money. He sold me a squib so I could 'pull a prank' at a party. Only my prank was done on set and nearly fatal. But Norman had to go. He was noticing too much. Hovering around Jerry. Watching everything closely."

"And Fred figured out what happened, didn't he, Kylee?"

"For a stupid old ox, Fred did manage to figure that out. That stupid ox was hard to kill, too. The fentanyl I added to his coffee cup that morning didn't do the trick. It only sent him to the hospital—"

"You pulled that stunt with the snake, right in front of me."

"I needed time. Fred wanted more blackmail money, so I had to do him the same way I did Jerry here." Kylee waved the gun. "The old-fashioned way."

Kylee's eyes flared with fury.

"You and your stupid coffee! It was *easy* to poison the Driftwood coffee. Everybody's name was on the cup, and they just set the drinks out to sit on the counter. I pounded a pill into powder, mixed it with water, and squeezed my eyedropper of fentanyl into Jerry's coffee that morning, too, but he stopped drinking the Driftwood swill. After he tasted *yours*, he wouldn't touch theirs. He switched to orange juice, and they kept it in a fridge behind the counter, so I couldn't tamper with it—"

Kylee was ranting wildly, but the gun never wavered. The entire time she kept it aimed at my heart.

"With Fred gone and nobody watching the weapons, it was easy to switch the blank for a real bullet. But Jerry switched the script on me, and that barista got shot instead!"

Kylee's face contorted as she relived her frustrations.

"I wanted to try the fentanyl on Jerry again, but your *stupid* baristas made all the coffee drinks fresh to order and handed them right to everyone! I couldn't tamper with the coffee—or the food because your staff watched it like hawks."

She cocked her head and put one finger against her temple.

"So, I'm thinking . . . since I can't get to Jerry again, I'll take out Billy. Tipping off the cops was insurance. There should have been a big scandal and the set shut down. But NO! That didn't happen, either! All I got was more cop scrutiny and a narc on set. Then the narc left. It was my last chance to get what I wanted, and I took it. It would have worked, too, except for YOU!"

Kylee suddenly frowned, and I saw a bizarre mood shift in her expression.

"You know what, Clare?" she said. "This has become boring."

Then she shot me—twice.

And nothing happened.

That's because Hutch put only a single blank in the gun, and I wasn't wearing a squib, like Jerry.

Kylee stepped back in horror when Jerry got up. At the same moment, Hutch and the two camera operators emerged from hiding. (Jerry had insisted two cameras be used for coverage, both high-speed to capture as much light as they could in the shadowy coffeehouse.)

Kylee dropped the gun and turned to flee.

But Detectives Lori Soles and Sue Ellen Bass were behind her, waiting. Sue Ellen was the one who cuffed the pop queen turned actor.

Kylee appeared too stunned to protest.

Mike Quinn and Sergeant Franco emerged from the coffeehouse pantry.

"That was a heck of a performance, Coffee Lady," Franco said.

Behind me, Lori Soles addressed Kylee. "You have the right to remain silent . . ."

"Yeah," Jerry cracked as Hutch began helping him out of his fake-blood-stained jacket, "and you should take it!"

As Detective Soles finished advising Kylee of her rights, her partner slipped on white cotton gloves and retrieved Kylee's handbag.

"Yep," Sue Ellen announced. "There's a gun in here. An eyedropper, and look at this . . ."

She waved a sealed glass vial. Inside was a collection of pills that the detective said resembled the latest batch of fentanyl-laced street drugs.

"I don't believe it!" Jerry cried.

"What part?" I asked.

But Jerry wasn't talking about the gun or the drugs. He was pointing at our front door. "It's, it's—"

I turned to see Lizzy Meeks rushing in.

"Jerry! What's going on?" Lizzy saw the fake blood all over him, and her face went pale. "Oh, no! You're hurt!"

"I'm okay. I'm okay!" Jerry said. And for the first time in ages, he embraced his biggest fan.

"I got an anonymous text message that you were in danger!" Lizzy shuddered. "It said I should come to the Village Blend, right away." Glancing around in confusion, she noticed the camera operators. "I guess someone was pulling a prank on me. I'm sorry if I interrupted your filming."

"We're not filming the show," Jerry told her. "This is real."

"Real?!"

"That's right, you stupid cow!" Kylee cried out—ignoring her right to remain silent. "This should be YOU in handcuffs, not me!"

Detectives Soles and Bass exchanged glances, and I knew what they were thinking. *If this perp wants to talk, we're going to let her.*

Meanwhile, Jerry knew a cue when he saw one. As Lizzy approached Kylee, he silently twirled his index finger—and the cameras started rolling again.

"I don't understand," Lizzy said to the enraged young woman. "Did *you* send me the text?"

"You were supposed to rush here to *save Jerry*," Kylee said in a mocking tone. "But all you were going to find were two dead bodies and a bullet for yourself. I had it all figured out! Murder-suicide with all the evidence in a handbag at your side. It was brilliant! It would have worked!"

"I knew you were bad news," Lizzy told her, shaking her head. "From the very start."

"And you're just an old witch!"

"Don't you dare insult my friend," Jerry said, stepping between them. "You know, Kylee, I was like you once. I saw everything through blinders. And I killed, too, with my stupid mistakes. I killed careers, opportunities, and what should have been a lifelong friendship."

He turned to Lizzy. "I owe you an apology. You were right all along. Instead of pushing you away, I should have listened."

"Go to hell!" Kylee spat. "You can *all* go to hell!"

"Maybe we will," Jerry said. "But I know one thing. You're going first."

And with that, Lori Soles took Kylee by the arm and led her to a police van. There was a police car outside, too, and pulling up to the curb.

Turning from the window, I looked up, into Mike's blue eyes. He'd been wary of this crazy stunt when I proposed it to him, and worried about my safety, but I was determined to set this trap and see it through.

"These are show business people," I'd told Mike. "Why not use their tricks of the trade to trick our criminal into confessing?"

Now he was looking at me with extreme relief, admiration, and something else, something that touched my heart. I knew how he felt.

"I'm glad that's over," I said. "It's been a long day. And a busy night."

Mike pulled me close and whispered in my ear.

"If we're lucky, it will get even busier."

EPILOGUE

∞∞∞∞∞∞∞∞∞∞∞∞∞∞∞∞∞∞∞∞∞∞∞∞∞∞∞∞

MIKE and I were lucky that night. Things did get busier, and the results were blissful.

Afterward, I slept deeply and in peace with the knowledge that I'd helped stop a deranged killer before she claimed three more innocent lives—my own among them.

Unfortunately, things looked very different in the harsh light of day.

In the weeks that followed her arrest, Kylee Ferris cast herself in a brand-new role: the Defendant. She pleaded innocent to all charges and hired the best criminal defense lawyer money could buy—and Kylee had plenty of it. In fact, she was making more now than ever because her notorious reputation fueled a worldwide resurgence of her pop music.

After her indictment on two counts of murder, Kylee's defense team flew various trial balloons to a headline-hungry press. They began with the angle that poor Kylee had been the victim of an entrapment, that her so-called confession was recorded illegally and anything she said should be dismissed as evidence. The prosecution immediately pointed out that New York was a one-party consent state. Only one person being filmed or recorded had to give permission. As the manager of the Village Blend, I'd consented to the filming, so that more or less ended that ploy.

Next came the "innocence exploited" defense.

Poor Kylee, so young and naive in the ways of Hollywood, signed an unfair three-season contract. She was forced to work unreasonably long hours, was put in danger by doing her own fighting stunts and by working on an unsafe set—yes, the same set that she herself had set on fire. Of course, Kylee denied setting the fire. She also claimed she was terrorized during the shooting, and denied planting the snake, as well.

Kylee also charged that she had been exploited for her acting talent by a "recovering drug addict" of a director whose career was on the rocks, and finally, that she was impugned in public and in private by one Elizabeth "Lizzy" Meeks, the president of the Jerry Sullivan Fan Club.

When Jerry heard about it, he was livid. "Apparently, Kylee doesn't need Sebastian around to act after all."

Meanwhile, behind our Village Blend coffee bar, Tucker claimed some insight on Kylee's strategy.

"I know actors and I know egos. Kylee thinks she can sway the jury by playing the role of victim in what is shaping up to be the celebrity trial of the twenty-first century." He arched an eyebrow. "I'm no Sebastian Albee, but I've directed some of the best farces and melodramas in off-off caba-ret, and Kylee's not *that* good. The jury will see right through her."

"Her lawyers must agree with you," Esther said. "I heard they quit. I wonder why."

Thanks to Mike, I knew the answer. "From what I understand, the prosecution disclosed findings on the ballistics test of Kylee's gun, the one they found in her handbag. The DA not only linked that gun to Fred Den-ham's shooting in Central Park, but they also discovered the gun was taken from his own armorer's kit."

Tucker blinked. "No one noticed the gun was missing?"

"No. After you were shot, Hutch locked up all of Fred's guns without bothering to take inventory. And since Jerry no longer wanted real guns on the set, Hutch had no reason to open the kit again."

Tucker sighed. "What did Kylee say when she was told Fred was killed with his own gun?"

"She said he must have committed suicide."

Tucker's jaw dropped. "That girl wants a jury to believe that a man blew his own head off in Central Park and was found minutes later—by you and the police—with no gun in his hand? How will she explain hav-ing the murder weapon in her handbag?"

I shrugged. "I guess she needs a scriptwriter as well as a new lawyer."

"She'll need a good publicist, too," Tuck said, "especially after the bombshells in that true crime podcast. Did you both hear it?"

Esther and I nodded. The ambitious podcaster had hooked up with a local reporter from Kylee's hometown, along with a retired sheriff and some of her former classmates. They recounted so-called accidental deaths of people around Kylee during her early years.

The causes of these mysterious deaths bore an unsettling resemblance to the crimes around the *Only Murders in Gotham* set—a fall from a building that killed one of Kylee's middle school rivals; a suspicious fire that ended the life of an unpopular teacher; and the tragic death, by drug overdose, of a touring company's musical theater star for whom a young Kylee happened to be the understudy.

"Frankly, I was surprised there were no gun crimes," Esther said.

"Probably because she didn't learn how to use one until she played a cop on Jerry's show," Tucker replied.

Tucker was right, and the podcaster covered that, too.

During the press coverage for the show's first season, Kylee gave multiple interviews on how she trained for her police officer's role, recounting how Fred Denham, the production's armorer, taught her to handle, load, and shoot. Publicity footage even captured Kylee at a firing range, shooting the gun that they found in her handbag.

"The very one she killed Fred with," I said with a shudder.

Esther rolled her eyes. "That girl is going down for sure. She should have taken the plea deal!"

Tucker waved his hand. "It's not in her nature. Kylee is obviously determined to play the lead role in a big show trial."

"Tucker's right," I said. "And with her high profile, I have no doubt she'll find a new attorney."

"You mean a new *producer* in attorney's clothing," Tucker said. "Of course, with all the delays, it may end up being the trial of the *twenty-second* century . . ."

CRIME and punishment aside, Kylee managed to achieve one major victory. She stopped Jerry's show dead in its tracks.

With a murder trial looming, both the prosecution and the defense petitioned the streaming service to halt production and never air the second season with Kylee, given the crimes she was accused of committing during filming. The streaming executives agreed.

And so the unfinished, unaired second season of *Only Murders in Gotham* was permanently shelved in a legal move that sank a lot of hearts.

Tucker was crushed. He'd almost been shot by a real bullet, then came back to give the best comedic slapstick of his career—and it was all for naught.

Esther lamented that one of her finest slam poetry performances was now owned by a streaming service that would never air it.

Ironically, the Village Blend managed to thrive. All the publicity surrounding the crimes brought the international attention we all thought the show itself would bring. People lined up around the block just to get a glimpse of the interior of our shop and take a picture with Tucker Burton, whom the press had dubbed the Bulletproof Barista.

Not surprisingly, Dan Coffey and Jerry Sullivan were the most disappointed of all.

I knew because one night near closing time, the two comedians showed up at the Village Blend. I served them at the coffee bar while they bemoaned their situation.

"We rekindled our act after decades, created some of the best comedy of our careers, only to have it buried like the Ark of the Covenant in that *Indiana Jones* flick," Jerry said.

"Yeah, it's déjà vu all over again." Dan Coffey shook his big head. "You'd think the ghost of Fletcher Ulmer was getting his revenge from beyond the grave."

"I even lost my assistant," Jerry wailed.

He was right about that.

As it turned out, Drew Merriweather was secretly brewing up something on the side, but it wasn't sabotage. Drew's dream of producing a show of his own was about to come true. And he was doing it with the help of (surprise!) Jerry's fired cowriter, Tate Cabot.

Young and attuned to pop culture, Drew had noticed the popularity of *The Beverly Hillbillies* reruns, primarily due to the viral sensation of Jethro Bodine social media memes and pirated T-shirts with sayings like:

"Go soak your head in the cement pond!"
"Back off, I'm a double-naught spy!"
"Ain't nobody gonna hickory-switch me!"
"I hate to break your heart, Uncle Jed, but I ain't gonna be no brain surgeon."

Now the trades were abuzz about Drew's upcoming reboot of the old CBS show, which was quickly green-lighted by its streaming platform. According to the *Hollywood Reporter*, this "edgy new take on the hills of Beverly," titled *Jethro's World*, would retell the origin of the Clampett family from the point of view of young cousin Jethro, "an innocent country boy who comes to Hollywood with stars in his eyes and cow plop between his toes."

Tate Cabot, who knew a little something about arriving in Hollywood in cowboy boots, had penned the pilot and agreed to serve as head writer.

"Face reality," Dan told Jerry over cappuccinos at my coffee bar. "To Drew, you were his version of Fletcher Ulmer. Or should I say F.U.?"

"No way! I was never like that!"

"Come on, admit it. You treated that boy with total condescension."

"Hey, can I help it if the kid can't take a joke?"

"And he wasn't the only employee to give up on you," Dan pointed out.

"Lizzy Meeks *did not* give up on me!" Jerry protested. "When I finally go back to Vegas, she's going to manage my fan club personally again. In the meantime, she's hired an assistant to oversee it while she pursues new opportunities . . ."

As the men talked, I learned that back on the night Kylee was arrested, Jerry at last had seen the value of having Lizzy Meeks by his side. The next day, he'd asked her to join him on the set *and* help manage his career.

To Jerry's absolute shock, she'd turned him down.

Now that she knew Jerry was safe, Lizzy would be moving to the West Coast to take on a new challenge. She'd accepted Drew Merriweather's offer to manage all merchandizing, licensing, and fan club business for *Jethro's World*.

The move was also personal because Lizzy wanted to be close to the "lovely man" with whom she'd started a romantic relationship (surprise again), Tate Cabot.

As for Jerry and Dan, on that first night they met up at the Village Blend after the season was canceled, the pair stayed, talking and joking around, long past our closing time. They were great company, and (to my delight) they returned the next night. This time, they brought a pen, a pad, and a digital recorder.

"We're going to figure out our next move," Jerry told me, over a plate of our special Chocolate Chip Cookies.

"And this is the perfect place to do it," Dan said, licking his lips between bites. "Right where our creative partnership first took off."

For weeks after that, I listened to them laugh, and plot, and plan.

I finally knew how Madame felt when she ran the Village Blend all those years ago and watched two of the greatest comedy talents of their generation cook up sidesplitting jokes and clever routines right before her eyes.

The pair came so often that I finally gave Jerry his own key and told him to lock up when he and Dan were done. Many mornings, I'd come back downstairs at the crack of dawn and find the pair sitting there with stubble on their faces, empty pizza boxes piled up, cookie crumbs on their notes, looking haggard but happy, often still laughing their asses off.

It wasn't long before Jerry confided their solution to their dead series problem—

"Kylee may have killed the second season of *Only Murders in Gotham*, but she didn't end the show's life . . ."

He and Dan had spent all those nights writing fresh scripts for a *brand-new* season by combining the scripts for the second and third seasons and bringing in the former boy-band idol Justin Trevor right away.

"Sebastian Albee is on board," Jerry told me one evening at my coffee bar. "He and his wife are living in Chelsea now, and he's excited to begin again. Sebastian tells me that with the magic of cinema, he can use a lot of what we shot already. That will cut the reshoot budget by nearly half."

Then Jerry leaned forward in his bar chair, the old spark back in his sharp gray eyes.

"Of course, we'll need to film a lot of new scenes right here in the Village Blend. And we'll need craft services, too, a team that provides excellent eats and the very best coffee. Are you up for it, Clare?"

"Are you kidding? My baristas will be thrilled."

"Then it's a deal?" Jerry asked with that silver-screen smile.

Doing it all again would be exhausting work, and the challenge did give me pause. But I always was a Jerry Sullivan fan, and I always would be. How could I say anything but—

"Yes, Jerry. You've got a deal."

Recipes & Tips
From the Village Blend

Visit Cleo Coyle's virtual Village Blend at
coffeehousemystery.com
for a free illustrated guide to this section
and even more recipes, including:

Pizza Pinwheels
Baked Ziti (meatless)
Strawberry Shortcake Muffins
Irish Oatmeal Cookie Muffins
Cherry Streusel Pastry Cake

CLEO COYLE RECIPES

The Village Blend's Café-Style Chocolate Chip Cookies with Hints of Caramel and Sea Salt

The rich flavor notes of buttery caramel and sea salt make these delectable chocolate chip cookies a favorite at the Village Blend. The large cookies bake up on the thin side, producing crispy edges and chewy centers, perfect when sharing afternoon coffee breaks or late-night laughs with your favorite comedian. Yet another reason why Clare Cosi continues to find joy behind her coffee bar. To see a photo of these crispy-chewy rounds of bliss, visit Cleo Coyle's online coffeehouse at coffeehousemystery.com, where you can download an illustrated guide to this recipe section.

Makes about 8 large flat cookies (or 16 medium-sized)

1 stick (½ cup or 8 tablespoons) unsalted butter, melted and cooled

4 teaspoons pure vanilla extract

⅛ teaspoon finely ground sea salt

4 large egg yolks

½ cup white, granulated sugar

½ cup light brown sugar, firmly packed

½ teaspoon baking soda

1 cup all-purpose flour (spoon into cup and level off)

½ cup + 2 tablespoons mini semisweet chocolate chips (see recipe note below)

(optional) 3 tablespoons finely chopped walnuts

Step 1—Prep step: In a microwave-safe bowl, melt the butter and set it into the fridge to cool for 5 minutes while you preheat the oven to 350°F and separate the eggs. You're only using the yolks for this recipe. Lightly beat them with a fork.

Step 2—Make the batter: Once the butter feels cool to the touch, whisk in the following ingredients in this order: the vanilla and salt; the beaten egg yolks; and the two sugars (white and light brown). Whisk in the baking soda. Measure in the flour and switch to a rubber spatula to stir into a sticky, loose dough. Finally, fold in the mini chocolate chips (and nuts if using).

Step 3—Bake: Line a baking sheet with parchment paper. Drop the dough in large, equal-sized mounds on the lined pan, leaving plenty of space between the cookies for spreading. Bake in your preheated 350°F oven for 9 to 10 minutes, depending on cookie size. Remove cookies when golden brown but still slightly underdone. Allow to finish cooking by sitting on the hot baking sheet, outside of the oven, for another 8 minutes. Do not skip this step. Cool on a rack before handling to prevent breakage and eat with chocolate chip joy!

Recipe note: For best results, use mini chocolate chips. If you only have standard chips, discs, or chocolate chunks on hand, chop them into smaller pieces and measure after chopping.

The Village Blend's Caramel-Dipped Meltaway Cookies

These delightful cookies marry the joy of tender, melt-in-your-mouth shortbread with the buttery sweetness of caramel. Caramel is one of the most popular flavors for coffeehouse lattes, which is why this recipe is so popular at Clare Cosi's Village Blend. Because these cookies pair so beautifully with coffee, they make a great addition to after-dinner dessert trays. For the holidays, Clare sometimes adds extras, and you can, too. The caramel side of the cookies can be finished with nuts, colored sprinkles, and other tasty garnishes. For more variety on your cookie tray, you can even replace the caramel and dip some of the cookies with melted dark, milk, or white chocolate. To see a photo of these finished cookies, visit Cleo Coyle's online coffeehouse at coffeehousemystery.com, where you can download an illustrated guide to this recipe section.

Makes 3 to 4 dozen cookies, depending on thickness

1 cup (2 sticks) unsweetened butter, softened to room temperature
½ cup powdered sugar
¼ cup light brown sugar, firmly packed
1 large egg yolk
½ teaspoon baking powder
½ teaspoon table salt (or finely ground sea salt)
2¼ cups all-purpose flour

For Dipping

50 soft caramels or 2 cups Caramel Bits
2 tablespoons light cream or half-and-half
(Finishing options at the end of the recipe)

Step 1—Make the dough: Using an electric mixer, cream the softened butter, powdered sugar, and brown sugar. Add the egg yolk and blend until smooth. Add the baking powder and salt and beat again until incorporated. Finally, add the flour and mix on low speed until blended.

Step 2—Form log and chill: Use your hands to squeeze together dough pieces. Knead a little, working with the dough until it is smooth. Form it into a ball. Turn the dough onto a parchment paper–covered surface and shape it into a thick, long log about 2 inches in diameter. Wrap the log in the parchment paper, using the paper to finish shaping and smoothing the log. Chill the wrapped log in the fridge for at least 1 hour. If you are going to chill it longer (overnight or up to 2 days), wrap the log tightly in plastic wrap to keep it from drying out.

Step 3—Bake: Preheat the oven to 300°F. Line a baking sheet with parchment paper. Slice the chilled dough log into thin cookies. Bake 10 to 12 minutes. The centers should still be creamy and the edges golden brown. The cookies are tender when warm. Allow them to cool before handling or dipping.

Step 4—Dip: Place the unwrapped caramel candies (or Caramel Bits) and light cream (or half-and-half) in a nonstick saucepan. Continually stir over low heat until the candies melt. If the melted caramels are still too thick for dipping, add in a bit more light cream (or half-and-half). When the consistency is right, turn the heat to low. Gently dip half of each cooled cookie into the saucepan of melted caramels, allowing excess caramel to drain away. Gently rest on a wax paper–lined pan until set. Enjoy!

Finishing options: To create variety on your cookie tray, these cookies can be finished in different ways. Place ½ cup of any of the following garnishes into a shallow bowl and lightly roll the freshly dipped caramel side of some (or all) of your cookies into chopped nuts (such as hazelnuts, walnuts, or almonds). Or try shredded coconut or mini chocolate chips. For the holidays, colorful sprinkles or festive edibles like nonpareils are an option. You can even swap out the caramel and instead dip some (or all) of your cookies in melted dark, milk, or white chocolate.

Clare Cosi's Chocolate Espresso Cupcakes with Espresso Buttercream

Close your eyes, take a bite, and enjoy the sensuous delights of these outstanding cupcakes as chocolate drenches your palate. Every tender little cake is topped with a light, creamy cloud of mouthwatering buttercream laced with espresso. As chefs and bakers know, the roasted note of espresso boosts the flavor of chocolate in any recipe, which is why this buttercream icing is the perfect complement to the rich chocolate cakes beneath. That's also why, the night Mike brought a cupcake to

Clare's bedroom, she knew the tempting nature of what he was offering. Eyeing the frosting at the edges of his mouth, she quickly sent her worries about crumbs in the sheets right out the window. To see a photo of these finished frosted cupcakes, visit Cleo Coyle's online coffeehouse at coffeehousemystery.com, where you can download an illustrated guide to this recipe section.

Makes 12 cupcakes

1 cup plus 2 tablespoons all-purpose flour

½ cup unsweetened cocoa powder

1 teaspoon baking powder

½ teaspoon baking soda

¼ teaspoon finely ground sea salt (or table salt)

½ cup (1 stick) unsalted butter (softened)

¾ cup white, granulated sugar

¼ cup light brown sugar

1 large egg, at room temperature

½ cup whole milk

1 teaspoon pure vanilla extract

½ cup espresso or strong brewed coffee (cooled)

1 teaspoon instant espresso powder

¾ cup mini semisweet chocolate chips (must be mini!)

Espresso Buttercream (recipe follows)

Step 1—Prep pan: First, preheat the oven to 350°F. Line a cupcake pan with paper liners. To prevent sticking of the baked cupcakes, lightly spray the papers and pan top with nonstick cooking spray.

Step 2—Mix dry ingredients: Whisk together the flour, cocoa powder, baking powder, baking soda, and salt, and set aside.

Step 3—Make batter: Cream the butter and two sugars together until fluffy. Beat in the egg. Stop the mixer and add the milk, vanilla, and cooled espresso or brewed coffee (with the instant espresso powder dissolved into it). Beat in the flour mixture from Step 2. Do not overmix at this stage, but be sure that all the raw flour is incorporated into the batter. Finally, fold in the mini chocolate chips. (They really should be mini chips for the best results. In a pinch, you can chop standard-sized chocolate chips or discs, but do not use standard chips for this recipe.)

Step 4—Bake: Divide the batter among the 12 lined cupcake cups of your pan. Bake about 18 to 22 minutes or until a toothpick inserted in the center of a cupcake comes out with no batter clinging to it. (Be careful not to mistake melted chocolate chips for unbaked batter!) Cool the cupcakes *completely* before frosting them. See the next recipe for instructions on making the Espresso Buttercream.

Espresso Buttercream

Makes enough to frost 12 cupcakes

> ½ cup (1 stick) unsalted butter, at room temperature
> 1½ cups powdered sugar
> 1¼ teaspoons instant espresso powder
> 1 teaspoon pure vanilla extract
> 2 tablespoons brewed coffee or espresso

Using an electric mixer, whip the softened butter until light and fluffy. Reduce the mixer speed and add the powdered sugar a little at a time. After the powdered sugar has been incorporated, scrape down the sides of the bowl. Whisk the instant espresso powder into the vanilla extract and brewed coffee and then beat it into the frosting until it is beautifully fluffy and ready for the tops of your delicious Chocolate Espresso Cupcakes. Top with chocolate shavings or a chocolate-covered espresso bean!

The Village Blend's Coffee Cake Streusel Muffins with Vanilla Glaze

The Village Blend has trouble keeping these delicious streusel-layered muffins in their pastry case. They're a customer favorite, and it's no wonder.

These tender little cakes with sweet crumb topping are great paired with coffee. The muffins are even finished like coffee cake, with a drizzle of vanilla glaze. The only downside is they disappear quickly—as Clare discovered when she found Matt eating the last one. To see a photo of these finished muffins, visit Cleo Coyle's online coffeehouse at coffeehousemystery.com, where you can download an illustrated guide to this recipe section.

Makes 12 muffins

For the Muffins

1½ cups Crumb Topping (Streusel), recipe follows this one
½ cup (1 stick) butter, softened
½ cup white, granulated sugar
½ cup light brown sugar
¾ teaspoon table salt (or finely ground sea salt)
½ teaspoon cinnamon
1½ teaspoons vanilla extract
2 large eggs, lightly beaten with fork
¾ cup sour cream
¼ cup whole milk
1½ teaspoons baking powder
½ teaspoon baking soda
2 cups all-purpose flour

For the Vanilla Glaze

2 tablespoons butter
1 cup powdered sugar
½ teaspoon vanilla extract (for a whiter glaze, use clear vanilla)
1 tablespoon whole milk (more or less)

Step 1—Preheat, prep pans, mix streusel ingredients: First, make the streusel filling and topping (that recipe follows this one). Now preheat the oven to 350°F and place paper liners in 12 muffin cups.

Step 2—One-bowl mixing method: In a large bowl, use an electric mixer to cream the softened butter and sugars. When light and fluffy, beat in the salt, cinnamon, vanilla, eggs, sour cream, baking powder, and baking soda. Continue beating for another minute. Stop the mixer and measure in the flour. Mix everything until you have a batter that is smooth, but do not overmix or you'll develop the gluten in the flour and the muffins will be tough instead of tender.

Step 3—Layer muffin cups and bake: You will now need the streusel topping that you already prepared. Into your paper-lined muffin cups, drop a generous dollop of batter. Sprinkle a layer of streusel onto the batter and top with more batter. Finish with a generous sprinkling of crumb topping (streusel). Bake for 18 to 20 minutes. Muffins are done when a toothpick inserted comes out with no wet batter clinging to it. Remove from oven and take the muffins out of the hot pan promptly or the bottoms may steam and toughen.

Step 4—Make the vanilla glaze: In a small saucepan, over medium-low heat, melt the butter. Sift in the powdered sugar (or sift the sugar first and then add). When all of the sugar is melted into the butter, remove from heat and stir in the vanilla. Finally, whisk in the milk, a little at a time, until the glaze is smooth and the right consistency to drizzle over the muffins. See the next step on how to test for doneness.

Step 5—Glaze the cooled muffins: Test the glaze by drizzling it from a fork onto a clean plate. If the glaze is too thick, whisk in a bit more milk. If it's too thin, whisk in a bit more powdered sugar. To finish the muffins, dip a fork in the warm glaze mixture and drizzle it in a back-and-forth motion over the cooled muffin tops.

Crumb Topping (Streusel) for any Muffin or Coffee Cake

Makes about 2 cups, enough for 12 muffins or 1 small (8-by-8-inch) coffee cake

¾ cup all-purpose flour
½ cup light brown sugar
¼ cup white, granulated sugar

1 teaspoon cinnamon
⅛ teaspoon finely ground sea salt (or table salt)
5 tablespoons unsalted butter (very cold), cubed

Food processor method: Place all ingredients in the processor and pulse until you see coarse, pea-sized crumbs. Store any extra in a sealed plastic container in the refrigerator.

Low-tech method: Using your hands and/or a fork or pastry blender, work the butter into the dry ingredients (squeezing and rubbing if using your hands) until you get coarse, pea-sized crumbs. Once made this way, chill in the refrigerator before using in the recipe (your hands will warm the butter and you'll want to firm it up before baking). Store any extra in a sealed plastic container in the refrigerator.

Clare Cosi's Skillet Lasagna

Clare has fond memories of her nonna's hearty lasagna. When she doesn't have the time (or energy) to make her grandmother's many-layered casserole, she likes to whip up this quickie skillet version for herself and Mike Quinn. Given Clare and Mike's interest in other kinds of comfort, they don't always get around to eating this dinner right away, which is why this dish is perfect for them—because it makes great leftovers. Heat and reheat. Good advice for this lasagna, as well as couples in long-term relationships. To see a photo of Clare's simple stovetop lasagna, visit Cleo Coyle's online coffeehouse at coffeehousemystery.com, where you can download an illustrated guide to this recipe section.

Serves 4

6 ounces curly lasagna noodles
1 yellow onion, finely chopped
1 cup baby bella mushrooms (optional), chopped
2 cloves garlic, minced
½ pound lean ground beef
½ pound ground pork or chicken

1 (28-ounce) can whole peeled tomatoes, drained and chopped
(you can use a food processor for this)
¼ cup tomato paste
1 tablespoon Italian seasoning or a mix of dried rosemary, basil, and oregano
Handful of fresh Italian (flat-leaf) parsley, chopped
¾ cup ricotta cheese (whole milk will give the best flavor)
½ cup mozzarella cheese, shredded (whole milk will give the best flavor)
Sprinkling of grated Romano or Parmesan cheese, to taste

Step 1—Boil lasagna noodles: Bring a large pot of water to a boil. Break lasagna noodles into 3-inch pieces and cook according to the package directions. Drain well and set aside.

Step 2—Meat and vegetables: Lightly coat a large skillet with olive oil and set over medium heat. Add chopped onion. Cook and stir for 5 minutes, until translucent. Add the mushrooms (if using) and garlic and cook another 2 minutes. Stir in ground beef and pork (or chicken), breaking up and cooking until meat is browned and no longer pink, about 5 to 7 minutes. When the meat is cooked, add chopped tomatoes, tomato paste, and Italian seasoning, stirring frequently, until thickened, about 6 minutes. Stir in parsley.

Step 3—Finish with noodles and cheese: Add in the cooked lasagna noodles and gently stir until heated through, about 5 minutes. Use a spoon to evenly top the mixture with big dollops of ricotta. Sprinkle the shredded mozzarella on top. Cover and cook a few more minutes, until everything is heated through. Dish out helpings and garnish with a sprinkling of grated Romano or Parmesan cheese. To reheat, add more mozzarella, cover, and melt. *Molto bene!*

Clare Cosi's Chicken Marsala

A favorite on the craft services menu, Chicken Marsala is also one of the most popular dishes in Italian restaurants worldwide. The chicken melts like butter, and the mushrooms provide an earthy richness, but the key ingredient (and the secret to this dish's charm) is dry Marsala, a fortified wine from Sicily similar to sherry or port. Clare adds an extra step when she makes this one-skillet version in her kitchen—an easy marinade. Her advice for an amazing dish: Do not skip this step! The marinade truly heightens the flavor, bringing this dish to a whole new level. Though Chicken Marsala is traditionally dished up over pasta, Clare and her craft services team served it the way many Italian eateries in New York City do—on a crispy, fresh Italian roll, the perfect lunch, dinner, or late-night sandwich for anyone as busy as a film crew shooting on location.

Serves 4

1 to 1½ pounds boneless, skinless chicken breasts
1¾ cups dry Marsala, divided
4 tablespoons olive oil, divided
6 cloves garlic, smashed
¼ teaspoon kosher salt or ground sea salt, divided
¼ teaspoon freshly ground black pepper, divided
½ cup all-purpose flour
3 tablespoons butter, divided
1 large onion, diced
3 cups sliced mushrooms (baby bellas, cremini, button, or a mix)
1 cup chicken stock

Step 1—Prep the chicken and marinate: Wash chicken breasts and slice horizontally. On a cutting board, use a meat hammer to pound breasts thin. (Or you can buy pre-filleted breasts, but because the goal is tenderness, you still must pound the chicken.) In a bowl or plastic container with a lid, mix ¾ cup Marsala with 1 tablespoon olive oil, the garlic, ⅛ teaspoon salt, and ⅛ teaspoon pepper. Place the chicken in the marinade, cover the bowl with plastic wrap (or seal the container), and refrigerate for 30 minutes, or up to 3 hours.

Step 2—Dredge marinated chicken and sauté: Remove chicken from marinade, do not rinse. (Discard the liquid.) Dredge in ½ cup all-purpose flour. Heat 3 tablespoons olive oil in a large skillet over low heat. Add 1 tablespoon butter to the hot oil, then gently sauté the coated chicken until golden brown (3 minutes per side should do it, turning once). When the chicken is cooked through, remove from the pan and set aside.

Step 3—Sauté the aromatics: Add the diced onion to the oil, and cook over medium heat until the onions are clear and tender (about 5 minutes). Add 1 tablespoon butter to the skillet. When melted, throw in the sliced mushrooms and sauté. The mushrooms will quickly absorb the oil, but keep cooking until the edges are brown and they begin to release their juices again.

Step 4—Add wine, reduce: Now pour into the pan the remaining 1 cup of Marsala. Increase the heat and bring to a low boil. Simmer until the liquid has been reduced by half, 5 to 6 minutes. Add the chicken stock and simmer for another 3 minutes.

Step 5—Sauce the chicken: Return the chicken breasts to the pan along with any juices that might have accumulated in the holding dish. Lower the heat and cook until the chicken is heated through and the sauce thickens, about 5 to 7 minutes. Now toss in that final 1 tablespoon butter, 1/8 teaspoon salt, and 1/8 teaspoon black pepper. Serve hot.

Clare Cosi's French Dip

A French dip, also called a "beef dip," is a hot sandwich consisting of thinly sliced roast beef on a roll or baguette served with a dipping container of au jus. In French "au jus" refers to the natural pan drippings from the meat. Because natural drippings sometimes aren't enough to satisfy, Clare makes an American version of au jus, which amounts to a savory beef broth made with the meat drippings. The combination of tender beef and the crusty bread saturated with the savory beef juice makes a perfect meal. Create plenty of Clare's Au Jus for this dish, because reheating thin slices of beef by simmering them in the meat juice (with your pan over low heat) is the best way to warm and refresh any leftovers.

Clare's Roast Beef

Clare prefers using an "eye of round" cut of beef for roasting in this recipe, although any of the three types of rump roasts—top round, eye of round, or bottom round—will work well. If possible, look for a roast with a layer of thick fat; this will keep your meat juicy and tender and provide lots of drippings when you make Clare's Au Jus (that recipe follows this one).

Serves 6

1 boneless beef rump roast; top, bottom, or eye round (4 to 5 pounds)
1 tablespoon coarse sea salt
1 teaspoon cracked black pepper, coarsely ground
2 tablespoons cooking oil (olive, corn, or vegetable)

Step 1—Prep: Rinse the raw beef, pat it dry, and place it on the rack of your roasting pan. Allow the beef to rest outside of the refrigerator for at least 40 minutes or up to 1 hour. If you put cold meat in a hot oven, you risk uneven cooking and tougher meat.

Step 2—Encrust: Preheat the oven to 350°F. In a completely dry bowl, combine the sea salt and pepper. Mix thoroughly and pour on a flat dish or cutting board. Coat the beef completely with cooking oil, and roll all sides in the salt-and-pepper mixture, crusting well.

Step 3—Roast: Place the beef, fat side up, on the pan's rack. Roast the meat at 350°F for 17 to 20 minutes per pound for rare; 22 to 25 minutes per pound for medium; and about 30 minutes per pound for medium well to well-done. Clare roasts her beef to an internal temperature of about 160°F, but remember that the meat's internal temperature will rise about 10°F after it's taken out of the oven, so she actually removes the meat from the oven at 150°F.

Step 4—Rest: An important step. After the beef comes out of the oven, let it sit for at least 30 minutes before slicing, or all of those lovely meat juices will run out and you'll be left with a roast that's far too dry. Place a loose tent of aluminum foil over the beef to keep it warm.

Recipe tip: If you've never used an instant read meat thermometer, here's a helpful hint. Do not stick the meat too often with the thermometer or the meat will lose its juices. Wait until you're near the end of the cooking time to test the meat, and if possible, do it only once.

Clare's Beef "Au Jus" for French Dip

Serves 6

1 tablespoon olive oil
1 stalk celery, chopped
¼ cup red onion, chopped
1 teaspoon garlic, minced
1 tablespoon water (or white wine)
1 tablespoon Worcestershire sauce
2½ cups beef broth
All the pan dripping from your roast beef (see previous recipe)
1 teaspoon Wondra flour

Step 1—Prep the vegetables: Coat the bottom of a medium saucepan with olive oil and heat. Chop celery and onions, and mince the garlic. Caramelize the onions in the olive oil. Add celery and cook for 2 minutes. Add garlic and cook for 2 more minutes.

Step 2—Simmer: Deglaze the pot with the water or white wine, then add Worcestershire sauce and cook for another minute, stirring constantly. Add the beef broth and meat drippings and bring to a boil. Reduce heat and simmer for 30 minutes.

Step 3—Strain and finish: Pour hot broth through a strainer, then return it to the pot. Add the Wondra flour, which is specially formulated to dissolve quickly in gravies and sauces, and simmer 5 minutes or until it thickens.

Recipe tip: When reheating your beef, place thin slices in a gently simmering pan of this meat juice for two minutes, flipping once.

"Cold Oil" Pommes Frites

Love French fries but fear the fryer? Try this rustic "cold oil" recipe for delicious, crispy results. This "slow cook" method for frying potatoes takes a little more time, but they can simmer on the back burner while you're cooking up the main course, and you won't need a thermometer, either. This easy, low-tech method produces beautiful fries, aka pommes frites, *the perfect side for your French dip meal.*

Makes 4 servings

3 or 4 large russet potatoes (about 2 pounds), no substitutes!
6 cups (1.5 quarts) vegetable oil
Finely ground sea salt (to taste)

Step 1—Prep the potatoes: You want to rid the potatoes of as much starch as possible, which is the secret to crispy fries. Rinse and peel the potatoes. Cut them into matchsticks by first creating slices and then cutting those slices into long, thin sticks. Soak the potato sticks in cold water for 10 minutes. Change the water and re-soak for another 10 minutes. (You'll know the starch is gone when the soaking water remains clear.) When finished soaking, dry the fries well using paper towels. You want to remove any excess liquid that will slow the cooking time or cause the hot oil to splatter. Here's a good tip: Spread the dried-off potatoes on a pan and place them in the refrigerator for 30 minutes. The dry, cold air of the fridge does a great job removing any remaining surface moisture.

Step 2—Start the boil: In a large skillet or sauté pan (large enough so that there will be 2 inches between the oil and the top of the pan), add the dry potatoes and pour the oil over them. On high heat and uncovered, allow the potatoes to warm, stirring only enough so they don't stick together. The oil should reach a boil in about 9 minutes. Once the oil is boiling, cook for 20 to 30 minutes. Do not stir (until the very end of cooking). The fries will break apart if you do.

Step 3—Finish and serve: After 20 minutes or so the fries should show some color, turning from white to slightly tan or brown. But at least 5 or more minutes will be required for the potatoes to fully cook. These last minutes are crucial. Watch the pan closely, stirring *very* gently. When the fries turn golden brown they should be ready, but don't jump the gun and remove them from the oil too soon or they will be soggy. Taste the fries, and if you are happy with the result, use a spider or slotted spoon to move them to a paper towel–lined bowl. Season with finely ground sea salt and serve immediately.

Recipe tip: The best potatoes to use for this recipe are russets. They hold up wonderfully during this process. Other types will not, so accept no substitutions!

Babka's Whole Roasted Chicken with Sweet Garlic and Citrus

At Babka's famous New York restaurant, one of the most popular main courses is her Roasted Chicken with Sweet Garlic and Citrus. The dish takes time and preplanning to prepare, but the taste is worth the effort. The lime shines through because of the zest. The garlic deepens the flavor and helps to sweeten the dish, and a thin but delightful brown sugar glaze coats the bird. To see a photo of this delectable chicken, visit Cleo Coyle's online coffeehouse at coffeehousemystery.com, where you can download an illustrated guide to this recipe section.

Serves 4

1 whole chicken (3 to 4½ pounds)
4 to 6 limes
4 to 6 cloves of garlic, minced
4 tablespoons light brown sugar
½ teaspoon white or black pepper (ground fine)
3 tablespoons olive oil (divided)
1 tablespoon soy sauce
½ teaspoon coriander (optional)
Dash of MSG (optional for flavor boost)

Step 1—Create the marinade: Zest two of the limes, then juice them all—you should get 4 to 6 teaspoons of juice (more is better). In a large mixing bowl combine the zest, lime juice, minced garlic, light brown sugar, pepper, 1 tablespoon olive oil, soy sauce, coriander (optional), and MSG (optional for flavor boost). Whisk.

Step 2—Marinate: Clean the whole chicken and pat dry. Salt the cavity (optional). Place the whole chicken in a large resealable plastic bag and pour the marinade over it. Seal tightly and place in refrigerator for at least 24 hours (36 hours is optimal). See recipe note (below) for more tips.

Step 3—Roast: Preheat the oven to 325°F. Remove chicken from marinade (do NOT rinse). Place chicken in a foil-lined roasting pan and cover it with a thin coating of the remaining 2 tablespoons of olive oil. Place in the middle rack and roast for 90 minutes to 2 hours (about 25 minutes per pound of chicken).

Step 4—Serve: Remove from the oven and let the chicken stand for 20 minutes before carving. At Babka's restaurant this dish is served with white or brown rice and a garden salad.

Recipe note: Chicken must marinate at least 24 hours to achieve its flavor potential. But don't marinate more than 48 hours. The citrus will "bleach" the chicken skin white in 24 hours, which doesn't affect the flavor, but after 48 hours the chicken meat itself begins to break down.

Babka's Sweet Garlic and Citrus Chicken Wings

At the bar in Babka's restaurant (and in her underground nightclub and casino) this snack is a popular finger food. It pairs nicely with wine or cocktails.

Serves 4

3 to 4 pounds chicken wings (about 12 to 14 wings)
Marinade (see previous recipe)
1 tablespoon olive oil
¼ cup fresh cilantro, chopped

Step 1—Marinate: Create marinade (see previous recipe). Clean and pat dry the wings, then place them in a large, resealable plastic bag. Pour marinade over the wings and refrigerate for 12 to 24 hours.

Step 2—Roast: Preheat the oven to 325°F. Line a baking pan with parchment paper or foil and grease with 1 tablespoon olive oil. Remove wings from marinade (do NOT rinse) and arrange them on the baking pan so they're about ½ inch apart. Place in the middle rack and roast for 90 minutes. Sprinkle the wings with fresh chopped cilantro and serve.

Recipe note: These wings can also be grilled using your favorite method. They're guaranteed to be tender and will stay juicy, even when cooked over an open flame.

Clare Cosi's Fa-La-La-La-Lattes!

Every year, Clare adds seasonal coffee drinks to her Village Blend holiday menu. Enjoy these fun home-kitchen versions of her famous Fa-la-la-la-latte flavors. Unless otherwise indicated, the recipes that follow are for single servings.

Gingerbread Latte

1 shot hot espresso or strong coffee
1 tablespoon or to taste Homemade Gingerbread Syrup (recipe follows) or bottled syrup
⅔ cup milk or half-and-half
Whipped cream, for topping

Pour the espresso into an 8-ounce mug. Stir in the gingerbread syrup. Fill the rest of the mug with steamed milk. To create the milk, use an espresso machine steam wand, a store-bought milk frother, or my rustic stovetop method (see instructions on page 328). Top with a dollop of whipped cream.

Homemade Gingerbread Syrup

Makes enough for 4 lattes

2 cups water
1½ cups white, granulated sugar
2 tablespoons ground ginger
½ teaspoon ground cinnamon
¼ teaspoon vanilla extract

In a nonstick saucepan, combine the water, sugar, ginger, and cinnamon. Over medium-high heat, bring the mixture to a boil, stirring frequently to prevent burning. After the mixture comes to a boil, reduce heat to medium-low and continue simmering for 15 to 20 minutes, stirring every so often to prevent sticking or burning. The mixture will reduce and become slightly thicker. Continue stirring for 1 minute. Remove pan from the heat. When the mixture cools a bit, stir in the vanilla. Serve warm in your latte or try it over vanilla ice cream!

Eggnog Latte

½ cup cold eggnog
¼ cup cold milk
1 shot hot espresso or strong coffee
Pinch ground nutmeg, for garnish

Step 1—Combine the eggnog with the milk. Steam the liquid mixture using an espresso machine steam wand, a store-bought milk frother, or my rustic stovetop method (see instructions on page 328). Note that eggnog will scald faster than milk, so watch the steaming process closely.

Step 2—Pour the espresso into your mug. Fill the mug with the steamed eggnog mixture. Top the drink with a bit of foamed eggnog mixture. Garnish with ground nutmeg.

Winter White Chocolate Latte

½ cup milk
¼ cup white chocolate, chopped, or white chocolate chips
¼ teaspoon vanilla extract
1 to 2 shots hot espresso or strong coffee
Whipped cream (for topping)

Step 1—Combine milk and white chocolate in a heatproof bowl and place over saucepan about one-third full of boiling water. (The water level should be under the bowl edge but not touching it.) Stir constantly until the chocolate is melted. Do not allow this mixture to scorch or the flavor will be subpar.

Step 2—Using a whisk or electric mixer, whip in the vanilla. Continue to whip about 1 minute until the warm mixture is loosely frothy.

Step 3—Pour the espresso into a large mug. Add the steamed white chocolate milk, using a spoon to hold back a little of the froth. Stir the cup to blend the flavors. Top with the reserved froth. You can finish it with whipped cream, but it's not necessary. This is one heavenly beverage, especially for winter—like a rich, warm, coffee-infused-milkshake hug. Enjoy!

Candy Cane Latte

⅔ cup cold milk
1 shot hot espresso or strong coffee
1 candy cane
1 tablespoon Candy Cane Syrup (see next recipe)
Whipped cream (for topping)

Step 1—Froth the milk using an espresso machine steam wand, a store-bought milk frother, or the rustic stovetop method (see instructions on page 328).

Step 2—Pour the espresso into an 8-ounce mug and use the candy cane to stir in Candy Cane Syrup (or the two substitutes listed in the recipe note below).

Step 3—Fill the rest of the mug nearly to the top with steamed milk and stir a second time with the candy cane to distribute the flavors. Top the drink with whipped cream. Leave the whole candy cane in the mug for a festive serving touch!

Recipe note: You can substitute the following for the homemade Candy Cane Syrup: ½ tablespoon of kirsch (cherry liqueur) or cherry syrup and ½ tablespoon crème de menthe liqueur or peppermint syrup.

Homemade Candy Cane Syrup

Got extra candy canes? Then you can make this excellent syrup. It's delicious stirred into hot cocoa, drizzled over ice cream and cupcakes, and splashed into holiday cocktails. Or try using it the way Clare Cosi does—to make delicious Candy Cane Lattes.

Makes about 1½ cups of syrup

1 cup water
1½ cups white, granulated sugar
8 large candy canes, broken up

Pour the water and sugar into a large saucepan. Stir over medium heat until the sugar has dissolved. Add the candy cane pieces to the mix and continue stirring and cooking. When the candy canes begin to melt, the mix will turn a milky pink. Keep cooking and stirring until the mixture comes to a boil. Boil and continue stirring for 3 to 4 minutes, until the mixture begins to thicken up. The syrup is done when it's thick enough to coat the back of a spoon.

Remove from heat at that point. Allow the syrup to cool in the pan before transferring to a storage jar or plastic bottle. When chilled, this peppermint syrup will thicken up quite a bit. To reuse, simply put the squeeze bottle or jar of syrup into a warm-water bath.

Orange-Spice Yule Latte

⅔ cup cold milk
½ tablespoon Homemade Orange Syrup (recipe follows) or Grand Marnier liqueur
½ tablespoon Amaretto syrup or liqueur
Pinch allspice
1 shot hot espresso or strong coffee
Cinnamon stick
Whipped cream, for topping

Step 1—Froth the milk using an espresso machine steam wand, a store-bought milk frother, or try my rustic stovetop method (see instructions on page 328).

Step 2—Measure out the flavored syrups or liqueurs into an 8-ounce mug, add the allspice, pour in the shot of hot espresso, and stir well with the cinnamon stick to distribute the flavors.

Step 3—Fill the rest of the mug nearly to the top with the steamed milk and stir a second time with the cinnamon stick to mix the flavorings through the drink. Leave the cinnamon stick in the mug to continue adding spiced flavor. Top the drink with whipped cream.

Homemade Fruit Syrup

Makes about 2 cups of syrup

2 cups water
1½ cup white, granulated sugar
1 cup of your favorite flavor of jam, jelly, or fruit preserves
Flavor suggestions: raspberry, orange, strawberry, peach,
apricot, blueberry, mango, mint

In a nonstick saucepan, stir together water and sugar with your favorite jam, jelly, or preserves. Bring to a boil over medium-high heat, stirring often to prevent burning or sticking. Reduce heat and simmer for 20 minutes, stirring frequently. After 20 minutes, mixture should be slightly reduced and thicker. Remove from heat and strain through a fine-mesh sieve. (Strain a second time if needed.) Allow to cool to room temperature in a bowl and remove any skin that forms. Transfer syrup to a plastic squeeze bottle and store in refrigerator. To rewarm syrup, simply place the plastic bottle in warm-water bath.

Recipe note: If using an "all-fruit" preserve—the kind sweetened with fruit juice or concentrate—add about 10 minutes to the simmering process. You may have to boil this mixture down a bit longer for the same result.

How to Create Rustic Steamed Milk
for a Latte or Cappuccino

No, it is not the same as professional, coffeehouse-quality foamed milk, and Clare would never try to pour latte art with it. For true microfoam nirvana, you should visit your local barista! To have some fun at home, however, this stovetop method allows you to create a rustic version of a coffeehouse cappuccino and latte in your own kitchen without a store-bought milk frother, which is always an option if you enjoy coffeehouse-style drinks. In the meantime, here's a low-tech solution for creating foam at home.

Step 1—Fill a medium-sized saucepan about one-third full with water. Place the pan over high heat until the water begins to boil. Turn the heat down to medium and allow the water to simmer.

Step 2—Select a heatproof mixing bowl from your cupboard that is large enough to sit on top of the saucepan. (You are creating a double boiler.) Make sure the simmering water beneath the bowl is not touching the bowl's bottom. Pour fresh, cold milk into the bowl and allow it to warm over the boiling water for 1 minute, no longer! How much milk? About ⅔ cup per serving.

Step 3—With an oven mitt on one hand to hold the hot bowl and a hand-held electric mixer in the other, tip the bowl enough to tilt all the milk into one deep, concentrated pool and then whip it. Whip it good! Use the fastest speed available on your mixer and simply hold the mixing beaters in the center of the milk pool—do not move the mixer around. In a matter of seconds, you'll see the warmed white fluid froth up. Whip the milk 20 to 90 seconds, depending on how much foam you'd like to create, and you're done! Do not overwhip the milk. You won't be able to foam up every molecule of milk with this method, and if you whip it too much, you'll just be breaking down the foam you've created.

Troubleshooting: To make this rustic frothing method foolproof, keep these four suggestions in mind:

(1) Never try to re-froth milk that has been whipped and has fallen. It won't work. You must always start with cold, fresh, undisturbed milk. Pour it straight from the fridge to your measuring cup to the bowl. That's it.

(2) Don't try to start whipping at a low speed and increase it. Whip it like crazy from the start, using the highest speed possible on your blender—if there's not enough immediate, vigorous whipping action, the milk won't properly foam up.

(3) To infuse spices or flavorings into your latte or cappuccino, stir them into your hot espresso shot. Do not add syrups, flavorings, or ground spices into the milk before trying to froth it.

(4) Finally, do not allow the milk to warm much longer than a few minutes over the boiling water. Steaming milk properly brings out its sweetness. If the milk is overheated, however, your latte will have a terrible scorched taste instead of a sweet one. That's why this rustic frothing method is done double-boiler style instead of in a pan directly on the stove burner. It's the best way to control the heat and prevent your milk from scorching.

Easy Iced Mocha

Makes one 8-ounce serving

⅓ cup coffee (4 coffee ice cubes)
⅓ cup milk (low-fat is fine)
2 teaspoons white, granulated sugar (or more if you like your drink sweeter)
¼ teaspoon vanilla extract
¼ teaspoon unsweetened cocoa powder
Whipped cream
Chocolate curls (recipe follows)

Fill an ice cube tray with leftover coffee and freeze. Remove four coffee ice cubes (per 8-ounce serving) and place in blender. Add milk, sugar, vanilla extract, and cocoa. Pulse the blender to chop the coffee ice cubes into fine particles. You can create a very icy drink with small ice chips (like a frozen margarita) or you can run the blender full speed until the mixture is completely liquefied yet still cold and frothy. The drink is delicious either way and a great use for your leftover joe. To finish, pour this frosty refresher into a glass mug, top with whipped cream and chocolate curls (see the next recipe).

How to Make Chocolate Curls

To create chocolate curls, start with a block of room-temperature chocolate. Using a vegetable peeler, scrape down the block and you'll see curls of chocolate peel away. Chocolate curls make a wonderful garnish for coffee drinks, hot cocoa, cakes, cupcakes, and puddings. Or use them to decorate a dessert plate. Chill or even freeze the curls for more sturdiness and longer life on a serving plate or dessert table.

Home Kitchen Caffè Mocha (aka Mochaccino)

Makes one 8-ounce serving

½ cup milk
¼ cup dark or milk chocolate, chopped from good-quality block
¼ teaspoon vanilla extract
1 to 2 shots hot espresso or strong coffee
Whipped cream (for topping)

Step 1—Combine milk and chopped chocolate in a heatproof bowl and place over saucepan about one-third full of boiling water. (The water level should be under the bowl edge but not touching it.) Stir constantly until the chocolate is melted. Do not allow this mixture to scorch or the flavor will be subpar.

Step 2—Using a whisk or electric mixer, whip in the vanilla. Continue to whip about 1 minute until the warm mixture is loosely frothy.

Step 3—Pour the espresso into a large mug. Add the steamed chocolate milk, using a spoon to hold back a little of the froth. Stir the cup to blend the flavors. Top with the reserved froth. If you like, garnish with chocolate curls. See the previous recipe for tips on how to make them.

**From Clare, Matt, Madame, and everyone at the Village Blend . . .
May you eat and drink with joy!**

Don't Miss Cleo Coyle's
Next Coffeehouse Mystery!

For more information about what's next for Clare Cosi
and her merry band of baristas, visit Cleo Coyle at her website:
coffeehousemystery.com.

ABOUT THE AUTHOR

CLEO COYLE is a pseudonym for Alice Alfonsi, writing in collaboration with her husband, Marc Cerasini. Both are *New York Times* bestselling authors of the long-running Coffeehouse Mysteries—now celebrating twenty years in print. They are also authors of the national bestselling Haunted Bookshop Mysteries, previously written under the pseudonym ALICE KIMBERLY. Alice has worked as a journalist in Washington, D.C., and New York, and has written popular fiction for adults and children. A former magazine editor, Marc has authored espionage thrillers and nonfiction for adults and children. Alice and Marc are also both bestselling media tie-in writers who have penned properties for Lucasfilm, NBC, Fox, Disney, Imagine, Toho, and MGM. They live and work in New York City, where they write independently and together.

VISIT CLEO COYLE ONLINE

CoffeehouseMystery.com

🅕 CleoCoyleAuthor

🐦 CleoCoyle

📷 CleoCoyle_Author